Henry James

The Secret of Swedenborg

Henry James

The Secret of Swedenborg

ISBN/EAN: 9783337366759

Printed in Europe, USA, Canada, Australia, Japan

Cover: Foto ©Andreas Hilbeck / pixelio.de

More available books at **www.hansebooks.com**

THE

SECRET OF SWEDENBORG:

BEING AN ELUCIDATION OF HIS DOCTRINE

OF THE DIVINE NATURAL

HUMANITY.

By HENRY JAMES.

BOSTON:

FIELDS, OSGOOD, & CO.,

SUCCESSORS TO TICKNOR AND FIELDS.

1869.

UNIVERSITY PRESS : WELCH, BIGELOW, & Co.,
CAMBRIDGE.

ADVERTISEMENT.

THE following essay comprises an article which appeared in the North American Review for July 1867, and a large amount of additional matter. I had not space in the Review to do more than enter upon a theme previously so unwrought, and I am afraid I have done it only scant justice since. The subject is one however which invites and will well reward any amount of rehandling; and I cannot, just now at all events, afford the time to treat it more exhaustively. I am content to have outlined it in so conscientious a manner as that any one interested may easily work out the necessary details for himself; so I leave it for the present.

While deism as an intellectual tradition continues doubtless to survive, it seems at the same time to be losing all hold upon the living thought of men, being trampled under foot by the advance of a scientific naturalism. Paganism and science are indeed plainly incompatible terms. The conception of a private or unemployed divine force in the world — the conception of a deity unimplicated in the nature, the progress, and the destiny of man — is utterly repugnant to human thought; and if such a conception were the true

logical alternative of atheism, science would erelong
everywhere, as she is now doing in Germany, confess
herself atheistic. But the true battle-field is not nearly
so narrow as this. The rational alternative of atheism
is not deism, but christianity, and science accordingly
would be atheistic at a very cheap if not wholly gratuitous rate, should it become so only to avoid the deistic
hypothesis of creation. The deistic hypothesis then
is effectually dead and buried for scientific purposes.
That it is rapidly becoming so even for the needs of the
religious instinct also, we have a lively augury furnished
us in the current popularity of two very naive and
amiable religious books, which unconsciously put a new
face upon the atheistic controversy by attempting to
give revelation itself a strictly rational aspect, and so
bring it within the legitimate domain of science. One
of these books is named *Ecce Homo*, the other *Ecce
Deus*. They are both of them interesting in themselves, but much more so, I think, as indicating a certain
progress in religious thought, which tends to the disowning of any deity out of strictly human proportions,
out of the proportions of our own nature; or, what is
the same thing, tends to disallow all personal and admit
only a spiritual infinitude, which is the infinitude of
character. I for my own part rejoice extremely in this
brightening of our intellectual skies. I hope the day is
now no longer so distant as once it seemed, when the
idle, pampered, and mischievous force which men have
everywhere superstitiously worshipped as divine, and
sought to placate by all manner of cruel, slavish, and
mercenary observances, may be utterly effaced in the

resurrection lineaments of that spotless unfriended youth, who in the world's darkest hour allied his own godward hopes with the fortunes only of the most defiled, the most diseased, the most disowned of human kind, and so for the first and only time on earth avouched a breadth in the meanest human bosom every way fit to house and domesticate the infinite divine love. Long before Christ, the lover had freely bled for his mistress, the friend for his friend, the parent for his child, the patriot for his country. History shows no record however of any but him steadfastly choosing death at the hands of fanatical self-seeking men, lest *by simply consenting to live* he should become the object of their filthy and fulsome devotion. In other words, many a man had previously illustrated the creative benignity in every form of *passionate* self-surrender and self-sacrifice. He alone, in the teeth of every passionate impulse known to the human heart — that is to say, in sheer despite of every tie of familiarity, of friendship, of country, of religion, that ordinarily makes life sweet and sacred — surrendered himself to death in clear, unforced, spontaneous homage to universal love.

But then it must be frankly admitted on the other hand that a certain adverse omen declares itself in the religious arena; not however among the positive or doctrinal orthodox sort, so much as among those of a negative or sentimental unitarian hue. It is fast growing a fashion, for example, among our so-called " radical" religious contemporaries, vehemently to patronize Christ's humanity, by way of more effectually discountenancing his conventional divine repute. I too dislike the altogether musty and incoherent divinity ascribed to Christ by the church — a divinity which is intensely accidental and no way incidental to his ineffably tempted, suffering, and yet victorious spiritual manhood. But it is notoriously bad policy to confirm one's self in a mere negative attitude of mind, especially on questions of such intellectual pith and moment as this, and I therefore caution the movers of the new crusade to bethink themselves in time, whether, after all, the only divinity which is capable of permanent recognition at men's hands must not necessarily wear their own form? I find myself incapable, for my own part, of honoring the pretension of any deity to my allegiance, who insists upon standing eternally aloof from my own nature, and by that fact confesses himself personally incommensurate and unsympathetic with my basest, most sensuous, and controlling personal necessities. It is an easy enough thing to find a holiday God who is all too selfish to be touched with the infirmities of his own creatures — a God, for example, who has naught to do but receive assiduous court for a work of creation done myriads of ages ago, and which is reputed to have cost him in the doing neither pains nor patience, neither affection nor thought, but simply the utterance of a dramatic word; and who is willing, accordingly, to accept our decorous sunday homage in ample quittance of obligations so unconsciously incurred on our part, so lightly rendered and so penuriously sanctioned on his. Every sect, every nation, every family almost, offers some pet idol of this description to your worship.

But I am free to confess that I have long outgrown this loutish conception of deity. I can no longer bring myself to adore a characteristic activity in the God of my worship, which falls below the secular average of human character. In fact, what I crave with all my heart and understanding — what my very flesh and bones cry out for — is no longer a sunday but a week-day divinity, a working God, grimy with the dust and sweat of our most carnal appetites and passions, and bent, not for an instant upon inflating our worthless pietistic righteousness, but upon the patient, toilsome, thorough cleansing of our physical and moral existence from the odious defilement it has contracted, until we each and all present at last in body and mind the deathless effigy of his own uncreated loveliness. And no clear revelation do I get of such a God outside the personality of Jesus Christ. It would be gross affectation then in me at least to doubt that he, whom all men in the exact measure of their own veracious manhood acknowledge and adore *as supreme among men,* will always continue to smile at the simulated homage — at the purely voluntary or calculated deference — which is paid to any unknown or unrevealed and transcendental deus, who is yet too superb to subside into the dimensions of his sacred human worth.

CAMBRIDGE, MASS., January, 1869.

CONTENTS.

CHAPTER IV.

CHAPTER V.

CHAPTER VI.

CHAPTER VII.

CHAPTER VIII.

CHAPTER IX.

CHAPTER X.

CHAPTER XXV.

CHAPTER XXVI.

—————

APPENDIX.

THE SECRET OF SWEDENBORG.

THE fundamental problem of Philosophy is the problem of creation. Does our existence really infer a divine and infinite being, or does it not? This question addresses itself to us now with special emphasis, inasmuch as speculative minds are beginning zealously to inquire whether creation can really be admitted any longer, save in an accommodated sense of the word; whether men of simple faith have not gone too far in professing to see a hand of power in the universe absolutely distinct from the universe itself. That being can admit either of increase or diminution is philosophically inconceivable, and affronts moreover the truth of the creative infinitude. For if God be infinite, as we necessarily hold him to be in deference to our own finiteness, what shall add to, or take from, the sum of his being? It is indeed obvious that God cannot create or give being to what has being in itself, for this would be contradictory. He can create only what is devoid of being in itself: this is manifest. And yet what is void of being in itself can at best only appear to be. It can be no real, but only a phenomenal existence. Thus the problem of creation is seen to engender many speculative doubts. How reconcile the antagonism of real and phenomenal, of absolute and contingent, of which the problem is so full? By the hypothesis of creation, the creature derives all he is from the creator. But the creature is essentially not the creator, is above all things himself a created being, and therefore the utter and exact opposite of the creator. How then shall the infinite creator give his finite creature projection, endow him with veritable selfhood or identity, and yet experience no compromise of his own individuality? Suffice it to say that what has hitherto called itself Philosophy has had so little power fairly to confront these difficulties, let alone solve them, as to have set Kant upon the

notion of placating them afresh by the old recipe of Idealism ;
that is, by the invention of another or *noumenal* world, the world
of " things-in-themselves." No doubt this was a new pusillanimity on the part of Philosophy, but what better could the philosopher do ? He saw plainly enough that things were phenomenal ; but as he did not see that this infirmity attached to them
wholly on their subjective or constitutional side, while on their
objective or creative side they were infinite and absolute, he was
bound to lapse into mere idealism or scepticism, unrelieved by
aught but the dream of a noumenal background.

We may smile if we please at the superstitious shifts to which
Kant's philosophic scepticism reduced him ; but after all, Kant
was only the legitimate flower of all the inherited culture of the
world, the helpless logical outcome of bewildered ages of philosophy. Philosophy herself had never discriminated the objective or absolute and creative element in knowledge from its subjective or merely contingent and constitutional element. And
when Kant essayed to make the discrimination, what wonder
that he only succeeded in more hopelessly confounding the two,
and so adjourning once more the hope of Philosophy to an indefinite future ? But Kant's failure to vindicate the philosophic
truth of creation has only exasperated the intellectual discontent
of the world with the cosmological data supplied by the old the-
ologies. Everywhere men of far more tender and reverential
make even than Kant are being driven to freshness of thought ;
and thought, though a remorseless solvent, has no reconstructive
power over truth. Men's opinions are being silently modified in
fact, whether they will or not. The crudities, the extravagan-
ces, the contradictions of the old cosmology, now no longer
amiable and innocent, but aggressive and overbearing, are compelling inquiry into new channels, are making it no longer possible that the notions which satisfied the fathers shall continue to
satisfy the children. A distinctly supernatural creation, once so
fondly urged upon our faith, is quite unintelligible to modern
culture, because it violates experience or contradicts our observation of nature. Everything we observe in nature implies to our
understanding a common or identical substance, being itself a
particular or individual form of such substance. If then the objective form of things were an outward or supernatural com-

munication to them, it would no longer be their own form, inasmuch as it would lack all subjective root, all natural basis, and confess itself an imposition. Thus, on the hypothesis of a supernatural creation, every natural object would disclaim a natural genesis ; and nature, consequently, as denoting the universal or subjective element in existence, would disappear with the disappearance of her proper forms.

Now if nature, in her most generic or universal mood, return us at best a discouraging answer to the old problem of creation, what answer does she yield in her most specific — which is the human or moral — form ? A still more discouraging one even ! In fact, the true motive of the intellectual hostility now formulating to the traditional notion of creation, as an instantaneous or magical exhibition of the divine power, as an arbitrary or irrational procedure of the divine wisdom — by which the universal or substantial element in existence is made, by a summary outward fiat, to *involve* its higher or individual and formal element — is supplied by our moral consciousness, by the irresistible conviction we feel of our personal identity. That moral or personal existence should be outwardly generated, should be created in the sense of having being communicated to it supernaturally, contradicts consciousness. For moral or personal existence is purely conscious or subjective existence, and consciousness or subjectivity is a strictly *natural* style of existence, and hence disowns all supernatural interference as impertinent. It is preposterous to allege that my consciousness or subjectivity involves any other person than myself, since this would vitiate my personal identity, and hence defeat my possible spiritual individuality or character. If, being what I am conscious of being, namely, a moral or personal existence invested with self-control or the rational ownership of my actions, I yet am not so naturally or of myself, but by some supernatural or foreign intervention, then obviously I am simply what such intervention determines me to be, and my feeling of selfhood or freedom is grossly illusory. Thus morality, which is the assertion of a selfhood in man commensurate with all the demands of nature and society upon him, turns out, if too rigidly insisted on — if maintained as a divine finality, or as having not merely a constitutional, but a creative truth, not merely a subjective or phenomenal, but also an objective or real validity — to be essentially atheistic, and drives those who are loyal rather to the inward spirit than the outward letter of revelation to repugn the old maxims of a supernatural creation and providence as furnishing any longer a satisfactory theorem of existence.

Faith must reconcile herself to this perilous alternative, if she obstinately persist in making our natural morality supernatural by allowing it a truth irrespective of consciousness, or assigning it any objectivity beyond the evolution of human society or fellowship. It is not its own end, but a strict means to a higher or spiritual evolution of life *in our nature;* and they accordingly who persist in ignoring this truth must expect to fall intellectually behind the time in which they live. Some concession here is absolutely necessary to save the religious instinct. For men feel a growing obligation to co-ordinate the demands of freedom or personality with the limitations of science ; and since Kant's remorseless criticism stops them off — under penalty of accepting his impracticable noumenal world — from postulating any longer an objective being answering to their subjective seeming, they must needs with his successors give the whole question of creation the go-by, in quietly resolving the minor element of the equation into the major, man into God, or making the finite a mere transient experience of the infinite, by means of which that great unconsciousness attains to selfhood. For this is the sum of the Hegelian dialectic, to confound existence with being, or make identity no longer serve individuality, but absorb or swallow it up : so bringing back creation to intellectual chaos, which is naught.

I myself, in common with most men doubtless, feel an instinctive repugnance to these insane logical results ; but instinct is not intelligence, and sophistry can be combated only by intelligence. Now, to my mind, nothing so effectually arms the intellect against error, whether it be the error of the sceptic or the error of the fanatic, whether it reflect our prevalent religious cant or our almost equally prevalent scientific cant, as a due acquaintance and familiarity with the ontological principles of Swedenborg. Emanuel Swedenborg, I need not say, is by no means as yet " a name to conjure with " in polite circles, and, for aught I opine, may never become one. Nevertheless numerous independent students are to be found, who, having been long hopeless of getting to the bottom of our endless controversies, confess that their intellectual doubts have at last been dispersed by the sunshine of his ontology. It would be small praise of Swedenborg to say that he does not, like Hegel, benumb our spiritual instincts, or drown them out in a flood of vainglorious intoxication brought about by an absurd exaltation of the subjective element in life above the objective one. This praise no doubt is true, but much more is true ; and that is, that he *enlightens* the religious conscience, and so gives the intellect a repose which it has lacked throughout history — a repose as natural and therefore as sane and sweet as the sleep of infancy. Admire Hegel's legerdemain as much as you will, his ability to make light darkness and darkness light in all the field of man's relations to God ; but remember also that it is characteristic of the highest truth to be accessible to common minds, and inaccessible only to ambitious ones. Tried by this test, the difference between the two writers is incomparably in favor of Swedenborg. For example what a complete darkening of our intellectual optics is operated by Hegel's fundamental postulate of the identity of object and subject, being and thought. "Thought and being are identical." Such indeed is the necessary logic of idealism. Now doubtless our faculty of abstract thought is chief among our intellectual faculties; but when it is seriously proposed to build the universe of existence upon a logical abstraction, one must needs draw a very long breath. For thought by itself affords a most inadequate basis even to our own conscious activity ; and when, therefore, our unconscious being is in question, it confesses itself a simply ludicrous hypothesis.

But in reality Hegel, in spite of his extreme pretension in that line, never once got within point-blank range of the true problem of ontology ; and this because he habitually confounded being with existence, spirit with nature. By being he never meant being, but always existence, the existence we are conscious of; so that when he would grasp the infinite, he fancied he had only to resort to the cheap expedient of eliminating the finite. It is precisely as if a man should say : "All I need in order to procure myself an intuitive knowledge of my own visage, is not to look at its reflection in the looking-glass."

Think the finite away, said Hegel, and the infinite is left on your hands. Yes, provided the infinite is never a positive quantity, but only and at most a thought-negation of its own previously thought-negation. But really, if the infinite be this mere negation of its own negation, that is, if being turns out to be identical with nothing, with the absence of mere *thing*, then I must say, in the first place, that I do not see why any sane person should covet its acquaintance. Being which has been so utterly compromised, and indeed annihilated, by its own phenomenal forms, as to be able to reappear only by their disappearance, is scarcely the being which unsophisticated men will ever be persuaded to deem infinite or creative. But then I must also say, in the second place, let it be true, as Hegel alleges, that being is identical with the absence of *thing*, that is, with nothing, I still am at an utter loss to understand how that leaves it identical with pure thought. I need not deny that I hold thing and thought to be by any means identical; but I am free to maintain nevertheless that if you actually abstract things from thought, you simply render thought itself exanimate. For thought has no vehicle or body but language, and language owes all its soul or inspiration to things. Abstract things then, and neither thought nor language actually survives. You might as well expect the body to survive its soul.

But in truth this metaphysic chatter is the mere wantonness of sense. The infinite is so far from being negative of the finite, that it is essentially creative — and hence exclusively affirmative — of it. The finite indeed is only that inevitable diffraction of itself which the infinite undergoes in the medium or mirror of our sensuous thought, in order so to adapt itself to our dim intelligence. It is accordingly no less absurd for us to postulate a disembodied or unrevealed infinite — an infinite unrobed or unrepresented by the finite — than it would be to demand a father unavouched by a child. The infinite is the sole reality which underlies all finite appearance, and in that tender unobtrusive way makes itself conceivable to our obtuse thought. Should we get any nearer this reality by spurning the gracious investiture through which alone it becomes appreciable to us? Is a man's intelligence of nature improved, on the whole, by

putting out his eyes? If, then, the infinite reveals itself to our
nascent understanding only by the finite — i. e. by what we
already sensibly know — how much nearer should we come to
its knowledge by rejecting such revelation? We who are not
infinite cannot know it absolutely or in itself, but only as it veils
or abates its splendor to the capacity of our tender vision, —
only as it reproduces itself within our finite lineaments. In a
word, our knowledge of it is no way intuitive, but exclusively
empirical. Would our chances of realizing such knowledge be
advanced, then, by following Hegel's counsel, and disowning
that apparatus of finite experience by which alone it becomes
mirrored to our intelligence? In other words, suppose a man
desirous to know what manner of man he is: were it better for
him, in that case, to proceed by incontinently smashing his looking-glass, or by devoutly pondering its revelations? The question answers itself. The glass may be by no means achromatic;
it may return indeed a most refractory reply to the man's inter-
rogatory; but nevertheless it is his only method of actually
compassing the information he covets, and in the estimation
of all wise men he will stamp himself an incorrigible fool if
he breaks it.

But the truth is too plain to need argument. There is no
antagonism of infinite and finite except to our foolish regard.
On the contrary, there is the exact harmony or adjustment between them that there is between substance and shadow: the
infinite being that which really or absolutely *is*, and the finite
that which actually or contingently *appears*. The infinite is
the faultless substance which, unseen itself, vivifies all finite
existence; the finite is the fallacious shadow which nevertheless *attests* that substance. The shadow has no pretension
absolutely to be, but only to exist or appear as a necessary
projection or image of the substance upon our intellectual
retina; and when consequently we wink the shadow out of
sight, we do not thereby acuminate our vision, we simply
obliterate it. That is to say, we do not thereby approximate
our silly selves to the infinite, but simply degrade them out
of the finite into the void inane of the indefinite. To you
who are not being, being can become known only as finite or
phenomenal existence. If then you abstract the finite, the

realm of the phenomenal, you not only miss the infinite substance you seek to know, but also and even the very shadow
itself upon which your faculty of knowledge is suspended.
Such, however, was the abysmal absurdity locked away in
Hegel's dialectic, which remorselessly confounds infinite form
and finite substance, real or objective being with phenomenal
or subjective seeming; which in fact turns creation upside
down, by converting it from an orderly procedure of the divine
love and wisdom into a tipsy imbroglio, where what is lowest
to thought is made to *involve* what is highest, and what is
highest in its turn to *evolve* what is lowest: so that God and
man, creator and creature, in place of being eternally individualized or objectified to each other's regard, become mutually undiscoverable, being hopelessly swamped to sight in the
ineffectual mush of each other's subjective identity. But
what is Hegel's supreme shame in the eyes of philosophy,
namely, his utter unscrupulous abandonment of himself to the
inspiration of idealism, will constitute his true distinction to
the future historiographer of philosophy. For idealism has
been the secret blight of philosophy ever since men began to
speculate ; and what Hegel has done for philosophy in running idealism into the ground, has been to bring this secret
blight to the surface, so exposing it to all eyes, and making
it impossible for human fatuity ever to go a step further, in that
direction at all events.

The correction which Swedenborg brings to this pernicious
idealistic bent of the mind consists in the altogether novel
light he sheds upon the constitution of consciousness, and
particularly upon the fundamental discrimination which that
constitution announces between the phenomenal identity of
things and their real individuality ; between the subjective or
merely quantifying element in existence, and its objective or
properly qualifying one. The old philosophy was blind to this
sharp discrimination in the constitution of existence. It regarded existence, not as a composite, but as a simple quantity,
and consequently sank the spiritual element in things in their
natural element — sank what gives them individuality, life, soul,
in what gives them identity, existence, body; in other words
sank the *creative* element in existence — what causes it absolutely

or objectively to *be* — in its *constitutive* or generative element, in what causes it phenomenally or subjectively to *appear*. For example, what was its conception of man ? It regarded him simply on his moral side, which presents him as essentially selfish or inveterately objective to himself, and left his spiritual possibilities, which present him as essentially social, or spontaneously subject to his neighbor, wholly unrecognized.* In short, it separated him from the face of deity by all the breadth of nature and all the length of history ; and suspended his return upon some purely arbitrary interference exerted by deity upon the course of nature and the progress of history.

Swedenborg's analysis of consciousness stamps these judgments as sensuous or immature, and restores man to the intimate fellowship of God. Consciousness according to Swedenborg claims two most disproportionate generative elements ; — one universal, subjective, passive, organic ; the other, particular, objective, human, active, free. The former element gives us fixity or limitation ; *universalizes* or *identifies* us, by relating us to the outward and finite, i. e. to nature. The latter element gives us freedom, which is *de*-limitation or *de*-finition ; *particularizes* or *individualizes* us, by relating us to the inward and infinite, i. e. to God. This latter element is absolute and creative, for it gives us potential being before we actually exist or become conscious. The other element is merely phenomenal and constitutive, making us exist or go forth to our own consciousness in due cosmical place and order.

Now the immense bearing which this analysis of consciousness exerts upon cosmological speculation, or the question of creation, becomes at once obvious when we reflect that it utterly inverts the long-established supremacy of subject to object in existence, and so demolishes at a blow the sole philosophic haunt of idealism or scepticism. The great scientific value of the Critical Philosophy lay in Kant's making manifest the latent malady of the old philosophy by dogmatically affiliating object to subject, the *not-me* to the *me*. His followers only proved

---

* The best and briefest definition of moral existence is, *the alliance of an inward subject and an outward object ;* and of spiritual existence, *the alliance of an outward subject and an inward object.* Thus in moral existence what is public or universal dominates what is private or individual ; whereas in spiritual existence the case is reversed, and the outward serves the inward.

themselves to be his too apt disciples, in endeavoring to paint and adorn this ghastly disease with the ruddy hues of health, by running philosophy into pure or objective idealism. For if the subjective element in existence alone *identifies* it or gives it universality, then manifestly we cannot allow it also to *individualize* it or give it unity, without making the being of things purely subjective, and hence denying it any objective reality. Kant is scrupulously logical. He accepts the deliverance of sense as final, that the *me* determines the *not-me;* that the conscious or phenomenal element in experience controls its unconscious or real one; and hence he cannot help denying any absolute truth to creation. He cannot help maintaining that however much the creator may *be*, he will at any rate never be able to *appear;* that however infinite or perfect he may claim to be in himself, that very infinitude must always prevent him incarnating himself in the finite, and consequently forbid any true revelation of his perfection to an imperfect intelligence. And Mr. Mansel, who is Kant's intellectual grandson, is so tickled with this sceptical fatuity on the part of his sire, as to find in it a new and fascinating base for our religious homage; and he does not hesitate accordingly to argue that the only stable motive to our faith in God is supplied by ignorance, not by knowledge; or, what is the same thing, by fear, not by love.

Swedenborg, I repeat, effectually silences these ravings of philosophic despair by simply rectifying the basis of philosophy, or affirming an absolute as well as an empirical element in consciousness, an infinite as well as a finite element in knowledge. He provides a real or objective, no less than a phenomenal or subjective, element in existence; an element of unconditional being as well as of conditional seeming; a creative element, in short, no less than a constitutive one. This absolute or infinite element in existence is what *qualifies* the existence, is what gives it distinctive life or soul, and so permits it to be objectively *individualized* as *man, horse, tree, stone;* while its empirical or finite element merely *quantifies* it, or gives it phenomenal body, and so permits it to be subjectively *identified* as *English*-man, *French*-man; *race*-horse, *draught*-horse; *fruit*-tree, *forest*-tree; *sand*-stone, *lime*-stone. Or let us take some artificial existence, say a statue. Now of the two elements which go to make up the statue, one ideal, the other material, — one objective or formal, the other subjective or substantial, — the latter, according to Swedenborg, finites the statue, fixes it, incorporates it, gives it outward body, and thus universalizes or identifies it with other existence; while the former *in*-finites it, frees it from material bondage, vivifies it, gives it inward soul, and so individualizes it from all other existence. Thus the statue as an ideal form, or on its qualitative side, is absolute and infinite with all its maker's absoluteness and infinitude; and it is only as a material substance, or on its quantitative side, that it turns out contingent, finite, infirm.

This discrimination, so important in every point of view to the intellect, gives us the key to Swedenborg's ontology, his doctrine of the Lord or Maximus Homo. Swedenborg's cosmological principles make the natural world a necessary implication of the spiritual, and consequently make the spiritual world the only safe or adequate *explication* of the natural. In short, his theory of creation assigns a rigidly natural genesis and growth to the spiritual world; and as this theory is summarily comprised in his doctrine of the God-Man or Divine Natural Humanity, I shall proceed to test the philosophic worth of this doctrine, by applying it to the problem of our human origin and destiny. But before doing this it may be expedient briefly to recall who and what Swedenborg was, in order to ascertain whether his private history sheds any light upon his dogmatic pretensions.

I.

It is known to all the world that Swedenborg, for many years before his death, assumed to be an authorized herald of a new and spiritual divine advent in human nature. Similar assumptions are not infrequent in history, and it cannot be denied that our proper *a priori* attitude toward them is one of contempt and aversion. But Swedenborg's alleged mission, both as he himself conceived it and as his books represent it, claimed no personal or outward sanction, and accepted no voucher but what it found in every man's unforced delight in the truth to which it ministered. He was himself remarkably deficient in those

commanding personal qualities and graces of intellect which
attract popular esteem; and I am quite sure that no such insanity ever entered his own guileless heart as to attribute to
himself the power of complicating in any manner the existing
relations of man and God.

Swedenborg, as we learn from his latest and best biographer,
Mr. White,* — whose work is almost a model in its kind, and
does emphatic credit both to his intellect and conscience, — was
born at Stockholm in 1688.   His father, who was a Swedish
bishop distinguished for learning and piety, christened the infant
Emanuel, " in order that his name might continually remind
him of the nearness of God, and of that interior, holy, and
mysterious union in which we stand to him."   The youth thus
devoutly consecrated justified all his father's hopes, for his
entire life was devoted to science, religion, and philosophy.   His
history, as we find it related by Mr. White, was unmarked by
any striking external vicissitudes; and his pursuits were at all
times so purely intellectual as to leave personal gossip almost no
purchase upon his modest and blameless career.   He held the
office for many years of Government Assessor of Mines, and
appears to have enjoyed friendly and even intimate personal
relations with Charles XII., to whose ability as a mathematician
his diary affords some interesting testimonies.   While he was
not professionally active, his days were devoted to study and
travel; and by the time he had reached his fiftieth year, his
scholarly and scientific repute had been advanced and established
by several publications of great interest.   We may say generally
that the pursuits of science claimed all his attention till he was
upwards of fifty years old; that his life and manners were pure
and irreproachable, and his intellectual aspirations singularly
elevated.   To arrive at the knowledge of the soul by the
strictest methods of science had always been his hope and
endeavor.   He conceived that the body, being the fellow of the
soul, was in some sort its continuation; and that if he could
only penetrate therefore to its purest forms or subtlest essences,
he would be sure of touching at last the soul's true territory.
Long and fruitless toil had somewhat disenchanted him of this

* Emanuel Swedenborg: his Life and Writings. By William White. London,
1867. 2 Vols. 8vo. See Appendix, Note A.

illusion previously; but what he calls "the opening of his spiritual sight," which event means his becoming acquainted with *the spiritual sense of the scriptures*, or the truth of the DIVINE NATURAL HUMANITY, effectually put an end to it, by convincing him that the tie between soul and body, or spirit and letter, is not by any means one of sensible continuity, as from finer to grosser, but one exclusively of rational correspondence, such as obtains between cause and effect. From this moment, accordingly, he abandoned his scientific studies, and applied himself with intense zeal to the unfolding of the spiritual sense of the scriptures "from things seen and heard in the spiritual world." This internal sense of the scriptures is very unattractive reading to those who care more for entertainment than instruction, and I cannot counsel any one of a merely literary turn to undertake it. But it is full of marrow and fatness to a philosophic curiosity, from the flood of novel light it lets in upon history; its substantial import being, that the history of the church on earth, which is the history of human development up to a comparatively recent period, has been only a stupendous symbol, or cover, under which secrets of the widest creative scope and efficacy, issues of the profoundest humanitary significance, were all the while assiduously transacting. It is fair to suppose, therefore, that our sense of the worth of Swedenborg's spiritual pretensions will be somewhat biassed by the estimate we habitually put upon the church as an instrument of human progress. If we suppose church and state to have been purely accidental determinations of man's history, owning no obligation to his selfish beginnings on the one hand, nor to his social destiny on the other, we shall not probably lend much attention to the information proffered by Swedenborg. But if we believe with him that the realm of "accident," however vast to sense, has absolutely no existence to the reason emancipated from sense, we shall probably regard the church, and its derivative the state, as claiming a true divine appointment; and we *may* find consequently in his ideas of its meaning and history an approximate justification of his claim to spiritual insight. At all events no lower justification of his claim is for a moment admissible to a rational regard. As I have already said, his books are singularly void of literary fascination. I know of no writer with anything like his intellectual force who is so persistently feeble in point of argumentative or persuasive skill. His books teem with the grandest, the most humane and generous truth; but his reverence for it is so austere and vital, that, like the lover who willingly makes himself of no account beside his mistress, he seems always intent upon effacing himself from sight before its matchless lustre. Certainly the highest truth never encountered a more lowly intellectual homage than it gets in these artless books; never found itself so unostentatiously heralded, so little patronized in a word, or left so completely for its success to its own sheer unadorned majesty.

It must be admitted also that the books, upon a superficial survey, repel philosophic as much as literary curiosity, by suggesting the notion of an irreconcilable conflict between our conscious or phenomenal freedom and our unconscious or real dependence. To a cursory glance they appear to assert an endless warfare between the interests of our natural morality on the one hand, and of our spiritual destiny on the other. It seems, for example, to be taught by Swedenborg, that human morality serves such important theoretic ends in the economy of creation, that it may even be allowed to render the creature utterly hostile to the creator, or endow him with a faculty of spiritual suicide, and yet itself incur no reproach. In other words, our moral freedom is apparently made to claim such extreme consideration at the divine hands, in consequence of its eminent uses to the spiritual life, as justifies it in absolutely deflecting us, if need be, from the paths of peace, and landing us ultimately in chronic spiritual disaffection to our maker. Such no doubt is the surface aspect of these remarkable books — the aspect they wear to a hasty and prejudiced observation; and if the reality of the case were at all conformable to the appearance, nothing favorable of course would remain to be said, since no sharper affront could well be offered to the creative perfection, than to suppose it baffled by the inveterate imbecility of its own helpless creature.

But the reality of the case is by no means answerable to this surface seeming; and it is only from gross inattention to what we may call the author's commanding intellectual doctrine — his doctrine of the Lord or Maximus Homo — that a contrary impression prevails to the prejudice of his philosophic repute. This doctrine claims, in the estimation of those who discern its profound intellectual significance, to be the veritable apotheosis of philosophy. What then does the doctrine practically amount to? It amounts, briefly stated, to this: that what we call nature, meaning by that term the universe of existence, mineral, vegetable, and animal, which seems to us infinite in point of space and eternal in point of time, is yet in itself, or absolutely, void both of infinity and eternity; the former appearance being only a sensible product and correspondence of a relation which the universal heart of man is under to the divine love, and the latter, a product and correspondence of the relation which the universe of the human mind is under to the divine wisdom. Thus nature is not in the least what it sensibly purports to be, namely, absolute and independent; but, on the contrary, is at every moment, both in whole and in part, a pure phenomenon or effect of spiritual causes as deep, as contrasted, and yet as united, as God's infinite love and man's unfathomable want. In short, Swedenborg describes nature as a perpetual outcome or product in the sphere of sense of an inward supersensuous marriage which is forever growing and forever adjusting itself between creator and creature, between God's infinite and essential bounty and our infinite and essential necessity. But these statements are too brief not to require elucidation.

II.

Let it be understood, then, first of all, that creation, in Swedenborg's view, is of necessity a composite, not a simple, movement, inasmuch as it is bound to provide for the creature's subjective existence, no less than his objective being. The creature, in order to be created, in order truly to be, must exist or *go forth from* the creator; and he can thus exist or go forth only in *his own form*, of course. Thus creation, or the giving absolute being to things, logically involves a subordinate process of *making*, which is the giving them phenomenal or conscious form. In fact, upon this strictly incidental process of formation, the entire truth of creation philosophically pivots;

for unless the creator be able to give his creature subjective
identity (which is natural alienation from, or *otherness than*,
himself), he will never succeed in giving him objective individuality, which is spiritual oneness with himself.   In other words,
the creature can enjoy no real or objective conjunction with the
creator, save in so far as he shall previously have undergone
phenomenal or conscious disjunction with him.   His spiritual
or specific fellowship with the creator presupposes his natural
or generic inequality with him.   In short, the interests of
the creature's natural identity dominate those of his spiritual individuality to such an extent that he remains absolutely
void of being, save in so far as he exists or goes forth in his
own proper lineaments.   If creation were by possibility the
direct act of divine omnipotence, which men superstitiously
deem it to be — in other words, if God could create man magi-
cally, i. e. without any necessary implication of man *himself*,
without any implication of his mineral, vegetable, and animal
nature — then of course creator and creature would be undistinguishable, and creation fail to avouch itself.   Thus the total
truth of creation spiritually regarded hinges upon its being a
reflex not a direct, a composite not a simple, a rational not an
arbitrary exertion of divine power — hinges, in short, upon
its supplying a subjective and phenomenal development to the
creature every way commensurate with, or adequate to, the objective and absolute being he has in the creator.

  We may clearly maintain, then, that the truth of creation is
wholly contingent upon the truth of the creature's identity.   If
the creator is able to afford the creature valid selfhood or
identity, then creation is philosophically conceivable, otherwise
not.   All that philosophy needs, in permanent illustration of
the creative name, is to rescue the creature subjectively regarded from the creator, or put his identity upon an inexpugnable basis.   To create or give being to things is no doubt an
inscrutable function of the divine omnipotence, to which our
intelligence is incapable of assigning any *a priori* law or limit.
But we are clearly competent to say *a posteriori* of the things
thus created, that they *are* only in so far as they exist or go
forth in their own form.   That is to say, they must, in order
to their being true creatures of God, not only possess spirit-

ual form or objectivity in him, as the statue has ideal form or objectivity in the genius of the sculptor, or the child moral form or objectivity in the loins of his father, but they must actually go forth from him, or exist in their own proper substance, in their own constitutional identity, just as the statue exists in the appropriate constitutional substance which the marble gives it, or the child in the proper constitutional lineaments with which the mother invests it. The legal maxim is, *de non apparentibus et non existentibus eadem est ratio.* The philosophic demand is broader. It says, no *esse* without *existere;* no reality without corresponding actuality; no soul without body; no form without substance; no being without manifestation; in short, no creation on God's part save in so far as there is a rigidly constitutional response and reaction on ours.

The creative perfection is wholly active; that is to say, God is true creator only to the extent that we in our measure are true creatures. Thus, before creation can be worthy of its name, worthy either of God to claim it or of us to acknowledge it save in a lifeless, traditional way, it implies a subjective experience on our part, an historic evolution or process of formation, by which we become eternally projected from God, or endowed with inalienable self-consciousness, and so qualified for his subsequent spiritual fellowship and converse. In other words, creation is practically and of necessity to our experience a formative or historic process, exhibiting a descent of the divine nature exactly proportionate to the elevation of the human, and so presenting creator and creature in indissoluble union. This is the inexorable postulate of creation, that the creature be *himself* — have selfhood or subjective life — a life as distinctively his own as God's life is distinctively his own. Not only must the creature aspire, instinctively and innocently aspire, " to be like God, knowing good and evil," i. e. to be sufficient unto himself, but the creative perfection is bound to ratify that aspiration, and endow its creature with all its own wealth of goodness and wisdom. The aspiration itself is the deepest motion of the divine spirit within us. It is impossible to be spiritually begotten of God without desiring to be like him; that is, to be wise and good even as he is, not from constraint or the prompting of expediency, but spontaneously, or from a serene inward delight in goodness and

2

wisdom. Evidently no fellowship between God and our own souls is possible until this instinct be appeased; for up to that event all our life will have been only the concealed motion of his spirit in our nature. He alone will have been really living in us, while we ourselves will have only seemed to live — will have been, in fact, mere unconscious masks of his life.

Now how shall creation ever be seen to bear this surprising fruit? From the nature of the case, creation must be a purely spiritual operation on God's part, since he alone is, and there is nothing outside of him whence the creature may be summoned. By the hypothesis of creation, God alone is, and the creature exclusively by him. How is it conceivable, therefore, to our intelligence, that the creature should possess selfhood or subjective identity, without a compromise to that extent of the divine unity? How is it conceivable that God, the sole being, should himself create or give being to other existence without impairing to that extent his own infinitude? The creature has no being which he does not derive from the creator; this is obvious. And yet the hypothesis of creation binds us to regard the creator as communicating his own being to another, without any limitation of its fulness. The demand of our intelligence is insatiable, therefore, until it ascertain how these things can be — until it perceive how it is that the creator is able to impart selfhood or moral power to the absolutely dependent offspring of his own hands, the abjectly helpless offspring of his own perfection. By an indomitable instinct the mind claims to know, and will never rest accordingly until it discover, what it is which validly separates creature from creator, and so permits their subsequent union, not only without violence to either interest, but with consummate reciprocal advantage and beatitude to both interests.

It is exactly here — in giving us light upon this most momentous and most mysterious inquiry — that what Swedenborg calls "the opening of his spiritual sight," or his discovery of "the spiritual sense of the scriptures," professes to make itself of endless avail. What the literal sense of revelation is, we all know familiarly. We have been too familiar with it, in fact, not to have had our spiritual perceptions somewhat overlaid by it. It represents creation as a work of God conceived and accomplished in space and time, and consequently makes the relation of

creator and creature essentially outward and personal. Now
"the spiritual sense" of scripture as reported by Swedenborg
is not a new or different literal sense. It is not the least literal,
inasmuch as it utterly disowns the obligations of space and
time, and claims the exclusive authentication of an infinite love
and wisdom. In short, by the spiritual or living sense of
revelation, Swedenborg means the truth of God's NATURAL
humanity; so that all our natural prepossessions in regard to
space and time and person confess themselves purely rudimental
and educative, the moment we come to acknowledge in nature
and man an infinite divine substance. It is true, no doubt,
that Swedenborg's doctrine of creation falls, without constraint,
into the literal terms of the orthodox dogma of the incarnation.
But then the letter of revelation bears, as he demonstrates, so
inverse a relation to its living spirit, that we can get no help but
only hindrance, from any attempt to interpret his statements by
the light of dogmatic theology. Dogmatic theology is bound
hand and foot by the letter of revelation; and the letter of
revelation "is adapted," says Swedenborg, "only to the apprehension of simple or unenlightened men, in order that they
may thus be *introduced* to the acquaintance of interior and
higher verities." Again he says, "Three things of the literal sense perish, when the spiritual sense of the word is
evolving, namely, whatsoever belongs to *space*, to *time*, or to
person"; and still again, "In heaven no attention is paid to
person, nor the things of person, but to things abstracted from
person; thus angels have no perception of any person whose
name is mentioned in the word, but only of his human quality
or faculty." Hence he describes those who are in spiritual ideas
as never thinking of the lord from person, "because thought
determined to person limits and degrades the truth, while
thought undetermined to person gives it infinitude"; and he
adds, that the angels are amazed at the stupidity of church
people, "in not suffering themselves to be elevated out of the
letter of revelation, and persisting to think carnally, and not
spiritually of the lord, — as of his flesh and blood, and not
of his infinite goodness and truth." *

* Arcana Celestia, 8705, 5253, 9007; and Apocalypse Explained, 30.

III.

It is manifestly idle, then, to attempt coercing the large philosophic scope of Swedenborg's doctrine within the dimensions of our narrow ecclesiastical dogma. There is as real a contrast and oppugnancy between the two to the intellect, as there is to the stomach between a loaf of bread and a paving-stone. For example, it is vital to the dogmatic view of the incarnation to regard it as an event completely included in space and time, and yet brought about by supernatural power, acting in direct contravention of the course of nature. A dogma of this stolid countenance bluffs the intellect off from its wonted activity no less effectually, of course, than a stone taken into the stomach arrests the digestive circulation. With Swedenborg, on the other hand, the christian facts utterly refute this supernatural conception of the divine existence and operation, or reduce it to a superstition, by proving nature herself, in the very crisis of her outward disorder, to have been inwardly alive with all divine order, peace, and power. According to Swedenborg, the birth, the life, the death, the resurrection of Christ were so remote from supernatural contingencies as to confess themselves the consummate flowering of the creative energy in *universal* nature, i. e. the universe of the human mind, embracing heaven and hell quite equally. No doubt the flower is a very marked phenomenon to the senses, filling the atmosphere with its glory and fragrance. But its total interest to the rational mind turns upon those hidden affinities which, by means of its aspiring stem and its grovelling roots, connect it at once with all that is loftiest and all that is lowliest in universal nature, and so turn the flower itself into a sensuous sign merely or modest emblem of a secret most holy marriage, which is forever transacting in unseen depths of being, between the generic, universal, or merely animate substances of the mind, and its specific, unitary, or human form. So with the incarnation. The literal facts have no significance to the spiritual understanding, save as a natural ultimate and revelation of the true principles of creative order, the order that binds the universe of existence to its source.

What are these principles? They are all summed up in the truth of the essential divine *humanity*. According to Swedenborg, God is essential Man; so that creation, instead of being primarily a sensible product of divine power, or a work accomplished in space and time, turns out first of all a spiritual achievement of the divine love and wisdom in all the forms of human nature, and only subordinately to that a thing of physical dimensions. Swedenborg enforces this truth very copiously in the way of illustration, but never in that of ratiocination. His reason for this abstention is very instructive. Swedenborg distinguishes as no person has ever done between two orders of truth — truth of being. ontological truth, truths of conscience in short; and truth of seeming. phenomenal truth, truths of science in short. The distinction between these two orders of truth is, that the former is not *probable*, that is to say, admits of no sensuous proof; while the latter is essentially probable, i. e. capable of being proved by sensuous reasoning. The French proverb says, *the true is not always the probable*. Now with Swedenborg, the true — the supremely true — is *never* the probable, that is, finds no countenance in outward likelihood, but derives all its support from the inward sanction of the heart. Facts — which are matter of outward observation or science — may be reasoned about to any extent, and legitimately established by reasoning. But truth — which is matter of inward experience or conscience — owns no such dependence, and invites no homage but that of a modest, unostentatious Yea, yea! Nay, nay! The philosophic ground of this state of things is obvious. For if the case were otherwise, if truth. truths of life, could be reasoned into us, or be made ours by force of persuasion, then belief would no longer be free; that is to say, it would no longer reflect the love of the heart, but control or coerce it. In other words, the truth believed would no longer be the truth we inwardly love and crave, but only that which has most outward prestige or authority to back it. In that event, of course, our affections, which ally us with infinitude or God, would be at the mercy of our intelligence, which allies us with nature or the finite. And life consequently, instead of being the spontaneous indissoluble marriage of heart and head which it really

is, would confess itself at most their voluntary or chance concubinage.

I have no pretension, of course, to decide dogmatically for
the reader whether what Swedenborg calls the Divine Natural
Humanity be the commanding truth he supposes it to be, or
whether it be a mere otiose hypothesis. But I am bound
to assist him, so far as I am able, to decide these questions
for himself; and I cannot do this more effectually than by
fixing his attention for a while upon what is involved in the
middle term of Swedenborg's proposition, since we are apt to
cherish very faulty conceptions of what nature logically comprises. Swedenborg's doctrine summarily stated is, that what
we call nature, and suppose to be exactly what it seems, is in
truth a thing of strictly human and strictly divine dimensions
both as being at one and the same moment a just exponent of
the creature's essential want or finiteness, and of the creator's
essential fulness or infinitude. In other words, where people
whose understanding is still controlled by sense, see nature
absolute or unqualified by spirit, Swedenborg, professing to
be spiritually enlightened, does not see nature at all, but only
the lord, or God-Man, carnally hidden indeed, degraded, humiliated, crucified under all manner of devout pride and self-
seeking, but at the same time spiritually exalted or glorified by
a love untainted with selfishness, and a wisdom undimmed by
prudence. Manifestly then, in order to do justice to Swedenborg's doctrine, we must rid ourselves first of all of certain
sensuous prejudices we cherish in regard to nature; and to
this aim we shall now for a moment address ourselves.

Nature is all that our senses embrace; thus it is whatsoever
appears to be. Now the two universals of this phenomenal or
apparitional world are space and time; for whatsoever sensibly
exists, exists in space and time, or implies extension and duration. Space and time have thus a fixed or absolute status to
our senses, so furnishing our spiritual understanding with that
firm though dusty earth of fact or knowledge, upon which it
may forever ascend into the serene expansive heaven of truth
or belief. But now observe; just because space and time,
which make up our notion of nature, are thus absolute to our
senses, we are led in the infancy of science, or while the senses

still dominate the intellect, to confer upon nature a logical absoluteness or reality which in truth is wholly fallacious. We habitually ascribe a rational or supersensuous reality to her, as well as a sensible ; or regard the universe of space and time, not only as the needful implication of our subjective or conscious existence, but as an ample *explication* also of our objective or unconscious being. And every such conception of the part nature plays in creation is puerile, and therefore misleading or fatal to a spiritual apprehension of truth.

This may be seen at a glance. For if you consent to make nature absolute as well as contingent — that is, if you make it be irrespectively of our intelligence, which you do whenever you reflectively exalt space and time from sensible into rational quantities — then, of course, you disjoin infinite and finite, God and man, creator and creature, not only phenomenally but really ; not only *ab intra* or *in se*, but also and much more *ab extra*, or by all the literal breadth of nature's extension, and all the literal length of her duration : so swamping spiritual thought in the bottomless mire of materialism. For obviously if you thus operate a real or spiritual disjunction between God and man, you can never hope to bring about that actual or literal conjunction between them which Swedenborg affirms in his doctrine of the Divine Natural Humanity, save by hypostatizing some preposterous mediator as big as the universe and as ancient as the world. In short, you will be driven in this state of things spiritually to reconcile God and man, or put them at-one, only by inventing a style of personality so egregiously finite or material as literally to embody in itself all nature's indefinite spaces, and all her indeterminate times.

Thus, according to Swedenborg, sensuous conceptions of truth — the habit we have of estimating appearances as realities — are the grand intellectual hindrance we experience to the acknowledgment of a creation in which creator and creature are spiritually united. Evidently, then, our only mode of exit from the embarrassments which sense entails upon the intellect, is to spurn her authority and renounce her guidance. Now the lustiest affirmation sense makes is to the unconditional validity of space and time, or their existence *in se ;* and this means inferentially the integrity of nature, or the dogma of a physical creation. The great service, accordingly, which Swedenborg does the intellect is, that he refutes this sensuous dogmatizing by establishing the pure relativity of space and time; so vindicating the exclusive truth of the spiritual creation. I defy any fair-minded person to read Swedenborg, and still preserve a shred of respect for the dogma of a physical creation. He utterly explodes the assumed basis of the dogma, by demonstrating that space and time are contingencies of a finite or sensibly organized intelligence; hence that nature, being all made up of space and time, has no rational, but only a sensible objectivity. He demonstrates, in fact, and on the contrary, that nature rationally regarded is the realm of pure subjectivity, having no other pertinency to the spiritual or objective world than the bodily viscera have to the body, than the shadow has to the substance which projects it, than darkness has to light, or death to life — that is, a strictly *reflective* pertinency. The true sphere of creation being thus spiritual or inward, it follows, according to Swedenborg, that any doctrine of nature which proceeds upon the assumption of her finality, or does not construe her as a mere constitutional means to a superior creative end — as a mere outward echo or reverberation of the true creative activity in inward realms of being — is simply delirious.

Swedenborg's doctrine then of the Divine Natural Humanity becomes readily intelligible, if, disowning the empire of sense, we consent to conceive of nature after a spiritual manner, that is, by reducing her from a principal to a purely accessory part in creation, from a magisterial to a strictly ministerial function. There is not the least reason why I individually should be out of harmony with infinite goodness and truth, except the limitation imposed upon me by nature, in identifying me with my bodily organization, and so individualizing or differencing me from my kind. Make this limitation then the purely subjective appearance which it truly is, in place of the objective reality which it truly is not, — make it a fact of my natural constitution, and not of my spiritual creation, a fact of my phenomenal consciousness merely, and not of the absolute and infinite being I have in God, — and you at once bring me individually into harmony with God's perfection. Our discordance was never internal or spiritual, was never at best anything but phenomenal, outward, moral, owing to my ignorance of the laws of creation, or my sensible inexperience of the spiritual world, of which nevertheless I am all the while a virtual denizen. Take away then this fallacious semblance of the truth operated by sense, and we relieve ourselves of the sole impediment which exists to the intellectual approximation and equalization of creator and creature, of infinite and finite, and so are prepared to discern their essential and inviolable unity.

Thus the supreme obligation we owe to Philosophy is to drop nature out of sight as a real or rational quantity intervening between creator and creature, and hiding them from each other's regard, and to conceive of her only as an actuality to sense, operating a *quasi* separation between them, with a view exclusively to propitiate and emphasize their real unity. In a word, we are bound no longer to conceive of nature as she appears to sense, i. e. as utterly independent or unqualified by subjection to man ; but only as she discloses herself to the reason, that is, as rigidly relative to the human soul, and altogether qualified or characterized by the uses she promotes to our spiritual evolution.

IV.

Certainly we have no right after this to attribute to Swedenborg an obscure or mystical conception of nature. Nature bears the same servile relation to the spiritual creation that a man's body bears to his soul, that the material of a house bears to the house itself, or that the substance of a statue bears to its form, namely, a merely quantifying, by no means a qualifying, relation. It fills out the spiritual creation, substantiates it, gives it subjective anchorage, fixity, or identification, incorporates it, in a word, just as the marble incorporates the statue. For the statue is primarily an ideal form, affiliating itself to the artist's genius exclusively, and is only derivatively thence a material existence. So I primarily am a spiritual form, that is to say, a form of affection and thought, directly affiliated to the creative love and wisdom ; and what my body does is merely to fill out this form, substantiate it, define it to itself, give it consciousness, allow it to say *me, mine, thee, thine.* What my body then does for my spirit specifically, nature does for the universe of the human mind, or the entire spiritual world; namely, it incorporates it, defines it to itself, gives it phenomenal projection from the creator, and so qualifies it to appreciate and cultivate an absolute conjunction with him. My body reveals my soul — i. e. reveals the spiritual being I have in God — to my own rude and blunt intelligence; and the marble of the statue is an outward revelation of the beauty which exists ideally to the artist's brain. So nature reveals the spiritual universe to itself, mirrors it to its own feeble and struggling intelligence, invests it with outward or sensible lineaments, and, by thus finiting or imprisoning it within the bounds of space and time, stimulates it to react towards its proper freedom or its essential infinitude in God.

I cannot too urgently point the reader's attention to this masterly vindication of nature, and the part it plays in creation. Creation, as Swedenborg conceives it, is the marriage in unitary form of creator and creature. For the divine love and wisdom, as he reports, "CANNOT BUT BE AND EXIST in other beings or existences created from itself"; and nature is the necessary ground of such existences, as furnishing them conscious projection from the infinite. But let me throw together a few passages illustrative of his general scheme of thought.

"It is essential to love not to love itself, but others, and to be lovingly united with them; it is also essential to it to be beloved by others, since union is thus effected. The essence of all love consists in union; yea, the life of it, or all that it contains of enjoyment, pleasantness, delight, sweetness, beatitude, happiness, felicity. Love consists in my willing what is my own to be another's, and feeling his delight as my own; this it is to love. But for a man to enjoy his own delight in another, in place of the other's delight in him, *this is not to love;* for in this case he loves himself, while in the other he loves his neighbor. These two loves are diametrically opposed: they both indeed are capable of producing union, though the union which self-love produces is only an apparent or outward union, while really or inwardly it is disunion. For in proportion as any one loves another for selfish ends, he afterwards comes to hate him. How can any man of understanding help perceiving this? What sort of love is it for a man to love himself only, and not another than himself, by whom he is beloved again? Clearly no union, but only disunion, results from such love; for union in love supposes reciprocation, and reciprocation does not exist in self alone. Now when this is true of all love, it cannot but be infinitely true of the creative love: so that we may conclude that *the divine love cannot help being and existing in others whom it loves and by whom it is beloved*. It is not possible, of course, that God can love and be beloved by others who are themselves infinite or divine; because then he would love himself, for the infinite or divine is one. If this infinitude or divinity adhered in others, it would be itself, and God would consequently be self-love, *whereof not the least is practicable to him, because it is totally contrary to his essence.*" * " In the created universe nothing lives but God-Man alone, or the lord; and nothing moves but by life from him; and nothing exists but by the sun from him: thus it is a truth that in God we live and move and have our being." † " Creation means, *what is divine from inmost to outmost, or from beginning to end*. For everything which is from the divine begins from himself, and proceeds in an orderly manner even to the ultimate end, thus through the heavens *into the world, and there rests as in its ultimate*, for the ultimate of divine order is cosmical nature." ‡

Thus in all true creation the creator is bound, by the fact of his giving absolute being to the creature, to communicate himself — make himself over — without stint to the creature: and the creature, in his turn, because he gives phenomenal form or manifestation to the creative power, is bound to absorb the creator in himself, to *appropriate* him as it were to himself, to reproduce his infinite or stainless love in all manner of finite egotistic form; so that the more truly the creator alone *is*, the more truly the creature alone *appears*. Now in this inevitable immersion which creation implies of creative being in created form, we have, according to Swedenborg, the origin of nature. It grows necessarily out of the obligation the creature is under

---

* Divine Love and Wisdom, 47–49.   † Ibid., 301.
‡ Arcana Celestia, 10, 634.

by creation to *appropriate* the creator, or reproduce him in his own finite lineaments. It overtly consecrates the covert marriage of infinite and finite, creator and creature. By the hypothesis of creation the creator gives sole and absolute being to the creature ; and unless therefore the creature reverberate the communication, or react towards the creator, the latter will inevitably swallow him up, or extinguish the faintest possibility of self-consciousness in him. And the only logical reverberation of being is form or appearance. Being is extensive ; form is intensive. Being expropriates itself to whatsoever is not itself ; form impropriates whatsoever is not itself to itself. Thus in the hierarchical marriage of creator and creature which we call creation, the creator yields the creature the primary place by spontaneously assuming himself a secondary or servile one ; gives him absolute or objective being, in fact, only by stooping himself to the limitations of the created form. Reciprocity is the very essence of marriage. Action and reaction must be equal between the factors, or the marriage unity is of its own nature void. If, accordingly, the creator contribute the element of pure being — the absolute or objective element — to creation, the creature must needs contribute the element of pure form or appearance, its phenomenal or subjective element ; for being and form are indissolubly one.

It is a necessary implication, then, of the truth of the Divine Natural Humanity, that while the creator gives invisible spiritual being to the creature, the creature in his turn gives natural form — gives visible existence — to the creator ; or, more briefly, while the creator gives reality to the creature, the creature gives phenomenality to the creator. In other words still, we may say, that while the creator supplies the essential or properly creative element in creation, the creature supplies its existential or properly constitutive element — that element of hold-back or resistance without which it could never put on manifestation. Nature is the attestation of this ceaseless give-and-take between creator and creature ; the nuptial ring that confirms and consecrates the deathless espousals of infinite and finite. In spite, therefore, of its fertile and domineering actuality to sense, it is as void of all reality to reason as the shadow of one's person in a glass. It is, in fact, only the outward image or shadow of itself which is cast by the inward or spiritual world upon the mirror of our rudimentary intelligence. And inasmuch as the shadow or subjective image of itself which any object projects of necessity reproduces the object in inverse form, so nature, being the subjective image or shadow of God's objective and spiritual creation, turns out a sheer inversion of spiritual order; exhibits the creator's fulness veiled by the creature's want, the creator's perfection obscured, or negatively revealed, by the creature's imperfection. Spiritual or creative order affirms the essential unity of every creature with every other, and of all with the creator. Natural or created order must consequently exhibit the contingent or phenomenal oppugnancy of every creature with every other, and of all with the creator; or else furnish no adequate foothold or flooring to the spiritual world.

Nature is thus, according to Swedenborg, an inevitable implication of the spiritual world, just as substance is inevitably implied in form, i. e. as serving to give it selfhood or identity. This is her sole function, to confer consciousness upon existence, or give it fixity, by denying it individuality or affirming its community with all other existence. Nature identifies existence or gives it finiteness, while spirit alone individualizes it or gives it infinitude. In truth, nature is a pure spiritual apparition, having no reality to the soul, but only to the senses. It exists only to a sensibly organized and therefore limited intelligence; and hence, however absolute it appears, it is really all the while nothing whatever but a ratio or mean between a finite and an infinite mind. We as creatures, that is, as finite by constitution, can have, of course, no intuitive, but only a rational discernment of infinite or uncreated things. We cannot know divine goodness and truth in a direct or presentative way, but only in an indirect or *representative* one, that is, only in so far as they abase themselves to our natural level, or accommodate themselves to our nascent sensuous understanding. And nature is the proper theatre of this stupendous divine abasement and accommodation — of this needful obscuration, or *veiling-over*, of the divine splendor, in order to adapt it to our gross carnal vision. Throughout her total length and breadth, accordingly, she is a mere correspondence or imagery of what is going on in living or spiritual realms; but a correspondence or imagery which is vital nevertheless to our apprehension of creative order. For the very fact of our creatureship insures that we should have remained forever incognizant of the creator, and antipathetic to his perfection, unless he, by condescending to our limitations, or reproducing himself within the intelligible compass of our own nature and history, had gradually emancipated our intelligence, and educated us into living sympathy with his name.

Such, concisely stated, are the leading axioms of Swedenborg's ontology. Creation, spiritually regarded, is the living equation of creator and creature. But in order to the latter's attaining to the vital fellowship of the former, he must put on conscious or phenomenal form, must become clearly *self*-pronounced, that so being made aware, on the one hand, of his own essential and inveterate limitations, he may become qualified, on the other, to react spiritually towards the creator's infinitude. In other words, creation implies a strictly subordinate or incidental realm, a realm of preliminary *formation*, as we may say, in which the creature comes to self-consciousness, or the conception of himself as a being essentially distinct from, and antagonistic to, his creator. The logic of the case is inexorable. If creation at its culmination be an exact practical equation of creator and creature, the *minus* of the latter being rigidly equivalent to the *plus* of the former, then it incorporates as its needful basis a sphere of experience on the creature's part, in which he may feel himself utterly remote from the creator, and abandoned to his own resources; an empirical sphere of existence, in fine, which may unmistakably identify him with all lower things, and so alienate him from (i. e. make him consciously *another than*) his creator. Thus creation with Swedenborg, being at its apogee a rigid equation of the creator's perfection and the creature's imperfection, necessitates *a natural history*, or provisional plane of projection upon which the equation may be wrought out to its most definite issues. Creator and creature are terms of an inseparable correlation, so that we can no more imagine a creation to which the one does not furnish its causative element, the other its constitutive element, than we can imagine a child in which father and mother are not coequal factors, the one conferring life or soul, the other existence or body. No doubt their relation is a strictly conjugal one, proceeding upon a hierarchical distribution of the factors; one being head, the other hand; one being object, the other subject; one ruling, the other obeying. But their unity is all the more and none the less assured on this account; for notoriously the truest objective harmony is that which reconciles the intensest subjective diversity.

To sum up all that has been said, creation, with Swedenborg, challenges a subject earth, no less than an all-encompassing heaven; a natural constitution or body, no less than a spiritual cause or soul; an experimental or educative sphere for the creature, no less than an absolute one for the creator; a realm of phenomenal freedom or finite reaction on the part of the former, no less than one of real force or infinite action on the part of the latter. In a word, creation means, to Swedenborg, the creature's spiritual *evolution* in complete harmony with his creator's perfection; but if this be true, and certainly philosophy tolerates no lower conception, then obviously creation demands for its own actuality the natural *involution* of the creator, or his complete unresisting immersion in finite conditions. Which is only saying in other words, that creation — being a spiritual achievement of creative power within the limits of the created consciousness — involves to the creature's experience a rigidly natural generation and growth, with root and stem and flower all complete.

V.

We have now elucidated the logical grounds of the law by which alone, according to Swedenborg, creation becomes possible or conceivable, — the law of the creature's finite constitution, as it may be called, or of his apparent life in himself, in order to his finding real life in God, that is to say, the law of his phenomenal or subjective disjunction with the creator in the interest of their real and objective conjunction. The creator, as we have seen, is bound, in the interest of the creature's immortal spiritual being, to endow him with natural or subjective seeming, since otherwise he would remain destitute of selfhood or identity. Such is the creative law. The creature must at least *seem* to live of himself — must at least *feel* himself to be absolute or unconditioned in all the range of his natural appetites and passions, in all the breadth of his constitutional affections and thoughts — or else remain utterly void of that natural imagery of God, upon which all the possibilities of their subsequent spiritual sympathy and communion are contingent. It is clear that I must exist to my own consciousness, before I can act or function even animally ; *a fortiori*, therefore, before I can function morally or as a man, i. e. before I can make that appropriation to myself of good and evil, upon which my conscience towards God, and all the results of such conscience to my spiritual individuality or character, are suspended. And what is a necessity for one man is a necessity for all.

But now let us prepare to scrutinize the exact method of this grand creative operation as reflected in the facts of consciousness, in order that we may cease to think of creation as a voluntary or capricious exertion of irresponsible power, and learn to conceive of it only as an orderly going forth of infinite love and wisdom in all the forms of human nature. For this and nothing less than this it is. Creation, by Swedenborg's showing, is not that frivolous, irrational event in space and time which men have hitherto deemed it ; is not that mere arbitrary and ostentatious parade of the divine power which superstition delights in making it appear. It is, on the contrary, in its largest sense, a sincere and stupendous work of redemption wrought by God within the limits of human nature, by which it becomes gradually freed from its inherent corruption and death, and progressively invested with God's own infinity and eternity. Thus low or material conceptions of creation in the abstract will be fatal to our understanding of Swedenborg's cosmologic doctrine, and the reader will bear with me if I attempt to mark out the true boundaries of thought in this direction, or put him on his guard against permitting his imagination to run away with his reason in estimating the creative method — the method in which the creator utterly abases himself to the lowest level of the creature's egotism and cupidity, in order that he may gradually lift the latter to the otherwise impracticable heights of his own perfection.

There could be no difficulty in rightly estimating the prob-

lem of creation — it would be perfectly easy, in other words, to
regard it as a strictly rational or orderly achievement of divine power — if it were not for the grossly material aspect
which it is the habit of the sensuous imagination to impose upon
the relation of creator and creature.   Imagination, enlightened
only by sense, reports an insuperable distance or disagreement
between infinite and finite, perfect and imperfect, between that
which essentially *is* and that which essentially *is not*.   " How
shall that," we incessantly demand of our owlish wisdom,
" how shall that which alone really *is* make that which really *is
not* actually to be ? "   It has been the standing puzzle of philosophy, since the world began, to ascertain how creation becomes
possible or even conceivable on the hypothesis of the creator
remaining always infinite, the creature always finite.   And
the puzzle was a reasonably honest one, so long as science was
incompetent to disclose the true and altogether ministerial or
subordinate part that nature plays in the drama of creation — the
part of a handmaid, not of a heroine.   But it is no longer honest on the part of our philosophic guides to keep up this mysti-
fication, and palm off their own wilful imbecility upon the
simple as a necessity of the intellect itself, when we have in
Swedenborg's doctrine of God's NATURAL HUMANITY a sufficing
solution of this grand philosophic mystery, a perfect key to the
riddle of creation.   The honest desideratum of philosophy —
although philosophy has not always been intelligently conscious
of her *desideria* — was to discover some point of contact between
infinite and finite, some middle or undefined territory which
should effectively neutralize their envenomed hostility, by
blending what really *is* and what really *is not* in the bosom of
its own actual unity.   And Swedenborg, as we have seen, has
fully supplied this desideratum to philosophy, in his doctrine
of the God-Man, or Divine *Natural* Humanity — a doctrine
which for the first time sheds upon nature the light of a higher
day, and lifts it out of the vulgar bone of contention it has
hitherto been to the fanatic on one hand and the sceptic on
the other, into a superb majestic hieroglyph of the spiritual
creation, into a frank and luminous mirror of the spotless
ineffable marriage which in invisible depths of being forever
unites the divine and human natures.

3

Nature, according to Swedenborg, is all that *exists*, or *appears to be*. Its very being is form or appearance ; its total *esse* is *existere ;* that is to say, nature is what neither really *is* nor really *is not*, being in truth an actual marriage of the two which makes what really *is* appear as if it were not, and what really *is not* appear as if it were.* We may say, then, that nature is the realm neither of *being* (i. e. love) nor of *not being* (i. e. self), but all simply of *existence* (i. e. self-love), which blends these two factors in the unity of a conscious subject. For love (being) is of its own nature infinitely objective ; that is to say, it tends to *exist* or go forth from itself to whatsoever is not itself, to whatsoever indeed is most opposed to itself; and it can only so exist or go forth of course in subjective or created form, in which it may dwell as in itself and communicate its infinite blessedness. And self (not-being) is of its own nature infinitely subjective, that is, tends *to be*, tends to stay within itself, and subjugate to itself whatsoever is not itself, — whatsoever is in the least degree opposed to itself; and it can only thus *be* of course, by appropriating objective or creative substance which freely lends itself to its embraces, and ministers unreservedly to its lusts. There is no rational escape, as it appears to me, from Swedenborg's disclosures on this subject. Love of its own nature, of its own fulness or perfection, tends *to create*, i. e. tends *not to be in itself*, but only in forms created from itself to which it may thus communicate its own eternal felicities. It tends to forget itself, to abandon itself, to lose or merge itself in whatsoever is not love, but self; just as self, in its turn, becoming thus incited or vivified, tends of its proper nature, of its proper want or imperfection, *to be loved* infinitely, i. e. tends to seek itself and find itself in whatsoever is not itself, namely, infinite love. And this reciprocal tendency of love to be finited by not-love or self, and of self to be infinited by not-self or love, results logically in the universe of creation which we call nature.

---

* If indeed "to exist " or "appear to be " were equivalent to really "being," we might call nature, not so much a marriage of what really *is* to what really *is not*, as a compromise of the former in the latter's behalf, whereby the one abdicates being to the same extent as the other claims it. But this is absurd, for *to exist* or *to appear to be* is not really or absolutely *to be*, but only to be relatively to something else ; and the creator can endow the creature with any latitude and longitude of being in this sense, without the slightest compromise of his infinity.

Nature accordingly proclaims itself beyond all question that indispensable *tertium quid* of which, whether consciously or not the philosopher has always been in search : that needful middle-term or neutral ground between being and not-being, wherein what really *is* is seen giving subjective being to what is not ; and what really is not is seen in its turn giving objective existence to what is.

Nature is thus a purely subjective work of God, an actual going forth of creative love by every method of formative wisdom into every variety of creaturely manifestation or consciousness. It is not the objective or spiritual creation, but only the shadow of itself which that creation necessarily projects upon a carnal or sensibly organized intelligence ; and it is a sheer intellectual insanity to regard it in any higher light. The lion and the lamb, for example, both exist in nature, but has either lion or lamb the least title to be esteemed the objective or spiritual creature of God ? What nonsense to think of such a thing! If then the lion and the lamb, the serpent and the dove, the leopard and the kid, the bear and the calf, naturally exist or appear to be to my intelligence, what is the inference ? Not that such things spiritually exist or have absolute being in God, but that they pertain exclusively to the created consciousness, having no other function than outwardly to image or represent the things of human affection and thought, which alone make up the spiritual creation, or are alone objective to the divine mind. Our true or spiritual and objective consciousness is conditioned upon our phenomenal or bodily and subjective existence, so that we are incapable of apprehending interior and spiritual verities save as they image themselves to us in sensible forms. None of these sensible things really or spiritually are and exist ; for really or spiritually God alone *is*, and man alone really or spiritually *exists* from him. But they necessarily exist or appear to our finite consciousness, to our sensuous intelligence. Why *necessarily?* Because otherwise that intelligence or consciousness would be without form and void of substance. My sensibility and intelligence, my feeling and knowledge, are by no means absolute possessions of mine ; they do not belong to me as personally dissociated with nature, and independent of her resources, but only as I am intimately one with her, only as I partake her life, or am in organized contact with external things. They are not faculties which inhere in me objectively regarded, or as unconditioned upon nature, but only as subjectively regarded, that is, as rigidly conditioned upon mineral, vegetable, and animal existence, and dependent upon it as the child is dependent upon the mother's womb. Within the whole range of my subjective feeling and knowledge I never for an instant stand aloof from nature or outside of it, looking down upon it, that is to say, I am never in the least objective to it. On the contrary, I invariably stand under it, or inside of it ; I am in fact rigidly shut up or included in it, and yearn towards its instruction as devoutly as the child yearns towards its mother's breasts. In short, nature, so far as my feeling and knowledge are concerned, is wholly and intensely objective to me, shaping my subjectivity or giving it lavish body just as the mother shapes the fruit of her womb, and builds it up or fills it out with her own ungrudging substance.

Thus by creation I am in myself, in my own right, a helpless subject of nature, being dependent upon her stringent objectivity for all that I feel and know, for all that I consciously am and enjoy. If accordingly nature did not exist or appear to me in all her sensibly contrasted forms of light and dark, hot and cold, high and low, hard and soft, rough and smooth, great and small, strong and weak, beautiful and ugly, artless and cunning, innocent and noxious, pleasant and painful, my animal sensibility would afford no anchorage to my moral instincts, or those rational intuitions of good and evil in human character, upon which all my subsequent knowledges of spiritual, celestial, and divine things are of necessity to be moulded. If I had had no sensible observation of the difference between serpent and dove, fox and sheep, wolf and lamb, I should lack all basis of discrimination in regard to my own rational or moral attributes ; all ground for my subsequent recognition of myself as a moral agent, or for that discrimination of men into good and evil, true and false, wise and simple, by which our conception of moral existence or human unity is generated. If my senses did not familiarize me with the treachery of the serpent nature and the innocence of the dove nature — if, in short, my sensible experience did not furnish my rational understanding with a complete livery or symbolism of abstract human nature, with an infinitely modulated key wherewith to unlock all the secret chambers of the human heart, all the infinite possibilities of character among men — I should be forever destitute of moral perception, should never be able in thought to attribute good and evil, truth and falsity, either to myself or others ; because thought is impossible without language ; and language derives all its substance or body from things, or the contents of our sensible experience.*

Such is Swedenborg's idea of nature, and the relation of strict subservience it bears to our mental development. He regards it as a mere though exact and copious hieroglyph of spiritual existence ; a living inventory, so to speak, or exquisite picture-language, revealing all the otherwise ineffable mysteries of that marriage of the divine and human natures which alone constitutes the spiritual creation. It is a literal record, a faithful correspondence to sense, of whatsoever rationally befalls the intercourse of infinite creator and finite creature in inward invisible depths of being; so that if we once attain to an adequate doctrine of nature, or a just intellectual insight of the stupendous rational uses she subserves, we shall possess an infallible clew to all spiritual problems.

In short, Swedenborg holds nature to a strict and abject REVELATION of the creative perfection, and utterly denies it all substantive functioning. Only, as all the life of nature culminates in the human or moral form, so nature as a divine revelation becomes of necessity complicated with man's historic evolution ; and it is not until history consequently has attained to its apogee in the advent of human society or brotherhood upon the earth, that nature is able at last to justify her apocalyptic pretension, and vindicate the infinite goodness, truth, and beauty which have always lain concealed under our native egotism, lust, and vanity.

But we must not anticipate our subject.

* Language is an instinctive manifestation of mind or spirit in nature. It is the instinctive effort of the human mind to reproduce itself — to realize its own sole unity — in the universality of nature's phenomena.

VI.

It is easy to see that a reader unused to the line of thought here exposed may conceive it liable to a charge of pantheism. But it will be quite as easy to show that there is no real ground for such an imputation. What is the essence of pantheism? It consists in making creation a direct, not a redemptive process of the divine power; in making the creature *continuous*, as it were, from the creator. That is to say, it denies him the very boon of natural or subjective identity, upon which, according to Swedenborg, his spiritual or objective individuality is inevitably conditioned; and so leaves his creation, in any honest sense of the word, as completely indeterminate or unavouched, and indeed unattempted, as the generation of a child would be, which claimed a paternal or causative action, but disallowed a maternal or constitutive reaction. Thus Hegel bases his ontology upon the identity of being and nothing, i. e. he makes being (the creator) a logical *evolution* of not-being (the creature) : so that creation is no actual vivification of the created nature by the creator, whereby the creature's spiritual or individual conjunction with the creator becomes assured, but is on the contrary a grossly illusory appearance whereby the creator, under cover of a creaturely disguise, attains himself to subjective consciousness, and leaves his creature proportionably defrauded. He thus utterly falsifies, or degrades into childish make-believe, the great fact of a natural creation which is fundamental to Swedenborg's scheme of thought; for he interprets what appears to be creation into the so-called creator's essential incapacity *to be himself*, without a perpetual fillip from the so-called creature. He concedes, of course, a *quasi* reality to the creature; but as, upon his theory, the creator himself is no objective but a purely subjective or selfish style of being, so he cannot really exist or go forth from himself in lower subject forms; and the creature consequently remains void, not only of real objectivity, but of true subjectivity as well. Like all pantheists or idealists, Hegel commits the common but abject blunder of invariably *objectifying* to his own imagination the contents of consciousness, or what after all is only the subjective side of existence; and hence regards the pretension of the *me* as absolute and not contingent. And knowing but one legitimate absolute — but one real objectivity — he does not hesitate a moment to run all phenomenal individuality into that, so making the creative process to mean henceforth, not the orderly and fruitful marriage of the creative and created natures in every form of social and æsthetic action, but a peevish, snarling, and bewildered muddle of the two in a hopeless effort to escape from each other's grasp, or accomplish each other's extinction.

No doubt if Swedenborg set out from similar intellectual data to these, he would not be long in reaching a similar result. But his intellectual principles run strikingly counter to those of idealism or pantheism. That is to say, the *me* or subjective element has not the slightest claim, in his hands, to the finality or absoluteness which superficial observers ascribe to it. He maintains, on the contrary, its essential contingency to a higher outlying objectivity, or makes its total reality lie in the use it promotes to such objectivity. He has no trouble, accordingly, in demonstrating the unimpeachable veracity of our natural consciousness, since he makes it a necessary implication of God's objective work in creation ; an indispensable means to an eternal spiritual conjunction of creator and creature, and hence itself instinct with infinite love and wisdom.

And yet, though Swedenborg is no pantheist — though his doctrine of the Divine Natural Humanity betrays no lurking taint of idealism, but sturdily repugns all commingling and confusion of infinite and finite, creator and creature, in creation — it must be owned, as we have already intimated, that he has done almost nothing himself to help out the logic of the situation, and evidently considers his duty to the reader discharged by simply affirming the situation itself. Nor is any one entitled, as I conceive, to take up the least quarrel with him on this score ; for his purpose in writing was not synthetic or inductive, but purely analytic or deductive. It was not to argue principles, but simply to state and illustrate them by facts of experience and observation, leaving the reader to do the needful argumentation for himself according to the wants of his heart and the measure of his understanding. And the reason of this reserve is palpable. For I cannot remind the reader too often for his own advantage, that Swedenborg was all simply a *seer*, and in no sense a dogmatist or "thinker." That is to say, the grand truth he reports to us — the truth of God's *natural* humanity — is neither a truth of sense like pleasure and pain, nor a truth of science like equality and difference, nor yet a truth of conscience like good and evil, but exclusively a truth of life or spiritual perception : of which therefore no one can ever become convinced by any amount of reasoning, but only by a process of the strictest inward growth or refinement. "What you call nature" — says Swedenborg in effect — "what you call nature, and suppose to be infinite in extent and eternal in duration, has really no existence in itself, but is a pure superstition of our ignorance and folly ; all that is real about it being the providential use it promotes *as such superstition* to our self-consciousness. It has an apparent truth in itself, a truth to our senses, but it is void of absolute truth, being a sheer accommodation or concession of the divine love and wisdom to our spiritual fatuity. If accordingly we now saw with spiritual instead of carnal eyes, we should no longer discern this dead immovable nature, but see in the place of it an infinite Man, instant creator and redeemer of all men, carnally crucified no doubt and buried from sight under all the hallucinations of our native selfishness and conceit, but spiritually resurgent and shining forth as a risen sun in every reality of our *social* or regenerate experience and activity."

And how could any mere logical skill avail to make a doctrine so shocking to prejudice — in fact so intellectually revolutionary — as this, acceptable to minds unprepared by living culture to receive it ? But though one may not hope to convey the vital truth of the doctrine to the understanding of another, as you would convey a mathematical formula to his memory, it may nevertheless be quite within one's competence to dissipate some of the prominent fallacies and fantasies which hinder its reception. And this humble function I shall now, to the best of my ability, endeavor to discharge.

VII.

Let us begin by rightly interpreting to ourselves the nature of the selfhood which God is said to give us, as the condition of our perfect spiritual fellowship with himself. That is, let us be sure to view it as a composite, not a simple, phenomenon ; as a strict fact of conscience indeed primarily, and only by inference or derivation thence a fact of science. We read in the book of Genesis that "God created man in his image ; in the image of God created he him ; male and female created he them." Now the composite character here ascribed to human nature in the abstract — for as yet, according to the record, no concrete man existed upon the earth to till the ground, Adam, much more Eve, being still unformed — must be determined of course by what it is said to image, namely, the creative perfection. Man is by creation an image of God, and as such image he is both male and female. What connection is there between these two facts? What justification, in other words, does the creative perfection afford to this alleged duality in the creature? Swedenborg is full of instruction on this point to every one who has caught a glimpse of the profound spiritual or philosophic meaning which underlies the mystical letter of revelation, and I beg my reader's attention while I seek to reproduce it.

The origin of all created existence, according to Swedenborg, as we have already seen, is infinite or perfect love : meaning by that, a love so essentially unlimited by selfish or prudential regards as to be spontaneously creative. An infinite or perfect love, by his showing, is a purely objective love, i. e. it is so intent upon the blessing of others as to be utterly indifferent to self. It is a love so essentially untainted with subjective ends as to find its supreme felicity in *communicating* itself to others created from itself, in whom it may be and forever abide as in itself.

But obviously a love of this infinite quality implies a proportionate wisdom to carry it out. For it can never realize itself in action, save by vivifying *the nature* of the creature in a manner so absolute or thorough, as to make him seem to himself an unquestionable subject of nature, and lead him therefore instinctively to revolt at the imputation of direct creatureship. And what infinite skill or address is requisite to accomplish such a result! What an infinite wisdom, what a stupendous order, must the universe of existence exhibit, in order that the creature of God may find *himself* there without a risk of mistake or misconception ; may arrive at a form of consciousness so definite and absolute, as to defy the faintest suspicion in his mind of the real truth of the case, and leave him on the contrary so complacently self-poised as to render him an eternally fit subject of God's spiritual indwelling !

Our own love, finite and imperfect as it is, illustrates, in its way, the hierarchical adjustment here alleged between the divine love and wisdom. Our love is practically true and perfect, just as its action is guided by intelligence, by a judicious estimate of the wants of those we love. I may love my friend with what seems to myself a pure love ; but if I am not previously well informed in the nature of my friend and the needs that illustrate it, my love will go forth in very unwise acts, and probably do him more harm than good. Just so of the divine love. It would be utterly incapable of realizing itself in action, unless it were methodized by a proportionate wisdom, based upon an unflinching experimental acquaintance with the nature of those whom it would serve. Were it not thus methodized, thus schooled or guided, it would of course flow forth blindly or without measure, in utter indifference to any faculty of reaction and hence of reception on the part of its objects, and would consequently deluge or drown out under its merciless insane floods the very seeds it was intended to fertilize. The divine love then glorifies itself — i. e. avouches its essential perfection as love — by embodying itself in the lineaments of a perfect wisdom — a wisdom so intimately conditioned upon, or bound up with, the nature of those to whom its activity is addressed, as to be necessarily formative of it.

Understand me. The nature in question is confessedly a *created* one. That is to say, it is in itself sheer and absolute naught, being dependent for whatsoever appearances of life it exhibits upon a wholly gratuitous quickening received at the divine hands. Practically then, or at bottom, the divine wisdom is only the divine love *manifesting itself in creaturely form ;* existing or going forth in the endlessly diversified lineaments of the created nature ; endowing its creature with an apparently absolute selfhood, with a seemingly unconditioned consciousness. It is in fact the creative love *alienating* itself from itself in the interest of the creature's identity. Swedenborg accordingly always calls wisdom or truth *the manifestation* which the divine love makes of itself in creation; the inevitable *existere* (going-forth) of the infinite uncreated *esse* in the nature of its own finite creature; hence the middle-term, matrix, mould, or means by which the creative love energizes the *spiritual* creation, or brings forth results every way congruous with its own infinitude.

There is clearly no escape for the creative love from the obligation here imposed, short of renouncing its infinitude. If it would give itself unstintedly to the creature, if it would make itself over to him in the plenitude of its own resources, it must first of all give him subjective identity or projection from itself. The creature is in himself or by nature simply zero; and if therefore the creative love would communicate itself with all its unimaginable potencies and felicities to him, it must first of all *quicken him within all the compass of this natural destitution of his*, and so afford him a true ground of consciousness adequate to all the needs of his ultimate spiritual renovation, or reaction towards the creator. Thus our natural self-love and worldliness must inevitably degrade the creative wisdom to our own level, must infallibly impose upon it the aspect of " a man of sorrows and acquainted with grief." But surely no blame can by possibility attach to us on this account, since we are not our own creation, but God's. On the contrary, only a higher glory accrues in this way to the creative name, which cheerfully encounters all possible opprobrium, in order that the creature who is unconscious of the love which thus humbles itself to his service may thereby at least come to self-consciousness, and in that acquisition possess the pledge of his eventually perfect spiritual conjunction with the creator.

All this, I repeat, is an obligation of the creative love growing out of its own perfection. That love cannot become truly operative — that is to say, it cannot realize its own majestic spiritual ends — save in so far as it actually vivifies *the nature* of the creature; and to vivify the nature of the creature means to quicken his absolute and essential want or finiteness in a manner so ungrudging, as that he may feel *an instinct* of life within him, or claim to exist by simple right of nature, as it were, and without any direct divine interposition. In carrying

out this obligation the creative love undergoes of necessity the
utmost obscuration or humiliation. For how shall it succeed in
quickening our finite nature — in vivifying with its own unstinted substance our yawning and rapacious appetites and passions — without *ipso facto* assuming the responsibility of our
natural infirmities, sufferings, and griefs, without for the time
being taking upon itself the burden of all our iniquities, trans-
gressions, and sins? Thus it is by no means in itself that the
creative goodness incurs humiliation, but only in us ; that is to
say, in its manifested aspect, or as it is reproduced in created
form, and submits to be reviled, persecuted, and crucified at the
will of its own dependent but wholly unconscious, incredulous,
and ungrateful offspring. In short, it experiences no humiliation in its own essential or absolute character as love or goodness, but only in its existential or contingent aspect as truth, the
truth of form or appearance it takes on in our natural vivification. It is humiliated in us exclusively, at the hands of our
essential shabbiness and imperfection, our native egotism, tyranny, and lust. It is, however, a humiliation none the less real
and necessary on that account, since our creation, or coming to
natural consciousness, is inexorably conditioned upon it ; and
without it we should have missed all those capacities of spiritual
life to which that consciousness furnishes the indispensable anchorage.

We can now see our way very clearly, I think. For evidently the creative wisdom, in going forth into actual manifestation, or descending into created form, must be above all things
else solicitous to guarantee the integrity of the creature's consciousness, or dike out his personality against any chance leak-
age (*endosmosis*) of the infinite divine substance. The creature, regarded on his natural side, incurs no danger but from
the creator, in whom he lives and moves and has his being, and
who might, accordingly, if his love had the slightest subjective
infirmity, or were in the least conceivable degree debilitated by
a regard to self, incontinently drown him out at any moment.
Thus the creator is bound by the interest of his own good-name,
steadfastly to abjure every incursion into the creature's territory,
diligently to withhold himself from all interference with the
creature's consciousness, let its actual untried issues be what they

will; though they should plunge him, if need be, into the embrace of death and hell. To be created means, so far as the creature is concerned, to attain to subjective identity, to be separated from the infinite by becoming his own finite conscious self; and as nature is the exclusive medium of this creaturely experience, so no matter to what universality of dimensions nature enlarges us, our finite consciousness will never be enfeebled but only strengthened thereby, while our sensible remoteness from the infinite will be all the while most agreeably caressed, soothed, and flattered. But let the least ray of the infinite substance penetrate the deep divine darkness of our finite consciousness — the dense divine obliviousness upon which that consciousness is moulded, or out of which it is fashioned — instantly the total heat and light of our life vanish, and nature, with all her wealth of unnumbered worlds, shrivels from sight like a scroll in a furnace.

Now the armor of proof in which the creative wisdom arrays the created consciousness, in order to guard its integrity, is concisely hinted to our perception when we are told that "*God creates man male and female*": the *male* in this collocation being the grand cosmical or unconscious man designated by the latin word *homo*, and embracing the entire realm of physics from the lowest mineral up to the highest animal form of existence; and the *female* being the petty domestic or conscious man, designated by the latin word *vir*, and embracing the entire realm of our free and normal historic evolution.* For by this concise statement is signified that the creator endows his creature with an essentially finite genesis, or suspends his self-consciousness upon a strict equilibrium between the element of identity or universality in his nature, and that of difference or individuality; between the element of force or necessity, and that of freedom or contingency; between the interests of the broadest humanity in short and those of the narrowest conventional virtue. And surely nothing can so effectually separate creature from creator as his subjection to this finite experience. For in

---

* It is the identical contrast which is expressed by the antagonism of Nature and History, and by the terms "physical or organic" and "moral or voluntary" life, applied to man. The same contrast enlivens the graduated meaning we attach to the phrases *a humane* and *a virtuous* man.

the creator love and wisdom, heart and head, force and freedom, justice and mercy, universality and individuality, are one and inseparable, and it is only in the creature that the two principles are found in envenomed mutual hostility, being held both alike in rigid abeyance to that purely empirical reconciliation with each other, which is signified by the *social* destiny of the race.

Here then, at last, we have it. To be created male and female is to have a finite genesis, is to be conscious of one's self as the neutrality or indifference of two forces as wide apart as zenith and nadir, or heaven and hell. And to have a finite genesis is to be only an image of God, and consequently to stand in subjective antagonism to him, as the image necessarily stands in subjective antagonism to its original. Man is the image of God only as *finitely* constituted, i. e. when the fire of self-love in his nature disputes the sway of universal love ; and this is to be completely undivine, is to be the exact logical opposite of God. The image of God is a projection of the divine personality or character on some foreign substance. It is not God, but only what God appears to be in a form of opposition to himself, i. e. in *created* form. It is by no means what he is in himself; on the contrary, it is precisely what he is *not* in himself, but exclusively in others created from himself. To be God is to be essentially infinite, i. e. it is to be love without any alloy of self; a love that invariably *loses itself in its object.* To be an image of God, on the other hand, is to be essentially finite, i. e. it is to be love upon a basis or background of self; it is to be *self-love* in fact, a love that invariably *seeks itself in its object.* My love is organic, therefore passionate or coerced, leading me to subjugate all that is objective to me to the compass of my own subjectivity. The divine love is inorganic, and therefore free or unimpassioned, tending evermore to the enfranchisement of its proper objects from itself, or the investing them with their own inalienable subjectivity. In a word, the one love is altogether active or creative, the other altogether passive or reactive. And the whole problem of creation being to find a wall of partition between infinite creator and finite creature which shall be practically impervious or inviolable, nothing offers so clean and complete a solution of the problem as to find *the created consciousness itself constituting that wall :* the creature confessing himself no direct or living presentation of the divine perfection, but only and at best an indirect or negative *re*-presentation of it; only and at best an inverse subjective form and dead image of it.

VIII.

And now let us sum up all that has gone before, in preparation for what remains behind.

Man is the true creature of God, the creation of a really infinite love and wisdom. But the creature of God, *regarded in himself or subjectively*, must either be nothing — in which case creation, in any honest sense of the word, is impossible, being swallowed up of a remorseless idealism — or else he must be the total and exact opposite of his creator. For it is contrary to the creative perfection to conceive any existence as possible, which in itself or subjectively simulates that perfection.

Do I mean then to say that the creature of an infinite power is shut up to an eternal subjective antagonism with his creator? Unquestionably, if that subjectivity be a purely natural one or end with itself; that is to say, unless his nature undergo some modification at the creative hands, by lending itself to his subsequent spiritual redemption. The strict logic of the case forbids any other conclusion, under penalty of vitiating the integrity of creation. If any two notions are radically opposed on their subjective side, it is those of creator and creature. Objectively, or in creation, creator and creature are one and undistinguishable. But in their subjective aspect nothing can be so intensely antagonistic to the conception of a creator as that of a creature. To create is one thing, to be created is the total and exact opposite of that thing. For what is one's *nature* as a creature? It is abject want or destitution. To be created is to be void of all things in one's self, and to possess them only in another; and if I am the creature accordingly of an infinite creator, my want of course must be infinite. The nature of a thing is what the thing is in itself, and apart from foreign interference. And evidently what the creature is in himself and apart from the creator is sheer nothingness, that is to say, sheer want or destitution, destitution of all things, whether of life, of existence, or even of being. So that to give the creature natural form or

selfhood, is merely to vivify the infinite void he is in himself;
is merely to organize in living form the universal destitution he
is under with respect to the creative fulness.

I attempt no apology, accordingly, for Swedenborg's doctrine
on this subject, but applaud it with all my heart. I perfectly
agree with him that redemption and not creation avouches the
proper glory of the divine name. Creation is not, and cannot
be, the final word of the divine dealings with us. It has at
most a rigidly subjective efficacy as affording us self-consciousness, and not the least objective value as affording us any spiritual fellowship of the divine perfection. To be naturally created
indeed — to be created an image of God — is to be anything except a spiritual likeness of him. The law of the image is subjectively to invert the lineaments of its original, or reflect them
in so negative a form as that the original shall be wholly lost
sight of in itself and the image alone appear; all that is light in
the one being dark in the other, and *vice versa.* And to be
spiritually *like* God is inwardly to undo this subjective inversion
of the divine perfection to which we find ourselves naturally
born or created, and put on that direct or objective presentation
of it to which we are historically re-born or re-created. The
difference between the two states is the exact difference between
bondage and freedom, between being a servant and being a son.
So that if our natural creation were not strictly subservient to
something infinitely superior to itself, we should remain forever
at a hopeless though unsuspected spiritual remove from God.

Creation necessarily, as we have seen, *in*volves the creator
and obscures his perfection, in the exact ratio of its evolving the
creature and illustrating his imperfection. Unless therefore the
creature *himself* reproduce the creative infinitude concealed in
his nature, it must be forever obliterated from remembrance.
The bare fact of his creation stamps him in himself, or on his
subjective side, the utter uncompromising enemy of his creator;
and unless he can in some way *react upon himself,* or rise above
his natural level, the level of his proper subjectivity, that enmity
must remain forever unappeased. And this capacity of reaction
in the creature is precisely what his natural division into male
and female provides for, in rendering him both objective and
subjective to himself; in permitting him to be in himself both

the proper object and the proper subject of his own activity. The creative love as we have seen, the love of creator to creature, is essentially infinite, as being without any taint or drawback of self-love. And the created love, the love of creature to creator, is essentially finite, being a pure love of self, untinged by any love to the neighbor. If then the creative wisdom can inwardly so attemper the created nature, as gradually to bend this subjective love of the creature, or supreme regard for himself, into an objective love or supreme regard for society, the creature will, *ipso facto*, become unclad of his native corruption, and clothed upon with his creator's health. And it is, I repeat, exclusively to provide for this great contingency that the creature is created both male and female; that is to say, both organic and functional, static and dynamic, generic and specific, physical and moral, cosmical and domestic, universal and particular, public and private, outward and inward, common and proper, objective and subjective. For the reciprocal opposition of these elements is so great as to leave them finally no choice but marriage; that is, such a hierarchical adjustment of their conflicting claims as may render them freely prolific, or forever fuse them in the unity of a new nature. This spontaneous marriage of man as man with woman as woman — or, what is the same thing, of the objective and subjective, or physical and moral, contents of human nature — is what is meant by society, which is the consummation of human destiny. This marriage is prolific of an entirely new self-consciousness in man; amounts, in fact, to that new creation of God for which the dumb earth has so long groaned and been in inward unintelligent travail; that divine resurrection in our flesh which will ally us no longer negatively or inversely, but positively and directly, with infinite power, peace, and innocence.

What is legitimately meant by the selfhood or subjectivity which God is said to give us ought now to be clear. No sensible or material *thing* is meant, no outward and visible quantity whatever, but solely a fact of inward life or consciousness due to the essential marriage which exists in creation between creator and creature. We mean by it that inward sense of freedom and rationality which we enjoy as men by virtue of God's unstinted indwelling in our nature, and without which we should soon

4

forfeit every vestige of the human form. Selfhood, personality,
is not anything which you can sensibly discern, or reduce to
mathematical measurement, for it is a fact of life or consciousness exclusively, and the mathematics deal only with facts of
existence or sense. Nothing in the least explains it short of the
creative truth, the truth of the divine NATURAL humanity, which
teaches us that what God creates is no mere pictured or sculptured
reality, like the works we glory in; nor yet any mechanism,
like the clocks and steam-engines which exercise our maturer
genius; but a purely living or conscious form, which freely or
of its own nature reacts to his inspiration, and reproduces in
negative or inverse imagery every feature of his perfection. No
doubt the creature, taught by his senses, denies this great truth,
or separates himself to his own thought in a very vital manner
from the creator. But all this is a childish illusion on the creature's part, due to his native ignorance and imbecility in spiritual things; the real truth of the case being all the while, that
when he feels himself to be most absolute and independent, he
is then precisely the most abject puppet or dependent creature
of the creative wisdom.

This fact that the creature, by virtue of his native arrogance
and stupidity in divine things, inflates himself to absolute dimensions, ought not to challenge the serious intellectual homage
which philosophers are wont to accord it. In fact, philosophy
has been fed hitherto upon excrementitious food. Men have
always and everywhere so persistently defiled their infantile
simplicity and innocence, in eating of the tree of finite knowledge, as really to fancy themselves the source of their own
good and evil, and hence to exhibit states of alternate elation
and despair towards God, which reflect the gravest discredit
upon his stainless name. And what could philosophy do, having
no higher testimony to appeal to, and disdaining the light of
revelation, but accept this garbage of the moral or subjective
consciousness as final or absolute, and proceed to live upon it
as upon so much celestial manna? But the *data* of the moral
consciousness are a ghastly mockery of celestial truth. The
angel, according to Swedenborg, is so far from cherishing his
moral consciousness, or attributing the good and evil he is made
aware of in his own bosom to himself, that he habitually refers

the former to the lord, and the latter to evil association. He
is invariably described by Swedenborg as being utterly unwilling to appropriate to himself the least particle of good or of
evil : because he finds that just in proportion as he does so he
forfeits his inmost essential peace and beatitude. He is unfeignedly averse to claiming any selfhood or personality of his
own : unfeignedly averse to credit himself with the least subjective discrimination from the most wanton imp of satan. For
the heavenly atmospheres, as Swedenborg reports them, are so
instinct with objective use, are so inspiriting to every form of
productive action, that every one who respires them becomes
liberated from his finite ties, and actively associated with the
infinite power and loveliness. And how shall minds thus enlarged by contact with the real substances of the world diminish themselves again to the purely figurative and fallacious
dimensions of the moral or subjective consciousness ? Do men
who have known at last what life truly is relish it so little as
to revert deliberately to death ?

Bear diligently in mind, then, that our natural creation is a
purely spiritual operation of God, and that space and time, which
to our silly thought seem so essential to it, are, on the contrary,
sheerly existential to it, as abasing it to the level of our sensuous cognizance. They have nothing whatever to do with our
creation in the way of involution, but only in that of the most
reverent and obedient evolution. It involves them as the expressive symbols, as the patient pliant vassals, of human affection and thought; while they, in their turn, assidnously evolve
it, as having no primary pertinence to themselves, but only to
the sovereign form of man. Thus our natural creation, truly or
spiritually regarded, claims the dew of eternal youth. It is as
fresh and vigorous now, at this day and in this land, as it ever
was in the virgin heart of Eden, under suns whose heat and
light have been myriads of years extinct.

IX.

I do not see how the least doubt of my meaning can now
survive, when I talk of God's giving us natural selfhood or subjective identity. For it is plain, that I mean to allege no out-

ward and finite, but an inward and infinite, giving on his part ;
in fact, just that complete surrender of himself to us, in the
plenitude of his perfection, *which constitutes our natural creation,*
or is equivalent *to our being vivified by him in all the height and
depth, and length and breadth, of our native oppugnancy to him.*
This is the only true or philosophic conception of creation,
namely, the abandonment of yourself to what is not yourself
in a manner so intimate and hearty, as that you thenceforth
shall utterly disappear within the precincts of its existence —
shall become phenomenally extinct within the entire realm of its
personality — while it alone shall appear to be. For example,
you are sometimes said, in popular parlance, to *create* the products of your genius, say a statue. Now your creative action
here restricts itself to the ideal form of the statue, its material
substance being already supplied to your hand in nature. Accordingly, just in proportion as your statue is faultless in point
of art — which means, just as its *opus* subjugates its *materies,*
just as its base earthly substance becomes indissolubly wedded
with, or glorified into, ideal form — will your creative power
avouch itself, and the perfect work swallow up the personality
of the workman. Just so with the divine creation. It is an
utter, total, unstinted self-abnegation (as it must always appear
to our selfish intelligence) on the part of the infinite love,
whereby the creature being naturally vivified or made to appear
as if he had life in himself, and thereupon freely avouching himself the impassioned enemy of the divine infinitude, the creator
is seen frankly acquiescing in such enmity as his only suitable
or worthy ground of action, and proceeding at once to vindicate
his proper power by converting this created evil and falsity into
a good which shall be infinite, and a truth which shall be absolute.

Perhaps what I said just now about creation always and of necessity *appearing to our eyes* to be a self-denying operation of
the divine love, may strike the reader as still unimproved. Let
me then briefly try to make good to his understanding the
ground of this proposition.

When we call God's love infinite or perfect, what do we mean
by that predicate ? No doubt we mean something essentially
congruous with the subject, and the subject of the predicate

being love, we can only mean of course in calling it infinite or perfect, to allege that it is a love without any alloy of self; that it has no subjective ends ; that its aims are altogether objective, or tend to the aggrandizement of whatsoever is not itself. Now we can claim no intuitive knowledge of such love as this, but only a reflective one. For we are naturally prone to love ourselves primarily, and our neighbor derivatively, so that if any conflict of interests diversify our intercourse, it costs us a strong effort of self-denial to do him justice. In this manner self-denial, self-sacrifice, has become to our minds the symbol of pure love — love disengaged from sense and putting on spiritual attributes. In proportion as our love is void of passion or claims an active quality, it involves an element of self-abasement, or disowns all subjective and acknowledges only objective ends. Notoriously the purest form of passion known to us is a mother's love for her child. And the reason is that there is ordinarily far more of spontaneity in it than in any other passion ; that it habitually exhibits a greater degree of self-forgetfulness. And this being the case — namely, that the divine love is the pure love it is because it is unimpassioned, or has no selfish ends, being wholly addressed to the blessing of whatsoever is most remote from and opposite to itself; while ours, on the other hand, is the impure thing it is, because it is a merely organic or passionate love, being addressed to selfish ends, that is, to the aggrandizement of such as are in relations, not of remoteness and opposition to ourselves, but only of nearness and agreement — it is at once evident that the divine love must either remain wholly unknown and impracticable to us, or else must reveal itself in finite imagery, in lineaments adapted to our sensuous intelligence, and so alone find its chance of awakening our responsive sympathy.

This was all I meant in saying that the creative love must always wear a self-denying aspect to our natural understanding. The obligation grows out of the inevitable ignorance and inexperience we are under by nature in divine things ; and unless therefore the creative wisdom tenderly accommodated itself to these natural exactions, we should remain dead to the faintest possibility of spiritual life.

But now that I have made this explanation, let us prepare for a new aspect of our subject, and begin looking at creation no longer in its strictly universal or generic aspect, as a *descending* movement of the divine life in man, but in its particular or specific aspect, as an *ascending* movement of that life. Hitherto we have been more intent upon the statics of creation than its dynamics. That is to say, we have been looking too exclusively at *nature*, mineral, vegetable, and animal, as serving to give the creature selfhood or subjective identity, which is a conscience of alienation from (*otherness than*) his maker. But our attention is due in at least an equal degree to *history* also, as an emphatic counter-movement to nature in the interest of the creature's spiritual freedom or individuality, whereby he reacts against this finite impulsion, and seeks to reunite himself with the infinite. Nature is a centrifugal movement of the creative providence, whereby the creature becomes projected or set off to his own consciousness from the creator, by all the breadth of mineral, vegetable, and animal existence. History is an answering centripetal movement of the same providence, whereby the creature becomes gradually lifted out of his mineral, vegetable, and animal thraldom, into properly human proportions, or endowed with conscience. And creation consequently would be very inadequately conceived by us, if we should slight either of these majestic and coequal factors, either nature or history. They are both alike essential to the conception, nature as symbolizing its finite maternal side, history its infinite paternal one; nature as supplying the generic element, the element of identity in the creature which makes him objective to himself, or furnishes the fixed immutable ground of his consciousness, and history as supplying the specific element, the element of individuality in the creature, which makes him objective to God, or invests him with moral character, i. e. with a conscience of good and evil, and so furnishes the free, contingent, movable ground of his consciousness.

Let the reader diligently note the force of what has here been said. Nature and history are both alike and most strictly *involved* in the philosophic idea of creation, and they have themselves no other function than sedulously to *evolve* it. It is impossible that creation should *really* take place, save in so far as it takes place *actually*. In other words, the creature can possess no real or absolute being in God, save in so far as he possesses actual or phenomenal existence in himself. And any creation therefore would pronounce itself palpably inchoate, which should pretend to establish the creature's derivative being upon any other basis than that of his own underived form, or avouch his spiritual individuality by any other evidence than that of his natural identity. Thus nature and history are both alike necessary portals of the true or spiritual and eternal world; but they are nothing more than portals, and furnish no glimpse, save in the way of inverse correspondence, of the interior things belonging to it. They are both alike an inevitable preliminary matrix or mould of God's spiritual creation, which is man; but they are absolutely nothing whatever but such actual matrix or mould: nature, in its direct or objective bearing upon man, attesting the descent of the creator to the creature's level; while history, which is man's subjective protest or reaction upon nature, attests the creature's consequent rise to the level of the creator.

This is that dual consciousness which man is said to own by creation, and which is symbolized in sacred writ under the terms *male* and *female*; the former term corresponding to nature, the latter to history. * His nature, simply because it is a created one, is made up of two utterly disproportionate elements, one infinite and absolute, the other finite and contingent; one active or creative, the other passive or reactive; one generic or universal, the other specific or particular; one utterly objective or unconscious of self, the other profoundly subjective or self-conscious. Such is man's natural genesis, such his inevitable make as a created being. Every man, by virtue of his natural creation, has this conjoint inward and outward consciousness, this conjoint objective and subjective parentage, i. e. claims both an implicit community or identity with all existence, and an explicit individuality or difference from it.

No philosophy accordingly is worth a moment's regard, but confesses itself on its face unspeakably shallow and futile, which

* The reason why the former constitutes a descending movement of providence, and the latter an ascending one, is that in the natural man (*homo*) the human or specific principle, the principle of individuality (Eve), which allies us with the inward and infinite, is subject to the cosmical or generic principle, the principle of universality (Adam), which allies us with the outward and finite; while in the historic and moral development of the race (*vir*) the latter principle serves, and the former rules.

attempts to construct a doctrine of being upon the assumed
absoluteness of nature and history. Real, which is spiritual,
existence is utterly inexplicable upon any such basis, since the
life we derive from nature and history is only phenomenally
ours, while in reality it is altogether the creator's life in us.
For suppose creation fully accomplished in the exact equation
of creator and creature; the creature after all has no real but
only a phenomenal existence. Suppose the creator, on his part,
to have furnished the creature an ample basis of self-consciousness by vivifying his nature, or graduating it to his sensuous
recognition under the successive masks of mineral, vegetable,
and animal existence; and suppose the creature, on his side, to
have arrived consequently at the amplest and most vivacious
self-consciousness. What then? Why, after all, the creature
has not attained to true, but only to phenomenal being; for however much he alone all the while appears to be, it is nevertheless God alone who all the while really *is*, under that appearance.
No doubt the creature seems to himself absolutely to be, to be
naturally, as it were, or by inherent right; and on the strength
of that appearance manages to simulate spiritual character by
freely appropriating good and evil to himself, or charging himself with positive merit and demerit in God's sight. But he is
and remains a mere image or shadow of real existence. The selfhood or freedom which he feels to be so absolute is a pure providential concession to him in the interest of his ultimate emanci-
pation from nature and history, or his eventual spiritual evolution. It is all the while God's veritable and sole life in his nature, mercifully consenting to appear as his life. It is the creative love existing or going forth from itself in creaturely form;
and although the form or appearance thence resulting is that of
the creature alone, the total being or reality of the appearance
refers itself to the creator, and must eventually be recognized
in that light by the creature, unless he would remain forever
swamped in spiritual ignorance and folly. What an egregious
sciolism accordingly every philosophy must present, which attempts to account for existence upon its own data, or without
deference to the commanding light of revelation which alone
declares its true *raison d'être*.

You see at a glance then what a profound abyss, to Swedenborg's judgment, separates being from existence, spirit from nature. You see, in short, how infinitely remote from spiritual sonship to God our natural creation leaves us, and how obligatory it is upon him therefore, if he would ever spiritually affiliate us to himself, to give us redemption from our own nature. And this great redemption, how shall it ever be able to come about? By the very nature of the case, *the sphere of its evolution is restricted to the limits of the created consciousness*, so that the creator can command absolutely no enginery to effect it, which is not supplied exclusively by the resources of that consciousness. The creator is bound indeed to fulfil the obligation by his own sheer unassisted might; but this might will be weakness save in so far as he is able to sink himself in the created consciousness, or make the creature's unaffected selfishness and cupidity the all-sufficient gauge and fulcrum of his power. How then shall this grand drama of redemption, intimately complicated as it is with the immutable laws of creation, ever be conceived as actually traversing those laws, so as to bring forth the most definite spiritual issues to the human consciousness, without in the slightest degree violating their sanctity, or enfeebling their validity?

This is the question of questions to the philosophic mind; and if I can succeed in conveying to the reader even a clouded ray of the light I get from Swedenborg in regard to it, I shall not only, I am persuaded, have given him a key to all the metaphysic doubts which vex his intellectual progress, but I shall have supplied him a grateful stimulus also to a more close, earnest, and energetic prosecution of his most urgent practical duties, which are those he owes to the great truth of human society, fellowship, or equality.

X.

History, according to Swedenborg, resolves itself into the existence of the church on earth; and the existence of the church, spiritually understood, means the purgation of human nature by divine power. That is to say, there could have been no such thing as an historic resurrection of the human consciousness, but man's life must always have remained sunken in the mud of mere animality, unless our natural loves, which are those of self and the

world, had been permitted from the beginning to organize themselves in *religious* form, and assume the initiative in human affairs
under a *quasi* divine sanction.   The necessity of this providential
permission is obvious.   For if by nature man is the spiritual opposite of God — and he must be that in order to be anything at all
— it is clear that he can never be brought into living or spiritual
harmony with God, unless the natural loves which base his
action become interested factors in that result.   It is true they
will be very infirm factors, but they are nevertheless the only
ones the case admits of, since it is evident that no outward constraint can be practised upon a spiritual subject, nor any change
effected in him without his own consent and co-operation being
to some extent enlisted.   It is natural or logical enough, no
doubt, in the potter, to spurn the clay which will not lend itself
to his plastic advances; because the potter does not stand in a
creative, but only in a formative relation to the work of his
hands.   That is to say, he does not himself provide the clay
out of which his work is to be fabricated, but only the mould or
form into which the clay is to be run.   But it would be extremely derogatory to the divine name to suppose him quarrel-
ling with the material of human nature out of which alone his
spiritual results are to be fashioned; for he stands in an absolutely creative relation to those results.   That is to say, he alone
gives us physical existence, he alone vivifies it, animates it with
selfhood, or renders it capable of moral life; and he alone consequently is answerable if it should finally prove recreant to his
spiritual requirements.

Never accordingly for an instant does Swedenborg report the
creative relation towards the creature, in his very lowest moral
states, as a quarrelsome or even as a querulous one.   On the contrary he invariably represents the divine love as never *breaking*,
but always most tenderly *bending*, our perverse moral states to the
purposes of a mercy which is really infinite as embracing the salvation of the whole human race, and which otherwise must have
appeared altogether finite, as embracing the destiny of a comparatively few persons.   Thus heaven and hell, as portrayed by Swedenborg's impartial pen, argue — inasmuch as they exist only
by each other's antagonism — a finite love in the creator;
that is to say, a love which is not at harmony with itself, or has

no unitary end ; and hence they logically confess themselves to be mere *incidents* of human progress, mere stepping-stones to the end which God proposes to himself in the vivification of human nature.

" *The lord's love*," says Swedenborg, " *is the salvation of the whole human race* "; and such being his love, such also must be the aim of his providence.* Its salvation from what, pray ? Why, from the spiritual evils and falsities which are strictly incidental to its finite experience, or its innate and essential ignorance of the creative name and ways. Remember, I say the race's *finite* experience ; for the race of course comes to integral self-consciousness, to the consciousness of its own unity, only through the experience of its individual members gradually inducting human society or fellowship. The race itself has no existence apart from the individuals which compose it, and hence, being neither good nor evil in itself, has no evils nor falsities of its own to answer for. But of the innumerable multitude of persons who compose the race, some — let us for convenience' sake say the half — unaffectedly conceive themselves to be *good* men, while the remainder quite as unaffectedly agree in pronouncing themselves *evil* men. And as good and evil, like light and darkness, do not cohere in themselves or directly, but only in some third or neutral quantity, these two kinds of men, so distinctly antagonized by their own consciousness, inevitably go asunder in divine things, and by their reciprocal contrariety produce that bipolar aspect of the spiritual world which Swedenborg characterizes under the familiar names of *heaven* and *hell* : the only difference between his notion of the subject and that which is popularly entertained being, that with Swedenborg it is those alone who feel themselves to be good men that constitute hell, and those only who feel themselves to be evil men that constitute heaven.

While this discordant state of things endures in the spiritual world, or the higher regions of the mind, there can obviously be no unitary consciousness of the race on earth, or nothing but an enforced harmony in the lower degrees of the mind ; nation being divided against nation, family against family, and man

* See Arcana Celestia, 1676, 1813, 2034, 2222, 2227, 2819, 6371 – 6373, 6720, 8273, etc.

against man. That is to say, whilst our consciences are so un-enlightened in divine things as to pronounce one man or one class of men absolutely, and not alone relatively, good, and another man or another class of men absolutely, and not alone relatively, evil, it is evident that human society, fellowship, or equality (which alone gives unity to the race, or endows it with permanent self-consciousness) cannot come about; and man's life consequently must remain utterly chaotic or unredeemed, save in so far as certain providential instrumentalities, certain great social lieutenancies, arise to institute a *quasi* or provisional order in human affairs.

Let me be perfectly understood. What I say is, that all society or fellowship among men is simply impossible or unendurable, so long as one man or one class of men is held to be absolutely void of evil, and another man or another class of men absolutely void of good. For in that case the former must appear personally or in himself acceptable to God, and the latter must appear personally or in himself hateful to God, so that a religious obligation would constrain the good man to exclude the evil man from his society or fellowship in every possible way. If the evil man is personally revolting to God, how shall I dare to offend God by extending my personal countenance or sympathy to him? Nothing surely can be plainer than this. Very well then, transfer your view for a moment to the spiritual world, as made up of the contrasted spheres of heaven and hell. Do you not see at once that if this contrast be absolute — i. e. if heaven and hell reflect an actual divine decree, and not the mere unfettered play of human freedom — the mind of man in nature, depending as it does for its heat and light upon the inflow of spiritual good and truth, must necessarily repugn the *social* conception of human destiny; must necessarily revolt from it in fact, as from the grandest conceivable profanation of the divine name? It is the pretension of human society to take up the good and evil alike in its bosom, and shower its sunshine and its rain equally upon the just and the unjust. If then the spiritual world be established upon the absolute bipolarity of good and evil, that is to say, if the angel and the devil exhibit the same actual contrast to the divine regard that they do to ours, nothing can be more odious to the divine mind, nothing more contrary

to his providence, than a state of things upon earth which puts
forth the pretension, as society unquestionably does, practically
to efface all distinction of good and evil among men, by lifting
all men, saint and sinner, just and unjust, alike into the bosom
of its own regenerate unity.

Practically how stands the case then? What light does
Swedenborg shed upon the constitution of the spiritual world?
Does he affirm, so far as it was open to him to observe and
ascertain, any *absolute* difference between heaven and hell, between angel and devil? That is to say, did he discover that
the angel claimed any personal superiority to the devil in the
divine regard, any superiority in himself? Or did he discover
that the difference between them was purely relative, being altogether contingent upon the disproportionate attitude they bore
with respect to the truth of human brotherhood, fellowship, or
equality?

Unquestionably the latter verdict is the one invariably rendered
by Swedenborg. After a quarter of a century's unbroken intercourse with angel and devil, he declares that in themselves or
absolutely they are both alike; that so far as their *proprium* or
selfhood is concerned, there is nothing to choose between them.
Those who are familiar with Swedenborg's books will need no
testimonies from them to this effect, since such testimonies
abound to their knowledge on every page. But I may properly
cite a few of his innumerable *dicta* upon the subject, which may
prove interesting perhaps, and even inspiring, to readers of a
philosophic turn who have not had the same advantage.

I quote first of all a pregnant statement of general principles in regard to personality, which may fitly introduce the other
extracts.

" In heaven no thought is given to persons, nor to the things
of person, but to things abstracted from person. Hence the
angels have no recognition of a man from his name or other personal attributes, but only from his distinctive human faculty or
quality. The thought of persons limits the angelic idea, or
finites it; while that of things does not limit it, but gives it infinitude. No person named in the word is recognized in heaven,
but only the human quality or substance symbolized by that person; neither any nation or people, but only the human quality

of such nation and people. Thus there is not a single fact of scripture concerning person, nation, or people which is known in heaven, where the angels are totally unconcerned about the personality of Abraham, Isaac, and Jacob, and see no difference between Jew and Gentile, but difference of human quality. The angelic idea, refusing in this manner to be determined to persons, makes the speech of the angels as compared with ours unlimited and universal." *

" Every man, regenerate though he be, is such that, unless the Lord withheld him from evils and falses, he would cast himself headlong into hell." †

" Every one now-a-days supposes that evils and falsities in man are dispersed and abolished while he is regenerating, so that when he becomes regenerate nothing of evil and falsity remains, but he is clean and righteous like one cleansed and washed with water. This, however, is utterly untrue. For no single evil or falsity in man can be so broken up as to be abolished, but on the contrary whatever evil belongs by inheritance to a person or has been actually contracted by him persists; so that every man, even the regenerate, is in himself nothing but evil and falsity, as livingly appears after death. This truth flows from the fact that all the good and truth in man are the Lord in him, and all his evil and falsity are himself; so that every man, spirit, and angel, if left in the least to themselves, would plunge spontaneously into hell. This is why in scripture the heavens are

---

* Arcana Celestia, 5225, 8343, 9007.

† Arcana Celestia, 789. It must be remembered, in connection with these statements of Swedenborg, that he always represents *delight* to be the essence of hell as of heaven also ; only the delights of one are *opposed* to the delights of the other. Thus as heaven with Swedenborg means a mental state in which the love of God and the love of the neighbor rule, and the loves of self and the world obey, so hell means a mental state in which this hierarchy is inverted, the lower loves governing, and the higher ones serving. Its delights accordingly are so intimate and exquisite as being bound up with the subject's self, that he with difficulty credits their infernal character and derivation, and inclines in fact to regard them as truly celestial. Swedenborg, in his profoundly interesting book on the *Divine Providence*, says that he had been " let in to the delights of the *selfish* love of rule," and he found it " to exceed all the delights in the world." It was " a delight of the whole mind from its inmost to its ultimate substances, but it was only felt in the body as a certain pleasurable and gladsome inflation of the breast. I perceived that from this supreme delight, as from their fountain, flow all evil delights, such as adultery, fraud, revenge, blasphemy, etc." Divine Providence, 215.

called impure. The angels confess this truth, and no one who does not do so can relish their society. It is God's mercy alone which frees them from evil, yea, which draws them and keeps them out of hell, to which they have a headlong inclination." *

"There is no moral or intellectual rectitude which is to be ascribed to the angel himself, but only to the lord in him. The most celestial angel is in himself altogether false and evil, what is good and true in him being not really but only apparently his own." †

"All good and truth is of the lord, and what is his remains his in those who receive it; for it is divine, and refuses to be the private property of any man. He consequently who appropriates the divine to himself" — i. e. takes any merit to himself for his moral or personal excellency — "really defiles and profanes it." ‡

"It has been demonstrated to me by lively experience, that every man, spirit, and angel, viewed in himself or as to what is peculiarly *his own* in him, is the vilest excrement, and that if he were left to himself he would breathe only hatreds, revenges, cruelties, and foulest adulteries. These things are his *proprium* or distinctive selfhood. This is evident to reflection from the fact that man in his native state is viler than all beasts; and when he grows up and becomes his own master, unless external bonds which are of the law, and the bonds he instinctively assumes in order to grow greatest and richest, prevented him, he would rush into every iniquity, nor ever rest until he had subjugated everybody else to himself, and possessed himself of their substance, showing no favor to any but those who should become his abject slaves.§ Such is the nature of every man, however ignorant he be of the fact in consequence of his want of power to act himself out; but give him the power, and release him from the obligations of prudence, and his inclination would not belie his opportunity. The beasts are not so bad as this, for

* Arcana Celestia, 868.
† Arcana Celestia, 633.
‡ Apocalypse Revealed, 758. These facts shed light upon another statement of Swedenborg, to the effect that " there is no enforced or arbitrary authority in heaven ; *since no angel in his heart acknowledges any one superior to himself but the lord alone."* Apocalypse Explained, 735.
§ One would say that Swedenborg had had a glimpse of the second French Empire.

they are born into a certain order of nature. Those that are fierce and rapacious do indeed inflict injury, but only from self-preservation, devouring others to appease hunger, and ceasing from violence when this want is satisfied." *

These citations amply suffice to show that Swedenborg detected no manner of difference, so far as their selfhood or personality was concerned, between angel and devil, but on the contrary an absolute identity. That is to say, he discovered nothing in the angel which was the least degree meritorious towards God, and nothing in the devil which constituted the slightest ground of ill desert towards him. In short, he found the utmost actual difference between the two; but this difference was no way subjective as reflecting any personal merit upon the one, or any personal demerit upon the other, but purely objective as reflecting a difference of relation in them to something not themselves.

XI.

No doubt the statements we have just been canvassing may be said to be untrue; which is an easy, but by no means a reasonable, way to dispose of them. I myself see very clearly that they labor under the disadvantage which attaches to all spiritual or highest truth, namely, that it appears true only to those who wish it to be true, that it has only an intrinsic probability to back it, being destitute of all extrinsic likelihood, of all outward form and comeliness. But I am sure that to those who are prepared by previous culture to receive Swedenborg's statements on their own evidence — and the number of these I conceive cannot be small — they cannot help possessing a profound philosophic significance. For they go clearly to establish this fact, that the insufficiency of the moral hypothesis to account for existence — the hypothesis of our personal independence or absoluteness, as maintained, for example, by Fichte — is a fundamental postulate of angelic wisdom. And this is something quite new to philosophy, which has always had its hands so absurdly full of doubt and denial in regard to physical realities, as to permit it neither time nor inclination to harbor the slightest suspicion in

* Arcana Celestia, 987.

regard to the reality of the moral world. If then it is only our
physical experience that we can reckon upon as stable, while
our moral or subjective consciousness is the true realm of illusion, forever mocking us with hopes that mislead and betray,
philosophy has still a capital chance to get upon its legs, by simply adjusting itself for the first time in history, no longer to the
specious appearance of things, but to their absolute reality.   If
it be true, as Swedenborg reports, and I for one have no misgiving upon the subject, that all celestial and all spiritual intel-
ligences, in proportion as they are wise, agree in renouncing
the moral hypothesis of creation, or in holding the creator to be
influenced in his work by no subjective or personal aims, but by
ends purely objective and impersonal, I do not see how philosophy can fail on the instant to perceive an incomparable enlargement of her borders, literally such an aggrandizement of her
horizon as her annals have never yet recorded.   For her only
stumbling-block from the beginning has been the subjective
datum in consciousness, or our imbecile conceit of our own absoluteness.   And here, at last, comes Swedenborg with an induction for the first time adequate to the facts, being as broad as
human nature itself — i. e. as high as heaven and profound as
hell — which shows us that there is in truth nothing so little
absolute, so largely fallacious, as our moral or subjective consciousness ; that is to say, nothing so intensely dependent, so
subtly contingent, so exquisitely and essentially relative to some
thing else.   So that if philosophy would only consent to look
at these astonishing books, she would no longer feel any need to
spend money for that which is not bread, and her labor for that
which satisfieth not.

W hat, then, *is* this grand " something else" which is of such
poignant interest to philosophy, as reducing all our subjective pomp
and clamor to " an idiot's tale, full of sound and fury, signifying
nothing " ; as abasing, indeed, what we have always deemed the
majestic finalities of heaven and hell — the finished and sovereign personalities of angel and devil — to its own sheer and
exclusive constitutional ministry ?

It is the interest of REVELATION.   The grand controlling interest which all things, whether in heaven, on earth, or in hell,
obey, is the necessity *of an adequate revelation of the divine*

5

name. Spiritual existence — the existence of spiritual affection and thought — is indispensably conditioned, according to Swedenborg, upon a plenary revelation of the creative name in the created nature. Why? For the simple reason that the creature can claim no intuitive or *a priori* knowledge of the creator, and must come to know him therefore only as he is reflected in himself. He can know his creator *a posteriori* only, i. e. only through an actual *experience* of the creative presence and power, as revealed in the created nature. In a word, the created consciousness, the self-consciousness of the creature, is of itself and of necessity the sole measure and mirror of the creative perfection.

I am not going to argue the matter here set down, the alleged necessity of a divine revelation. I should be very loath to influence any one, even in what seems to me a good direction, against the impulses of his own heart; and those who are already disposed by independent or original culture to an affirmative view of this question will dispense with persuasion. But I nevertheless greatly desire to put the question in its true light before the reader, and I will, therefore, briefly restate it in the form it takes to my own intelligence.

In the first place let me say what is meant by revelation. The term is frequently, and indeed commonly, used as if it were synonymous with information, whereas it claims an utterly distinct and very much profounder meaning. To inform me of anything is to give me knowledge which is essentially level to the human faculties, or belongs legitimately to the realm of science; while revealed knowledge, properly so called, is knowledge which is essentially veiled or hidden from men's intelligence, and so transcends the legitimate grasp of science. Thus to reveal is to unveil what has been hitherto concealed under a veil of contrary appearances. The revelator, properly so called, is not a scientific genius, like Kepler, who sagaciously detects and exposes the hitherto unsuspected scope of natural law. He is rather, like Christ, a man of no scientific culture whatever, who yet, by force of his active humanitary sympathy and insight, livingly discerns and reproduces in himself the unknown spirit which animates all nature and history, but is persistently denied, dishonored, and crucified by their remorseless, insensate letter. Swedenborg gives me a great deal of information about spiritual things which I am very glad to get ; and I accordingly feel the same qualified esteem, in kind if not in degree, for him, that I do for Humboldt, or Fourier, or any other veracious man of science, whose labors, in any sphere of the mind, go to promote the race's progress. But he *reveals* absolutely nothing to me. That is to say, he sheds no new and living light upon the secret things of the divine providence, which have been hitherto obscured by the facts of nature and the events of history. On the contrary, his life was that of our average manhood, and the secrets he divulges in relation to the spiritual world, were not things inwardly discerned by him, but outwardly communicated to him by others ; they were, as he himself describes them, strictly *audita et visa*, the fruit exclusively of ocular and auricular experience amongst angels and spirits. He never pretends for a moment to bring mankind a new revelation, being altogether content to subside into the humble servant of the christian verity ; and if he had been a man of that stamp, we should doubtless have found his so-called " revelations " plainly attributing themselves to the same limbo of vanity which has spawned so much of the flatulent literature of our modern spirit-rapping.

Revelation then does not mean simple information, as it is corruptly used to do ; nor does it ask the least leave of the scientific intellect, since it is concerned with truths which are utterly beyond the original compass of the intellect to divine, however perfectly it may come afterwards to reflect them. Revelation discloses the existence in man of a higher than the moral or voluntary life, a life which has indeed always been symbolized by that, but which puts itself at a hopeless remove from it by rigidly disclaiming a finite genesis, and appealing only to infinite sanctions. Now science is the organ of the distinctively finite intellect, the intellect tethered to sense ; and though doubtless it will one day yield a prompt reverberation, a cordial flooring and support, to the instincts of this higher life, the two spheres are nevertheless as essentially distinct as those of freedom and bondage.

It is plain now what revelation does *not* mean, and incidentally to that of course what it does mean. And having ascer-

tained thus much, let us next proceed to inquire how it is that
revelation justifies itself, or is able to avouch its own supreme
necessity.

Revelation, according to Swedenborg, is essential to a true or
living acknowledgment of God, in contradistinction to a mere
doctrinal or traditional acknowledgment. An unrevealed God
is practically no God at all to the human understanding, but is
and must remain forever incognizable to every intelligence beneath his own; for a direct or immediate contact with the infinite would be obviously fatal to the finite understanding, and
the only alternative of such contact is the mediate or indirect
one which revelation affords. A direct or immediate knowledge
of God on our part would imply that there was some common
bond between him and us, something continuous from him to
us and from us to him, some point of identity or indistinction
which may livingly fuse the two, just as the marble fuses sculptor and statue in its own embrace, or the mother fuses father
and child in her own quickened bosom. But the hypothesis of
creation stringently excludes all such community or identity.
That hypothesis makes the creator all and the creature nothing
save by him; so that the very faculty of knowledge by which
the latter seeks to know the former, is his only in appearance,
while in reality it is the creator's power in him. Creation is, to
be sure, an exact equation of the creative and created natures,
but an equation in which one factor is wholly active and the
other wholly passive, or in which one really is while the other
only appears. To talk of the creature truly knowing the creator under these circumstances, is to talk arrant nonsense. The
statue, wrought by the sculptor out of the reluctant marble, is
infinitely nearer to a just appreciation of the character of the
sculptor, in the entire compass of his civil, religious, and domestic being. For the statue is a material existence at least, and
has thus one point of identity with the sculptor, which makes
it infinitely nearer to the latter than the latter himself is to God.
There is absolutely no such neutral point, or point of indifference, between creator and creature, for the very nature or
subjective identity of the latter, which to his own consciousness
disjoins him absolutely from the creator, is, after all, only a perpetual *permission* of the creative love in the interest of his sub-

sequent spiritual possibilities. The creator, no doubt, sinks or merges his infinitude in our finite lineaments; but as he, on his part, does not thereby cease to be, so we, on ours, do not thereby begin to be, but only to exist or appear to our own consciousness. In other words, God so vivifies by his own substance our native destitution of being, as that we thenceforward seem to live of ourselves, or, as we say, naturally; appear to ourselves absolutely to be, while he as absolutely disappears. But both the appearance and the disappearance are utterly fallacious, if we push them beyond their proper limits; that is, if they are not seen to be valid only within the compass of our finite consciousness, or to the extent of our sensuous understanding: the eternal truth of the case being all the while that God alone really *is*, in spite of his disappearance to sight, and that we ourselves really *are not*, in spite of our profuse semblance of being.

Or let me demonstrate the impossibility of a direct knowledge of God, from the necessary limitations of knowledge itself. We cannot know God immediately or independently of revelation, because the very nature of our knowledge forbids it.

Knowledge, properly speaking, is what relates us to outlying things — things that are external to ourselves. It always implies a basis of sensible experience. It is true that we often say that we know things when we do not really *know* them, i. e. as based upon sensible evidence, but only *remember* them, as based upon rational evidence, i. e. as having learned them. Thus we say that we know two and two to be *equal* to four, or the sum of the angles of a triangle to be *equal* to two right angles. But we know no such thing, in the proper sense of the word *knowledge*. It is, in fact, only a compact way of saying that we have been rationally convinced of such equality, or have learned it before now. *Equality* is a term of relation between two or more things, and relationships are cognizable only to the reason, never to sense. In this way we perpetually confound facts of memory which pertain to the rational or reflective understanding with facts of sense, which pertain to our bodily experience; but the two spheres are nevertheless perfectly distinct. We know only what our senses in some form or other avouch, that is, facts of finite existence. We believe only what our reason or

reflection in some form avouches, namely: that an infinite being *relates* all these existences in unity.   In short, sense is
the invariable ground of knowledge; reason, of belief; and the
two things should never be confounded in serious discourse.

If then, in this state of things, we should maintain that a
direct knowledge of God is possible to us, a knowledge irrespective of any revelation, the inference would be that God is an
external being to us, that he is related to us by our senses, and
hence is inferior to us ; for whatsoever lies outside of the mind
is below the mind, or inferior to it.   But this is the hoarse and
sottish croak of superstition.   No such God exists.   In the first
place, there is nothing absolutely, but only phenomenally, external
to the mind (or spiritual universe) ; all that sensibly exists being
but the mind's furniture, or existing only to proclaim and illustrate its spiritual unity.*   The sensuous or uncultivated mind
does indeed affirm the absolute as well as the relative objectivity
of the things of sense ; that is, it tacitly concedes to the tree
and the horse a virtual independence or immortality, in allowing
them to exist out of relation, not only to the individual consciousness (the *vir*), which is right, but also to the universal
consciousness (the *homo*), which is silly.   But the spiritual or
regenerate thought of man rectifies this shallow dogmatism, and
makes all sensible existence to fall within the unitary mind of
the race, makes it in truth to be simply constitutive of the mind
to its own recognition ; and consequently if everything that
sensibly exists does so only in relation to the mind of the race,
or falls under the human consciousness and not above it, why
then of course, we can bring God into external or sensible con-

---

* " Out of the ground the lord God formed every beast of the field, and every
fowl of the air, and brought them unto the man *to see what he would call them ; and
whatsoever the man called it, that was the name thereof.   And the man gave name to all
cattle, and to the fowl of the air, and to every beast of the field.* — Gen. ii. 19, 20.

Surely no one can for a moment seriously suppose this to be the record of a literal historic event ; every sober judgment, on the contrary, must regard it as an
expressive symbol of the great creative truth, that man (spiritually regarded) is
the measure of existence, that is, that all things in nature derive their specific
form and significance from the relation of use they bear to the human mind.
Name, in the science of correspondences, means *quality* ; and by " man giving
name " to all existence is signified therefore, that all the lower forms of nature,
mineral, vegetable, and animal, owe their specific genius or worth to the relation
of nearness they sustain to the human type of character.

tact with our intelligence only at the cost of transmuting the absolutely *creative* relation he bears to the mind, into a phenomenally *constitutive* relation ; that is, at the cost of degrading him from the throne of his infinitude into an abject article, neither more nor less, of the race's mental furniture.

XII.

I will assume, accordingly, without further parley, that a true or living knowledge of God is inevitably conditioned upon an authentic revelation of his name. The next question in order is, what is the method of this revelation ? How does it actually come about ? It must obviously do so in the most gradual manner, since its full accomplishment is contingent upon the advent of a true society or brotherhood among men upon the earth : the evolution of such society or brotherhood, again, being itself contingent upon a previous experience and exhaustion of the patriarchal, the municipal, and the national or political administration of human affairs. The truth of an absolute society, fellowship, equality among men, as the consummation of our earthly destiny, is indeed the hidden divine leaven which has been fermenting in all history, and even from its rudest beginnings moulding the mind of man into inevitable conformity with itself. But from the nature of the case its operation, during all these initiatory stages of progress, must be purely negative. For until society puts on positive form — that is, until the truth of man's rightful fellowship or equality with man becomes scientifically demonstrated — the two elements which go to constitute the social conception of human life are arrayed in inveterate hostility to each other. In all the rudimentary social forms, the family, the city, the nation, an utter enmity exists between the generic and the specific element in consciousness, between the universal and the particular interests of man. A most pronounced contrariety between the *homo* and the *vir*, between the masculine and the feminine force in history, between the physical and the moral life of man, is everywhere accepted and carefully organized in institutions, as the true law of human destiny ; and the order thence ensuing does not hesitate to claim for its support every guaranty of the most shameless force. At this rate, of course, society, which, spiritually or truly regarded, means the complete reconciliation of these jarring elements, is restricted to a purely negative exhibition, or makes itself felt, not as a friend, but rather as an enemy to the established order.

Understand me. When I represent society as a disturbing force in past history, as a perpetual menace to the existing civilization, I do not mean to say that the family, the city, the nation, are not in themselves very admirable institutions, eminently conducive to progress. I only mean to say that they are sure to become perverted in their practical administration to private ends, and that they hence provoke the just resentment of upright minds, of men in whose bosom the social sentiment has begun to be quickened. All of these institutions are so many nurseries of the social destiny of man ; so many divinely appointed *menstrua* for the purification of the social sentiment in the breast of the race. They are a purely *educational* device of the divine providence by which the brute intelligence of the race becomes quickened to discern its inherent selfishness and incapacity, and to aspire after humaner and wiser methods. But they have only this strictly ministerial efficacy, and they accordingly become instruments of the most unhallowed tyranny whenever they are administered in their own interest, or without regard to this exquisite subordination. At such times all that is divine in man rises in revolt, and unless wiser counsels speedily prevail, revolt grows into revolution, and the existing bonds of intercourse among men become violently ruptured.

But now by what recognized *organ* shall the social sentiment announce itself? Is any heart of man equal to the conception of a universal righteousness upon the earth, while as yet the earth is covered with fraud and violence? Is any intellect of man able to give adequate voice to the inspirations of such a righteousness?

Absolutely none. No man is either good enough or wise enough to forecast human destiny, until that destiny shall have at least negatively avouched itself to human hope by the historic desecration of *privilege* among men, or the gradual destruction of every institution, however conventionally sacred, which organizes human inequality. The bare conception of a righteousness truly divine upon the earth is rendered impossible, while the rightful inequality of man with man is enforced by institutions which still challenge human respect. The only thing that veils or obscures the divine name to men's eyes is the absence of any such living society or brotherhood of men as would justify them in ascribing human life to an infinitely wise and good and powerful source : in other words, is the *presence* of all those institutions which seek to guarantee order by force instead of freedom. And the only thing consequently which in this state of affairs can at all reveal or unveil the divine name to men's recognition is some purely *representative* bond, some merely *professional* brotherhood or fellowship among men, some strictly *formal* or *conventional* society, which may have no particle of substantive virtue, but is yet full of the richest prophetic worth, as symbolizing that perfected work of God in our nature, which unites us with him down to our flesh and bones, or gives us resurrection from death even this side of the grave.

This representative economy is called THE CHURCH. The church, as a visible or ritual institution, limits itself, according to Swedenborg, to this purely representative sanctity. Spiritually viewed, the church — what Swedenborg calls, accordingly, the new or final church, God's accomplished work in human nature — implies, of course, a deeper sanctity ; for it means that LIVING society, fellowship, brotherhood of men which shall perfectly reconcile or fuse in its own sovereign unity all the existing contrarieties of human temperament and character, and so cover the earth with the glory of God as the waters cover the sea. The ritual church has never had the least just pretension to constitute this grand and living reality, but only to reflect or represent it to man's dawning spiritual intelligence. And it has done this only by blindly, no doubt, but still unflinchingly upholding the literal divinity of Christ against all gainsayers, or persistently unmooring the hope of men from their own pygmy personalities, in order to anchor it afresh upon a great work of righteousness once for all achieved by absolute divine might in the very heart of their nature. I certainly set no value upon the technical "church" at this day in its ritual capacity. It has long since fulfilled all its legitimate uses in that line. It seems to me now, on the contrary, very much in arrears, spiritually, of its former competitor, "the world."

In fact, it very plainly cumbers the ground which it has grown impotent any longer to fertilize, so that the only use, divine or human, it now seems to enact, is that of alienating men's cordial respect and sympathy from the entire ecclesiastical scheme of thought. But when I look back to what the church *has* done for mankind by its blind unreasoning and yet sagacious adherence to the letter of the truth — when I think how, above all, it has kept alive in the earth the tradition of an original divine innocence in our nature, which will one day spiritually reproduce itself in every most abject finger and toe of our regenerate social and æsthetic consciousness, or obliterate in its infinite embrace every filthy and pitiful remainder of our moral righteousness — I know no bounds to my grateful respect and reverence for it. I feel indeed that all the vices which have attended its actual administration have been richly compensated by that prodigious service.

Revelation then, regarded as a full and impartial voucher of the divine name, is restricted to the same negative law of growth or evolution which society itself obeys, since it is identical with the very personality of society. So long, accordingly, as society itself is immature, so long as it is narrowed down by our native ignorance, conceit, and unbelief to a purely negative manifestation, so long of necessity must revelation reflect its adverse fortunes, and content itself with the merely negative exhibition it gets in the distinctively ecclesiastical life of the world, or at the hands of the established church.

This theory of the church as a strictly representative economy — as limited to conferring no real, but only a typical righteousness upon its subjects — is enforced and illustrated by every incident that Swedenborg relates of his intercourse with angels and spirits. That intercourse appears indeed to have surcharged him with curious and recondite information in regard to the states of the church before authentic history began ; but as usual, he makes no attempt to systematize his knowledge ; probably because he himself lived too near the era of the "last judgment" to be able to catch the key-note of the grand intellectual system to which all its developments are subservient.*

---

* His angelic acquaintances labored under an equal disability. Whenever he asked a judgment from them in regard to the intellectual prospects of the race,

He thus learned, for example, that all those long-lived generations mentioned in Genesis, which used to pique our juvenile admiration, from Adam to Seth, and Seth to Noah, and Noah to Eber, were not generations of persons by any means, as appears in the letter of the record, but only of churches which, in long succession, diversified the pre-historic annals of the race, and gradually hardened from the most fluid and infantile states of charity and faith into the rigidly fossil, or most unloving, unbelieving, and idolatrous thing, which the post-historic annals of the race prove the church to have been from the time of Abram to that of Christ. He gives us many beautiful, and, in a philosophic point of view, very interesting, glimpses of those early churches, and of the unaffected modesty, simplicity, and truth which characterized their tender genius. But I have no time, nor indeed inclination, to dwell upon these faint crepuscular gleams of the church in man. They are obviously one and all without any historic or scientific value (being thus only indirectly available to philosophy), because they one and all had no root in a redeemed nature of man, but only in certain specific differences of culture and character among men; hence no outward body corresponding to their inward soul; and they consequently lapsed into lower and ever lower states of natural innocence and integrity, until at last all savor of both was lost in that gigantic form of fraud and violence known as the Jewish church.

I am well aware that nothing can be more opposed to the loose thought of the time, whether religious or secular, than the entire drift of Swedenborg's teaching in regard to the nature and office of the church; but I have neither the presumption nor the inclination to offer myself as his apologist before the world.

they professed a complete ignorance, saying that all they knew was, that there would be a great increase of free thought in the church, inasmuch as the man of the church would thenceforth be spiritually free, the old bondage of the letter being now broken up. See "Last Judgment," 73, 74. In his "True Christian Religion," 123, he says: "The reduction of all things to order in heaven and hell" — that is, in the spiritual world — "is still an incomplete process, consequent upon the last judgment"; but he hoped to shed some light upon it when it was completed. He calls "this process *peculiarly that of redemption*"; but he died the year after this book was published, if I remember aright. At all events, he was not destined to do us this great service; one, moreover, for which, I cannot help thinking, the singularly simplistic character of his intellect did not specifically qualify him.

His statements, I doubt not, will sufficiently vindicate themselves in the long run to all minds seriously interested to understand them ; my sole concern with them meanwhile being to show how they justify themselves to my particular intelligence. He makes, indeed, very startling assertions. Over and over again, for example, he declares the church as a literal or ritual economy effete as to every divine and human use which once sanctified it ; * and announces in lieu of it a new and living church, built upon the altogether illiterate, unwritten, or internal scope of revelation, that is to say, upon the unfettered spiritual instincts of the race, which will enjoy all manner of spiritual peace or internal blessedness of life, because it will be instinct with true faith and true charity ; and which accordingly opens wide its arms of welcome and shelter to the whole religious world, whatever be its petty dogmatic distinctions.

Statements like these are doubtless very revolting to prejudice, but while none but a fool would believe them on Swedenborg's authority (as none but a fool would reject them for lack of any superior authorization), it must yet be admitted that myriads throughout christendom have a dawning conviction of the same truth in their own minds, however little they may be able intellectually to reconcile that truth with the advance of man's spiritual destiny. Multitudes of people perceive the church — as a visible institution distinct from the state — to be a mere spectre in the earth, moping, and moaning, and wringing wan ineffectual hands over the places it once inhabited, but now only infests. It may not always be as frankly avowed, but a host of honest minds feel the same conviction I myself have long felt, which is, that the religious life of man, claiming to have interests and aims essentially opposed or unreconciled to those of his

* It must not be imagined for a moment that Swedenborg is so base-minded as to include the *personnel* of the church in these denunciations. This would degrade him to the level of Joe Smith at once, and relieve all intelligent men of a desire to hear any further from him. On the contrary, he looks at the church purely in the light of an intellectual system, and has not the least apparent conception that it prejudices any man's spiritual prospects, save in those rare instances where its dogmas have been intellectually confirmed by pertinacious sophistical reasoning. See " Apocalypse Explained," 233, 250, and " Apocalypse Revealed," 426, where he shows the judgment upon the church to have respect to its dogmatic, not to its personal constitution. I will throw some quotations from Swedenborg bearing upon the general subject of the church into the Appendix. See note B.

secular life, has become at length a rank though unconscious
imposture; that it amounts, in fact, to the same ghastly and
grinning caricature of reality which the corpse exhibits to the
living man, or which the secular life, as opposed to the religious,
always modestly admits itself to be. And such persons doubtless
would gladly have their feeling become knowledge, their faith become sight; a result, as I conceive, wholly impossible, unless
we come to take essentially the same view of the nature and office
of the church that Swedenborg does, and deny it the least real,
while allowing it the utmost representative, significance in regard to spiritual things.

This then is the important question, Does the church properly
claim a positive, or a merely negative office? What has been its
historic mission, to nourish, or only to purify? Is the church
the really constructive institution it is vulgarly reputed to be,
capable of stamping one man or one class of men good before
God, and another man or another class evil? Or is it the rigidly detergent institution which Swedenborg proclaims it to be,
utterly incapable of originating, much more of confirming, any
personal differences among men, because its total providential
purpose is to efface all existing inequalities in human character,
and shut up all men alike, good and evil, virtuous and vicious,
wise and simple, learned and ignorant, religious and scientific,
devout and sceptical, great and small, rich and poor, white and
black, to the hope of God's sheer, unlimited, undistinguishing
mercy, to be yet fully revealed in the social regeneration of the
race?

Let us state the question in still another shape.

The vulgar notion of the church in its purest, most orthodox,
and therefore most vigorous or malignant form, is that it is a
divine assessor in the earth, appointed to take stock of the existing inequalities in human character, in order to build up an
eternal heaven out of one kind of men, and an eternal hell out
of another kind. Or we may say that it is a divine tariff imposed upon all earthly products intended for the skies; this
tariff running so high, in certain cases, as to be altogether pro-
hibitory, and actually consigning the excluded articles consequently to destruction.

Obviously this conception of the church involves a fatal

reproach to the divine name, inasmuch as it shows him dealing with his creatures no longer in an infinite and absolute, but in a finite and contingent manner ; or exhibits him as superfluously good to some of them, and as superfluously evil to others.

Swedenborg's conception of the church runs completely counter to this prevalent notion, whether we regard it in its more orthodox and insolent, or its more sentimental and mendicant modes of manifestation.

His idea of the church is, that it is at most a divine *witness* in the earth, holding out indeed to men's reverent attention a form of spiritual truth which will one day fall away and disclose the infinite divine substance so long imprisoned within it, but which is totally incapable, under any amount of culture, of itself fructifying into that substance. The church *witnesses* to God's creative presence in humanity, but of course does not *constitute* it, as it sometimes insolently pretends to do ; and heaven and hell are respectively nothing more nor less than the positive and negative sanctions which the human conscience freely accords to the truth of the church's testimony. They have neither of them the least particle of relevancy whatever to the presumption of any absolute difference in men's character and standing before God ; for, as Swedenborg proves, angel and devil are perfectly identical in themselves, and differ exclusively in the lord. Their contrarious existence consequently furnishes no conceivable augury of human destiny, but confesses itself a result, pure and simple, of the church's imbecile administration in divine things, that is, of its persistent inability to bear witness to the divine existence and character, without violating, in some sort, every instinct of man's freedom and rationality. Swedenborg shows, accordingly, throughout all his books, from their beginning to their close, that God has no joy in the angel, nor any grief in the devil, save as they stand favorably or unfavorably related to the prosperity of the church, i. e. tend to enforce or enfeeble the witness which it bears at once to the universality and the particularity of his presence and providence throughout the earth. The lord's love, as Swedenborg invariably reports it, is a universal love, being the salvation of the whole human race ; and no form of his church, therefore, can satisfy his regard, which is not practically identical with the interests of hu-

man society ; that is, *which does not in itself structurally reproduce and avouch the intimate and indissoluble fellowship, equality,
brotherhood of universal man.*

As the former conception of the church reflected a manifest
opprobrium upon the divine name, by changing his relation to
us from an absolute to a contingent one, from a spiritual or purely
inward to a personal or purely outward relation, so this latter
conception reverses that reproach, or implies the highest exaltation of the divine name, by universalizing his relation to us, or
showing that under whatever infirmities of administration his
name is really one and infinite, and utterly disavows, therefore,
the imputation of duplicity and finiteness which the enforced
antagonism of heaven and hell sheds upon it.

Let us then try briefly to settle this question in the light of
the principles we have already discussed.

XIII.

It has been abundantly demonstrated, in the earlier portions
of this essay, that our natural selfhood, or subjective identity,
is a pure exigency of the divine love and wisdom towards us,
in the interest exclusively of our spiritual or objective individuality.

There is nothing obscure in this proposition to any one who
has read what precedes. It simply implies that our life is twofold, that is, both natural and spiritual, conscious and unconscious, subjective and objective ; and then it alleges that the
former of these elements is *de jure* if not *de facto* subservient
to the latter. It is as if I should say that no child exists without the conjoint parentage of father and mother, and that in
every such existence the part of the mother subordinates that
of the father. Or, that every statue is the product of an ideal
force and a material reaction to such force ; the former element
in its production being primary, the latter secondary. Or, that
a watch is a unit of two forces — one functional or dynamic,
denoting its ability to keep time ; the other passive or static, denoting its mechanical organization : and that this latter component of its existence is wholly subservient to the former. In
all these cases the maternal force announces itself as giving ex-

istence to things, or phenomenally identifying them; and the paternal force as giving them being, or absolutely individualizing them.

These illustrations show what my proposition means to allege with respect to man. It implicitly alleges that man is a unit of two forces — one material, which finites or gives him conscious identity, and which we call nature; the other spiritual, which infinites him or gives him unconscious individuality, and which we call God: and that the former of these forces is in right, if not in fact, altogether secondary and ministerial to the latter.

Now such being the truth of things, the reader will agree with me, that nothing could more effectually tarnish the face of creation, or embarrass its practical working, than to find the creature taking a different view of creative order from that of the creator. If to the creative mind the natural interests of the creature are altogether secondary and subordinate to his spiritual interests, while to the understanding of the creature himself they are altogether primary and commanding, it is inevitable that creation must so far wear a disorderly aspect, or argue a conflict between its constitutional factors. It is evident, in fact, that creation will never attain to its sabbath or rest, in the perfect union of its infinite and finite elements, until this difference between them becomes practically overcome.

Now, as a fact both of his own experience and of his observation of others, every man knows that this conflicting estimate of natural and spiritual things actually exists between creator and creature. Every man knows that he is instinctively prone to over-estimate the actual and under-estimate the real; to indulge a high appreciation of natural goods, and a comparatively feeble one of spiritual goods. And he regards it accordingly as the legitimate aim of his best culture to reverse this unfortunate habit, and so bring himself into cordial and permanent adjustment with the mind of God.

Nor is this all. Every cultivated man — that is to say, every man who is not as yet hopelessly besotted either by the excess or the deficiency of nature's bounty towards him — perceives this actual adjustment of the finite with the infinite mind to be the total secret of human history; to constitute both the universal and the particular scope of what we call progress, meaning by that, man's providential destiny upon earth, or the completed education of the race.   No one is so dull as not to be able to recognize, either through himself or others, that a certain purifying process is going on in all history, public and private, whereby both the race and the individual are being gradually disciplined out of selfish into associated ends, and out of ignorant into enlightened methods, of action.   Progress, whether public or private, seems to take place in an invariably negative way, that is, it always exacts a preliminary experience and acknowledgment of evil and error.   Our vices and follies, collective and personal, have wrought us infinitely more advantage than our virtue and knowledge have ever achieved.   Our best learning has come to us in the way of unlearning prejudice, our best wisdom in the way of outgrowing conceit, our best action in the way of undoing what we have previously done of evil and false. In short, while the indisputable end of the creative providence is to endow us with its own infinitude, the invariable means it uses to effect this end is to saturate and nauseate us with the sense of our own inveterate finiteness.   So palpably true is all this, that the fundamental grace of the religious character throughout history is humility ; the primary evidence of a spiritual quickening in the soul, repentance.   And what can a fact of this magnitude mean, if notwithstanding we are to look upon the church as implying God's personal complacency towards one sort of men, and his personal ill-will towards another sort, that is, as supplying its subject with a positive and not a mere negative method of access to God ?

Such a notion of the church's efficacy would, in fact, stultify all history.   For she has been the incontestable historic representative and protagonist of this negative divine administration in human affairs.   Her proper function in the earth has always been to exalt men spiritually only by humbling them naturally, or making them heartily loathe the accidents of birth, temperament. and genius, which give them an adventitious superiority to other men.   Undoubtedly the church in its literal form has always exhibited a more or less gross perversion of this its original spirit ; that is to say, it has always contrived to replace the merely carnal or natural pride of the human heart. which it was appointed to discipline, by an infinitely more deadly religious or

6

spiritual pride, which nothing short of hell can discipline. But
some faint glimmer of spiritual life has always managed to keep
itself alive underneath the church's cumbrous and heathenish
ritual; and there never was a time accordingly, throughout
its history — until, perhaps, within a very recent period — when
some direct heavenly succor was not available through it to sin-
sick and weary souls. Even under its Jewish form the altogether purgative and sacrificial tenor of its ritual constrained
thoughtful minds to see that, though the worshipper was brought
outwardly nigh to God by the church, it was only with a view
to teach him by that unrighteous privilege his real or inward
remoteness, and so dispose him to that personal humility or
charity towards less privileged men, upon which alone all spiritual divine blessing pivots.

If this were the ever-latent virtue of the law, surely it is the
ever-patent virtue of the gospel. No intelligent reader of the
New Testament, it appears to me, can for a moment doubt that
Christ and his apostles looked upon the Jewish church as exert-
ing a strictly damnatory — never a justifying — power over all
who cultivated its prescriptive righteousness. Christianity itself
may be styled, in fact, a formal proclamation of the exhaustion
of religion as a ceremonial, and its revival as a life. It imported
the cessation of ritual or sacrificial worship as a means of access to God, and the substitution of an affectionate or heartfelt
devotion in the worshipper, *motived altogether upon God's revealed clemency to the unrighteous and the evil.* The cleansing
which the Jew derived from the law was a purely carnal one,
inferring no manner of spiritual nearness to God, but rather
spiritual distance from him, inasmuch as one whose heart coveted or even tolerated a ceremonial righteousness could not be
supposed to appreciate a living or real one. In Christ this be-
nighted ritualist was for the first time to lose his inward remoteness from the source of life, and be brought spiritually near;
was to be taught to renounce his literal or differential righteousness, based upon his assumed superiority in the divine sight to
other men, and to cultivate an exclusively spiritual one, based
upon his cordial fellowship or equality with all mankind. " Behold the days come, saith the lord, that I will make a new covenant with the house of Israel, and with the house of Judah.

This is the covenant I will make with the house of Israel, saith the lord: I will *put my law in their inward parts and write it in their hearts*, and I will be their God and they shall be my people. And they shall teach no more every man his neighbor, saying, Know the lord: for *they shall all know me from the least unto the greatest*, saith the lord: FOR *I will forgive their iniquity, and I will remember their sin no more.*" * "Remember," says the apostle to the Ephesians, "that ye being in times past gentiles in the flesh, who are called uncircumcision by that which is called the circumcision in the flesh made by hands, at that time were without Christ, being aliens from the commonwealth of Israel and strangers from the covenants of promise. But now in Christ Jesus ye who sometime were far off are made nigh by his blood. For he is our peace who hath made both one and hath broken down the middle wall of partition between us, *having abolished in his flesh the* [only ground of] ENMITY, *even the law of commandments contained in ordinances*, for to make in himself of twain one new man, so making peace. — Through him we both have access *by one spirit* to the father." So again the same apostle, addressing the Colossians, says: "And you, *being dead in your sins and the uncircumcision of your flesh, hath God quickened together with Christ, having forgiven you all trespasses, blotting out the handwriting of ordinances that was against us, which was contrary to us*, and took it out of the way, nailing it to his cross." †

Evidently then the iniquity in the church against which Christ protested and rebelled was its pretension to confer upon its followers a strictly legal or literal and personal righteousness — such a righteousness as implied a relation of merit on their part towards God, and a relation of demerit on the part of other people. And the righteousness he set before it was a purely spiritual one, or such a one as consists only in a temper of the most unreserved fellowship or equality with all men. In other words, the only church which Christ avouches is a living society, brotherhood, or fellowship of all mankind, which will disallow all distinction or privilege among men but that which grows out of the largeness and the zeal of the social spirit in their bosom;

---

* Jeremiah xxxi. 31, 33, 34 ; Hebrews viii. 8 – 12.
† Ephesians ii. 11 – 18 ; Colossians ii. 13, 14.

a spirit which is sure to abase whatsoever is proud or lofty, and to exalt whatever is lowly. Nor can it be denied that for a brief while the literal christian church itself appeared roughly to apprehend the spirit of its founder, and was intent upon bringing forth the best fruits it knew. For we read in the Acts of the Apostles, that "all who believed were together and had all things common, and sold their possessions and goods, and parted them to all as every one had need." *

Of course this was merely an effusion in the sphere of sentiment on the part of the early disciples, and as such entitled to its proper consideration. It was doubtless of great advantage to cherish this spirit of hearty mutual succor, when the christian church was barely germinating as a material institution, or pushing its way to light and air through the superincumbent layers of a totally inimical society. But the fact was without any strict philosophic value or permanent practical significance. For it must never be forgotten that the brotherhood of the church, or christian fellowship, is not based upon sentiment, i. e. does not admit a merely voluntary allegiance, but, on the contrary, claims a foundation of the most rigid equity or justice, and hence makes itself obligatory upon men. We must never forget, in other words, when we are speaking of the christian church, according to the idea of its founder, or as a spiritual economy, that it is a strictly universal administration, claiming the gentiles for its inheritance and the uttermost parts of the earth for its possession. The Old Testament prophecies and promises are replete with testimonies to this point. In Daniel's vision, for example, we read : "In the days of these kings shall the God of heaven set up a kingdom which shall never be destroyed ; and the kingdom shall not be left to other people, but it shall break in pieces and consume all these kingdoms, and it shall stand forever." Again : "I saw in the night visions, and behold ! one like the son of man came with the clouds of heaven, and came to the Ancient of Days — and there was given him dominion and glory and a kingdom that all people and nations and languages should serve him. His dominion is an everlasting dominion, which shall not pass away, and his kingdom that which shall not be destroyed." †

---

* Acts ii. 44, 45.
† Daniel ii. 44, and vii. 13, 14.

But there is no need to recur to the ancient seers, fascinating and majestic as their descriptions of the great redemptive sabbath are. Every reader, familiar with the New Testament, knows that christianity professes to be a universal religion, and promises to supersede or spiritually appropriate to itself all the religions of.the earth ; that its apostles were commissioned to go out into all the world and communicate the gospel of redemption to every creature ; and that, consequently, if we diminish it of this pretension by consenting to look upon the church, as it has hitherto *visibly* existed at any time, in the light of a fulfilment of Christ's idea, we at once reduce Christ to the level of a Moses, a Buddha, a Zoroaster, a Mahomet, and leave him, like them, stripped of all exhaustive divine significance. And if the christian church have this inevitable universality of scope — if, in other words, the society or brotherhood which Christ instituted among men be essentially a spiritual society or brotherhood — then clearly no past, no present, and no future exhibition of the church, in carnal or ritual form, can justly claim to be anything more than a matrix of this spiritual result ; bearing precisely the same relation to it that the shell of a nut does to its kernel, or the husk of wheat to the mature grain, namely, a relation of the strictest protection and nutrition during all the protracted period of the church's spiritual infancy, i. e. of our SOCIAL immaturity, and falling into contempt and oblivion whenever that use is accomplished.

XIV.

"Very well," I now think I hear my reader exclaiming, " I am ready to grant you that the primary office of the church has been to purify our consciences, by abasing the natural pride and covetousness in us which are so apt and eager to claim divine sanctions ; and that we are not entitled, consequently, to regard it in any more positive light than as, at best, a revelation or witness of God in the earth. But now tell me, I pray you, something about the beginnings of this revelation. How did it get itself started originally ? How, in other words, did the early church — the church in literal form — ever contrive to impose itself upon the popular belief as an authentic divine institution ?

It is very evident, for example, that the Mosaic revelation, if it
should take place in our day, would provoke, in spite of its unquestionable grandeur and dignity in a sensuous or picturesque
point of view, very much the same rational obloquy that the
sordid mormon imposture does.   It would be scouted, in fact,
as scientifically absurd by the greater part of christendom.
What makes the difference between then and now?   Is revelation altogether proportionate to the understanding addressed?
Give me your ideas in full on this subject.   Do you conceive
revelation to be a fixed, or only a contingent quantity?   Do
you regard it as absolute, or only relative to the human faculties?   Do you hold, for example, that the Mosaic revelation was
true for its own time and place, but untrue for our day?   Did
its authority, as a divine revelation, vest exclusively in its adaptation to the very narrow hearts and minds to which it was specifically addressed?   And does it challenge, consequently, no
such authority to our present regard?   In short, does it properly disclaim all pretension to that universality and perpetuity
which, as it seems to me, we are entitled to demand in a revelation from God?   For I find myself, not unwilling indeed, but
simply unable, to believe in any so-called revelation of the divine
name which is destitute of these two characteristics — universality
and perpetuity; which, in other words, does not embrace within
itself all space and all time, or proclaim itself identical with nature and history.   You yourself have been, virtually at least
if not actually, saying all along that no sufficing or permanent revelation is conceivable but upon these conditions.   And
what I want now, accordingly, is to get a more explicit statement of your views, that I may learn how you manage to believe, as firmly as you do, in the truth of revelation, without
perceiving the gross affront which every such pretension offers to
the inviolate progress of the mind, or, what is the same thing,
the continuity of natural and historic order."

The answer to all this doubt is, as it seems to me, very simple and salutary.   Briefly stated it is as follows: The human
mind, or natural and historic order, is itself only a process of
revelation of the creative name; and our technical " revelations," consequently, so far from affronting the mind's integrity,
do but confirm it; so far from invalidating nature and history,

do but foreshadow and induct their sovereign function ; do but
cradle and nurse, so to speak, their own highest and truest yet
most unsuspected significance.   But this statement is doubtless
much too brief.   Let me enlarge it.

I am taught, then, by Swedenborg's disclosures, not only to
look upon nature and history as the true theatre of the divine
revelation, but also to regard them *as having absolutely no other
purpose in existence than to serve as such theatre*.   That is to
say, they did not originally exist as finalities or on their own
account, and then become accidentally subjected to the apocalyptic function ; but their sole original title to exist derives from
their exquisite subserviency to that function.   This, in my opinion, constitutes Swedenborg's vast intellectual superiority to our
ordinary religious and scientific soothsayers, that he gives us
upon this subject no longer guesswork, but the fruit of positive
insight.   All our diviners, whether devout or sceptical, hold
nature and history to a final or absolute and independent significance ; and thus find themselves compelled either to adjust revelation to cosmical order in a very crude irrational way, or else
with my questioner to reject it altogether.   Swedenborg, on the
contrary, denies them the least independent worth, the slightest
substantive significance, and leaves them valid only as furnishing a basis of divine knowledge consonant with the ever-grow-
ing requirements of the human heart and understanding.   They
furnish a needful basis to the church in human nature, and have
absolutely no spiritual significance apart from that function.   The
vulgar prejudice, on the other hand, both religious and scientific,
is that nature is an objective work of God, consummated off-
hand before recorded history began, and that history is only the
subsequent subjective fermentation to which this work was liable ;
so that revelation, if it be admitted at all, cannot be admitted as
an inherent function of nature and history, but only as a supernatural achievement, or an event arbitrarily induced upon natural
and historic order.

Swedenborg has not the least intellectual complicity with this
prejudice.   He denies nature to begin with the faintest objectivity
to the divine mind, or affirms it to be a purely subjective work of
God in the interest exclusively of man's spiritual evolution.   It is,
in fact, as rigid an involution of the spiritual world — the universe

of affection and thought — as the glove is an involution of the hand, whose necessities alone call for its existence. And *a fortiori*, therefore, he denies history a natural origination, or turns it from a garish flowering of natural principles into an abject seed-place or seminary of spiritual truth and goodness, in whose necessities alone both it and nature find their sole and equal *raison d'être.* Holding these views of the essential subserviency both of nature and history to the spiritual world, or the evolution of a life divinely human, of course the question of a literal revelation could prove in no way embarrassing to him, but finds itself, in fact, implicitly if not explicitly solved by every word he says. For while he thus turns nature and history into an utterly servile correspondence or inverse imagery of the infinite divine substance which is always latent — in order that it may one day become patent — in the finite form of man, he at the same time transmutes all these literal so-called "divine revelations," which up to Christ's time had diversified the annals of the race, into so many partial glimpses of this grand universal verity, into so many premature attempts on the part of man to rifle the mystical heart of nature, or bring himself, by violence as it were, into accord with the great underlying but still unfathomable secret of history.

It seems to me that an incalculable intellectual advantage thus accrues to Swedenborg over the ordinary religionist and ordinary rationalist both, in respect to all these mooted points of the church's origin and history. What alone makes, and has ever made, these questions insoluble is, the pertinacity with which we cling to the notion of the church as a positive divine token in the earth, and not a mere negative one ; as a nutritive divine force in the world, and not a purely purgative one. If then, with Swedenborg, we consent to dismiss this irrational conception, and come to regard the church as a literal divine lieutenancy in the interests of the broadest human society or brotherhood on earth and in heaven — and bound, therefore, like all lieutenancies, to disappear when the true incumbent arrives — we see at a glance that it demands no other foundation than the instincts of the human heart, no other origination than it is sure to find in the free play of men's natural temperament and genius. The sole purpose of the church has been to purge the earth of its false gods, the gods authenticated by the native

arrogance and cupidity of the human heart, by the native ignorance and conceit of the human understanding ; and it carries out
this purpose of course only by first giving a *quasi* consecration
to these low instincts of our nature, and then gradually bending
and shaping them to higher issues. The rudest literal or symbolic form of the institution — the shape in which the church
originally challenges recognition, and which perfectly adapts it
to the comprehension even of sense * — is the antagonism of a
select race or family to the rest of mankind. The immemorial tradition of a divine seed in the earth, struggling for its dominion with the seed of the evil one, becomes easily appropriated to
themselves by persons or races of a devout temper, of a fanatical
genius ; and once appropriated, it is bequeathed of course as a
sacred inheritance to their offspring. This divine seed had been
for a long time previous to the christian era identified, to the
jewish imagination, with Abraham, the founder of their own
nation, and with the literal progeny descended from his loins.
In christianity this aspect of the church underwent a sheer and
sudden reversal, the jew being now authoritatively deposed
from the divine favor, and the gentile reinstated.   On what
ground ?   Manifestly that the jew, though distinguished above
the gentile by the carnal possession of the law, had yet become
by that very possession spiritually disaffected to its righteousness beyond all other people, and was hence incapable of reaping its promised satisfactions in the Christ.

Accordingly, from this period onward to our own day, the
name of Christ fills the historic page, and the church founded
by his apostles assumes to itself the rightful supremacy of the
whole earth.   What estimate does Swedenborg put upon these

---

* I can perfectly understand by sensible tuition what all my spiritual culture
disallows, namely, how one person may be acceptable to God and another abhor-
rent. I can even understand by that medium, and without any difficulty, how the
former person should be myself, and the latter person a man of another race,
family, or color. For sense of necessity views God as a far more grandly finite
or selfish being than man ; and to be more finite and selfish than man is to be
devilish ; that is, to love or hate all other beings without any reference to their
objective worth, but simply with reference to their subjective use and advantage to
one's self. No wonder that religion, with such an incentive, was so rife in early
times. No wonder that every family, or *gens*, in early times, boasted its special
tutelary divinity ; and that the entire *gentile* world was organized upon the inveterate mutual hostility of all religions, instead of their essential unity.

facts? How does he interpret Christ's personal and official significance? In what light does he exhibit the christian revelation — as a final or perfect, or as a transient and imperfect, manifestation of the divine name?

Altogether in the former and higher aspect. Let us see then, so far as we are able, on what grounds of reason he does this. We need not expect, as I have already said, to find him justifying himself in a strictly ratiocinative way, or as men deal with what they feel to be matter of opinion merely, but affirmatively rather, or as they deal with what they feel to be matter of precise knowledge. Nevertheless, he supports his affirmations by incessant reference to intellectual considerations, as well as by illustrations drawn from the recognized principles of common sense, or the race's rational experience, so that we need be at no loss after all to divine the true grounds of his induction.

XV.

We have seen that creation, philosophically viewed, involves a divided movement — one descending, generic, physical, by which the creature becomes set off, projected, alienated from the creator in mineral, vegetable, and animal form; the other ascending, specific, moral, by which the creature thus naturally pronounced becomes *conscious of himself* as separated from his creative source, and instinctively reacts against the fact, or seeks to reunite himself with God. Or, we may say that the former movement restricts itself to universalizing the creature, by giving him identity or community with all other things; while the latter aims to individualize him, by investing him with a conscience of selfhood or freedom sensibly distinct from all other things.*

* Hence it is that religion becomes specially addicted to, or cognizant of, this latter interest. For religion — from *re* and *ligo*, the prefix *re* in latin verbs having the same loosening or dissolving force as the prefix *un* in English verbs — means *the unbinding* of those who are in bondage to nature, in bondage to natural evil and error, and giving them the freedom which befits the children of God. No doubt the subject of nature, knowing as yet no higher objectivity, will be very sure to regard the bondage he is thus under as the truest freedom, and to look upon religion accordingly as his enemy. But the culprit is notoriously an unfair judge of the law; and whether we think well or ill of it, religion itself, viewed in its essence, and separated from all ecclesiastical alloy, has never meant anything but the enfranchisement of human life in every sphere of its activity.

But this is by no means all that we have seen. We have seen besides, that the generic or universalizing force in creation sensibly dominates its specific or individualizing force; and this is a fact of transcendent importance in its spiritual bearings, or its influence upon the development of the church. For it distinctly proves thus much, namely, that no direct effort which the moral subject makes to readjust himself to his creative source can ever spiritually avail him, or boast more than an illusory success; for the reason that his will is so contingent upon his instincts — his moral character so dependent upon his physical temperament — that his voluntary activity will always go to intensify his finite ties rather than abate them, to enhance his conscious remoteness from the infinite rather than abridge it. Let us glance, for example, at the beginnings of the religious life in man, or his ambition to bring himself *personally* near to the infinite. I feel an instinctive reverence for the divine name which disposes me to placate it, or render it personally propitious to me, by all the means in my power. But if I push this disposition beyond certain definite limits, I find myself gradually led into such wilderness states — states of frantic self-isolation — as brings erelong my inmost but hitherto latent selfishness and indifference to my kind into the broad gaze of consciousness, and fills me accordingly with any emotions but those of repose towards God. What I naturally covet, what all my innocent instincts crave, is the greatest possible experience of outward good, the greatest possible immunity from outward evil. But the moment I put my moral or personal force at the service of these instincts, and devoutly aspire to realize them, their innocence turns to shame in my bosom, and I become conscious — of course not *intelligently*, but *sensibly* conscious — of a growing inward distance from God, which bids fair to engulf all my nascent personal hopes in despair. I experience, in fact, what is properly called "a conscience of sin"; that is to say, I undergo such a sickening, disheartening sense of my utter inward disproportion to the infinite goodness, as paralyzes all the joy I have ever had in its remembrance. Indeed, so lively a conviction besets me, not merely of my actual or chance defilement, but of my essential and habitual corruption as illustrated by the light of God's holiness, that I feel a distrust and distaste of his once lovely name, hardly stopping short now of an inmost despair and hatred. Undoubtedly I cloak these disloyal emotions from my own acknowledgment, and even from my own suspicion. So sedulous indeed is my zeal in that behalf, that my prayer is sure to grow ever more vociferous as the lamp of my hope burns dim ; and as my real or inward enmity defines itself, the outward voice of my praise and adoration puts on an added fervor and frequency.

I need not say to any one who has ever felt a decisive creep of its horrors, that a more atrocious anguish than that here described as shut up in the religious conscience, wherever that conscience exists in its purity,* is unknown to the human bosom ; and it all grows out of the fact I am alleging, namely, the rigidly conditional nature of the moral consciousness, or the circumstance of its dependence for all its inspiration upon the finite organization. Man, as we have seen, is essentially a *social* being ; that is to say, he is created both male and female, both universal and particular, common and proper, generic and specific, physical and moral ; so that it is impossible for the *vir* (or inward man) to individualize himself absolutely to the divine regard without, to that extent, prejudicing the *homo* (or outward man), and hence defeating any schemes he may cherish upon deity by the very method he takes to carry them out. It is as if Eve, being consubstantiate with Adam, should nevertheless attempt to bring forth fruit of herself alone, or in spite of his concurrence rather than by its favor. It is however just this hallucination which according to Swedenborg bases the church in man, or underlies his distinctively religious life. The *vir*, or moral subject, enjoys a *sensible* absoluteness with respect to the *homo ;* that is, he *feels* himself to be independent of the race, or his kind ; and at the beck of this purely sensuous instinct (which in scripture symbolism is called *the serpent*), he aspires " to become like God, knowing good and evil " ; that is, to be good and wise in himself, irrespectively of his intimate unity or solidarity with all mankind. He instinctively aspires, in other words, to bring himself near to God, or achieve his spiritual safety, by the exercises of a devout self-love ; the invariable result being never to lift himself up to divine dimensions, but

* See Appendix, note C.

to degrade the deity to his own spiritual stature. Hence that life of inward self-abasement or anguish in the human bosom, which I have above pictured as constituting the sole spiritual reality of the church, the only true life of religion on the earth, being the literal descent of the divine to the human nature, and which will ultimately bring about that regenerate social sentiment of men on earth and in heaven, which constitutes the ascent of the human to the divine nature.

Let us linger here a little while that we may the more perfectly understand ourselves.

What in effect I have been saying all along is, that morality is not a personal or specific endowment of man, but a rigidly natural or generic one.* It is the badge, not of this, that, or the other man, but of all men alike, just in so far as they are men at all. It characterizes no special subject of human nature, but the very nature itself. It is indeed the essence of human nature; the logical *differentia* between man and the brute; being what characterizes him expressly as man, or in so far as he is neither mineral, vegetable, nor animal; so that no man is a man in the proper force of the word, unless he be a moral subject.

Now if morality be as here alleged the distinctive sign of human nature, that is to say, if a man is moral, not by virtue of what he is or has in contradistinction to his fellows, but solely by virtue of what he is or has in common with all other men, it is at once obvious that the moral subject, as such, must straightway disown every spiritual qualification, i. e. disavow any *direct* approximation to the infinite, any such approximation as does not rigidly presuppose that of his kind. He may claim to be spiritually affiliated to God, if he please, but not in his own

---

* Certain recent writers, ambitious to rejuvenate the old theology by giving it a *quasi* rational sanction, have labored hard to sophisticate this truth, by representing morality not as a natural but as a distinctly supernatural fact; but with no other effect than to signalize their own incompetence, since their whole labor is built upon a transparent quibble, that of confounding morality with moral goodness, so blinking moral evil out of sight. Certainly moral or voluntary goodness exists only by the antagonism of like evil; and if therefore moral good be supernatural or claim a divine source, moral evil has every right to be equally exacting. The more hardy leaders accordingly in this enterprise do not hesitate virtually to adopt the manichean hypothesis of creation, and trace back the existing evil of the creature to an "evil possibility" in the divine nature! See Dr. Bushnell's "Nature and the Supernatural."

right, and only by virtue of a previous spiritual affiliation of
the race.   In other words, the moral subject is self-debarred the
least spiritual attainment — the attainment, for example, of any
such bosom rectitude as argues in him the least legitimate superiority to his kind, or elevates him above the uniform level of
human nature.   No doubt a fallacious appearance of things is
apt to drown out the truth upon this subject to a superficial
observation.   No doubt many persons habitually ascribe to
themselves, and find others ready to justify them in so doing, a
spiritual rectitude or supernatural merit.   But this is only
because such persons are spiritually below the level of their kind,
rather than quite up to it, let alone above it.   That is to say, it
is because their intelligence is still childish or rank, is still controlled by sense in place of being served by it; or, what is the
same thing, because they are still in the habit of reasoning as
children do, from appearance to reality, from without to within,
and not as cultivated men do, from within to without, or from
reality to appearance.   But the truth utterly and invariably
rebukes their pretension.   The truth utterly falsifies every claim
the individual man puts forth to a measure of virtue which legitimately reflects the least spiritual discredit upon any other man,
however conventionally depraved he may be.   For it proves our
moral aspiration in every such case to be the fruit of a strictly
natural inspiration, the prompting or play in fact of an envenomed self-love; and in place therefore of justifying our easy
self-complacency, our habitual self-righteousness, it stamps us
as at best — or in our highest moral states — only fallaciously
individualized from our kind, while in reality we are more deeply
than ever implicated with it.

But if all this be true ; if it be true that the *vir*, which is the
feminine, specific, or moral element in consciousness, be thus
invincibly limited by the *homo*, which is its masculine, generic,
or physical element ; then it follows, unquestionably, that the
moral subject as such is inhibited any direct access to, or commerce with, God, and obliged to depend, consequently, for his
coveted reconciliation with him, upon some redemptive work of
God, which shall, if possible, revolutionize the constitutional
order of his consciousness, by making what has hitherto been
first in it last, and what hitherto has been last first.   Notori-

ously all divine prophecy or promise has been identified with the
" seed of the woman," not of the man ; but if the woman be
inveterately subject to the man — if, in other words, our moral
power is limited by our physical constitution — how shall these
grand immemorial prophecies ever be fulfilled ? Manifestly
only in one way ; by the actual regeneration of nature, which
means the marriage of the *homo* and the *vir*, or its male and
female elements ; which again means the eternal unification of
the distinctively human element in consciousness, with its distinctively cosmical element ; which still again means the perfect *humanization* henceforward, or exaltation to exclusively
human form, of mineral, vegetable, and animal substance.

Now this perfect marriage of the male and female elements
in creation — this complete unification or equalization of the
homo and the *vir*, of the cosmical and the domestic soul — manifestly appeals for its realization to the advent of a true society
or fellowship among men. It is only in the race's social evolution that our absolute and our contingent interests become harmonized ; that our physical interests, which are those of force
or necessity, put on an altogether conciliatory aspect towards
our moral interests, which are those of freedom or pleasure.
In a true society or brotherhood of men, and in this alone, our
organic appetites and passions, which constitute the realm of
necessity or force in us (so linking us with the outward and
finite), freely defer to our rational affections and thoughts, which
constitute the realm of freedom in us (so linking us with the
inward and infinite). But human society, human brotherhood,
human equality, is the slowest fruit of the ages, is indeed the
culminating truth of human destiny, and comes to consciousness
in the race, as we have already seen, only when the race shall
have definitively exhausted its domestic, its civic, and its political consciousness. Meanwhile what shall take the place of society, or proclaim itself its true vicegerent, so keeping the creative name and order temporarily alive in the earth, if not THE
CHURCH ; that is to say, that purely formal or provisional society,
that purely *representative* fellowship or brotherhood of man
with man, which has hitherto alone claimed a divine institution
upon the earth ?

Thus the church itself, according to Swedenborg, is no finality,

but a mere providential lieutenancy, instituted in the interests
exclusively of the divine righteousness, which is universal justice upon the earth ; such justice or righteousness being identical with human society, which means the frank and cordial
fellowship or equalization of every man of woman born, not
only with every other man, but with all other men put together,
and of all men consequently with each individual man.   He
found, by the opening of his spiritual sight, or his discovery
of the interior contents of revelation, that the sole reality or
justification of the church lay in the spiritual use it promotes
as a divine menstruum or sieve, to sift out the wheat of human
nature from its chaff, or separate its nutritive from its waste
material.   The wheat of humankind, spiritually regarded, are
those who acknowledge God's NATURAL HUMANITY, or give
man the primary place in the divine counsels, nature and history
a secondary and derivative one.   In other words, they hold man
to be no longer the finite subject, but the divine or infinite object of all created order.   And its chaff, of course, are those
who take the opposite view, or remain pertinaciously addicted to
the inspiration of sense, which teaches that nature and history
are a divine finality, or substance in themselves, when in truth
they are a mere sensuous correspondence of the absolute divine
substance which is latent exclusively in the human form.

The importance of the sifting function thus assigned by Swedenborg to the church, in its bearing upon the spiritual creation,
or the universe of human affection and thought, cannot be ex-
aggerated, when we consider that God is the sole substance of
that universe ; and that livingly to acknowledge him, therefore,
or to have our will and understanding inwardly open to the
access of his goodness and truth, is no less essential to our spiritual existence, than to be nourished by food capable of assimilation to our flesh and blood is essential to our natural existence.
We shall not be surprised, accordingly, at the immense intellectual significance Swedenborg puts upon the church, when
he represents it as promoting the same vital uses to the race's
spiritual body, that the heart promotes to man's natural body.
As the heart has a double office to fulfil, first a death-bearing
and then a life-giving one, so the church, according to Swedenborg, has both a literal and a spiritual aspect, both a body and a

soul ; the former allying us with hell, the latter alone with
heaven.   As the heart attracts to itself the vitiated blood of the
body, gross, lifeless, blackened with the foul humors discharged
into it through its long circuit, so exactly the church, as the
spiritual heart of mankind, attracts to itself, in its outward or
visible form, by the heavenly sanctions or lures it holds out to
our personal ambition and avarice, the most selfish, the most
despotic, the most worldly tempers among men.   And as the
heart, having gathered the corrupt or debilitated blood of the
body to its embrace, makes haste to hand it over to the lungs to
be defecated, washed, and renewed for use by contact with the
atmosphere, so in like manner the church, in spiritually or inwardly reacting against the ungodly influences which as a carnal economy it attracts, becomes itself renovated or washed
clean of defilement, shakes off its waste deciduous members,
purges itself, in other words, of all subjective aims and pretensions, by identifying itself ever more and more only with God's
impersonal and objective uses to all mankind.   In short, it becomes convertible with heaven ; heaven being a state of culture
in man in which charity or regard for others claims the first
place, and prudence or regard for self takes the second place.
The entire history of the church, by Swedenborg's showing,
amounts to this, neither more nor less, namely : such a sheer
humiliation on its literal or ritual side of the creative name to
the lowest level of men's carnal pride and concupiscence, as infallibly begets in the gentile conscience, or *common* mind of the
race, an inmost indifference and aversion to all consecrated authority, to all private or personal sanctity, to all exceptional or
privileged worth, and leads it eventually to associate God's living
honor and worship only with the reverence of every individual
man, however conventionally " common or unclean."

No one, of course, can be expected to do justice to Swedenborg's spiritual physiology, unless he constantly remind himself
that heaven and hell are only the sharply contrasted processes of
nutrition and waste, which go to the formation of the *maximus
homo*, the lord, or divine NATURAL man, and hence bear a strict
proportion to the varying states of the church on earth.   So
long as the truth of the divine NATURAL humanity, or of God's
strictly creative presence in our nature and history, is scientif

7

ically ignored by the human understanding, being at most only *representatively* avouched by the church, human life must necessarily exhibit a more or less conflicting aspect in every sphere of its activity. And when this conflict becomes at last intolerable, that is to say, when the principle of authority in the church (faith) becomes so envenomed and insolent as actually to overbear the free principle (charity), instant equilibrium ensues in "the world of spirits" (as Swedenborg names that province of the *maximus homo* which answers to the stomach in the finite organization), by an additionally stringent separation of evil spheres from good; or, what is the same thing, a freer elimination and excretion of the waste substances of the spiritual body.

The existence of hell, as a spiritual phenomenon, marks a superfluous divine energy in the earth; that is to say, an energy not as yet fully wrought into the tissue of human nature, not as yet fully authenticated and utilized by the tenor of our daily life, and liable to come forth consequently in perverse and disorderly modes of manifestation. As long as men believe in the unconditioned nature of morality, and therefore attribute to themselves a selfhood or freedom no less absolute in truth or reality than it is in fact or appearance, so long, of course, they will be unable to recognize the truth of the divine natural humanity; and while this truth remains unrecognized, men must continue to eat of the tree of finite knowledge, or hold good and evil to be essentially irreconcilable. That hell (or self-love) in this state of things should be allowed freely to precipitate itself from heaven therefore, and come under the permanent though unconscious subjection of the latter, is as much a provision of cosmical order or spiritual hygiene, as the separation of the waste matters of the body from our houses, and their incarceration in appropriate receptacles, is a provision of civic order or domestic hygiene. No doubt the church will one day lay off her tattered grave-clothes, the tarnished livery of death in which her persistent devotion to the letter of truth exclusively has hitherto bound her, and put on her resurrection garments in the acknowledgment of the divine *natural* humanity, or of God's living presence and power in every form of human life, whether conventionally sacred or profane, celestial or infernal. Then the church will have learned to disown all private ends, all purposes of self-seeking, whatsoever makes its interests as now alien to those of the secular or common life of man; will have learned, in short, to identify herself with the broadest human society or fellowship. At that time I presume the selfish or hellish element in our nature will have become so completely harmonized with the equitable or heavenly element, by their joint and equal subjugation to the uses of the divine natural humanity, which are the ends exclusively of a unitary society or universal fellowship among men, that no scientific but only a purely philosophic discrimination of hell from heaven will be any longer possible. That is to say, the mind of spiritual or philosophic culture alone will recognize hell, and that no longer as denoting a particular style of persons in humanity incapable of celestial assimilation, but as denoting the very principle of personality or selfhood in man universally, considered as absolute or independent. The christian hells, regarded as antagonizing the heavens, will thenceforth be "shut up," as Swedenborg describes the fate of the antediluvian hells, by ministering to no further scientific human use. Use is the only oxygen that ever kindled their lurid glow, and this being taken away, they must of sheer necessity collapse, become extinct, die out, just as a fire dies out deprived of vent. The church has now become elevated out of ritual into living dimensions; it is no longer a representative, but a real human society or brotherhood in heaven and on earth; and the evil principle in our nature (self-love) being thus shorn of its malignity by becoming reconciled to charity the good principle, constitutes in fact henceforth the truly divine and invincible guaranty of social tranquillity and order.*

---

* "It is a point of faith," says Swedenborg, "common both to the old and new dispensation, that the lord came into the world *to remove hell from man*, and that he effected this end by combats with and victories over it, so subduing it to himself, or making it forever orderly and obedient." — True Christian Religion, 2. Again he describes the "particular" faith of the new heavens and the new earth in human nature thus: "God is essential goodness and truth, and he manifested himself in Christ for the purpose of reducing all things in heaven, in hell, and in the church (or representative earth) to order, because at that period the power of hell or evil had got a greater purchase upon the human mind than that of heaven or good, and hence menaced a total destruction. This menace was averted by the lord's HUMANITY, which was the divine truth (or manifested form of the divine good), and hence angels and men became alike redeemed." — Ib., 3. See Appendix, note D.

XVI.

But the urgent question before us, towards the solution of which we have been all along steadfastly tending, is, How do the hells become actually "removed from man," as Swedenborg teaches us they must be, in order to the true revelation of the divine name? How, in other words, is the transition historically effected from the representative to the real church, that so we may know God no longer at second hand, or reflectively, but directly, or as we know ourselves? An obvious gulf separates the two churches; one being lifeless shadow, the other living substance; and what is capable of spanning it? The representative church exhibits the *vir*, or feminine element in consciousness, hopelessly subject to the *homo*, or masculine element; exhibits the distinctively human element in existence, which is that of individuality hopelessly immersed in the cosmical element, which is that of identity; and the antagonism, consequently, of Abel and Cain, of goodness and truth, of heart and head, of heaven and hell, in the human bosom, becomes of necessity indefinitely perpetuated. For so long as the woman in us is subject to the man — i. e. so long as our moral force is under the coercion of our physical necessities, and our distinctively human genesis refers itself, consequently, not to a divine or infinite source, but to what is merely mineral, vegetable, and animal in us — it is impossible that we should ever attain to true or spiritual individuality; and without this, of course, the only heaven capable of being formed is not "formed out of the human race," as Swedenborg says, but only out of infants and persons of a feeble moral force, whom the divine providence with infinite address *constrains* to their own advantage.

The new or real church reverses this state of things, or allows a heaven to be formed no longer out of the mere *débris* or off-scouring of humanity, but out of the very race itself, by avouching henceforth, not the antagonism but the marriage of the *homo* and the *vir*, the man and the woman. The new or final church, the fruit of God's long travail in our nature, exhibits the distinctively feminine and spiritual element in life, no longer in bondage to the masculine and material element, but rising superior to it, or conceiving and bringing forth directly of the infinite. For the new church is not a representative church, but a real one ; allowing no priesthood but that of the lord, or divine natural man, in whom alone we all live and move and have our being ; nor any instituted rites and ordinances, but those living ones which are inspired by the sentiment of the broadest human society, fellowship, or equality. The new and final church of God on earth is indeed identical on its literal side with this secular society or fellowship, and whosoever re- spires the social spirit — whosoever in heart acknowledges the grand essential brotherhood or equality of man with man, in spite of their petty or obvious moral inequalities — is in full spiritual communion with that church, and may securely aspire to enjoy whatsoever blessedness it has to offer either in this world or that to come. No hell can be bred of such a church accordingly. For the social evolution of human destiny means — and practically, or in fundamentals, it means nothing what- ever but this — such a thorough reconciliation, or marriage, in new forms of use of the two hitherto warring principles of force and freedom, self-love and charity, truth and goodness, as that their fruit shall henceforth be one and identical, or equally tend to the highest possible potentialization of human society. To the mind of the new or true church, hell can only signify a reasoned or confirmed denial of the divine natural humanity ; but our coming social evolution bars out the very possibility of such denial, by putting the senses themselves on the side of that truth, or bribing them to a more free and easy appreciation of it than is yielded even by the soul: though of course they will have no similar insight into its profound and comprehensive spiritual scope.

Such is the apparently hopeless conflict between the old and the new — the ritual and the real — church in humanity. How then, I repeat, does the chasm between the two become histori- cally filled up, so as that hell may at last be " removed from man," and the divine name consequently be hallowed, the divine kingdom come, and the divine will be done as in heaven so also on the earth — as in the spiritual world so also in the natural ? The obvious difficulty, as we have seen, in the way of this historic consummation is the limitation of human morality, or the impossibility of any man so far outgrowing the restraints of his hereditary consciousness, or his subjection to nature, as to feel himself really one with the infinite goodness, in spite of all appearances to the contrary. Our moral force is a strictly natural or hereditary one, and cannot rise above its source. In other words, our self-consciousness links us exclusively with the natural or material side of life, with what gives us subjective existence, or renders us phenomenal to ourselves; and to that extent, alienates us from the spiritual or paternal side of life, from what gives us objective being, or allies us with God: so that we have, as it were, inwardly to die — to undergo a conscious death to ourselves — before we can become emancipated from the shackles of the finite, and rise into the living discernment and participation of our true or infinite being. Self-consciousness restricts our regard to the *apparent* differences which separate us from other men, the differences which are obvious to sense; and never leads us to suspect accordingly that these superficial differences are only so many evidences of our profound substantial identity with all other men. We seem to our own eyes altogether different from others, now much better, now much worse. But this seeming is wholly shut up to our own shallow perception; the truth of the case being all the while that our conscious differences, the judgments of good and evil we apply to our own character, are only so many modulations of one identical moral substance, so many variations of one original theme. Freedom, selfhood, moral force, is our generic, not our specific qualification. It belongs to us each, only in so far as it first belongs to our *kind*, its whole end and purpose being to ascertain that kind, or vindicate its universality: first, by disengaging it from all lower kinds; and then by turning these latter from an apparently creative into an abjectly constitutive relation to it, or making them out of its incompetent tyrannical masters into its assiduous, obsequious servants. How is it even conceivable then, that you, or I, or any man, should ever so far disown this hereditary thraldom, this moral incarceration, or identification with his race, as really to emerge in spiritual life, and find himself in direct hand-to-hand commerce with the infinite? The pretension is manifestly preposterous. And yet the total problem of creation, about which alone the light of revelation revolves, is not to be solved short of the practical reconciliation of that contradiction. That is to say, somewhere in the progress of history some *vir* must be found able to transcend these hereditary moral limitations, or personally universalize himself to the dimensions of the *homo*, so bringing himself into conscious oneness with the infinite; or else the marriage of nature and man, of the *homo* and the *vir*, of the cosmos and the earth, must remain forever unconsummated, and human society turn out, not an eternal monument of the infinite divine love, but an abortive effort of his wholly incommensurate wisdom and power.

On Swedenborg's ontological principles, or intellectual method, as we have already to some extent seen, nothing is more practicable than the perfect solution of this problem. Undoubtedly his method affronts our sensuous prejudices, sacred and profane, religious and scientific. But this circumstance should rather conciliate than avert our respect, when we consider to what a complete blind-alley our intellectual prejudices of both sorts are bringing us: the devotee being afraid to trust his scientific instincts, lest his faith suffer shipwreck; and the sceptic being equally afraid to confide in his religious instincts, lest his knowledge undergo eclipse. Take any two men of equal culture who represent the existing reciprocal jealousy of science and faith, say Strauss and Neander, or Mill and Mansel. Can any one be so infatuated, or, as the phrase is, so good-natured, as to suppose that, between minds so mutually balanced or reciprocally limited as these, any reconciliation is possible upon the data already tediously trite and common to them both, that is, without some altogether new philosophic insight? *Credat Judæus Apella, non ego.* And if this hope has grown simply desperate, how incumbent is it upon all men of sense and uprightness who suffer from our existing mental chaos, to seek help wherever they can find it, even, if need be, at so unpromising a source as the books of Swedenborg!

I have already shown to some extent in what way Swedenborg helps the intellect, but much still remains behind; and in order to do the fullest possible justice to the subject, it is necessary that I define, even still more exactly than I have yet done, the prevalent but deep-seated and unsuspected intellectual malady which so piteously invokes divine medication.

Jew and Greek, devotee and sceptic, churchman and statesman, Mansel and Mill in short, perfectly agree in this, that the
realm of nature is *essentially* objective to man, and not merely
contingently so.   That is to say, they hold that nature is not
alone *sensibly* objective to him, as furnishing the proper ground
of his experience or knowledge, but also rationally objective to
him, as furnishing the definite goal of his beliefs ; so that when
any event occurs, like the alleged birth of Christ from a virgin,
or his resurrection from death, to embarrass or cripple his habitual belief, neither one nor the other ever dreams of resenting
the wholly arbitrary limitation thus put upon his intellect, but
both alike pusillanimously acquiesce in it, the only difference
between them meanwhile being, that Mr. Mansel timidly hastens
to save his faith by renouncing his reason, and Mr. Mill to save
his reason by renouncing his faith.   The event, according to Mr.
Mansel, transcends rational or scientific explanation, being addressed, not to our intelligence, but to our credulity, or instinct
of devout awe and wonder ; while Mr. Mill, on the other hand,
declares it to be incredible and inadmissible on any hypothesis
whatever, simply because it is unintelligible, or violates the
fundamental canons of the understanding ; and when the understanding is obliged to be paralyzed or set at naught to begin with
in divine things, it is of no practical moment whether we admit
or reject them, since in either case alike our action is sure to be
frivolous, unmeaning, and unmanly.

Clearly then the sceptic and the devotee both alike maintain,
in effect, that nature constitutes the legitimate object of which
man is the subject ; that it furnishes the inevitable boundary
both of his sensible and his intellectual experience.   And this
is only saying, in other words, that he is *essentially* finite, and
not merely *existentially* so ; finite not merely on his maternal or
constitutional side, wherein he stands related to nature and his
fellow-man, but also on his paternal or creative side, wherein
he stands related to culture or to spiritual goodness and truth.
Not merely are we finite, according to these disputatious gentlemen, on the side of our consciousness, or as we phenomenally
exist in ourselves, but we are equally finite also on our unconscious side, or as we really *are* in God.   For if I am nature's
unqualified subject — if I am her subject in an absolute as well

as a contingent sense, inwardly no less than outwardly, rationally as well as sensibly, specifically, or in all those respects wherein I am *individualized* from my kind, no less than generically, or in all those respects wherein I am *identified* with it — why then the manifest inference from such a state of things is, that I am not only apparently but essentially finite ; finite in myself and finite in my source ; finite in body and finite in soul ; naturally finite and spiritually finite ; in short, both actually and really, which means hopelessly and irremediably, finite.

We may say then that our prevalent intellectual malady, as measured against Swedenborg's robust sanity, consists in low and sensuous conceptions of the relation between man and God, or in a spiritual ignorance on the part of our religious and scientific guides, amounting to fatuity. And this statement, while it prepares us to estimate the advantage which Swedenborg's books will eventually confer upon true faith and true science — that is, upon a faith divorced from superstition, and a science divorced from sense — will also enable us to discern that precise and profound intellectual significance in them, which insures meanwhile that they shall prove a downright odium to Mr. Mansel, a downright folly to Mr. Mill.

XVII.

The first thing accordingly that strikes you in looking to Swedenborg for light upon this inglorious contention of faith and science, is that he palpably overlooks it, or takes no apparent interest in its fluctuating fortunes. But a second more attentive look explains this indifference, since it exhibits him industriously bent *upon vacating or exhausting the conceded intellectual foundations, upon which alone such an unfriendly rivalry becomes either possible or conceivable.* If you pay attention to what you read, you will easily hear him saying in effect or *sub voce* to both parties : " Your dispute, gentlemen, admits of no decision, but prorogues itself to an ever-indefinite future, because you are both alike destitute of that true intellectual insight — based upon a spiritual apprehension of creation — which alone can enable you to settle it, and are left meanwhile to espouse any plausible interest which happens to enlist your hereditary prejudices. You both alike maintain in truth, whatever you may do in fact, that nature is the limit, not the starting-point, of creation ; that it is the controlling end, not the servile means or pliant method, of the creative power: the consequence being that you, Mr. Mansel, from your point of view, have no occasion for a god who is not the jealous and implacable rival of nature ; nor you, Mr. Mill, from your point of view, any occasion for one who is not its unlimited servant, its idle and abject tool."

The regeneration, then, which Swedenborg's spiritual disclosures bring to faith and to science quite equally consists in a totally new conception of the creative power, whereby, on the one hand, nature, or the cosmos, is turned from an objective into a subjective work of God, which alone it is ; and man, on the other hand, is turned from a subjective work of God, which he is not, into an objective work, which alone he truly is.

Swedenborg's ontological starting-point, as we have seen all along, is that the life of man in nature is but an appearance, whereof the lord, or divine natural man, is the sole reality. To be sure, we habitually appropriate to ourselves an absolute or independent status, a freedom or selfhood unqualifiedly our own, which invests us to our own imaginations with an exclusive and inalienable property in our actions. And the creative wisdom, intent upon the interests of our natural renovation, of our eventual flesh-and-blood resurrection, which is our ultimate social evolution, mercifully authenticates this illusion meanwhile by endowing it with the sanctions of conscience, or suffering it to beget the provisional discrimination of heaven and hell in human character. But apart from this incidental or contingent use, the thing is all the while a gross hallucination. The true or spiritual creation ignores the sentiment of morality in its subjects, i. e. disallows the distinction of good and evil among men, as at all pertinent to the divine mind.* No angel that

---

* "People who are destitute of charity," says Swedenborg, "continually contemn and condemn others, save in so far as prudence constrains them to put on friendly manners. But they who are in charity can scarcely see another's evils ; on the contrary, while they note all that is good and true in him, they interpret whatsoever is evil and false in a favorable sense. *This disposition they derive from the lord,* WHO TURNS ALL EVIL INTO GOOD. The lord is as far from cursing and being angry with men, as heaven is far from earth. For who can conceive that the omniscient and omnipotent ruler of the universe, who is infinitely above all

Swedenborg encountered was ever so foolish as to attribute the good which was visible in him to himself; and no devil was ever wise enough not to do so. The fundamental difference, in short, between Swedenborg's angels and devils was the difference between humility and loftiness; the latter always cherishing an unsubdued selfhood, or pride of character, the former being always more or less cultivated out of it.

How does this ontological postulate of Swedenborg justify itself? On what ground are we entitled to regard our moral consciousness as a sheer fallacy of the sensuous understanding, save in so far as it is redeemed to truth by its uses to the spiritual evolution of human destiny? *On the ground of its being a distinctly generic, and not a specific endowment of the subject; or because it is what he has in strict community with his kind, and not, as he himself fondly conceives, in distinction from it.* Morality is the common possession of human nature just as inertia is a common possession of the mineral nature, growth of the vegetable, and motion of the animal, and utterly scorns, therefore, our private appropriation. That we do nevertheless privately appropriate it, is no presumption against the truth, but only a presumption of our ignorance of the truth. We habitually attribute to ourselves an absolute freedom, or personality: we habitually fancy that we are something in ourselves, not only generically, or as we stand identified with all other men, but also, and much more, specifically, or as we stand individualized from them; and are in no way surprised to learn accordingly from our foolish teachers and preachers, that we have each of us an absolutely good or evil *status* in God's sight, and must be prepared to expect his everlasting personal approbation or disapprobation. But all this is stigmatized by Swedenborg's higher spiritual insight as the grovelling wisdom of the serpent, or as the dictate of a purely sensuous intelligence, which makes natural fact or appearance a direct measure of spiritual truth or reality, and not the rigidly inverse one which alone it is.*

infirmity, should be angry with such poor and wretched dust as men are, who scarcely know anything they do, and can do nothing, of their own motion, but what is evil? There is nothing in the lord disposing him to anger, but only to mercy."— A. C. 1079, 1080, 1093.

* "Neither angel nor devil," says Swedenborg, "has the least inherent power; if they had the least particle, heaven would crumble to pieces, hell become a chaos,

While this immature mental condition of the race endures, God appears to our imagination as altogether like ourselves, only in aggravated form ; that is, as an intensely finite or personal being, a supreme self-lover in short, gracious to those that please him, and hateful to those who displease him ; so that heaven and hell (or a pronounced spiritual separation of mankind into sheep and goats) become an inevitable provisional necessity of human freedom.

What morality *is*, then, is very plain. It is the badge of human nature, the point of difference between man as man and all lower existences. And what morality — being what it actually is — really or spiritually *means*, i. e. what it implies with respect both to man's origin and destiny, is also becoming plain. It does not mean the aggrandizement of this, that, or the other petty person, but the aggrandizement of human nature itself to truly divine dimensions. It means the divinization, not of this, that, or the other *vir*, or specific man, but of the *homo*, or generic man, which is humanity itself, and its investiture with infinite attributes. It contemplates the exaltation of humanity itself out of those purely subjective and constitutional limitations of good and evil, wise and silly, great and small, celestial and infernal, bred of the *vir*, or specific man, into objective and unitary proportions, or the consciousness of its proper infinitude, as a universal human society or brotherhood. This is the distinction of the human from all lower forms of existence, whether mineral, vegetable, or animal, that it is a SOCIAL form, which means that its two component elements of genus and species, of identity and difference, are *essentially* matched or mated, and therefore eternally invoke each other, or seek a more free and intimate experimental union. It is a composite, not a simple form, and therefore disowns the mere concubinage which binds together the component elements of lower natures, while it

and with these every man would cease to exist." — Athanasian Creed, 34. " I once heard a celestial voice saying, that if a spark of life in man were his own, and not exclusively of God in him, heaven could not exist, nor anything belonging to heaven ; hence, no church on earth, and consequently no eternal life." — Intercourse of Soul and Body, 11. " The angels think that no man has a grain of will or prudence which is properly his own ; they say that if he had, heaven and hell would no longer hold together, and the whole human race would perish." — Divine Providence, 293.

makes marriage the very law of its existence. It is a form
which presents in itself the intensest objective unity or harmony
of two forces, which in all subjective aspects are as disproportionate and irreconcilable as heaven and hell, namely, an
infinite creative force, and a finite constitutive one : one being,
in reference to the other, merely generic or quantifying, and
therefore regarded as relatively mean or base ; the other, again,
with respect to that, specific or qualifying, and therefore regarded as relatively high or honorable. No such marriage
relation as this obtains out of human nature. No such society,
fellowship. or equality is ever felt between the generic tiger and
the specific tiger. The specific tiger is wholly incapable of
respecting his kind as he respects himself, or loving his brother
tiger's advantage no less than he loves his own. No animal,
much less any vegetable or mineral, of course, has ever betrayed,
since time began, any evidence of a social sentiment, any evidence of a higher objectivity than the indulgence of his selfish
instincts. No animal has ever exhibited the faintest evidence of
an inward conflict between his instinct and his aspiration, between his inherited nature and his acquired culture. In short,
no animal ever displays any traces of the existence or operation
of conscience, which is pre-eminently the citadel of the social
sentiment — the sentiment which makes us feel the fellowship
or equality of our *kind*, and which may be called therefore the
sentiment of *kind*-ness. Kindness is unknown except to the
human bosom, and consequently worship, which alone elevates a
man above himself. Occasionally, no doubt, a dog or a horse,
subjected to a regimen of fear, evinces an apprehension of chastise-
ment at its master's hands ; and many a man, subjected to a like
tyrannical discipline, proves to this extent a good horse or dog.
But no dog or horse. since the foundation of the world. ever
so far humiliated itself to his master as inwardly to condemn
itself, or feel a conscience of sin, for doing the will of the flesh
in lieu of its master's will. And consequently, no worshipful,
but only a mercenary relation binds the former to the latter.*

---

* No doubt the dog often exhibits a helpless attachment to the person of its
master ; but this is not because of a human quality in the dog. but because of a
canine quality in the master. The dog, in every such case, feels *himself* and loves
himself in the master ; he feels, of course, not intelligently but instinctively, how
grateful this fierce unreasoning devotion of his to his master's person proves to the

But human nature differs *toto cœlo* in this respect from all lower natures, being essentially reverential or worshipful. A relation, not of chance concubinage or lust, but of chaste wedded love, subsists between its generic and specific elements; a strict marriage unity, proceeding first upon no accord, but upon the frankest subjective discord, of the *homo* and the *vir*, or the cosmical and the domestic element in consciousness, and then upon their cordial objective harmony and co-operation.   But how is this essential marriage in humanity ever to become actual or prolific, so long as the parties to it are forever held asunder as they are in the old or representative church, and never personally confronted or brought together?   This was the impediment forever interposed by the ritual economy, that it estranged the human from the divine, the *vir* from the *homo*, the bride from the bridegroom, or perpetually postponed their nuptials.   That economy formally authenticated the subjective or phenomenal disagreement of the *homo* and the *vir*, of the cosmical and the domestic element in consciousness, and this was all it did ; for it lisped no word, except symbolically, of their prospective objective and real unity.   It exhibits the *vir* or specific element in consciousness (represented by the jew), blindly seeking to coerce the *homo*, or generic masculine element (represented by the gentile), into its bondage, instead of irresistibly attracting its love and homage by every graceful, tender, endearing art.   In other words, religion in its literal form is an extremely ascetic maiden, organizing a passionate warfare between our physical and our moral interests, between the element of fate or necessity and the element of freedom in our nature, or suspending our eternal beatitude upon the degree in which we have previously subjugated our flesh to our spirit, our bodies to our souls.*   Whereas the true tie between flesh and spirit, as

inmost pride of the latter ; how it soothes his self-love to be thus singled out from other men, and served without reference to his human or social, but only to his absolute or selfish, worth.   Thus the dog does not by any means love and serve its master because the latter is so far man, but only because he is so far dog. Take a man who has been spiritually cultivated out of his aboriginal cynicism — or his merely mineral, vegetable, and animal consciousness, and no dog will be found attaching itself to him ; for the simple reason that it will not find enough of the canine quality remaining in such a master to foster and reward its ..tach-ment.

   * The jewish law was admirably contrived accordingly, by its peculiar atoning

avouched by religion in its living or fulfilled form, is a marriage tie, which is one of essential freedom on both sides, owning no obligation but the spontaneous consent of the parties, and disowning force as intensely impertinent on either side. How get over this impediment then, so as at last to reconcile truth and fact, hitherto so utterly irreconcilable, and bring creator and creature, infinite and finite, into conscious unity?

Evidently only by the decease of man's ritual conscience towards God, and its resurrection in real or living form ; that is, by revolutionizing his consciousness to such an extent as that what has hitherto claimed the first place in it, as appearing to be properly objective, or infinite and divine (namely, the external or generic element, the macrocosm, or *homo*), shall henceforth take the last place, and confess itself altogether subjective or finite and human : while what has hitherto been accorded only the last place, as appearing strictly subjective or human and finite (namely, the internal or specific element, the microcosm, or *vir*), shall henceforth claim the first place in it, and avouch itself altogether objective, or divine and infinite : the indispensable pivot of this great historic revolution being, according to Swedenborg, the life, death, and resurrection of Jesus Christ.

Let me briefly but clearly indicate the leading intellectual grounds of this necessity.

XVIII.

There is no such thing possible on Swedenborg's intellectual principles as miracle, in the conventional sense of that word ; that is, no such thing as an outside divine interference with the order of nature : because nature, which exists only as an implication of man, affords but an inverse witness of God ; such a witness

ordinances and its perpetual implication of personal uncleanness in its votary, to suggest to every one of the least spiritual insight how futile this moral aspiration on our part is, since it is invariably energized by a carnal spirit, or is all the while pursuing really fleshly ends by apparently ascetic methods. This being the exact inward condition of the jewish church (and that church represents the distinctively religious conscience of man everywhere) — namely, that its zeal for sound morality was a mere cloak to its real unconscious immersion in all manner of carnal cupidity and uncleanness — it is not surprising that it outwardly at last, or correspondentially, fell under the roman yoke, which symbolizes the unbridled worldliness or ambition of the human bosom.

as restricts his *direct* presence and activity to the dimensions of moral or distinctively human form. The birth of Christ, for example, for the simple reason that it involves a departure from the seeming order of nature, has always been reckoned an essentially disorderly event, complicating the even tenor of existence by an outside or personal divine interference. It was a new thing under the sun, and as no one understood the grounds of it, or had the least intelligent perception of nature's being a mere mask of God's creative presence and power exclusively in man, the event which came especially charged with the revelation of that truth has remained, intellectually speaking, almost wholly inert and inoperative down to Swedenborg's day, if indeed it has not been usually interpreted in a sense exactly contrary to the truth. Swedenborg regards it on the other hand as the supremely normal event of history, the only positive revelation of law that ever took place, law infinite and eternal, or, what is the same thing, creative; the orbit of the law being for this very reason so vast and comprehensive as to defy scientific calculation, and adjourn its rational recognition to that enlargement and renovation of the common mind of the race which is coincident with our perfected social evolution. The event, though habitually ascribed to supernatural interference, if not indeed to influences contrary to nature, was in truth the spontaneous flowering of nature; only of nature in a sense so consummate, in a sense so grand and universal, as to be utterly beyond the ken either of a superstitious faith, or a sensuous science, and as to impress the votaries of both alike, consequently, as the realm of the vague, the unintelligible, the miraculous. For this great truth of the incarnation brings the spiritual universe itself within the realm of nature, i. e. nature elevated to human or moral form, since it proves our highest inward possibilities to be rigidly conditioned upon the due and orderly satisfaction of our humblest outward necessities. It in fact turns angel and seraph — nay, the infinite majesty itself — from the ineffable supreme voluptuaries we have hitherto tacitly reckoned them to be, into the cheerful, untiring, undaunted missionaries of every lowliest human want, and irresistibly invokes, therefore, a faith and a science whose past piddling dissensions will all be forgotten erelong in the access of a regenerate spiritual unity.

The creative law, as we have already abundantly seen, is that our *subjective or natural identity*, no less than our objective or spiritual individuality, *is a strict divine communication to us ;* and that without this incidental gift indeed the grander spiritual gift could never be secure to us, would be simply nugatory in fact. That is to say, we must *sensibly* exist in ourselves, or enjoy *phenomenal* self-consciousness, before we can pretend actually to image the divine perfection ; for that perfection, being spiritual or living, requires to be imaged in what *seems*, but *only* seems, to have life in itself. Of course, life cannot image itself in life (for life *is* life), but only in death, i. e. in what outwardly appears but inwardly is not. Besides, if we really should have life in ourselves, we should be uncreated ; and to be uncreated, would require us to be without selfhood, for selfhood means limitation, means the condition of a subject in relation to its own nature ; that is, a purely *conscious* or composite style of existence, whose unity consequently is not in itself, but is essentially referable to a higher source. But, although we are really devoid of being, we must nevertheless *seem* to ourselves absolutely to be, or else we shall have neither sense nor understanding, neither affection nor thought, nor any other attribute whereupon the truth of our existence may be grounded. If we thus unmistakably appear to ourselves to be, or possess moral consciousness, we have in that fact a basis for any amount of subsequent divine culture or discipline, whereby we may be gradually educated out of finite into infinite knowledge ; gradually elevated out of subjective or phenomenal existence into objective or real being ; gradually built up in fine out of the mere negative imagery of God, which we present by nature, into positive likenesses of his immortal spiritual perfection.

But let us not be duped by our own terms. When, for example, we say that God, and God alone, gives us selfhood, that is, natural or subjective identity, it is obvious that we use language suggested by material analogies ; and we must not allow any mere literal images of the truth to control, and so obscure, our perception of the spiritual reality. God does not give us selfhood in any outward manner, as I give a gift to my child ; for that would require us to exist before we were in existence, or to be on hand to receive our selfhood, before selfhood could be given to us. There is, and indeed can be, no proportion between God's giving and ours, inasmuch as he gives infinitely, i. e. gives himself; and we give finitely, i. e. do not give ourselves, but only what we have over and above ourselves, namely, our superfluity. In a word, God is a *creator*, who gives subjective or conscious life to the work of his hands; while man is at most a *maker*, who gives mere objective or unconscious existence to the conceptions of his genius. Let us beware, then, of reflectively picturing the creative procedure, in giving us selfhood or identity, as by any means an outward, personal, or moral act. In order to allow it to be that, we should be obliged, as I have just said, subjectively to antedate our own subjectivity. No, the creative throe is no mere rational adaptation of means to ends, like *our* highest activity ; much less, is it any act of simple will or caprice, like that of some flashy conjurer or magician, who would set off his own vain prowess by appearing to bring something out of nothing, or giving what is impossible a faint semblance of probability. It is not an act at all in the strict sense of that word, as being a something past and over, a mere deed of power begun and ended in space and time. For space and time are judgments of the finite intelligence exclusively ; and creation is never done and never past, but is renewed every moment, being instinct with and inseparable from the inmost love and life of God. It is what Swedenborg calls the perpetual *existere* of the divine *esse ;* that is to say, a most sincere, spontaneous, irresistible *going-forth* of the creative love in every method of formative wisdom — the creature himself being the real and inexpugnable voucher of that wisdom. No doubt the creature, misled by his senses or subjective consciousness, separates himself to his own immature thought in a very silly conceited way from the creator, and imagines himself when once created, or consciously afloat, to exist ever after on his own bottom, on his own independent or absolute merits. But this is a mere fantasy of our servile or finite understanding, the truth of the case being all the while that our selfhood, apparently so absolute, is a mere semblance or shadow of which the lord or divine natural man is the sole substance or reality.

This is what creation means to Swedenborg. It means that

our conscious or subjective life is but an arrest and appropriation
to ourselves of the objective or unconscious life we have in God.
It means, in fine, that God, and God alone, lives in us, when most
we appear to have life in ourselves ; whence it becomes instantly
evident that space and time, or nature and history, have absolutely nothing whatever to do with creation in its objective
aspect, or as it exists to the divine mind, but only in its subjective aspect, or as it exists to our infirm thought. They belong
to it, not as a result, but as a process. They are not laws of real
or spiritual being, but only of phenomenal or conscious existence, and characterize creation therefore, not as it appears to
instructed, but only to uninstructed thought. They have but a
representative function at most, as symbolizing to the created
intelligence laws of spiritual life and action, which must otherwise have remained forever incognizable and inconceivable to it.
They are not the true or spiritual creation but a rigid correspondence or reflection of it to a finite or sensibly-organized
intelligence, whereby the creator in methods perfectly level to
the created apprehension, becomes able fully to reveal himself to
every one who is inwardly disposed to be enlightened in divine
knowledge.

Let the reader ponder what is here said. This visible universe is by no means the true or spiritual creation, but only and
at best a lively image or correspondence of it to a sensibly-organized intelligence. The spiritual creation is not a work of God
begun and accomplished in space and time. It is an infinite and
eternal work, disclosing itself in space and time, or nature and
history, without doubt, but deriving all its form and substance
from the immediate divine presence and activity. The truth of
creation spiritually regarded is that of the lord or essential
divine humanity, which means the union of God and man, creator and creature, in first principles, that is, in affection and
thought ; so as that no intelligent angel or spirit shall ever doubt
for a moment, that however much his good and his truth may
seem to be his own they are nevertheless all the while the lord
alone in him. It is this that makes creation so inglorious an
attribute of the divine sovereignty, compared with that of
redemption. For creation leaves the creature at his highest a
merely natural existence — without personality — consequently

without any faculty of spiritual insight or sympathetic reaction towards his creator, and it leaves the creator accordingly and at best a sort of glorified clock-maker, intent no doubt upon mechanizing his creature to the best available issues, but utterly indifferent to his spiritual fellowship and co-operation, utterly insensible to the awful wants of his soul. One would gladly be exiled from such an Eden to a land producing only thorns and thistles, or where one should earn one's bread at the cost of his proper toil and sweat; for it would be bread honestly earned at all events, and would make life for the first time seem life in contrast with one's past beggarly existence. Swedenborg accordingly makes creation to pivot exclusively upon redemption, that is, upon a work of infinite and eternal mercy accomplished in the *nature* of the creature, or outside of his personal consciousness, whereby he becomes divorced from his native imbecility and impotence as a created being, and clothed upon with all divine power, innocence, and peace. Hence the universe of nature, and hence man its finished flower and fruit, whose individuality alone is commensurate with such universality; for he, although born in utter want and nakedness, and bred in weakness and infamy, has the task and has the power divinely given him of subduing all nature to himself, and so leading it back to him from whom it originally comes.

Thus Swedenborg disconcerts our existing religious and scientific empiricism, by vacating the sole intellectual ground or basis it possesses in the assumed integrity of nature, or the imputation of an objective reality to space and time. The intellectual fallacy which is common to the rival parties, and which alone indeed makes their rivalry possible, is, that a certain indisputable work of God exists which we call nature. If it were not so, the sceptic would never complain of the devotee for alleging *another* work of God, which he calls supernatural or miraculous as enforcing a temporary suspension of nature's laws. The sceptic and the devotee perfectly agree that nature is a positive achievement of God. But the former holds that it is his only achievement: while the latter maintains that a subsequent work takes place, which effectually revokes or supersedes the former one, and puts our knowledge of God consequently upon a much more authentic footing. Hence their interminable conflict, the noise of which Swedenborg instantly silences by denying their common premise ; or affirming that nature is no objective, but a purely subjective work of God, in the interest exclusively *of man's spiritual evolution in harmony with the creative perfection.* Nature serves, according to Swedenborg, and serves only to give God's true creature, which is man, a constitutional projection from his creative source, or a basis of self-consciousness, whereupon he may subsequently rise to any height which seems to himself good of interior communion or fellowship with infinite goodness and truth.

It is not difficult accordingly to hear Swedenborg saying in effect to both of these disputants : " The matter of your dispute is essentially trivial, or impertinent to philosophy, for the simple reason that it has no ground in objective reality. but only in your own subjective ignorance and fantasy. You, Mr. Mansel, are interested, for what doubtless seem to you good theologic reasons, in maintaining a possible divorce or disproportion between our knowledge and our belief; and you, Mr. Mill, for what seem to you equally good scientific reasons, are interested in the denial of that possibility. But your quarrel could never have arisen unless you both alike held, to begin with, that our knowledge is essentially objective, and not subjective ; that it is a knowledge of what really or absolutely *is*, and not alone of what actually or contingently *exists*. i. e. *appears* to be. Now, philosophy disowns and derides this pretension. Philosophy declares that being (which is *real* existence) is spiritual, and hence can never be sensibly, but only inwardly or livingly discerned — can never be known directly, or as it is in itself. but only as it is reproduced in what is not itself; so that existence (which is *phenomenal* being) confesses itself a sheerly reflex condition of things, and is therefore sure to turn the intellect upside down which regards it as a direct or positive exhibition of truth. Thus what both of you gentlemen subjectively know — what your senses reveal to you jointly — is, according to philosophy, no divine reality, but only the semblance of such reality to a wholly undivine — i. e. *created* — intelligence. How absurd then for either of you to attempt philosophizing upon that shallow provisional basis of knowledge ! What possible interest can philosophy feel, Mr. Mansel, in your devout assurance of faith ?

What greater interest can it pretend to take, Mr. Mill, in your
sceptical plea of ignorance ?   They are both alike worthless to
a philosophic regard, because they proceed upon the assumption
that our beliefs and our doubts, our knowledge and our ignorance, are exercised upon realities, whereas they have to do only
with the shadows of reality.   They both alike assume that
nature is not merely a sensible but a rational reality, whereas it
is the mere negative or inverse attestation of such reality.
What Mr. Mansel specifically believes or doubts in any case —
what Mr. Mill specifically knows or ignores in like case — is
never the objective reality but only the subjective show of
things.   Of what vital moment to philosophy therefore is the
vaunted faith of the one, or the vaunted science of the other ?
The things they are severally exercised upon, nature and history, belong exclusively to the phenomenal realm, never for a
moment exceed the compass of the subjective understanding,
and hence are destitute of the least objective significance.   To
go into a passion over them accordingly — above all, to assume
a philosophic strut on one side and the other, as if the business
of the universe had been at last completely settled — is about
as absurd as it would be for two children who, looking by turns
into a mirror, and seeing each a different face of reality projected, should thereupon fall foul of each other, and vituperate
each the other's innocent eyes, because they could not see the
same face.   God forbid that I should feel the least personal
complacency in your shortcomings to philosophy !   For I have
never for an instant dissembled the fact, that all my own knowledge upon the subject is owing to no superior intellectual acumen
on my part, but wholly to sensible angelic mediation.   But I
maintain that this knowledge, how little soever it may flatter
one's pride of independence, gives to every one that possesses it
a great intellectual advantage over those who do not, because in
the first place it confronts one with real, and so divorces him
from merely apparitional existences ; and in the second, it puts
an end to controversy, or converts that honest human force in
us which has been hitherto squandered in mere idle blood-
shed into a force of endless spiritual nourishment and edification."

Such is a perfectly fair report of Swedenborg's attitude towards our existing intellectual dissensions. I freely admit, at the same time, that nothing can be more dispiriting than this report to the mind which craves above all things some *authoritative* adjustment of these dissensions, in " giving reason," as the French say, to one side or the other. I cannot find a word of soothing addressed to that pusillanimous expectation in all Swedenborg's books, for he denies reason to both sides alike. In fact I seriously warn every one away from these books, whose mind preserves any considerable leaven of respect for " authority " of any sort, divine or human, religious or scientific ; i. e. who is not prepared to render a supreme obedience to his own convictions of goodness and truth whithersoever they lead him, and however much our best authenticated men of faith and men of science may refuse him countenance. We have indeed in the extraordinary lore with which Swedenborg's books make us familiar our first faint presentiment of an entirely new or regenerate intellectual existence — an existence whose fixed earth, or immovable foundations, *is laid exclusively in the ten commandments,* and whose free heaven, or infinite expanse, *is made up of love divine and human, universal and particular.* It is a world whose deepest night is our present intellectual day, whose remotest west is our kindling east, whose frostiest winter is our most blooming summer, the obvious solution of the enigma being, that our current intellectual life proceeds upon the acknowledgment of nature as a fixed achievement of the divine power, while these books represent it as an altogether fluid and obedient *medium* of such power. Our infallible doctors make nature a divine terminus, whereas Swedenborg makes it at most a starting-point of the creative energy. Our old intellect is fashioned upon a conception of nature, which reports her organizing a real or essential discrepancy between creator and creature. The new intellect beholds in nature on the contrary a real or essential marriage of the divine and human, and admits only a contingent or logical divorce. In short, while the old world regards nature as the realm exclusively of finite or created existence, and hence at best of fossilized or inactive divinity, the world to come, of which we catch in Swedenborg's books the tenderest vernal breath as it were, is built upon the recognition of the spiritual only in the natural, of the divine only in the human ; and hence exhibits the creature instinct and alive with the creative personality.*

XIX.

It thus appears that Mr. Mansel and Mr. Mill cannot help differing egregiously from Swedenborg in the estimate they make of Christ's nativity, inasmuch as they both alike look upon nature as an absolutely fixed existence, as an *essentially* finite quantity, wholly incapable of any adjustment or approximation to the infinite ; while Swedenborg regards it as an essentially indeterminate quantity, or indefinite existence, being in itself neither infinite nor finite, but the exact neutrality or indifference of the two, and standing therefore in equal and unforced proximity to either interest. Both Mr. Mansel and Mr. Mill conceive nature herself — the cosmos — whatever they may make of her shifting specific forms, to be her own end, to exist upon her own absolute basis, as exhibiting no normal subserviency to a distinctly superior style of life. With Swedenborg, on the other hand, nature is only an outward image or show, only a sensuous mask, of a living decease, so to speak — an inward obscuration and humiliation — a spiritual imprisonment and coercion — which the creative love undergoes in endowing its true creature, man, with subjective identity, or valid self-consciousness. For selfhood, or moral life, would be simply unattainable and indeed inconceivable to us, without a *quasi* natural basis, or physical background, to give it conscious relief ; without a something properly objective to it, interposing between it and the creator, and tempering his presence and activity in a way rationally to authenticate all its instincts of freedom and power ; so that the creative love, if it would endow us with moral subjectivity as a basis of our spiritual evolution, or objectivity to itself, is bound to immerse itself in mere mineral, vegetable, and animal conditions, is bound eternally to identify itself in all subjective regards with cosmical law and order.

The consequence of so fundamental a discrepancy, in their intellectual point of view, between Swedenborg of the one part and Mr. Mansel and Mr. Mill of the other, is that when nature

* See Appendix, note E.

is finally called upon to give up the ghost, confess her secret, and avouch the latent infinitude which sanctifies her most finite form, neither Mr. Mansel nor Mr. Mill is at all rationally equipped for the catastrophe ; the one feeling himself compelled to pronounce it miraculous or supernatural, the other to pronounce it an illusion or imposture; while Swedenborg, on the contrary, declares that this so-called catastrophe is precisely nature's normal business ; that her only true and honest function has ever been to subserve revelation ; that she actually exists *ab initio*, and has always been providentially graduated, shaped, and guided to that supreme issue : so that all our hot disputes as to whether things abstractly *are* or *are-not*, turn out to be of no philosophic account as bearing upon the doctrine of being, or determining what really *is*, but at most of a scientific moment, as bearing upon the doctrine of knowing, or determining what actually *appears*. Swedenborg says in effect to dogmatist and sceptic alike : " You have neither of you the least right to formulate an ontological judgment, until you shall have ceased, first of all, looking upon nature and history as finalities, and come to regard them as an abject correspondence or servile imagery of spiritual truth. It is simply ludicrous to hear one of you gravely pronouncing a certain historical event to be *supernatural*, and the other as gravely pronouncing it *intranatural*, when it is palpable to me that neither one nor the other has the faintest suspicion of what nature herself is. You have neither of you ever enjoyed any intellectual insight of nature, but only and at most a sensible contact with her. Had either of you ever been admitted to an unreserved intimacy with her, or an intelligent acquaintance with the heights of spiritual being whence alone she descends, he would have discovered that she was a real existence, a fixed quantity, only to a sensibly-organized intelligence, and hence that nothing can be more preposterous in the eyes of philosophy than to make her a standard of truth, or convert her from an abject servant into the controlling mistress of the mind. You might as well confound brick-making with architecture, or convert the moral law from a fixed earthly root of human culture into its free heavenly fruit. Nature and history are not objective, but exclusively subjective, divine experiences. They attest not the creator's infinitude or perfection, which is what he is in himself, but the finiteness or imperfection he necessarily contracts when he descends to the level of the created nature, or puts on the creature's lineaments. In creation he is utterly subject to the exigencies of our finite consciousness, so that there is no possible abyss of infamy through which his patient unsoiled love is not content to be dragged by us; and it is only in our spiritual redemption that we release him from this degrading thraldom, and allow him to become truly and intelligibly objective to us. It is very childish in us accordingly to attempt imprisoning the infinite within the finite, instead of allowing the latter freely to expand to the dimensions of the former. It is very absurd, in other words, for us to insist upon interpreting history by nature, reason by sense, high by low, and not contrariwise; beginning thereupon to wrangle about what *is* or *is-not*, as if we had some private access to divine knowledge, and were intellectually independent of the great light of revelation. It is not to be denied that you are both of you extremely clever men. You both possess uncommon ratiocinative resources, and are both alike capable consequently of making white seem black, or black white, at your pleasure. This, however, is no help, but rather a hindrance to you — unless indeed you distrust your own plausible gifts — in the discernment of truth. No cordial, disinterested lover of truth can long endure to reason about it. He willingly affirms or denies whatever is agreeable or repugnant to it; but he would be very sorry rationally to enforce its acceptance upon any unwilling mind.

" I repeat, then, that nature has not the least claim to be a direct revelation of God, any more than the body has to be a direct revelation of the soul, or the cuticle, which invests the body, has to be a direct revelation of its interior viscera. The body attests the soul only to those who are previously convinced of the soul's existence; and the skin illustrates the activity of the more vital organs only to those who are directly acquainted with these latter. So nature may be said to attest and illustrate the creative name only to those who have previously become acquainted with it in history or man; but whatever direct information it pretends to give is sure to be misleading. That is to say, it is an obedient mirror of divine revelation, but the light

which illumines it in that case is not supplied by itself, but exclusively by a reason emancipated from sense.   You have neither
of you consequently the least warrant to dogmatize positively
or negatively upon historic problems — the problems of our
human origin and destiny — until you have ascertained the
relation of nature to history.   I have not the slightest intention
nor desire to intimate that you are bound to accept mine or any
other man's view of that relation.   But I do say without any
hesitation that unless you arrive at *some* intellectual conclusions
upon this subject — unless you formulate to yourselves some
intellectual doctrine as to the kind of tie which binds nature to
spirit — you are both alike utterly incompetent to say what is
either true or untrue of the intercourse between God and man ;
both alike incompetent in fact to furnish even a shrewd guess at
the solution of any ontological problem.   Before you can be
philosophically qualified in this direction, you must have definitively settled it to your own mind : whether nature is an objective presentation of divine truth to an intelligence capable of
directly appreciating such truth ; or whether it is a sheer subjective abasement and humiliation of it to an understanding
infinitely below its level, and sure otherwise to remain out of all
acquaintance and sympathy with it.   No dodging of this issue
can be tolerated for a moment without peril to your philosophic
souls.   You are bound to postpone every derivative scientific
inquiry until you shall have first of all decided for yourselves the grand original problem of philosophy, whether nature is an absolute or purely contingent existence ; whether it is
what it appears to be, a substantive work of God achieved in
space and time, and presenting its justification therefore on its
face ; or whether it really is what it does not appear to be,
namely. a mere phenomenal manifestation. or reverberation to
sense. of an infinite and eternal work of God accomplishing in
the spiritual and invisible realm of the human mind, the realm of
man's living affection and thought."

Thus not *being* but *existence*. which is only a manifestation of
being. is Swedenborg's conception of the meaning both of
nature and history : nature expressing the subjective aspect of
existence. which means the descent of the creator to created
form ; and history its objective aspect, which means the conse

quent gradual ascent of the creature to a fellowship with the uncreated perfection. The two movements are hierarchically related as husband and wife are in marriage, where force is seen endowing weakness. They combine to constitute creation according to a law of definite proportions, as hydrogen and oxygen combine to produce water, or nitrogen and oxygen to produce atmospheric air, what is mere quantity in the one freely deferring to what is quality in the other. Thus what is greatest in existence, what is generic or universal, in short what is properly substantial, gravitates towards what is least in existence, what is specific or individual, what in short is strictly formal; and this in its turn vigorously reacts to that. The *homo*, which is the fixed or cosmical and masculine element in existence, yearns towards the *vir*, which is its free or domestic and feminine element; while the *vir* again responsively aspires to the *homo*, aspires to bring all nature, mineral, vegetable, and animal, into its embrace, and reproduce it in every form of its own teeming activity. Thus we may say that the great historic problem — the problem alike of our earliest religious and our latest philosophic culture — has been to reconcile nature and man, to fuse flesh and spirit, to wed force and freedom, to harmonize law and gospel, to marry mechanism and morals, in short permanently to unite the indefinitely great, which is the superb overbearing cosmos, with the indefinitely small, which is our humble domestic earth, the pleasant house of our abode, that so whatsoever is most outward or public and profane in existence may find itself authenticated by what is most inward or private and sacred; that so whatsoever is most absolute or material, and therefore domineering and cruel in experience, may become sanctified by association with whatsoever is most contingent, most moral or free, and therefore most gracious, pliable, and orderly.

Such is the tie which subsists between the two constitutive elements of creation, — a strictly conjugal tie, or one which exhibits the superior and creative element altogether merging and losing itself in the inferior and created one. Creation is manifestly inconceivable on any lower terms. For if the infinite creative substance should refuse to accommodate itself to the finite created form, the creature who is nothing but by the creator would fail to appear, would remain obstinately nonexistent ; just as air or water would fail to exist or appear if their constituent elements should not renounce their subjective differences, in order to become objectively fused and reproduced in the bosom of their harmless and beautiful offspring. Water is the type of all that is spiritually pure or true. It is the soft motherly womb, formless itself, out of which all form grows and defines itself. And nothing is so wholesome as the air which typifies the invisible divine breath or spirit by which we live. It is the warm paternal mantle wrapped about us, which — colorless itself — lets in infinite color, beauty, and distinction upon everything it touches. But air and water are thus gifted — are thus pure and strong and generous, thus fluid, searching, and caressing, in a word, are so little magisterial and so extensively ministerial to existence — only because they are the fruit of a strict marriage tie between two forces, which in themselves or subjectively are so frankly antagonistic as to be mutually incompatible, and which are incapable of combining therefore except objectively or in prolification, that is, in some third or neutral quantity which effaces every vestige of their intrinsic oppugnancy in its own concordant and unitary bosom.

So is it precisely with creation. In order to claim any validity in itself — in order to exhibit the least permanent worth or character — creation must be the fruit of a stringent indissoluble marriage between its infinite and finite factors. It must confess itself a perfect reconciliation in objective form of two powers which in themselves, or subjectively, are as reciprocally opposed as zenith and nadir, good and evil, light and dark, heaven and hell. This is the distinction between marriage and concubinage, that the one tie is objective, social, productive, while the other is subjective, selfish, prodigal. Concubinage is physical, instinctual, compulsory, having purely subjective issues, or expressing mere natural want, the want of some suitable ministry to reflect one's essential mastery. Marriage is moral, voluntary, free, claiming distinctively objective sanctions, or expressing the purely spiritual need one feels to supplement a feebler existence with his own force. In marriage the man so freely makes himself over to the woman, so cordially endows her with all his substance, as to make a spiritual resurrection or glorification for him in his offspring logically inevitable. Thus it is the essen-

tially objective nature of marriage, the fact that the parties to it
are utterly disunited in themselves, and united only in their offspring, which makes it undefiled and honorable, or invests it
with the social interest and prestige that distinguish human from
brute prolification. And it is the essentially subjective nature
of concubinage, the fact that the parties to it are one not
actively or in prolification, but passively or in themselves, or
that they contemplate — not that glorified or regenerate social
existence to which marriage partners find themselves summoned
in the person of their offspring, not that large and frank and
generous commerce with each other in all humane aspiration
and endeavor to which the interests of their offspring invite
these latter — but a mere transient, selfish, and mercenary
traffic in personal delights, terminable at the caprice of either
party, which puts an indelible stigma upon it. It would be
infinitely discreditable accordingly to the two factors in creation, if their tie were anything short of a marriage tie, i. e.
if it did not claim an exclusively *social* sanction, or profess to
stand only in that conscious, living reconciliation of the two
otherwise irreconcilable natures which the church has always
prophesied, but which is spiritually realized only in the grand
practical truth of "the divine NATURAL humanity," or the advent of that predestined perfect society, fellowship, equality of
men in heaven and on earth, which alone has power to bring
nature and spirit, the outward and inward, the universal and
particular, the cosmos and the earth, the *homo* and the *vir*, the
man and the woman, the world and the church, into living
unison, and so reduce the infinite creative majesty into the
keenest, most sympathetic fellowship, into the active efficient.
servitude, of every humblest organic want known to the experience of the meanest, most necessitous, most infamous of
created bosoms. Just conceive for a moment that creator and
creature, instead of being indissolubly married in creation, were
bound to each other only *par amours*, or as the artist is bound to
his work; and then ask yourself what would be the practical
result to creation. Why, I need hardly say that spiritual existence would instantly declare itself an impossible conception, for
spiritual existence is universally conceded to stand only in the
union of the divine and human natures; but I must say, what

is not so obvious, that physical and moral existence, or nature
and history, would in that case also disappear, since the subjective discrimination of these things has always been a mere provisional necessity of their eventual objective reunion in a perfect
society or brotherhood of men. In fact, the visible creation
would at once collapse from the living, breathing, organic unity
of force and freedom, of genus and species, of law and order,
which constitutes our actual cosmos, into a lifeless mush or
chaos infinitely below anything now extant even in mineral
nature outside the seething bowels of Ætna or Vesuvius.

XX.

I believe that I have now to some extent adequately venti-
lated the philosophic contents of the christian revelation, as
these are either directly explicated or indirectly implicated in
Swedenborg's books. I have no idea that in doing so I have
entirely succeeded in removing the scruples of any one who has
been hitherto prejudiced against the christian doctrine, on the
score of its proffering some apparent affront to what his heart
pronounces good. What we all of us need — in order to have
every prejudice and misconception thus honestly motived effectually met — is not a more conclusive argumentation on the part
of any one else, but a larger intellectual insight on our own
part; and this will not fail to be forthcoming in due season.
But I hope that I have nevertheless done something to help the
thought of those who, being heartily disposed to entertain the
christian verity — which is the truth of Christ's literal divinity,
or his flesh-and-blood resurrection from death — are yet more
or less unaware how profoundly rooted it is in the intellect. No
truly philosophic objection can be intelligently urged against it,
but at most a scientific one. The only plausible weapons forged
against it have always been supplied by the arsenal of sense, not
by that of the reason. Nothing indeed can be more absurd to
sense — or the imagination which looks upon nature not as a
mere implication of moral existence, but as existing in itself or
absolutely — than the pretension of a person so genuinely unostentatious as the Christ to constitute the only true and suffi-
cent revelation of the divine name. And every one accordingly

whose reason is controlled by sense, or who refuses to see in nature a mere echo or correspondence of the spiritual creation, the creation which falls exclusively within or above — not without or below — the realm of consciousness, will be sure to reject his pretension : the obvious philosophy of the fact being that sense necessarily views nature as the only just measure of the creative perfection, and regards every one therefore who is altogether devoid of native pomp or sumptuosity — who has no personal grace nor comeliness, no inheritance, no learning, no wit, no skill, no genius, no natural distinction of any kind to recommend him to popular favor — as obviously disowned or smitten of God.

But this judgment as we have seen is eminently fallacious, inasmuch as nature is in reality no just measure of the creative resources, any more than the materials out of which the Cologne cathedral is wrought are a just measure of its architect's genius. On the contrary, nature is an incessant foil to creation, operating a perpetual constraint, imposing an invincible limitation, upon the motions of the divine spirit, until it becomes historically taken up or reproduced in moral form ; until it becomes historically purged and renovated through man's enlarging self-knowledge, through his domestic, his civic, and his political experience, and so at last transfigured with an exclusively human substance or meaning. Sense has no hesitation in regarding nature as an objective work of God, or as furnishing the legitimate criterion of his power, just as the clock is an objective work of its maker as furnishing the proper measure of his activity. But the analogy is grossly fallacious and misleading for this reason, namely, the clock-maker does not stand in a *creative* relation to his clock, but only in a formative one. That is to say, he does not give it *natural* selfhood or generic identity, with a view to certain subsequent spiritual possibilities on its part, with a view, for example, to a certain specific or individual reaction on its part toward himself ; just as God endows man with natural subjectivity in order that he may thereby become forever spiritually objective to his maker. On the contrary, he simply *makes* the clock out of lifeless materials, or gives it a purely artificial existence with a view to supplement his own subjective infirmity, an existence of which the clock itself can have no enjoyment

nor any perception ; so that, instead of avouching its maker's
spiritual infinitude, it simply illustrates his natural limitations;
instead of proving a monument of his wealth and power, turns
out a humble confession of his want and impotence.   The foible
of the mechanician is that he stands in a purely objective relation to his work, and reduces his work therefore to his proper
subjection.   The glory of the creator and his strength is that
he makes his creature his exclusive and eternal object, and himself its loving subject.   Following our *a priori* instincts, or
judging according to sense, we should say that creation must
necessarily arrange itself upon the plan of the creature's proper
subjectivity to the creator, and the creator's proper objectivity
to the creature.   But the light of revelation stamps this judgment with fatuity in showing the creator invincibly subject to
the least or lowest of his creatures, and this least or lowest in
its turn invincibly objective to him ; so that creation spiritually
regarded turns out so exquisitely balanced an equation between
the creative and the created natures, as that all the iniquity,
transgression, and sin of the lower nature become freely assumed by the higher, and all the holiness, peace, and innocence
of the latter become freely made over to the former.

Thus, reason emancipated from sense, or what is the same
thing enlightened by revelation, disowns our *a priori* reasoning, and pronounces nature an altogether subjective divine work
enforced in the exclusive interest of man's spiritual evolution ;
just as the moral control I exert over myself is a subjective
work on my part enforced by my objective regard for society,
or my sense of human fellowship ; just as an artist's education
and discipline — which often are nothing more than his physical
and intellectual penury and moral compression — are a needful
subjective preparation for his subsequent objective or æsthetic
expansion.   Nature has no existence *in itself* to spiritual
thought, because it is a mere implication of man, just as the
works of a watch have no existence in themselves to rational
thought, but only as an implication of the watch ; or just as my
brain and heart, my lungs and liver, my stomach and intestines,
do not exist on their own account, but only as a requisite involution of my body.   Nature exists *in itself* only to carnal
thought, or an intelligence unemancipated from sense ; just as

9

the works of a watch would claim a substantive value only to a savage regard, or as the viscera of the body might claim a sensible existence independently of the body, or out of their due subordination to it, only to uninstructed thought. Nature and history do doubtless evolve or explicate the spiritual world, because they are first of all inexorably involved or implied in its life ; just as the works of a watch explicate the watch itself on its objective or functional side as a timekeeper, because they are rigidly implied in such functioning ; or as my bodily viscera explain the life of my body, because they alone furnish the conditions of its activity. But then we must remember that nature and history illustrate spiritual existence not to a servile, but to a free or qualified intelligence ; just as the mechanism of a watch illustrates its peculiar function, and the viscera of the body illustrate its proper life, only to the eye of the mind, only to an educated or regenerate intelligence, and by no means to the eye of sense.

What we call " the universe of nature," then, and conceive to exist in itself or substantively, i. e. in equal independence of God and man, is a gigantic superstition of our spiritual ignorance and imbecility. There is no universal natural substance, but only a universal spiritual substance, God the creator ; and there is no individual spiritual form answering to this substance, but only an individual natural form, man the creature. But these two, although they are indissolubly one in creation, or to the divine mind, are altogether distinct, and even antagonistic to consciousness, or the created imagination. For consciousness is built upon sense, and sense analyzes or dissolves existence, putting the universal before, and the individual after, or one here and the other there ; while it is only the reason emancipated from sense which synthetizes existence, or sees the universal only in the individual, the individual only in the universal. In fact consciousness or life would be wholly impossible to the creature, without this sharp discrimination of its physical or universal element from its moral or individual element ; for consciousness means the union of an inward subject and an outward object, being so much the more or less vivacious as the object is more or less identified with the nature of the subject. Thus, what creation when regarded from a spiritual or inward point of view unites — namely, infinite and finite, creator and creature, substance and form, reality and appearance, universal and particular, genus and species, *homo* and *vir*, man and woman — these it invariably divides when regarded from a sensible or outward point of view, presenting them together never in harmonious, but always in opposing fashion. They never produce a unitary, but always a reciprocally hostile impression upon the mind controlled by sense, God the creator being whatever, whenever, and wherever man the creature is not, and the latter of course standing in like contrariety to the former. Sense, in short, converts creation from a spiritual achievement of God in human nature exclusively, or the realm of consciousness, into a purely mechanical exploit of divine power in space and time, and hence puts an effectual end to the hope of any spiritual or free intercourse between creator and creature: so that a consciousness built upon sense requires to undergo a complete outward demolition and inward renewing, before it can be at all conformed to the truth of things.

But what especially interests philosophy in the facts we have just recited, as bearing upon the christian revelation, and what therefore it is especially incumbent on us to observe, is, that what is spiritually *greatest* in existence, i. e. what is uppermost to creative thought, namely, the creature himself, is naturally least, or of comparatively no account to created thought ; while, on the other hand, what is spiritually *least*, or of no account whatever to creative thought, namely, the creator himself, is comparatively so overpowering to the created imagination as almost to suffocate its capacity of spiritual life. I am not so presumptuous as to lament the fact; I only signalize it. For the helpless necessity of the case is, that what is first in creative order shall be last in created, and what is last first. This necessity inheres in the infinitude or perfection of the creative love. For God is infinite love ; that is to say, his love is a purely objective love, without any subjective drawback or reaction, being a pure love of others untempered by the least love of himself, so that he cannot help making himself over in the plenitude of his perfection to whatsoever is not himself. But whatsoever is not creator is creature, and how shall the former make himself over in the plenitude of his uncreated love to the latter, when the very fact of the latter's creatureship must transmute all that love into instant self-love? Of course there is no alternative if creation is really to take place. The creative love must either disavow its infinitude, and so renounce creation, or else it must frankly submit to all the degradation the created nature imposes upon it, i. e. it must consent to be converted from infinite love in itself to an altogether finite love in the creature. There is nothing in the creature but what is *a fortiori* in the creator, save the mark of his creatureship, which is "selfhood" or moral consciousness, being the wholly fallacious judgment he derives from the inspiration of sense as to his own absoluteness, or the fancied power of unlimited control he possesses over his own actions. If accordingly the creative love should scruple to permit *proprium* or selfhood to its creature — scruple to endow him with moral consciousness — it would withhold from him all conscious life or joy, and leave him at the highest a mere form of vegetative and animal existence. Creation, to be spiritual — i. e. to allow of any true fellowship or equality between creator and creature — demands that the creature be *himself*, that is, be *naturally* posited to his own consciousness, and he cannot be thus posited save in so far as the creative love vivifies his essential destitution, organizes it in living form, and by the experience thus engendered in the created bosom lays a basis for any amount of free or spiritual reaction in the creature towards the uncreated good.

One sees at a glance, then, how very discreditable a thing creation would be to the creator, and how very injurious to the creature, if it stopped short in itself, i. e. contented itself with simply giving the creature natural selfhood, or antagonizing him with the creator. Nothing could be more hideous to conceive of than a creation which should end by exhibiting the subjective antagonism of its two factors, without providing for their subsequent objective reconciliation; which should show every cupidity incident to the abstract *nature* of the creature inflamed to infinitude, while the helpless creature *himself* at the same time was left to be the unlimited prey of his nature. Certainly no such abortive creative conception as this attributes itself to the divine love, for that love is methodized by an infinite wisdom, a wisdom proportionate to itself. That is to say, creation, spiritually regarded, does *not* stop in itself, does not consist in giving the creature mere natural selfhood, or finite and phenomenal existence, but acknowledges itself at bottom a great purgative or redemptive process, whereby the very nature of the creature becomes finally freed from its intrinsic limitations, and eternally associated with infinite goodness and truth. For the creative power, properly so called, which consists in energizing the nature of the creature to the extent of affording him moral consciousness, or a *quasi* life in himself, is of necessity limited by that nature, and can never avouch its proper infinitude consequently but by overcoming the nature, i. e. by exalting it out of physical and moral into exclusively social and æsthetic lineaments. Thus while creation shows us the creature naturally or subjectively projected from his creative source, alienated from (i. e. made *other-than*) God. redemption shows us the creator joyfully acquiescing in that event, or invisibly accompanying him into the most intimate fastnesses of his alienation, in order *there* to bring about his spiritual or objective restoration.

Now, the providential machinery of this great revolution in our historic consciousness is supplied, as we have seen, by the church, which is the sole and unconscious guardian of the race's spiritual progress. I say "unconscious," because the church has always identified its interests with those of the natural selfhood in man, with the interests of his *quasi* life in himself, and, by washing it here and feeding it there. has vainly sought to make it bring forth positive divine or infinite fruit. The church has never had a misgiving as to the *absolute* nature of our moral experience. It has always taken for granted that conscience was a divine finality, the good man being absolutely good. or good in himself, and the evil man absolutely evil, or evil in himself; and has never so much as conceived consequently that heaven and hell, angel and devil. were only the positive and negative signs of a great unitary work of redemption yet to be accomplished, by divine might exclusively, in human nature itself. The church has always placed itself at the point of view of sense in divine things, and has greedily drunk in whatsoever that cunning old serpent has taught it of the essential or absolute, and by no means purely provisional. worth of the moral sentiment. It has always identified itself with the literal or merely created life of man as against his spiritual or regenerate possibilities; with the principle of fate or necessity in existence as against that of freedom or delight; with the generic or universal and masculine element in consciousness as against the specific or individual and feminine element; and has never had a suspicion accordingly that the day could dawn when its function would cease by its own limitation: i. e. when the *vir* or "woman" would renounce her enforced allegiance to the *homo* or "man"; when the sentiment of freedom in the human bosom would overtop that of fate or constraint, and our private life disavow its rightful subserviency to our public necessities. The church has always regarded the adamic or finite element in consciousness as absolute, and has never had a dream of its eventually confessing itself an abject foil or background to the interests of our spiritual life. And yet, in spite of the church's carnality, in spite of her dense stupidity in spiritual things, or rather indeed in virtue of it, she has been an unfaltering servant of human progress, an invaluable divine handmaid in the evolution of man's true destiny. For, by blindly avouching, as she has always done, not merely the logical but the absolute, not merely the phenomenal but the real, contrariety of creator and creature, or identifying herself with the honor of God *as against* that of man, she has so inflamed the fanaticism of the human bosom as gradually to provoke the disgust and indignation of all thoughtful and modest natures, and so reduce religion from its old magisterial to a now wholly ministerial efficacy in human affairs. She has always espoused the religious *as against* the secular life of man, and by running that interest out to its last gasp of blasphemous and insolent pretension in the pride of the ascetic conscience, has ended at last by organizing such a godly revolt and reaction in the secular or lay bosom, as must ultimately revolutionize the existing relations of creature to creator, or convert them from a polemic to a pacific character, and so bring about the complete eventual redemption of the race. It takes for granted, or assumes as unquestionable, the superiority — as given in the sensuous imagination — of the creator to the creature, of the creative to the created element in existence, of the divine to the human, of the *homo* to the *vir*, the man to the woman, of what merely *creates* or gives being to things to what *redeems* or gives them form, thus of the distinctively substantial or masculine and universal element in consciousness, to its distinctively formal or feminine and individual element; and by persistently pushing this assumption out to its logical and most inhuman issues, arouses at last so vigorous a resentment in the secular bosom, so righteous and reverential a reaction towards the outraged name of God, as end erelong in transfiguring the common mind of the race into the sole meet and adequate temple of the divine infinitude. The church ratifies *à outrance* the provisional despotism exercised by nature over man, by the cosmical or public interest in existence over the human and private interest, by the husband over the wife, by the parent over the child, by the strong over the weak, by the wise over the simple, by the flesh over the spirit, by our organic necessities over our spontaneous delights, by our sensuous appetites and passions over our rational affections and thoughts; and it thereby succeeds in engendering so desperate a resistance and so acute a suffering in the innocent bosom of the race, that the heart of God melts with compassion, and he makes the cause of the oppressed — the cause of *mankind* — his sole and righteous cause forevermore.

XXI.

Thus we are brought back through this long circuit to our original thesis, and have only to make a clear estimate of its philosophic significance, in order to see the end of our labor.

It is true that God creates the *homo* (Adam, man) male and female in his own image; and the *homo*, because he is a created being, is all unconscious of himself, — that is, without moral form, or inwardly void, being still immersed in mineral, vegetable, and animal conditions. The truth of creation necessitates that the creator be all in the creature, and the creature *in himself* nothing, so that unless the creator contrive in some way to give the creature selfhood, creation might as well have remained unattempted. Unless the creator be able to conceal his creative presence and power under a mask of the utmost imbecility and impotence, by making creation wear the aspect at most of a contingent truth, or allowing the creature to attribute to himself a strictly natural origin and destiny, the

latter will never put on form, will never come to consciousness.
So long as the truth of creation enjoins that the creator be all in
the creature, and the creature *in himself* nothing, it is evident
that creation can never attain to actuality unless the creator be
able utterly to sink himself out of sight, and let the creature
alone appear to be. In other words the creative power *must
vivify the created nature by giving it moral form, or endowing it
with selfhood*, before the creature will ever attain to that conscious, phenomenal, or subjective projection from his creative
source which is implied in the truth of his real or objective
creation. Of course no one can conceive of such a thing as a
real or absolute separation of creature from creator, enforced by
anything *accidental* to their relation : for by the hypothesis of
creation, which makes the creator all in the relation, and the
creature *in himself* nothing, everything conceivably accidental
to it is excluded : but only a logical or conscious separation,
which is rigidly *incidental* to the possibilities of their eternal
spiritual intercourse and conjunction.* And this conscious or
contingent separation of creature from creator is all that is
meant by the creator giving him natural selfhood, or *quasi* life
in himself. A creative — which of necessity is an infinite — love
can have no shadow of respect to itself in creating, but only to
the creature, or what is not itself. Hence its supreme aspiration must be to lift its creature at any risk out of dumb creatureship into intelligent sonship, i. e. out of fatal into free conditions of life, out of necessary into contingent relations with
itself, by endowing him with self-consciousness (which means
sensible *alienation from*, or *otherness than*, itself), that so his
subsequent frank and spontaneous reaction towards infinite
goodness and truth may be eternally secured and promoted.

It is clear then that while we say God creates the *homo*, we
cannot say that he creates, but only that he *begets*, the *vir*.
He creates the natural man, the *maximus homo*, male and female in his own image, — the grand, unconscious, universal, or
cosmical man, who embraces in himself the entire realm of
sense, all worlds wandering and fixed, and is attested by every

---

* Any conception contrary to this would imply that the creature is life *in himself*, and not exclusively in the creator — hence, that he is the creator himself
over again.

fact of existence, mineral, vegetable, and animal. But beneath the ribs of this sleeping Adam, this wholly unconscious *maximus homo*, or universal man, he inwardly builds up the *minimus homo*, the moral or conscious Eve, the petty, specific, domestic *vir* of our actual bosoms, who embraces in himself the entire spiritual world, the universe of affection and thought, and to whom all the facts of life, i. e. all the events of history, great and small, public and private, and all the results of experience, good and evil, true and false, exclusively pertain. Give particular heed to this discrimination, for it is what emphatically distinguishes Swedenborg's intellectual method from that of every philosophic system hitherto in vogue ; and if the method fail accordingly to justify itself to our understanding in this particular, it must utterly fail to do so, since all the data of spiritual observation and experience upon which it is based are vitalized exclusively by the discrimination in question.

Let me insist then upon being perfectly understood.

I am a conscious, which means a composite or unitary, and not a simple or absolute, form of life, because I am both objective and subjective to myself. On my physical side — my fixed, organic, passive, maternal side — by which I am related to nature or outlying existence, I am my own object. On my moral or personal side — my contingent, free, active, or paternal side — by which I am related to man or my kind, I am my own subject. Now in the former aspect of my existence I am a creature, identical with all that exists; in the latter I am spiritually begotten or inwardly formed, and hence am consciously individualized from whatsoever else that exists. It is indeed obvious that in this latter aspect of my personality, I can with no propriety be said to be created, but only generated or begotten ; because it stamps me consciously free, i. e. makes me to my own perception praiseworthy or blameworthy as I do well or ill. And no mere creature of a superior power can possess conscience, because conscience means autonomy or self-rule, and self-rule contradicts creatureship. Conscience, or the faculty of self-rule, implies that its subject be equal to its object. Thus, if God be the proper object and man the proper subject of the faculty, it implies so far a spiritual fellowship or equality between the two. Hence what I learn from Swedenborg is, that while on my physical or organic side, the side of my natural want, of my overpowering appetites and passions, I am God's abject creature, and hence wholly unredeemed from the fate which impends over mineral, vegetable, and animal, on my moral or conscious side, the side of my personal fulness, of my rational affection and thought, and the free activity engendered by these, I become released from this created vassalage and elevated into God's spiritual sonship, — the fact of my personal consciousness, of my felt selfhood or freedom, being the inexpugnable witness and fruit of the inward and invisible marriage which eternally unites the creative and created natures. In a word, so far as I am *homo*, and therefore only physically conscious, being generically identified with all existence, I am God's servile creature, knowing fulness and want, to be sure, or sensible pleasure and pain, but without any conscience of moral, i. e. supersensuous, good and evil. On the contrary, so far as I am *vir*, and therefore morally or personally conscious, being formally individualized from all lower existence, and identified only with man, I am God's veritable son, being spiritually begotten of him through his living absorption in the *homo*, and am consequently endowed with conscience, which is the faculty of discerning between good and evil, or, what is the same thing, of freely compelling myself away from a finite and illusory good to one which is infinite and real, and so coming at last into the deathless fellowship of his perfection.

This, then, is the remarkable addition made by Swedenborg to philosophy, — an addition which it is not too much to say recreates philosophy, or makes it from hitherto standing upon its head stand henceforth upon its feet. According to Swedenborg, man morally regarded, the *vir* or conscious man, is divinely begotten of the *homo* or cosmical man ; whereas, according to all authoritative or recognized philosophy, human nature is a mere helpless involution of cosmical nature, and man just as much the unlimited creature of God in his moral or specific aspect as he is in his physical or generic one. Thus the vulgar conception of creation is that nature absolutely separates between God and the soul, so that the moral or conscious subject is actually distanced from God, in place of being really brought near to him, by all the breadth of the cosmos. To Swedenborg this judgment is the mere dotage of sense. He makes the moral or conscious world involve the physical or unconscious one, just as cause involves effect, or form substance, or the body its viscera, i. e. not as deriving objective being or character from it, of course, but subjective existence or constitution. He makes man involve mineral, vegetable, and animal, precisely as the statue involves the marble, not of course as receiving spiritual form from these things, but material body. According to Swedenborg, human nature has no quantitative, but only a qualitative manifestation; what is quantity, substance, or body in it being supplied by mineral, vegetable, and animal existence; what is quality, form, or life being supplied by infinite love and wisdom. That is to say, man, *in so far as he is man*, does not exist to sense, but only to consciousness, and consequently human nature properly speaking is not a thing of physical but of strictly moral attributes. In so far as man exists to sense he is identical with mineral, vegetable, and animal; and it is only as he exists to consciousness that he becomes naturally differenced or individualized from these lower forms, and puts on a truly human, which is an exclusively moral, personality.*

Indeed, Swedenborg's ontological principles compel us to go further than this, inasmuch as they stamp the generic element in *all* existence, the element of *identity*, as strictly phenomenal, while they make the specific element, the element of *individuality*, alone real. He makes the subjective element in all existence — physical existence no less than moral — not real, i. e. purely phenomenal, because it is *created*, or possesses being not in itself, but in what is not itself; and he makes reality attach only to the objective or formal contents of existence, because these are not naturally created, but spiritually begotten. For example: the rose in its generic, subjective, or constitutional aspect, or in so far as it falls within the sphere of physics, is identical with all the other facts of physics, and is therefore

* Swedenborg makes spiritual perception to consist *in the removal or abstraction of quantities from qualities.* "Thus," he says, "spiritual thought (and spiritual affection also) is altogether alien to natural thought; so alien, in fact, as to transcend natural ideas, and make itself dimly intelligible only to an interior rational vision, and this — *non aliter quam per abstractiones seu remotiones quantitatum a qualitatibus.*" See the little tract *De Divina Sapientia*, VII., 5, at the end of the *Apocalypsis Explicata*.

without selfhood — that is, without anything to individualize or make it differ from universal nature; without anything to make it rose rather than lily or cabbage. But in its specific, object-ive, formal, or characteristic aspect, in which it is rose and nothing else, i. e. in so far as it transcends the realm of phys-ics and falls within that of mind, by becoming permanently objective to human affection and thought, it is strictly individ-ualized from all other existence, and claims a real or absolute in place of a contingent or phenomenal quality; claims in short to exist in its own proper form, in its own distinct and deathless individuality, and not alone in mere and sheer identification with all other existence. *Qua* plant the rose is undeniably identical with all plant life, just as the horse *qua* animal is iden-tical with all animality. But the rose *qua* rose, or the horse *qua* horse, is itself and nothing else, being individualized or differenced from all other existence. How? *By its alliance with the human consciousness, of whose structure it forms a component part.* The rose and the horse, which in themselves or subjectively possess only a phenomenal existence undistin-guishable from all other phenomena, nevertheless objectively, or in man, claim a real or absolute significance, being a part of the creative logos or word by which alone we love and think and speak and act. They are a constituent portion of our mental structure, so that if they were away the human mind would be to that extent impoverished, or out of correspondence with spiritual truth. Neither in universals nor in particulars does the mind permit itself to be regarded as of an abstract, but only as of a concrete nature. In both spheres alike (the universal and the particular) the mind claims to exist before it lives, — claims an unconscious substance before it has a conscious form, claims an unquickened body before it has a living soul. The body or substance of the mind in its universal aspect is identi-cal with love, for love is the unconscious life of the *homo;* all *homines* — mineral, vegetable, and animal — having sensation, and being therefore instinctual forms of affection. The body, or substance of the mind, again, in its individual aspect, is truth; for truth is the conscious life of the *vir*, all *viri* — good and evil, great and small, wise and simple, able and weak — pos-sessing knowledge, and being therefore instinctual forms of intelligence.   And neither sensation nor knowledge is an abstract, but purely a concrete quality, as no one can either feel or know but by an organic contact with the objects of feeling and knowledge.

Thus, according to Swedenborg, the generic element in all existence, or what identifies and universalizes it, is what stamps it phenomenal and perishable ; and the specific element, or what individualizes it from all other existence, is what alone stamps it real and absolute with all the reality and absoluteness of the mind itself.

But let us take another very important step in advance. Man morally regarded, the *vir* of consciousness, is divinely begotten of the *homo* or physical man ; is an outbirth of the divine spirit, not directly, but inversely, through the *homo*, — a precipitate, so to speak, in finite or personal form of the infinite love and wisdom pent up, imprisoned, degraded, drowned out in the cosmos.   But now, if the *vir* be an inversion of the *homo*, then we must expect to find what is first in the latter (namely, substance, the generic or universal principle, which means God the creator) becoming last in the former ; and what is last, (form, the specific or individual principle, which means man the creature) first.   Accordingly this is the exact difference the *vir* actually presents to the *homo*.   In the *homo* the race principle, the principle of universality, or community, is everything comparatively, and the family principle, the principle of individuality or difference, is comparatively nothing ; while in the *vir* the family principle is comparatively everything, and the race principle comparatively nothing.   So that the *vir* is an unquestionable inversion of the *homo* divinely operated or begotten.

But now what is the method of this great achievement? How can we rationally conceive of the *vir* being spiritually begotten by the divine power out of the *homo?*   In other words, what conceivable ratio is there between the wholly unconscious life of mineral, vegetable, and animal, and the wholly conscious life of man?   Between the blind instinctual groping of Adam, and the clear intelligent will of Eve ?   Between the utterly unselfish nature of the *homo*, and the utterly selfish nature of the *vir?*   Between the innocence which characterizes all our distinctively *humane* tendencies and affections, and the guilt which stains all our distinctively *virtuous* ones? We shall easily find the answer to this inquiry, but we must give a new chapter to the investigation.

XXII.

What is the question we seek to have answered?

It is a question about the genesis of consciousness, or as to the precise *nexus* that obtains between physical and moral existence. We wish to know how the *vir* is divinely begotten of the *homo*. How does man become extricated from his mineral, vegetable, and animal conditions, or stereotyped in properly human, which is moral, form?

The logical situation out of which the question proceeds cannot be too clearly conceived to begin with. It may be thus more explicitly restated: —

What is meant by *creating?* It means — strictly interpreted — giving being to things. Thus when we call God a creator, we mean to say that he and he alone gives being to things; that he and he alone constitutes the real or absolute truth of existence. But as the giving being to things necessarily implies that the things themselves phenomenally or subjectively exist, so the creative process involves a subordinate and preliminary process of making, or forming, whereby the things created attain to subjective dimensions. Thus when we say that God creates the universe of nature, we explicitly assert indeed that all natural existences owe their specific form or variety to him, but we implicitly affirm also that he gives them generic substance or identity as well, since without this as a background or basis their specific differences could not appear or exist. The universe is not a simple, but a complex phenomenon. It claims finite existence in itself as well as infinite being in God; phenomenal or contingent substance as well as real or absolute form; chaotic or communistic subjectivity no less than orderly or diversified objectivity; and what any cosmological doctrine, assuming to be philosophically competent, is concerned with specially is the former, not the latter, of these claims. The latter claim is self-evident. God the creator is himself infinite and eternal, and it is a matter of course, therefore, that he should communicate infinite and eternal being to his creature. The difficulty is to imagine him giving anything less than this; that is, to imagine him giving the creature finite and temporal existence. This is the obvious contradiction involved in the creative problem; and no doctrine of creation accordingly can stand a moment's scrutiny, which does not on its face resolve this contradiction.

Sensuously conceived, of course creation amounts to a simple conjuring trick or magical feat on the part of God, whereby a real something is produced out of apparent nothing. But to the philosophic apprehension creation means that God gives spiritual reality to existence only in so far as he gives it material actuality; that he gives specific form or differential quality to things only in so far as he endows them with generic substance or common quantity. This is the intimate and essential logic of the conception, that the objective truth or reality of creation is utterly contingent upon its subjective fact or appearance. We are ready enough to concede that God *qualifies* existence, or gives it visible form; but we are by no means so ready to perceive that he also *quantifies* it or gives it inward invisible substance as well. This latter *rôle* we conveniently assign to a certain metaphysic entity we call Nature, which has no fibre of actuality in the absolute truth of things, but which we in our ignorance of the creative power superstitiously summon to our aid nevertheless, whenever we would intellectually account for existence. No doubt we agree that this abstraction called Nature had some sort of mysterious being given it "once upon a time" by God, in order to quantify all subsequent forms of life which might appear, or give them projection from their creative source; indeed we are very forward to maintain creation in this ghastly chronic or fossil sense against all disputants. But that creation still exists in any acute or living sense of the word, that any and every concrete form of nature which we see begotten and born in endless series under our eyes, is yet in its measure a literal creation of God, deriving its entire actual or material substance, no less than its real or spiritual form, from his sole and active perfection. — this is a truth of which none of us have even any instinctual suspicion, much less any intellectual conviction.

Nevertheless, if we would maintain in good faith that the universe of existence is created, this is the intellectual obligation incumbent upon us, namely, to believe in creation as an altogether vigorous present reality, and deny its retrospective character, under penalty of lapsing into a childish and godless pantheism. A true or philosophic doctrine of creation imports that God is able to bestow spiritual or objective and unconscious being upon things, only by giving them material or subjective and conscious existence : and hence binds us if we would understand creation save in a superstitious unworthy manner, to cultivate assiduously the physical and moral sciences, or the study of nature and history. For example : if I should say that *God creates the rose*, what would my words imply to a philosophic ear? Clearly no direct or outward and literal action on God's part whereby the rose *qua* rose — or as to what specifically distinguishes it to man's intelligence from cucumber, cabbage, and all other forms of existence — is made really or objectively *to be ;* but rather an indirect or inward and spiritual passion on his part, whereby the rose *qua* plant — or as to what generically identifies it to my intelligence with all plant life, and through that with all existence — is made subjectively to exist or-appear. The rose *qua* rose, i. e. as to its metaphysic quality, as to what makes it logically appreciable to my intelligence, or stamps it an object of human affection and thought, obviously claims to exist in itself, claims to exist absolutely, and so far manifestly repugns creation. If then I still insist upon proving it created, I can only succeed in doing so by showing that it is not created directly as *rose*, — i. e. as to what gives it metaphysic quality, or makes it specifically and absolutely to be to my intelligence, — but only indirectly as *plant*, — i. e. as to what gives it physical quantity, or makes it generically exist as a contingent fact of nature, in organized subjection to the laws of space and time.*

* The rose *qua* rose has no existence to sensible or direct intuition, nor yet to scientific or reflective observation, but only to conscious or living perception, whose proper organ is faith. For sense regards only what is exceptional in existence. i. e. divine or supernatural ; and science only what is normal, i. e. human or natural ; while faith regards only what is spiritual in existence, or sees the exception and the rule, the divine and the human, the infinite and the finite, the absolute and the relative, blent in the unity of life. In its mineral or inorganic aspect of course the

Now if all this be true, if it be true that the creative activity properly speaking restricts itself to what is public, common, generic, universal, or subjective in existence, then it becomes obvious to the least reflection that the creature as such can have no pretension to moral, but only and at most to physical form; i. e. a form in which the generic element is altogether controlling, and the specific element altogether subservient or servile. I do not say that moral existence may not supervene to the creature's experience upon his creation; I only insist that it cannot be created. For moral existence is not simple but composite, the moral subject being both objective and subjective to himself, or claiming to be self-conscious, i. e. to possess a selfhood distinct from all other existence, and hence uncreated; while physical existence is simple or purely subjective, the physical subject not being his own object, but finding his proper objectivity outside of himself, and hence without self-consciousness: the exact distinction between the two being that in physical order the generic or substantial element. i. e. what gives subjectivity, rules, and the specific or formal element, i. e. what gives objectivity, serves; whereas in moral order, a distinctively converse state of things obtains, form or species being primary, substance or genus altogether secondary.

We may say then without fear of contradiction that the sphere of creation is identical in strict philosophic speech with the realm of physics, and excludes moral or metaphysical existence. In other words, we may say that God creates the *homo* alone; that is, gives being to man only in physical form, or in mineral, vegetable. and animal proportions: this limitation moreover upon the created nature being enforced by the creative perfection. For God is love — love infinite and eternal, as knowing no drawback of self-love — and whatsoever he creates or gives being to consequently cannot help turning out a purely subjective form of existence, as realizing its proper life in the uses

rose exists to sense, whose office is to affirm the absolute in existence; and *qua* plant or on its organic side it exists equally of course to science, whose office is to affirm the relative in existence. But *qua* rose, or in so far forth as it is itself alone, characteristically individualized from all other existence, being neither mineral nor vegetable, neither absolute nor relative, but the living unity of the two, it exists only to life or consciousness, and is affirmed only by faith which is the organ of life or consciousness. It is, in short, a mere index to the creative logos.

it promotes to something beyond itself. But a purely subjective form of existence is a servile or impersonal form, being destitute of all objective accord with, or intellection of, the uses it promotes to other existence. The sphere of creation properly speaking claims accordingly to be rigidly identical with the universe of nature, inasmuch as natural existence of whatever stripe, mineral, vegetable, or animal, is strictly servile or impersonal, being what it is and doing what it does in spite of itself, or without its own rational concurrence.

Observe well what has just been said. If God is love infinite and eternal, then whatsoever he creates or gives being to must image this spiritual or individual perfection of his only in a natural or universal way, by avouching itself at best an instinctual which is a servile and lifeless form of love, exhibiting only an interested subserviency to other existence. This limitation is obligatory upon the creature by virtue of its creation, which is its essential distinction from the creator. The creator, being by the hypothesis of creation both infinite (as having no limitation *ab intra*) and absolute (as knowing no limitation *ab extra*), is the one individual, while the creature, being by the hypothesis of creation finite (as self-limited,) and relative (as limited by what is not-self), is the one universal, i. e. the many. Consequently the creature must be in himself universality without any admixture of individuality, since otherwise he would be undistinguishable from his creative source. If there were the least flavor of individuality attaching to his universality, he would transcend his nature as a creature, or put on moral lineaments; for moral existence is not created but begotten.

But universal existence — existence which is purely generic or subjective, and noway specific or objective — is simple, and therefore chaotic: it is *me* without any *thee* or *him* to finite it, or render it morally conscious. Thus the *homo* divinely created (the universal man, Adam or earth) is in its own nature a chaos, and only by regeneration a cosmos. The bare fact of its creatureship stamps it " without form and void," i. e. without human or moral form, and void of rational or internal consciousness; for it *cannot help* being precisely what it is, and doing precisely what it does, inasmuch as all its life and action are imposed upon it by its creation. It is necessarily and utterly void of objective worth or character, — doing uses not spontaneously or of itself, but altogether instinctively or of natural constraint, — because, being a created existence, the creator is everything in it and itself nothing. Hence it must forever remain a mere dead or stagnant image — a strictly negative or inverse correspondence — of the creative perfection, unless the creative resources are so commanding as to supply this inherent defect of the created nature, and convert its inveterate death into exuberant life, by begetting a *vir* everyway answerable to the immortal want of the *homo*, or bringing forth a human, which is a moral or individual form, everyway commensurate with the universality of mineral, vegetable, and animal existence.

Thus the truth of creation invincibly implies that the creature bear a purely formal or outward and objective relation to the creator, while the creator sustains a strictly substantial or inward and subjective relation to the creature. The creator must constitute the sole and total subjectivity of the creature, and the creature in its turn must constitute the sole and total objectivity of the creator. No doubt that creation in this state of things will wear a sufficiently unhandsome aspect, inasmuch as the creature will lavishly appropriate, or make its own, whatsoever it finds of the creative personality thus invincibly subject to it. But its action in that case will be simple, not composite; i. e. will be wholly instinctual or fatal, and noway moral, rational, or free, as implying any consciousness of personality on its part, or any sentiment of difference between it and the creator. In short, the creature, *qua* a creature, will be a very good mineral, vegetable, or even animal existence, but it will have no pretension to the human form. It may claim mineral body, fixity, or rest, vegetable growth, and animal motion, but the fact of its creatureship must always inhibit it attaining to human, which are exclusively moral dimensions.

We have the amplest warrant then to deny that moral existence, or human nature, is included in creation proper; to deny that man is God's proper creature save as *homo*, i. e. on his organic, passive, unconscious side, in which he is physically identified with mineral, vegetable, and animal existence; while as *vir*, i. e. on his free, active, or self-conscious side, in which he is morally individualized from all other existence, he is manifestly the only begotten son of God. We read accordingly in the symbolic *Genesis*, that while all lower things take name from man (or derive their quality from their various relation to the human form), man himself (Adam or the *homo*) remains void of self-consciousness, void of moral or personal quality, remains in short wholly unvivified by the *vir*, until creation itself gives place to redemption, or nature becomes complicated with history, in that remarkable divine intervention described as the formation of Eve or the woman out of the man's rib: by which event is symbolized of course an inward or spiritual divine fermentation in man which issues at last in his moral consciousness, or his becoming subjective as well as objective to himself. The entire mythical history amounts in philosophic import to this: that the *homo* or physical man, divinely *created*, is utterly distinct from the *vir* or moral man divinely begotten out of the other; hence that humanity could never have attained to personal consciousness, could never have put on human as contradistinguished from mere animal lineaments, could never in short have drawn a breath of moral or rational life, unless the merciful illusion had been granted it to look upon itself not as exclusively objective to God, which is the eternal truth of things, but rather as exclusively subjective to him, which is the mere fallacious semblance of things. For how shall created existence ever be properly *subject* to its creator? By the very terms of the proposition its entire subjectivity resides in the creator; and how therefore shall it even so much as *seem* to be subjective to him, unless he graciously defer to its deep spiritual necessities by becoming himself formally reproduced within the created nature, or putting on finite and phenomenal form in the *vir?*

The interesting question, I repeat, then, to philosophy is, What is the method of this hidden or spiritual divine operation? How is the *vir* (Eve) actually begotten of the *homo* (Adam)? How is moral life generated of mere physical existence? How does the dull opaque earth of our nature become translucent with heavenly radiance? How does the mere natural or lifeless image of God become converted into his spiritual or living likeness? How does God's dumb unconscious creature become glorified into his conscious son? In a word, how does the

chaotic darkness which invests universal nature, mineral, vegetable, and animal, become gradually lifted or effaced in the
light, order, and beauty which characterize man's individual
intelligence? For it is only Eve, *divinely quickened*, who brings
the carnal, gross, and grovelling Adam to final and adequate
self-consciousness; only the *vir* (the private specific man) who
is able to mirror or reproduce the *homo* (the public generic
man) to himself. The symbolic Adam is "in a deep sleep,"
while Eve is being divinely quickened within him. He has no
suspicion that she is formed out of his own lifeless clay; that
she is only his own relentless unconscious death divinely fashioned into *quasi* or conscious life; that she is but the phenomenal revelation of the most real but unrecognized being
which he himself has exclusively in God. He regards her on
the contrary as an absolute divine benefaction. cleaving to her as
flesh of his flesh, and bone of his bone, and betraying no misgiving — any more than we his distant descendants do at this
day — that the divinity with which she is instinct is one with
his own base flesh and blood, or inseparable from his lowest
mineral, vegetable. and animal characteristics. He takes it for
granted indeed — just as we his unintelligent offspring have
done ever since — that the selfhood or freedom of which he is
made sensibly cognizant in the person of the woman. is an unconditional divine surrender to him. is its own all-sufficient end,
being given to him for its own sake exclusively, and with no
view to any ulterior spiritual advantage.*

Let me repeat my question once more then. How does this
subjective equation of the creative and created natures, which is
implied in all the phenomena of consciousness, actually come
about? Moral existence implies such a literal indistinction of
creator and creature in all subjective regards, such an unstinted
vivification of the lower nature by the higher, such an absolute
identification of what is properly infinite in creation (substance)
with what is properly finite (form). as necessarily makes God
and man convertible quantities. or abases the divine to human,
and exalts the human to divine proportions. Our intelligence
consequently brooks no arbitrary refusal in its research after the
rationale of this stupendous creative achievement. It is the

* See Appendix, Note F.

urgent insatiate problem both of the world's dawning spiritual
faith, and of its dawning spiritual science, to know how the *vir*
becomes divinely begotten of the *homo*, how moral life is bred
of physical decay, how spirit is born of flesh, or nature is
quickened out of mineral, vegetable, and animal into human or
moral form.   And the altogether sufficing solution, as it seems
to me, which Swedenborg gives the problem, may be stated
substantially as follows.

The *vir* is begotten of the *homo* (or nature becomes spiritually
vivified) exclusively through the instrumentality of *conscience*,
which is a living though tacit divine word in every created
bosom, leading it to aspire only after infinite knowledge.   Conscience does not give this counsel to the *homo* in direct or explicit,
but only in indirect or implicit terms.   Its precept is negative, not
positive, saying, " thou shalt *not* eat of the tree of the knowledge
of good and evil (i. e. finite knowledge), for in the day thou
eatest thereof thou shalt surely die."   Two trees grow in the
garden of the created intelligence, which cannot be eaten of
simultaneously :   one called *the tree of the knowledge of good and
evil*, i. e. the knowledge of the finite, whose fruit is death ;
the other *the tree of life*, i. e. the knowledge of the infinite,
whose fruit is immortal life.   Or to drop figurative and con-
fine ourselves to scientific speech, there are two sources of
knowledge practicable to the created bosom :   1. Experience,
which gives us self-knowledge ;   2. Revelation, which gives
us divine knowledge.   And by Adam's being told " that he
should die if he ate of the tree of the knowledge of good and
evil," is symbolized that law of human destiny which makes
the seeming life but most lethal death we encounter in ourselves, or reap from our physical and moral experience, altogether subordinate and ministerial to the seeming death but
most vital life we realize in God, or reap from our spiritual and
historic culture — from our social and æsthetic regeneration.

Conscience in its literal or subjective requirements has respect
exclusively to the *homo ;* and it is only as a spiritual or objective administration that it contemplates the *vir*.   It is to
Adam alone, not Eve, that the prohibition to eat of the tree
of knowledge is addressed ; and though Eve in her dialogue
with the serpent chooses to associate herself with Adam in the

prohibition, and even superstitiously aggravates its force by alleging that they were forbidden also to *touch* the tree, the step is a strictly gratuitous one on her part, having no other warrant than her own instinctive identification of herself with Adam. The reason why Adam alone is forbidden to eat of the tree of the knowledge of good and evil — in other and less figurative terms, the reason why conscience as a letter has to do only with the animal, and not with the moral or rational man — is very obvious. It is that Adam is the abject *creature* of God, and hence is blindly *instinct* with — though by no means intelligently conscious of — the creative infinitude or perfection ; and to suppose him therefore " eating of the tree of the knowledge of good and evil " with impunity, i. e. finding life in his finite experience, is expressly to affront and mutilate his creatureship. Unquestionably what is mere " instinct " in the creature will eventually undergo conversion into will and intelligence ; in other words, man will infallibly outgrow his animal consciousness, and attain at length to truly human proportions, when he will no longer blindly or instinctively, but freely or spontaneously, react to the creative impulsion. And this being the case, his moral or rational experience, his experience of selfhood or freedom (symbolized by Eve, or the woman), becomes incidentally inevitable, because his free, spontaneous, or spiritual reaction towards the creator is rigidly contingent upon such experience. But it is strictly *incidental*, and no way final, its total purpose being to afford the creature that phenomenal or generic projection from God which alone may motive his subsequent real or specific conjunction with him. Conscience *is the veritable spirit of God in the created nature, seeking to become the creature's own spirit ;* and it can only do this, of course, in so far as it first of all leads the creature intelligently to apprehend and appreciate the distance between God and himself; between infinite love and wisdom and finite affection and thought ; between his nature and his culture ; between his inheritance and his destiny ; between his physical and his moral consciousness ; in short, between what gives him objective being to his own eyes as *homo*, and what gives him only subjective existence or appearance as *vir*. It is the *final*, not the immediate, office of conscience to reveal man to himself as a unit of two forces, one infinite, the

other finite; one spiritual, the other material; one specific or
private, the other generic or public; so vindicating at last the
sole and supreme truth of the divine natural humanity. Until
this great end is fully wrought out,—i. e. so long as the truth
of the divine natural humanity remains a mere letter or tradition, and is not spiritually or livingly believed,—the moral or
rational man seems of course to be the true end of the divine
providence upon earth, whereas he is a strictly *mediate* end to
the evolution of society; and all sorts of reproach, contumely, and
humiliation consequently attach meanwhile to the divine name.

Thus we must not for a moment forget that selfhood or moral
poise has a purely *constitutional* and by no means a *causative*
efficacy in the evolution of creation. That is to say, it is
what makes the creature phenomenally exist, but it has nothing directly to do with conferring real being upon him. It
gives him subjective consciousness, or the appearance of being
to himself; but it is very far indeed from constituting his objective or real being in the divine sight. For the creator
alone constitutes the being of the creature; and it is only in so
far as he ignores the creator consequently, that the creature
attributes being to himself. Thus the creature's self-knowledge
or subjective consciousness is inexorably conditioned upon his
sheer and absolute ignorance of the creative perfection; i. e. of
what gives him objective and unconscious being, or makes him
a reality to God; what we call his selfhood being a mere
ratio or means to the evolution of a spiritual life in him, and
having absolutely no other force. By the sheer fact of his
creatureship he is void of selfhood or moral force, void of
the human form or quality; and yet by the same irresistible
necessity he aspires to it with all his might. For how unworthy it would be of the creative infinitude to content itself
with leaving its creature a mere animate existence, utterly incapable of private or interior sympathy with itself! The sole
justification of the creator in creating—i. e. in vivifying an
inferior and opposite form of existence to himself—flows from
the hypothesis that he is infinite, as having no regard to himself
in creation but only to his creature, and intending to exalt
the latter to the plenary fellowship of his perfection. None
but the creator knows and, knowing, resents the limitations of

the created nature. None but he knows that the profoundest want and hence the controlling love of the creature is self-hood or freedom, and that to expect it to be anything or do anything incompatible with this fundamental want, or until its love of self is fully satisfied, would be a heartless mockery of its constitutional infirmity. He consequently breathes in the Adamic or created bosom no absolute, but an altogether qualified or conditional injunction, designed in the first place to keep it at bottom innocent under whatever superficial issues may subsequently arise to obscure that innocence, and in the second to stimulate and fashion in it the precise moral or rational consciousness in which as being created it is deficient. "Thou shalt not eat of the tree, etc., FOR in the day thou eatest thereof thou shalt surely die." Thus while conscience accommodates its utterances with the utmost strictness to the needs of the created nature, or makes the evolution of spiritual life in the creature, in his love to God and love to the neighbor, rigidly contingent upon his amplest previous experience and exhaustion of the death he has in himself, we at the same time learn from the symbolic narrative that this death which conscience brings to light in man is no vengeful judgment — no unworthy penal infliction — on the part of God, but on the contrary a strictly constitutional incident, or physiological necessity, of our immortal spiritual life. For is not Adam represented as saying — in full and reverent explanation of his fall, and at the same time in full and reverent attestation of his faith in God — the woman THOU GAVEST WITH ME, she gave me of the tree, and I did eat? Could anything more perfectly avouch his integrity so far as any real or spiritual offence towards God is implicated in the transaction, than the fact that he was led to do as he did by the irresistible influence of God's own best gift to him? Accordingly the inspired tradition, though it represents him duly incurring the death denounced upon his transgression — that death to our instinctual innocence and peace which is involved in every breath of the moral or voluntary consciousness — by no means reports him as having become personally obnoxious to the divine dislike. The serpent, which in symbolic speech denotes the senses, is cursed above all cattle, that is, is made to grovel upon the earth, because it misled the woman; and the ground, by which is symbolized *man's external life*, is cursed *for the man's sake;* the symbolic import of the otherwise puerile story being, that men should be led betimes by the evils which beset their outward life inwardly to renounce their physical and moral genesis, which is a purely phenomenal one, and cultivate instead their social and æsthetic aptitudes, which alone are divinely real. But neither Adam nor Eve is pictured as encountering the least personal inclemency at the hands of God. So far is this from being the case, that Eve, who was the leader in the transgression, hears a gracious promise of blessing and victory made in behalf of her prospective offspring.

Conscience then is the sovereign link or point of transition for which we have been seeking between moral and physical existence. In conscience the moral which is the individual or differential element in nature becomes disengaged from the physical, which is its strictly universal or identical element, and the conscious *vir* absorbs the unconscious *homo* in his deathless embrace, never henceforth to be reproduced save in the spiritual or regenerate lineaments of a perfect human society. That is to say, nothing is really universal but individuality; what we call the universal element in nature, meaning thereby what gives *genus* or substance to things, having no existence in itself, but being a mere implication of the individual element, which gives *species* or form: just as the viscera of the body and the works of a watch have no existence in themselves, or apart from the forms in which they constitutionally inhere. In other words, the creator is the sole reality of the creature, while the creature is only an appearance or manifestation of that reality; and as the creator is infinitely individual — which means that he is individual to the exclusion of universality or community — so consequently what we without misgiving call the universe of nature, and conceive upon the testimony of our senses to be absolute, is utterly destitute of being, and confesses itself a mere appanage of the human form. In the infancy of the human mind, no doubt the truth seems exactly contrary to this. So long as the subjugation of nature is not only unachieved but almost unbegun — i. e. while man's spiritual evolution is still in abeyance to the satisfaction of his physical and moral wants —

nature seems the only real, and man a strictly contingent existence; man himself being meanwhile a squalid savage, content
to live in abject dependence upon nature's caprice. and eke out
a beggarly subsistence upon the scraps her niggard larder affords
him. This, however. is but the initiament of human history.
Man can afford to sink his foundations very low, because he is
destined to build very high; destined. in fact, eventually to house
the creative infinitude in himself. Infinite love and wisdom are
his source, and as he cannot help spiritually returning sooner or
later to his source, it is expedient and even inevitable that his
merely natural genesis should degrade him below all mineral,
vegetable, and animal possibilities, degrade him in short to hell,
that so he may thence more efficiently react or rebound towards
his appropriate spiritual destiny. Thus no matter to what depths
of savagery his native instincts of infinitude originally incline
him, erelong the indwelling though unrecognized divine word or
logos begins to inspire his consciousness, and lift him out of
ignorance into knowledge, out of imbecility into wisdom, out of
bondage into freedom. out of penury into plenty.

Undoubtedly all this while man is the victim of a stupendous
though most merciful illusion. For he all the while regards himself not merely as consciously or phenomenally disjoined with
God by nature, but as really or absolutely so, and hence strives
though in vain to conjoin himself anew by the zealous cultivation
and practice of virtue. He strives in vain, because virtue in
proportion to the sharpness of its aims, and the earnestness of its
aspirations, shuts the votary up to himself, or separates him from
his fellow, while all the resources of the divine providence are
leagued to break down human isolation or selfishness, and exalt
the broadest human fellowship to its place. But man in his
moral beginnings has no intuition of this truth. The beginnings
of conscience in us invariably exhibit the *vir*, or moral and conscious subject, freely identifying himself with the finite and created side of things. that is, with the *homo* or physical and unconscious man [*thy desire shall be to thy husband. and he shall rule
over thee*]. while he recoils at the same time in abject dread and
estrangement from the spiritual world, or the infinite and creative side of existence. How, indeed, could it be otherwise?
How is it possible that I, when all my feeling and knowledge

stamp me to my own perception as finite, or ally me exclusively with nature, should ever worthily apprehend my invisible spiritual source, ever feel myself to be inwardly enfranchised of God, ever see in the balanced good and evil of the moral world only a stupendous mask of the creative presence, behind which, in silence and secrecy, it slowly but surely builds up for itself a faultless temple of inhabitation in our nature? The thing is manifestly impossible. My physical organization itself baffles every such conception of truth on my part; for isolating me as it does to my own consciousness from all other men, and relegating me to the perpetually recurring sway of my finite necessities, it makes the rise of any really spiritual or divine worth in me rigorously attributable, not to a spontaneous evolution of my nature, but to the exercise of a more or less severe self-denial on my part. And self-denial is the very essence of virtue. Thus to all the extent of my peculiar *virtus*, manhood, or moral consciousness, I of necessity antagonize all other men, deny their fellowship or equality, feel *my* self to be at essential and internecine odds with *theirs*, in short proclaim myself an utterly unsocial or selfish being; and so practically refer all true *virtus* — all real manhood — to a divine and infinite personality.

Conscience is thus the true and living matrix in which the infinite creative substance puts on finite created form. All the phenomena of our moral history go to show the *homo* or created man, the man of interior affection and thought, utterly unconscious of the infinite goodness and truth which alone give him *being*, and joyfully allying himself with the *vir* or finite conscious man, the man of mere organic appetite and passion, who gives him contingent *existence* only, or renders him phenomenal to himself; shows him, as the symbolic narrative phrases it, "*leaving his father and mother, and cleaving unto his wife until they become one flesh.*" In this way the creature, from being only physically objective to the creator (as the clock is to its maker, or the statue to its sculptor), becomes morally subject to him (as the wife is to the husband, or the child to the parent); while the creator, in his turn, from being literally constitutional to the creature (as substance is to form, or the material of a house to the house itself), becomes spiritually creative of it (as form is creative of substance, or a house creative of its material). This

is the grand secret of creation, the dense and otherwise impene-
trable mystery of our nature and history, that a certain inversion is divinely operated in the field of consciousness, whereby
the *homo* or merely *created* man, who is wholly unconscious
and therefore undistinguishable from his creator, being a mere
universal or animal and passive force, becomes taken up into the
vir, or puts on the semblance of an individual or moral and active force, and so attains to self-consciousness or that apparently
absolute projection from his creative source, which is the needful prerequisite of his subsequent spiritual reaction towards it.
And conscience is the dazzling inscrutable mask under which
this great divine operation conceals itself. It is in reality
a subtle and exquisite mirror wherein all the imperfection
inherent in the abstract unconscious nature of the creature, or
in mineral, vegetable, and animal existence, emerges, i. e.
becomes luminously reproduced or reflected in his concrete,
conscious self; and all the perfection consequently which is
inherent in his creative source becomes for the time hopelessly
immersed, i. e. obscured if not obliterated. Please observe that
there is nothing arbitrary in the inversion thus alleged to be
wrought in conscience. For if, as we have seen, the *vir* or concrete conscious man be the offspring of divine or infinite power
begotten out of the *homo*, or abstract unconscious human nature,
then it is evident to a glance that *his individuality must constitute
an exact and veritable equation of these unequal factors :* i. e. must
be perfectly commensurate on its inward, spiritual, or paternal
side with all the resources of infinite or creative love ; and on
its outward, material, or maternal side with all the defects of
mineral, vegetable, and animal, or simply created existence :
so that the only true subject of conscience, the only one who
really fulfils all its righteousness, must be at once perfectly
divine and perfectly human — or perfectly infinite and perfectly
finite — in his proper person.

XXIII.

Let me here observe that my reader would greatly mistake the
true state of the case, if he should suppose me animated by any
personal designs towards him; if he should suppose me, for

example, aiming to convert him from a sceptical to a believing state of mind. I have, indeed, far too much reverence for the divine prerogative in all things spiritual, to attempt substituting my own foolish reasonings for his unerring initiative. I have not the least ambition to modify my reader's religious convictions, or invade in any manner the sacred precincts of his heart. My aim in writing is exclusively philosophic, not religious. It is not to persuade, but only to instruct. I would not if I could persuade any one who doubts the truth of creation to believe in it, because I am sure that my labor would be soon undermined in that case by the hidden currents of his soul. But I have a great desire to commend this truth itself to men's speculative regard, that they may know both what is philosophically included in it, and what is philosophically excluded from it, and so feel themselves at perfect liberty thenceforth to obey their hearts' supreme instincts without fear or favor. To this end, and this end solely, I have shown that creation deals only with universals, or stops short in physics, hence that man on his moral or distinctively human side is not a creature of God, but a son spiritually begotten, and that the method of his generation is identical with the authority of conscience.

But here let us be frank with ourselves. Such extremely vague notions in regard to the nature and function of conscience are unhappily prevalent, not only in vulgar but in technically enlightened minds, that we shall hardly be able to proceed a step further, intelligently, without some preliminary clearing of the way.

Conscience is commonly interpreted as a divine revelation to the intellect, whereby men are put in favorable relation to truth or moral science. That is, it is not thought to possess a constitutive efficacy with respect to moral existence, but only a regulative one. Thus it is by no means commonly reputed to be the exclusive organ or voucher of the difference which all men recognize between good and evil, infinite and finite, God and man ; on the contrary, this difference is assumed to be somehow absolute and eternal, and conscience is regarded as coming in thereupon merely to prescribe the duties which are appropriate to the relation. And it is astonishing to observe the amount of cleverness men sometimes waste in attempting to demonstrate the fallacy of this alleged revelation, on the ground that some men are wont to deem that right which others deem wrong, and that wrong which others deem right. I say this cleverness is wasted, because it is addressed after all to the refutation of a false theory of the moral instinct. No doubt the widest diversities of opinion and practice obtain among equally conscientious races: and why not? For conscience was never intended to operate a direct restraint either upon the affections or the thoughts of men, but only indirectly upon the action in which affection and thought legitimately issue, and in which alone they permanently reside. It was never intended to produce any uniformities of intellectual culture or conventional practice among men, but only to avouch the human principle itself, under every contrasted form of culture and practice, by sharply discriminating man from the brute, or antagonizing moral and physical existence. It was intended in short only to signalize the fundamental discrepancy which exists between the human form and all lower forms of life, as lying in the absolute right of property, or exclusive power of control, which every man as man attributes to himself with respect to his own action.

Hence if men had not conscience — i. e. *if they had no inward perception of the inexpugnable difference between good and evil, high and low, infinite and finite, God and man,* which is exactly what conscience affirms, and is all that it affirms — they would not be men, but animals, inasmuch as they would be no longer masters, but slaves of their organic appetites and passions. The distinctive quality of manhood lies in its subject's ability to recognize a law of action for himself superior to pleasure and pain, in his power to discern a good more intimate than any particular gratification of his appetites and passions, and an evil more poignant than any particular postponement of them. And this power he derives exclusively from conscience, i. e. from a supreme divine presence, or living divine word, in his soul, affirming the inextinguishable contrariety of good and evil. Thus the seat of conscience is neither the affections, nor the intellect, but the life. Its primary office is not to tell us what is good and true, or teach us how to feel and think, but to tell us what is evil and false, or teach us what to avoid. Its aim, in a word, is not to regulate our opinions, but our practice; not to mould our senti-

ments, but our lives. Were men without it then, they would
be like the animals, utterly indifferent to the quality of their actions. Manhood is not primarily physical and derivatively moral.
On the contrary, it is primarily moral and only derivatively physical. In other words, my action is not mine because my heart
conceived, and my thought planned, and my hand executed it:
a thousand acts, claiming just this sort of affiliation to me, I daily
loathe and disown: but simply because my conscience approves
it; i. e. because I inwardly feel it to be right and not wrong for
me to have done it, and hence gladly identify myself with it.
It is childish accordingly to attempt discrediting conscience as a
divine regimen, merely because it allows and even authenticates
the most contrarious intellectual judgments among men. It is
an instinct of the soul, not an intuition of the reason, much less
an induction of the understanding. If accordingly the sceptic,
instead of pursuing his present tactics, would seek to invalidate
conscience as the soul's own instinct of deity, by showing that it
is *as such* an uncertain light, declaring no absolute or real, but
only a contingent or phenomenal opposition between good and
evil, between God and man, between infinite and finite, then I
admit his effort would be more reputable in point of logic, but
certainly quite as fruitless in point of result. For conscience is
not what it is commonly reputed to be, a mere miraculous
endowment of human nature, liable therefore to all the vicissitudes of men's hereditary temperament, much less is it a mere
divine trust to the intellect of men, liable, therefore, to all the
vicissitudes of our natural genius and understanding. On the
contrary, and in truth, it is *the divine natural humanity itself;*
and its light, consequently, is as clear and unflickering as that
of the sun at noonday, which in fact is but the servile image of
its uncreated splendor.

No better proof can be desired of the truth here alleged,
namely, that conscience masks the actual divine presence itself
in human nature, than the fact that every man is inexorably
characterized or spiritually individualized by it to his own perception. That is to say, every man unhesitatingly pronounces
himself either *good* or *evil* relatively to all other men, precisely
as he obeys or disobeys it. And certainly no law has power to
stamp me, a free subject, good or evil to my own profoundest

conviction, unless it be an essentially formative law, the law of my very being or form as man. The only valid natural superiority I can claim to the animal lies in the fact that I have conscience, and he has not. And the only valid moral superiority I can claim to my fellow-man is, that I am more hearty in my allegiance to it, and he less hearty. Thus deeper than my intellect, deeper than my heart, deeper in fact than aught and all that I recognize as myself, or am wont to call emphatically *me*, is this dread omnipotent power of conscience which now soothes me with the voice, and nurses me with the milk of its tenderness, as the mother soothes and nurses her child, and anon scourges me with the lash of its indignation, as the father scourges his refractory heir.

But this is only telling half the story. It is very true that conscience is the sole arbiter of good and evil to man ; and that persons of a literal and superficial cast of mind — persons of a good hereditary temperament — may easily fancy themselves in spiritual harmony with it, or persuade themselves and others that they have fully satisfied every claim of its righteousness. But minds of a deeper quality soon begin to suspect that the demands of conscience are not so easily satisfied, soon discover in fact that it is a ministration of death exclusively, and not of life, to which they are abandoning themselves. For what conscience inevitably teaches all its earnest adepts erelong is, to give up the hopeless effort to reconcile good and evil in their own practice, and learn to identify themselves, on the contrary, with the evil principle alone, while they assign all good exclusively to God. Thus no man of a sincere and honest intellectual make has ever set himself seriously to cultivate conscience with a view to its spiritual emoluments — i. e. with a view to placate the divine righteousness — without speedily discovering that every such hope is illusory, that peace flees from him just in proportion to the eagerness with which he covets it. In other words, no man, not a fool, since the beginning of history, has ever deliberately set himself " to eat of the tree of the knowledge of good and evil " — i. e. *to prosecute his moral instincts until he should become inwardly assured of God's personal complacency in him* — without finding death and not life to his soul, without his inward and spiritual obliquity being sooner or later made to abound in the exact ratio of his moral or outward rectitude. I have no idea, of course,

11

that a man may not be beguiled by the insinuating breath of sense into believing himself spiritually or in the depths just what he appears to be morally or in the shallows. Vast numbers of persons, indeed, are to be found in every community, who — having as yet attained to no spiritual insight or understanding — are entirely content with, nay, proud of, the moral "purple and fine linen" with which they are daily decked out in the favorable esteem of their friends, and are meanwhile at hearty peace with themselves. All this in fact is strictly inevitable to our native and cultivated fatuity in spiritual things; but I am not here concerned with the fact in the way either of denial or of confirmation. What I here mean specifically to say is, that every one in whom, to use a common locution of Swedenborg, "the spiritual degree of the mind has been opened," finds conscience no friend, but an impassioned foe to his moral righteousness or complacency in himself, and hence to his personal repose in God. For example: conscience limits my self-love, or zeal for my own welfare, to a just or equal zeal for the welfare of my fellow-men; that is to say, it suspends all my hope of personal righteousness upon my practically deferring to my brother to such an extent — in case of any conflict between us — as that the interests of absolute justice be promoted, if need be, at any personal cost to myself, and any personal advantage to my rival. But it is the very essence of self-love to spurn control, and make one's own welfare the practical measure of the welfare of other men. Hence, and of necessity, conscience wears an implacable front towards the *vir* or specific interest in humanity, unless the latter conciliate it by freely accepting death at its hands, or, what is the same thing, studiously compelling itself into all manner of actual conformity to the *homo* or generic interest.

A living death then, which is a death to all one's distinctively personal pretension, is the sentence which conscience enforces in the breast of every child of Adam who attempts seriously to fulfil its righteousness. It is indeed idle to conceive that any mere child of Adam should ever be able, while the world stands, positively to fulfil the law of conscience, or avouch himself a true unit of the divine and human natures. A stream cannot mount above its source, and no mere creature of God will ever be able to transcend his nature, and attain to God's spiritual sonship. Even if such an aspiration were possible to him, it would be defeated by its own genesis, since the only motive it could attest on his part would be an unsocial or selfish one, consisting in the lust of personal aggrandizement. When I earnestly aspire to fulfil the divine law — when I earnestly strive after moral or personal excellence — my aim unquestionably is to lift myself above the level of human nature, or attain to a place in the divine regard unshared by the average of my kind; unshared by the liar, the thief, the adulterer, the murderer. But the same law which discountenances false-witness, theft, adultery, and murder binds me also *not to covet:* i. e. *not to desire for myself what other men do not enjoy:* so that the law which I fondly imagined was designed to give me life turns out a subtle ministry of death, and in the very crisis of my moral exaltation fills me with the profoundest spiritual humiliation and despair. It is an instinct doubtless of the divine life in me to hate false-witness, theft, adultery, and murder, and actually to avert myself from these evils whenever I am naturally tempted to do them. But then I must hate them *for their own sake,* exclusively, or because of their contrariety to infinite goodness and truth, and not with a base view to tighten my hold upon God's personal approbation. I grossly pervert the spirit of the law, and betray its infinite majesty to shame, if I suppose it capable of ratifying in any degree my private and personal cupidity towards God. or lending even a moment's sanction to the altogether frivolous and odious separation which I devoutly hope to compass between myself and other men in his sight. The spirit of the law is love, love infinite and eternal; and it consequently laughs my personal homage to scorn, however conventionally faultless it may be, so long as it is moved by so selfish a temper on my part, or freely imputes to him "who is of too pure eyes to behold iniquity" the meanest of human characteristics. namely, "a respect of persons."

It must be abundantly clear by this time, I think, that conscience is the distinctive badge of human *nature,* having no manner of respect to any man's personal virtue, but aiming, on the contrary, to inflame and nourish in every bosom the human sentiment exclusively, the sentiment of every man's invincible

solidarity with his kind, which is indeed fatal to all personal pretension, whether virtuous or vicious. That is to say, conscience
is what specifically disengages man from all other existence, in
spite of any generic complicity with such existence on his part;
and it is what, therefore, generically confounds every man with
every other man, whatever specific diversity may exist between
them. It is, on the one hand, the true logical *differentia*, or point
of individuation, between man and animal; and consequently it
is, on the other hand, the true point of indifference, indistinction,
or identification, between man and man. In short, conscience
characterizes the *homo* or generic interest in humanity, primarily,
and pays only an incidental regard to the *vir* or specific interest;
its aspect towards the former being altogether positive and salutary, towards the latter invariably negative and disastrous.

Now what is the meaning of this great fact? Why — to all its
sincere or qualified experts — does conscience practically turn
out this inveterate savor of death unto death, rather than of
life unto life? In other words, why does this internecine conflict obtain between our moral interests on the one hand, or
the life we apparently possess in ourselves, and our spiritual
interests on the other, or the life we really have in God?

The reason, after what has gone before, seems hardly to need
restatement, being found exclusively in the social bearings of
conscience, or the influence it exerts upon human brotherhood,
fellowship, or equality.

The entire historic function of conscience has been to operate
an effectual check upon our gigantic natural pride and cupidity
in spiritual things, by avouching a total contrariety between
God and ourselves, so long as we remain indifferent to the truth
of our essential society, fellowship, or equality with our kind,
and are moved only by selfish or personal considerations in the
devout overtures we make to the divine regard. In other
words, conscience is addressed exclusively to the purgation of
human *nature* itself, and its consequent thorough reconciliation
with the divine nature; and it pays accordingly no manner of
obeisance to the imbecile claims which any particular subject of
that nature may prefer to its respect. The only respect it ever
pays to the private votary is to convince him of sin, through a
previous conviction of God's wholly *impersonal* justice or right-

eousness, and so divorce him from the further cultivation of a
mercenary piety, while leading him to make common cause with
his kind, or frankly disavow every title to the divine esteem
which is not quite equally shared by publican and harlot. We
are naturally under a fatal delusion with respect both to God
and ourselves. That is to say, our sense of selfhood is so absolute and expansive as to drown our judgment of spiritual truth,
or lead us to infer that our being is not only apparently but
really our own, whereas in truth it is exclusively God's being
in our nature. Thus my senses affirm my absoluteness, and
hence leave me not only wholly unconscious but even wholly
unsuspicious of the divine being and existence; so that I am
actually shut up for any knowledge I may claim on that subject
to an immemorial tradition zealously cherished by my race.
Sense has of course no cavil to allege against a tradition so universally respected — the tradition of a physical and moral creation of God which took place "once upon a time," an indefinite number of ages ago. On the contrary it stoutly assumes
the truth of that superstition, and in doing so binds the mind
to infer that what took place only "once," or in the beginning
of history, takes place no longer, but that men, having been
supernaturally created at the start, have been ever since and at
most only naturally begotten and born: so that God no longer
stands in an inward or spiritual and creative relation to men, *as
vivifying their very nature,* but only in an outward or legal and
personal relation as determined by the relative merits and de-
merits of their petty *selves.*

Now conscience or religion is the divinely appointed menstruum of our purgation from this sensuous mental captivity,
and our consequent eventual edification in all right knowledge
of the relation between man and God. It is the cherubic sword
which flames every way to guard the mystic "tree of life"; or
flashes dismay into every bosom thus persistently mistaught of
sense, and fills it with the pungent odor of mortality. Religion,
as I have argued on a previous occasion.* exerts, rightly understood, no repressive, but a purely liberative or detergent influence upon the mind, its office being not to bind but to *unbind*

* *Substance and Shadow, or Morality and Religion in their Relation to Life.* Second Edition. Ticknor and Fields, Boston. 1867.

(*re*-ligare) a victim already fast bound in the fetters of sense. My sensuous reasonings all lead me to suppose that there is some infallible *ratio* between God and myself — some middle-term or law in which we may freely coincide or become one — and that if I can only divine this *ratio* and faithfully execute its behests, I shall be sure to make myself a partaker of the divine life. Now religion or conscience apparently flatters this fallacious prepossession on my part, but only that it may the more effectually emancipate me from it, by convincing me in the end that no such *ratio* or law is possible between man and God. That is to say, it first conciliates my native instincts to the extent of giving me a *quasi* or so-called divine law, contained in fleshly ordinances, and suspending my life upon its obedience; but I no sooner engage, as I conceive, in its hearty service than I find a new world — a hitherto unsuspected social or spiritual realm of life — opening up within me, in the light of which all my nascent laurels turn pale and die. I find in fact, the more honestly I endeavor to obey the divine law, that a totally prior law to this claims my allegiance — *the law I am under to my own race or nature* — and that until I am perfectly absolved from this prior and profounder law it will be idle and hopeless to attempt fulfilling the other. The mother stands in a much more intimate and tender relation to the child than its father does, and easily *attracts* a love and reverence from it which the latter is totally impotent to *command*. Just so mother Nature exerts a far more potent sway over my affections than father God; and the best service accordingly which this *quasi* divine law does me, is to convince me of this necessary but hitherto unsuspected truth, and so prepare me betimes for a plenary divine descent to my nature, which shall enlarge that nature to truly infinite dimensions, and consequently fill me its subject with a filial feeling towards God — or a spontaneous love and worship — which will forever do away with the thought of any paltry legal and personal relations between us.

Thus it has always been the historic function of conscience to undermine the sensuous and merely traditional conceptions we entertain in regard to our God-ward origin and destiny, by gradually convincing us that neither the physical nor the moral man, neither Adam nor Eve, neither the *homo* nor the *vir*, has ever had any just claim to be considered God's true or spiritual creation: but only that regenerate social and æsthetic man in whom Adam and Eve, the *homo* and the *vir*, the physical and the moral man, are freed from their intrinsic oppugnancy — from their reciprocal limitations — and reproduced in perfect unity, and in whom alone consequently the divine and the human natures are completely reconciled. Conscience is a really divine presence *in our nature* — being in fact its sovereign though latent distinction from all lower natures — so that no mere *vir* can ever fulfil its righteous exactions save by spiritually exalting himself to infinitude : which means, enlarging himself to the proportions of the *homo*, or universalizing his distinctively personal sympathies and aspirations to all the extent of man's common or generic want towards God. In other words, no one who seeks to appropriate this divine life in our nature, or make it his own by reproducing its righteousness, can ever hope to succeed save in so far as he exhibits in himself a virtue every way identical with the broadest humanity, and therefore commensurate with the divine perfection : save by proving himself so frankly and spontaneously dead to every personal hope and aspiration, every craving after mere moral excellence, in short every inspiration of his native egotism and vanity, as to feel absolutely no conflict whatever between his private interests and those of universal man. Conscience announces a fundamental discrepancy between our private and our public life, i. e. a deficient *social* force in our nature ; and as the sole end or sanction of discord is harmony, so accordingly no one can pretend to harmonize these contrasted spheres, who is lacking above all things on the private side, or in whom the sentiment of self antagonizes that of kind. If conscience be the veritable door of immortal life, and if it avouch at the same time a fundamental practical antagonism between the universal and the individual interest in our nature, then clearly it must prove an open door only to those in whom this antagonism has been actually confronted and reconciled, and a closed door to every one else.

Scarcely any doubt need linger now, I apprehend, upon the philosophic import of conscience. It is the badge of human *nature* itself, considered as being inwardly qualified or quickened by God's infinitude, and at the same time outwardly quantified or substantiated by any amount of finite limitation, any amount of mineral, vegetable, and animal matter. It is nothing short of ludicrous, accordingly, to imagine any man capable of fulfilling conscience, or the creative law of human nature, whose personality does not exhibit a perfect reconciliation of its opposing factors, infinite and finite, God and man, a perfect harmony or adjustment of its twin poles, high and low, good and evil. Whoso fulfils the law of conscience must infallibly present in his proper person that rigorous and exact equation of the creative and created natures which all its righteousness implies; and he can only do this by, first of all, renouncing his personal con sciousness — that is to say, whatsoever specific virtue or pride of character may conventionally approximate him more closely to God than other men, and frankly identifying himself in sympathy and aspiration only with man's generic or universal want, the want in which all men are one, want of society, fellowship, equality, brotherhood. The law is meant to be fulfilled of course, since otherwise human nature, or the human race, would confess itself a failure; but, in the nature of things, it can only be fulfilled by a man who, being in thorough sympathy, on the one hand, with God's infinite majesty, is no less sympathetic on the other with man's most sordid misery; or who, being on one hand in perfect accord with God's stainless love or mercy, is on that very account emphatically able to justify man's most abject natural selfishness and worldliness. Such a man of course will be qualified to fulfil the law of conscience, but he will do so only by inwardly disowning all that exceptional virtue which legally distinguishes one man or one family of men from the communion of their kind, and publicly identifying himself with whatsoever normal vice and unrighteousness bind them to it.

Remember that conscience, or the spiritual creation, is a unit. That is to say, the two factors given in science or the material creation as divided — God and man, infinite and finite, spirit and flesh, the one all fulness the other all want — are exhibited in conscience, or the spiritual creation, as perfectly reconciled, married, put at one; while in the material creation the higher factor or creative element is held in invincible subjection, being bound hand and foot to the necessities of the lower or created element. The palpable logic of creation — considered as an exact equation between the creative fulness and the created want — is that the former be utterly swallowed up of the latter, or actually disappear within its boundless stomach. In other words, in order to the creature coming to self-consciousness, or getting projection from the creator, it is necessary that the latter actually pass over to the created nature, cheerfully assume and eternally bear the lineaments of its abysmal destitution : so that practically, or in its initiament, creation takes on a wholly illusory aspect, the creature alone appearing, and the creator consequently reduced to actual non-existence, or claiming at most a traditional recognition. Now conscience — regarded as the law of the spiritual creation, or of the evolution of the human mind — corrects this fallacy of the sensuous understanding in us, by convincing us that this is only the true and inalienable life of the creative love — only its sublime necessity, so to speak — to disappear within the precincts of the created consciousness, or freely abandon itself to every caprice and exaction of our finite nature, since otherwise the creature himself could never come to consciousness, nor present consequently any natural basis for his subsequent spiritual evolution in all divine perfection : so that what we call nature, and suppose to be absolutely set off from the creative personality, is in truth or at bottom only the creator swamped or submerged in the created consciousness, in order thence alone to effect and energize the spiritual creation. Of course if the creator should *really* exist apart from or out of relation to the created nature — if, in other words, his resources should not be visibly and wholly absorbed in the created consciousness — then it would be impossible to conceive of the creature ever coming to self-consciousness ; for he *is* only by virtue of the creator, and he can never therefore phenomenally exist or appear to himself, but by the creator's perpetual tacit connivance and assistance. And if this be the inflexible logic of creation, it is perfectly obvious that no professing subject of conscience can legitimately pretend to reproduce its righteousness, save by perfectly reconciling in himself these phenomenally divided natures, or crowning man's lowest conventional infamy with God's spotless sanctity.

XXIV.

It would be difficult to express the exquisite peace which flowed into my intellect, when this great discovery began to shape itself out of the multitudinous but accordant details of Swedenborg's marvellous yet most veracious *audita et visa*. If there had been anything habitually unquestioned to my conviction, it was the indefeasible sovereignty of conscience on the one hand, or the literal finality of its judgments in all the field of a man's relations to God, and the truth on the other hand of every man's complete personal adequacy to all the demands of its righteousness, provided he were only actuated by good-will; and I spared no pains accordingly to cultivate such good-will, and so conciliate its austere regard. I never questioned the absoluteness of all the *data*, good and evil, of my moral experience. I never doubted the infinite and eternal consequences which seemed to me to be wrapped up in my consciousness of personality, or the sentiment I habitually cherished of my individual relations and responsibility to God. I had never, to my own suspicion, been arrayed in any overt hostility to the divine name. On the contrary, I reckoned myself an unaffected friend of God, inasmuch as I was a most eager and conscientious aspirant after moral perfection. And yet the total unconscious current of my religious life was so egotistic, the habitual color of my piety was so bronzed by an inmost selfishness and indifference to all mankind, save in so far as my action towards them bore upon my own salvation, that I never reflected myself to myself, never was able to look back upon any chance furrow my personality had left upon the sea of time, without a shuddering conviction of the abysses of spiritual profligacy over which I perpetually hovered, and towards which I incessantly gravitated. And I have accordingly no hesitation in expressing my firm persuasion that nothing kept me in this state of things from lapsing into a complete despair, and a consequent actual loathing and hatred of the divine name, but the infinite majesty of Christ; that is to say, a most real and vital divine presence *in my nature* deeper than my *self*, deeper than consciousness, deeper than any and every fact of my moral or personal experience, which was able, therefore, to rebuke and control even the pitiless rancor of conscience itself, and say with authority to its tumultuous waves, Peace, be still!

I do not mean to say that I had any clear idea of this truth at the time. Familiar as my intellect had always been with the letter of revelation, it was — not indeed altogether, but — comparatively blind to its spiritual scope, until I found in Swedenborg all the light it was possible to crave in that direction. My traditional faith bound me to look upon Christ as a mere succedaneum to Moses, or practically subordinated the gospel in my estimation to the law; so that the only use I ever made of the christian facts — whenever the voice of conscience was loud in my bosom, proclaiming the inextinguishable difference of good and evil, or God and man — was to worry out of them some more or less plausible pretext of consolation against the wrath of God, still presumably impending upon all manner of unrighteousness. I do not think I overstate my intellectual obligations to Swedenborg, when I say that his spiritual disclosures put an effectual end to this insane worry and superstition on my part forever. For these disclosures made plain to my understanding, what the Scriptures themselves had long before made plain to my heart, namely, that the law, with whatever pomp it had been sometimes administered, boasted of no independent worth, that its total sanctity lay in its negatively adumbrating to sense a coming righteousness in our nature so truly divine or infinite as to forbid all positive anticipation of it without instant wreck to the mind's freedom. Swedenborg showed me, in fact, in the discovery he for the first time makes to the intellect of spiritual laws, the laws of the divine creation, that the conception of law or conscience as a basis of intercourse between God and the soul is no longer tenable in philosophy, but must give place at once to the truth of a present or actual divine life in the very heart of human nature. He shows the empire of law, of conscience, of religion in human affairs, to be superseded henceforth by the christian truth, the truth of God's NATURAL humanity, and he allows the soul no permanent refuge against spiritual illusion and insanity but what it finds in that supreme verity. What renders this lapsed *régime* of law or conscience or religion spiritually odious and intolerable to me, is that it proves a sheer and invariable ministration of death to all my personal hopes God-ward; it proves this, and cannot help proving it, because its ends are primarily public or universal, and mine are primarily private or individual. What I crave with the whole bent of my nature is that God should be propitious to me personally, whatever he may be to all the rest of mankind. I have naturally a supreme regard to myself, although I habitually conceal that fact both from my own sight and that of other people under a flowing drapery of professional benevolence; and what conscience or the law — regarded as a literal divine administration — does, is to inflame my cupidity towards God to such a pitch, as that the thick scales fall at last from my eyes, and I am ready not only to perceive what an unclean and beggarly lout I have always spiritually been in his sight, but also to agree that it were better there were no God at all, than that he should be capable of lending a benignant ear to my hypocritical or dramatic worship.

Understand me here, I beg. I have not the least idea of representing myself as ever having been especially obnoxious to the rebuke of conscience. On the contrary, I am willing to admit that I have been tolerably blameless in all the literal righteousness of the law. It is probable, no doubt, that I have borne actual false-witness on occasion, or committed here and there actual theft, adultery, and murder. I am not in the least interested either to admit or deny any literal imputations of this sort. But the habitual tenor of my life has been undeniably contrary to these practices; and it is only in my spiritual aspect accordingly that I find myself a reprobate. For example, I have been living all my days in great comfort and plenty, when the great mass of my fellow-men are sunken in poverty, and all the ills physical and moral which poverty is sure to breed. From the day of my birth till now I have not only never known what it was to have had an honest want, a want of my nature, ungratified, but I have also been able to squander upon my mere fantastic want, the will of my personal caprice, an amount of sustenance equal to the maintenance of a virtuous household. And yet thousands of persons directly about me, in all respects my equals, in many respects my superiors, have never in all their lives enjoyed an honest meal, an honest sleep, an honest suit of clothes, save at the expense of their own personal toil, or that

of some parent or child, and have never once been able to give
the reins to their personal caprice without an ignominious exposure to severe social penalties. It is, to be sure, perfectly
just that I should be conveniently fed and lodged and clad, and
that I should be educated out of my native ignorance and imbecility, because these enjoyments on my part imply no straitening
of any other man's social resources, and are indeed a necessary
condition of my own social worth. But it is a monstrous affront
to the divine justice or righteousness, that I should be guaran-
teed, by what calls itself society, a life-long career of luxury
and self-indulgence, while so many other men and women every
way my equals, in many ways my superiors, go all their days
miserably fed, miserably lodged, miserably clothed, and die at
last in the same ignorance and imbecility, though not, alas! in
the same innocence, that cradled their infancy. It is our wont,
doubtless, to submit more or less cheerfully to this unholy social
muddle or chaos, and many of us indeed are to be found rejoicing
in it as the fit opportunity of their own lawless aggrandizement, material and moral. But be assured that no one, be he
preacher or philosopher, statesman or churchman, poet or phi-
lanthropist, artist or man of science, can reconcile himself in
heart to it, can reflectively justify it on grounds either of reason
or necessity, either of principle or expediency, without *ipso
facto* turning out an unconscious but most real abettor of spiritual wickedness in high places, and reaping a spiritual damnation
so deep that he will himself be the very last to feel or suspect
its reality.

Now I had long felt this deep spiritual damnation in myself
growing out of an outraged and insulted divine justice, had
long been pent up in spirit to these earthquake mutterings and
menaces of a violated conscience, without seeing any clear door
of escape open to me. That is to say, I perceived with endless
perspicacity that if it were not for the hand of God's providence visiting with constant humiliation and blight every secret
aspiration of my pride and vanity, I should be more than any
other man reconciled to the existing most atrocious state of
things. I knew no outward want, I had the amplest social recognition, I enjoyed the converse and friendship of distinguished
men, I floated in fact on a sea of unrighteous plenty, and I was

all the while so indifferent if not inimical in heart to the divine justice, that save for the spiritual terrors it ever and anon supplied to my lethargic sympathies, to my swinish ambition, I should have dragged out all my days in that complacent sty, nor have ever so much as dreamed that the outward want of my fellows — their want with respect to nature and society — was in truth but the visible sign and fruit of my own truer want, my own more inward destitution with respect to God. Thus my religious conscience was one of poignant misgiving towards God, if not of complete practical separation, and it filled my intellect with all manner of perplexed speculation and gloomy foreboding. Do what I might I never could attain to the least religious self-complacency, or push my devout instincts to the point of actual fanaticism. Do what I would I could never succeed in persuading myself that God almighty cared a jot for me in my personal capacity, i. e. as I stood morally individualized from, or consciously antagonized with, my kind; and yet this was the identical spiritual obligation imposed upon me by the church. Time and again I consulted my spiritual advisers to know how it might do for me to abandon myself to the simple joy of the truth as it was in Christ, without taking any thought for the church, or the interests of my religious character. And they always told me that it would not do at all; that my church sympathies, or the demands of my religious character, were everything comparatively, and my mere belief in Christ comparatively nothing, since devils believed just as much as I did. The retort was as apt as it was obvious, that the devils believed and trembled, while I believed and rejoiced; and that this joy on my part could not be helped, but only hindered, whenever it was allowed to be complicated with any question about myself. But no: the evidently foregone conclusion to be forced upon me in every case was, that a man's religious standing, or the love he bears the church, takes the place, under the gospel, of his moral standing, or the love he bore the state, under the law; hence that no amount of delight in the truth, for the truth's sake alone, could avail me spiritually, unless it were associated with a scrupulous regard for a sanctified public opinion.

Imagine, then, my glad surprise, my cordial relief, when in this state of robust religious nakedness, with no wretchedest fig-

leaf of ecclesiastical finery to cover me from the divine inclemency, I caught my first glimpse of the spiritual contents of revelation, or discerned the profoundly philosophic scope of the
christian truth. This truth at once emboldened me to obey my
own regenerate intellectual instincts without further parley, in
throwing the church overboard, or demitting all care of my religious character to the devil, of whom alone such care is an inspiration. The christian truth indeed — which is the truth of
God's incarnation in our nature, and hence of the ineffable
divine sanctity of our natural bodies, not only in all the compass
of their appetites and passions, but down even to their literal
flesh and bones — teaches me to look upon the church's heartiest malison as God's heartiest benison, inasmuch as whatsoever
is most highly esteemed among men — namely, that private or
personal righteousness in man, of which the church is the special protagonist and voucher — is abomination to God. The
church maintains a jealous profession of the.divinity of Christ,
and fills the earth with the most artfully reiterate and melodious
invocation of his name ; but when it comes practically to interpret this divinity, and apply it to men's living needs. the result
turns out a contemptible quackery, inasmuch as this alleged
union of the divine and human natures endows us helpless par-
takers of the latter nature with no privilege towards God, but
leaves us, unless we are consecrated by some absurd ecclesiastical usage, as far off from the sheltering divine arms, as any
worshipper of Jupiter or the Syrian Astarte. Revelation. on the
contrary, teaches me that Christ's divinity is an utterly insane
pretension, in so far as it implies any personal antagonism on his
part with the rest of mankind, or claims to have been exerted
on his own proper behalf, and not on behalf exclusively of universal man, good and evil, wise and simple, clean and unclean.
In other words, spiritual christianity means the complete secu-
larization of the divine name, or its identification henceforth only
with man's common or natural want, that want in which all men
are absolutely one, and its consequent utter estrangement from
the sphere of his private or personal fulness, in which every
man is consciously divided from his neighbor: so that I may
never aspire to the divine favor, and scarcely to the divine tolerance, save in my social or redeemed natural aspect ; i. e. as I

stand morally identified with the vast community of men of whatever race or religion, cultivating no consciousness of antagonist interests to any other man, but on the contrary frankly disowning every personal hope towards God which does not flow exclusively from his redemption of human nature, or is not based purely and simply upon his indiscriminate love to the race.

Such, as I have been able to apprehend it, is the intellectual secret of Swedenborg; such the calm, translucent depths of meaning that underlie the tormented surface of explication he puts upon the spiritual sense of scripture. In spite of my reverence for the christian letter, perhaps to a great extent because of it, I had never enjoyed the least rational insight into the principles of the world's spiritual administration, until I encountered this naïve, uncouth, and unexampled literature, and caught therein, as I say, my first clear glimpse of the vast intellectual wealth stored up in its new philosophy of nature, or its doctrine of the divine *natural* humanity. The obvious disqualification of my intellect, no doubt, spiritually viewed, lay in my habitually identifying nature, to my own thought, with the created rather than the creative personality. That is to say, inasmuch as the creature to my sensuous imagination appeared to exist absolutely or in himself, and not exclusively in and by the creator, I could not logically help making him responsible for his nature, or whatsoever is legitimately involved in himself. By the *nature* of a thing we mean whatsoever the thing is in itself, and apart from foreign interference ; and so long consequently as we ascribe real and not mere phenomenal personality or character to the creature, we cannot possibly help saddling him with the responsibility of his own nature. The only way to evade this necessity is to deny him all real, and allow him a purely phenomenal, existence, by making his actual life or being to inhere, not in himself, but exclusively in his creator. But who, before Swedenborg, ever dreamt of such a thing? The moral pretension in existence has always been regarded outside of the church as altogether absolute and unquestionable ; and inside the church no machinery exists for its confutation or exhaustion, but the two initiatory rites of Baptism and the Lord's Supper, upon which alone the church was founded : the one rite inferring its subject's complete purgation from any amount of moral defilement his conscience may have contracted, the other his consequent free impletion with any amount of spiritual divine good.

No more than any one else, however, had I compassed the least spiritual apprehension of the church, or divined save in the dimmest manner the endless philosophic substance wrapped up in its two constitutive ordinances. Thus, although I rendered faultless ceremonial homage in my soul to the supreme lordship of Christ (as traditional God-man, or God in our nature), I yet all the while had no distinct conception that the divinity thus ascribed to him implied any really creative or comprehensive relation on his part to our immortal destiny. In fact I utterly ignored his pretension to constitute an utterly new and final — because spiritual — divine advent upon earth, nor ever for a moment therefore supposed it to be pregnant with hostility and disaster to all that our natural understanding has been wont to conceive of under the name of God, and our natural heart has been wont dramatically to worship under that specious and grandiose appellation. Along with the entire christian world, on the contrary, I always conceived of Christ's divinity as an eminently personal and restrictive one, based upon his conceded moral superiority to all mankind, whereas in truth it is a purely spiritual or impersonal one, based upon his actual and undisguised moral inferiority to the lowest rubbish of human kind that faithfully dogged his footsteps, and hung enchanted upon his lips.

The world has had gods many and lords many, but they are one and all eternally superseded and set at naught by the christian revelation of the divine name as being essentially inimical and repugnant to the moral hypothesis of creation, or the existence of any personal relations between the soul and God. It is true that the christian church has never been just to the idea of its founder, has been indeed anything but just to the altogether spiritual doctrine of the divine name he confided to it. From the day of the apostle John's decease down to that of our modern transcendentalism, a midnight darkness has rested upon the human mind in regard to spiritual things — a darkness so palpable at last, so utterly unrelieved by any feeblest starshine of faith or knowledge, that a church has recently set itself

12

up among us which claims to be nothing if not spiritual, and yet, forsooth, excludes Christ from a primacy in its regard, because it can get no conclusive proof of his having been *morally* or *personally* superior to certain other great men, of whom history preserves a memorial! This indeed has been the animus of the church throughout history, to naturalize rather than spiritualize, —to moralize rather than humanize,—the creative name, by identifying it with certain personal interests in humanity rather than those of universal man; by showing it instinct in short with a sectarian or selfish rather than a social or loving temper. It could not possibly have done otherwise in fact, without violating its function as a literal or a ritual economy, which has always been to represent or embody in itself the instincts of the purely natural mind, of the strictly unregenerate heart, towards God.

The church has thus spiritually or unconsciously crucified the divine name, while intending literally or consciously to hallow it. For no man by nature has any other idea of God than that of an almighty and irresponsible being creating all things — not out of his own infinite love and wisdom yearning to communicate their own potencies and felicities to whatsoever is simply not themselves — but out of stark and veritable naught, and merely to subserve his own personal pleasure, his own selfish and vainglorious renown. The conception we naturally cherish of God in his creative aspect is that of an unprincipled but omnipotent conjuror or magician, who is able to create things — i. e. to make them *be* absolutely or in themselves, and irrespectively of other things — by simply willing them to be; and to unmake them therefore, if they do not happen to suit his whim, just as jauntily as he has made them. Now there is no such unprincipled and almighty power as this, nor any semblance of such a power, on the hither side of hell. And the church, accordingly, by massing or embodying in its own distinctive formulas this superstition of the carnal heart, and affording it a *quasi* divine authentication, only succeeds in furnishing the creative spirit in our nature the very imprisonment or appropriation it needs—the identical crucifixion or assimilation it demands—in order finally to transfuse our natural veins with the blood of its own resurgent and incorruptible life. But in spite of all this — in spite of the church's owning only a negative worth, only a representative sanctity — we cannot too gratefully appreciate its proper historic use, which has been to induct the common mind into a gladsome recognition of God's NATURAL HUMANITY, by gradually disgusting or fatiguing it with the conception of an abstract — i. e. an idle, unemployed, or unrelated — divine force in the world.

Deism, as a philosophic doctrine, enjoys only a starveling existence. To be sure, nothing is more congruous with the uncultivated instincts of the heart, than the conception of a self-involved or self-contained deity, — a deity who is essentially sufficient unto himself, and who is therefore a standing discredit, reproach, and menace to whatsoever is not himself. For we who are by nature finite and relative can contrive no other way of honoring God than by making him intensely opposite to ourselves, or projecting him in imagination as far as possible from our personal limitations, from our own finite experience. We do not hesitate to attribute simple or absolute — which is sheerly idiotic — existence to him, an existence-in-himself, or before the world was, and utterly irrelative to his creature; we endow him with all manner of passive personal perfection, such as infinitude of space and eternity of time ; and by way of conclusively establishing his subjection to nature, while at the same time avouching his personal superiority to ourselves, we call him omniscient, omnipresent, and omnipotent, or suppose him literally cognizant of every event in time, literally present in every inch of space, and literally doing whatsoever he pleases, while we do only what we can. No doubt this proceeding is none the less useful for being inevitable on our part. No doubt we thus adequately objectify the divine being to our regard, or get him into conditions at once of such generic nearness to us, and at the same time of such specific remoteness, as to constitute a very fair basis of evolution to any subsequent spiritual intercourse which may take place between us. But this is the sole justification we can allege of the devout natural habit in question. For God has really no absolute but only a relative perfection, no passive but a purely active infinitude. His perfection is no way literal, but a strictly spiritual or creative one, being entirely inseparable save in thought from the work of his hands ; his infinitude a wholly actual or living one, standing in his free communication, or spontaneous abandonment, of himself to whatsoever is not himself. He has in truth no absolute or personal and passive worth, such as we ourselves covet under the name of virtue; no claim upon our regard but a working claim; a claim founded not upon what he is in himself, but upon what he is relatively to others. Our native ignorance of divine things to be sure is so dense, that we cannot help according him a blind and superstitious worship for what he presumably is before creation, or in-himself and out of relation to all other existence. But this nevertheless is sheer stupidity on our part. His sole real claim to the heart's allegiance lies in the excellency of his creative and redemptive name. That is to say, it consists, first, in his so freely subjecting himself to us in all the compass of our creaturely destitution and impotence, as to endow us with physical and moral consciousness, or permit us to feel ourselves absolutely to be; and then, secondly, in his becoming by virtue of such subjection so apparently and exclusively objective to us — so much the sole or controlling aim of our spiritual destiny — as to be able to mould our finite or subjective consciousness at his pleasure, inflaming it finally to such a pitch of sensible alienation from — or felt *otherness* to — both him and our kind, as to make us inwardly loathe ourselves, and give ourselves no rest until we put on the lineaments of an infinite or perfect man, in attaining to the proportions of a regenerate society, fellowship, brotherhood of all mankind.

XXV.

The very great obscurity which attaches to the problem of creation is not, I am persuaded, intrinsic, but altogether extrinsic, arising from our instinctive and inveterate proneness "to put the cart before the horse" in spiritual things, by making what is first in creative order, namely, the object, last, and what is last, namely, the subject, first. The fundamental logic of creation is, that it is real only in so far as it is actual, and not contrariwise; thus that its form determines its substance, or its objective element its subjective one. In other words, the law of all spiritual existence is that doing determines being, or that character is based upon action, not action upon character. Whatsoever one actually does when one is free from the coercion of necessity or the constraint of prudence is the measure of what he really is.

Thus his action when freely exerted determines his being or character, and is itself wholly undetermined by it.

But we are inveterately prone in our instinctual judgments to reverse this law. We habitually conceive that the subjective element in existence or action qualifies the objective one; thus that a man's being qualifies his doing, his character his action; so that, applying this fallacious mental habitude to divine things, we readily conclude that it is the creator who limits or qualifies the creature, and not exclusively the creature who limits or qualifies the creator.

The truth, however, is exactly contrary to this. The subjective element in existence has no other function than to quantify it, i. e. give it material substance or filling out; while its objective element alone qualifies it or gives it spiritual form. My subjective being merely quantifies me, or gives me natural identification with all other men, while my objective action alone qualifies me, i. e. gives me spiritual individuality or characteristic distinction from other men. But if this rule hold true in reference to our ordinary existence and action, it is emphatically true in the sphere of creative action, where we see the creator contributing only the substantial or quantifying element in the result, and the creature himself furnishing its formal or qualifying one. Creation indeed is inconceivable on any less generous terms. What sort of a creation would that be, where nothing was created? And how shall anything be created — i. e. have *being* communicated to it — unless it first exist in its own form, or have selfhood? And what is it "to exist in one's own form," or "to have selfhood." but to exist *naturally*, i. e. to be the joint product of a generic or common substance and a specific or differential form? The statue has no natural base, thus no selfhood or form of its own, to serve for the communication to it of its inventor's being. Hence the statue cannot properly be said to be created, but only invented, imagined, devised. The sculptor does not create it, because he is all unable *to communicate himself* to it, to pass over to it, bag and baggage, in the shape of the material marble. If the sculptor *could* do this, — if he should himself give maternity as well as paternity to his work, give it generic substance as well as specific form, by himself animating the marble out of which the statue is wrought,

so that the statue itself might thenceforth be seen to flower out
of the marble as the grass flowers out of the earth — then indeed
the sculptor might truly be said to create his work, and the statue
would feel a brimming life of its own animating its members.
For this is *fundamental* to the idea of creation, that the creator
give natural existence or self'hood to his creature, since otherwise
the creature will feel no possible ground of spiritual reaction towards the creator; and this can be done of course only by the
creator passing over unreservedly to the created *nature,* making
himself over in all the wealth of his power a prisoner to the nature of his creature, in order that the creature, feeling this infinite potentiality in his nature incessantly stimulating him to like
infinite action, may himself in his turn put on truly divine dimensions. Thus the statue, though it might enjoy physical
consciousness, or the sentiment of its own identity, could never
attain to moral consciousness, or the sentiment of its own individuality, save in so far as the sculptor could afford to immerse
or lose himself to sight in the maternal marble, in order to undergo a resuscitated or glorified existence in the personality of
the statue. If the marble could so completely obscure, i. e. so
completely absorb or take up into itself, the sculptor's being and
activity, as to betray no evidence of his presence in it, so that the
statue should never suspect the truth of the case, nor hesitate
consequently to look upon its material substance as absolutely
its own substance, then of course the statue, in formulating this
judgment to itself, would to its own thought perfectly exclude the
sculptor from the periphery of its conscious life or the sphere of
its subjective experience — that is, from any inward and spiritual
relation to it — and thereby compel him into purely outside or
formal and objective conditions.

Undoubtedly this judgment on the statue's part, and consequent appropriation to itself of its creator's being, would be
strictly fallacious, when viewed absolutely; because in very truth
the sculptor alone furnishes all its subjective being to the statue,
while the statue in its turn supplies him only with objective existence. But yet, evidently, the natural existence of the statue,
or its living creation, would be conditioned upon this same fallacy,
since without it the statue would be forever void of self'hood,
void of subjective life or consciousness, and hence of any real

or objective participation in its sculptor's being. But in point of fact the statue is not created, disclaims any living basis, because it lacks that generic or identical substance, that common quantity, which we call nature (but which in reality is God-in-us, God-man, the lord), and which is essential to all living existence ; and possesses only the specific or individual form, only the differential quality, it derives from man. Hence it is an inanimate or artificial existence, in ghastly contrast with all that lives or grows.

Such then is the indispensable condition of the creator's ever becoming objective, i. e. cognizable to his creature, that he be utterly swamped so to speak in the created *nature*, utterly lost to sight in the creature's subjective consciousness, and know no resurrection from that death but in a new and spiritual or objective creation. Creation means, first of all, giving the creature subjective consciousness, which is felt freedom or selfhood ; it means the endowing of the creature with its own conscious life, its own natural form ; and in order to this the creator must himself *be* its unrecognized generic substance, must himself constitute the sole, patient, unflinching, invisible reality imprisoned in its visible natural form or phenomenality ; because otherwise the creature would be without selfhood or conscious life, and hence without any faculty of spiritual insight, or sympathetic conjunction with its maker. This natural form or appearance of the creature will be indelibly his own, but it will be his by no absolute or unconditional right, but simply because the creator himself is its sole underlying spiritual substance or being, eternally hidden from view, eternally masked from discovery, under the gross mental superstition — the dense mental incubus — we call the world or nature.

It takes but a glance to see how repugnant this entire strain of doctrine is to established maxims, whether practical or speculative. If we cannot help magnifying the subjective element, the element of self, in all our moral and æsthetic judgments,* we surely cannot help doing so with added emphasis and good-will in our judgment of spiritual and divine things. Who of us ever

---

* See Appendix. Note G, for some illustrations of the way in which our practical judgments are habitually betrayed by the absurd preponderance we give to the subjective or phenomenal element in consciousness.

doubts that in creation the creator remains essentially aloof from the created nature, essentially uncommitted to it, when in truth what we call the created *nature* is itself a mere shadow or reflection of the creative effulgence stamped upon our mental horizon, in order to give the creature that necessary background or relief which he requires for his own self-recognition? There is no such *thing* as the created nature. It is a mere phantom of the creature's ignorance by which, in the absence of any spiritual insight, he seeks and contrives to account for his own existence. My moral part, which individualizes me from all lower existence and identifies me only with man, is absolute and suffices unto itself, being a pure fact of consciousness. But my physical part, which identifies me with all lower existence and individualizes me only from man, being a fact of sense, not of consciousness, is anything but absolute, and utterly refuses therefore to be accounted for on any hypothesis short of nature, i. e. short of some middle term between God and myself, giving us that needful subjective distance from each other which is implied in our subsequent objective contact or approximation to each other. Thus nature regarded as existing absolutely, or apart from the mind, is a mere superstition or abject fetch of our ignorance in regard to God, whereby we make out to account for creation on mechanical — whilst we are still untaught to do so on dynamical — principles. Being able as we are to distinguish between creator and creature in thought, we presume they are also distinguishable in fact; whereas in fact they are so utterly undistinguishable — so indissolubly blent, so chaotically commingled or confused — that we inevitably mistake what is logically the creative element (nature) for the created, and what is logically the created (man) for the creative.

In short we never suspect that God is creative only in and by the creature, but, on the contrary, hold him to be so absolutely, or in and by himself exclusively. That is to say, we invariably suppose that the creator is subjectively not objectively constituted. We have no idea that the husband or father is subjectively constituted, for we see very plainly that he is objectively constituted, being what he is as husband and father, not in virtue of himself, but only in virtue of wife and child. Yet we never tire of making this glaring mistake in the higher relation, and insist upon making God subjectively creative, instead of objectively so; creative in and by himself, instead of in and by the creature exclusively; creative by right of *being*, and not by right exclusively of *doing*. We suppose him to be somehow *essentially* a creator, whereas he is only *existentially* so; i. e. he creates only in so far as he objectively exists, or goes forth from himself, from his own subjectivity, from his barren and bleak infinitude, and takes up his abode in the finite, or what is not himself, in what indeed from the nature of the case must logically be the exact and total opposite of himself. The strict truth of creation — which is that the creature owes himself wholly to God, and has no breath of underived being — necessitates that he shall not even appear to be, save by the creator's actual or objective disappearance within all the field of his subjective consciousness; save by the creator's becoming objectively merged, obscured, drowned out, so to speak, in the created subjectivity. The relation between the two is that of substance and form, and you can no more rationally discern where one ends and the other begins than you can sensibly discriminate what is purely material or substantial in the statue from what is purely spiritual or formal. As then the substance of things *is* exclusively by their form, while their form *exists* only from their substance, so whatsoever in existence is created (as having inward *being* given to it) logically exists only by what is creative; while whatsoever is creative (as having outward *existence* given to it) logically subsists only by what is created.

Creator and creature then are strictly correlated existences, the latter remorselessly implicating or involving the former, the former in his turn assiduously explicating or evolving the latter. The creator is in truth the subjective or inferior term of the relation, and the creature its objective or superior term; although in point of fact or appearance the relationship is reversed, the creator being thought to be primary and controlling, while the creature is thought secondary and subservient. The truth incurs this humiliation, undergoes this falsification, on *our* behalf exclusively, who, because we have by nature no perception of God as a spirit, but only as a person like ourselves, are even brutally ignorant of the divine power and ways. But it *is* a sheer humiliation nevertheless. For in very truth it is the creator alone who gives subjective seeming, or phenomenal constitution, to us, only that we, appearing to ourselves thereupon absolutely to be, may ever after give formal existence or objective reality to him. Thus creation is not a something outwardly achieved by God in space and time, but a something inwardly wrought by him within the compass exclusively of human nature or human consciousness; a something subjectively conceived by his love, patiently borne or elaborated by his wisdom, and painfully brought forth by his power; just as the child is subjectively conceived, patiently borne, and painfully brought forth by the mother. Creation is no brisk activity on God's part, but only a long-patience or suffering. It is no ostentatious self-assertion, no dazzling parade of magical, irrational, or irresponsible power; it is an endless humiliation or prorogation of himself to all the lowest exigencies of the created consciousness. In short, it is no finite divine action, as we stupidly dream, giving the creature objective or absolute projection from his creator; it is in truth and exclusively an infinite divine passion, which, all in giving its creature subjective or phenomenal existence, contrives to convert this provisional existence of his into objective or real being, by freely endowing the created nature with all its own pomp of love, of wisdom, and of power.

It is easy to see what an immense revolution Swedenborg accomplishes in philosophy by thus humanizing nature, or resolving it into the mind, into man's subjective consciousness, and so vacating its claim to the rational objectivity which we, misled by sense, erroneously ascribe to it. What we call nature — the generic or universal element in existence — has no right, on Swedenborg's principles, to exist in itself or subjectively, but only as an implication of the human mind. It is a mere outcome or effect in the sphere of sense — a mere lifeless imagery, echo, or correspondence — of a spiritual work of God which is taking place in the invisible depths of the mind, or the realm exclusively of the human consciousness. And if therefore we persist in regarding it as a divine *ens* or finality, we shall not only miss the signal advantage it might, as an image or echo, have rendered us, in making us acquainted with an otherwise inscrutable original, but our intellectual faculty itself will become spiritually bastardized by being put out of all lineal or direct

relation to the divine mind. What alone is objective to the
divine mind is man ; and if therefore we would put our intelligence in harmony with God's, we must be content to see in
nature a mere phenomenal outcome or appanage of man, a mere
shadow or correspondence of the human mind. The natural
universe, on Swedenborg's principles, does not exist to the divine
mind, being destitute of all reality outside of consciousness. It
exists only as an inevitable implication of created thought, its
use being to give logical substance, background, continuity,
coherence, identity, to all the specific or individual details
of the creature's sensible experience. All universals are mentally, not physically, realized. The family, for example, is a
universe of relationship, mentally constituted, extending between
persons who have sprung from the loins of a certain pair, associated for procreative ends. The tribe again is a unit of relationship, mentally constituted, existing among many families ;
and the city in like manner unites or gives universal mental
form to many tribes ; while many cities in their turn go to make
up the mental unity called the nation, which is the highest universality yet realized in human thought. If however the unity
of the race itself had been practically realized by the mind, it
would confess itself a strict unit of relationship existing among
all nations and peoples, and would thus illustrate in its measure
the truth I am enforcing, namely, that the generic or universal
element in existence is always and exclusively a necessity of our
thought, representing or expressing that identity of substance,
that community of being, which to our intelligence subtends
all specific or differential forms. It is in all cases a strict logical
induction, or mental generalization, from a greater or less amount
of specific experience, and it is utterly destitute of real or absolute validity. In short nature is a purely mental fact. It constitutes, itself, indeed the identical mind of the race, what we
call *the common mind* of man ; and we are each of us mentally
qualified or endowed — each of us intellectually energized — in
the degree, not of our merely sensible or isolated and absolute,
but of our rational or relative and associated, discernment : our
discernment, not of mere visible existence, but of the invisible
ratio or relationship which binds all existence in unity. And if
all this be true, then the reader sees at a glance how mistaken

he has always been in viewing human nature, or the human
race, as a physical and not a purely mental or metaphysical
quantity, as a fixed or absolute and not as an exclusively free or
contingent fact.   There is no such *thing* as human nature, outside of men's consciousness ; no such thing as a *race* of man
existing in itself, or independently of our mental experience.
The phrases in question attest no substantive reality, but only an
inevitable infirmity, only a gross superstition, of our carnal
thought, whereby, in our ignorance of God's living or spiritual
perfection, we are prone to account for existence on purely
mechanical or pseudo-rational principles.   Thus human nature is
no fixed or absolute, but an altogether free or empirical quantity,
conditioned at its highest upon such a harmony of interests between each and every man, as amounts to an actual incarnation
of the law of conscience in every individual bosom ; and at its
lowest consequently, upon such a conflict of interests between
man and man as degrades human life to a lower level than that
of the brutes.   The human race, human nature, has no pretension in other words to be livingly or spiritually constituted,
until the twin elements of our consciousness — self and the
neighbor, delight and duty, interest and principle — have been
freed from their inveterate subjective antagonism, and definitively
reconciled or married in an objective society, fellowship, or
brotherhood of man with man throughout the earth.   Conscience, as we have seen, is the sole qualifying, i. e. *creative*,
law of human nature, inasmuch as it alone individualizes man
from the brute, and alone identifies him with himself ; and
what conscience with irresistible sovereignty enforces is the un-
mitigated society, fellowship, equality of all men with each man,
and of each man with all men, throughout the illimitable realm
of God's dominion.

It is all very true then that the generic or universal existence
which we ascribe to things is a purely mental, not a physical experience on our part.   We know only specific or individual
form, and the generic or universal substance we ascribe to such
form under the term " nature," is only a prejudice or superstition
growing out of our ignorance of God's creative perfection, or
of his spiritual and living presence in all existence.   What we
call nature in fact is only a gigantic shadow cast upon the mind

by specific or individual — which is spiritual — form ; a shadow
whose sole substance is the lord, or God-Man : that is, society.
And we must allow it no intellectual tolerance but as such
shadow. But now if we are faithful to this obligation, we shall
at once separate ourselves intellectually from all that is called
religion, or philosophy, or even science almost, upon the earth.
All the recognized leaders of human thought cherish this pesti-
lent superstition in regard to nature's absolute universality ; a
superstition which keeps our reason at the level of sense in
spiritual things, or degrades it into an occasional *haunt* of the
spiritual world, at most, when it ought to be its orderly and permanent home. The current superstition is twofold, as implying,
first, that nature (the world or macrocosm) exists universally or
as a whole, in itself, and without reference to the spiritual world,
which is supposed in fact, if admitted at all, to be simply secondary and subservient thereto ; and secondly, that as such universe
or whole it of course involves man (the mind or microcosm).
Such is the traditional hallucination belonging to our orthodox
ways of thinking both in science and philosophy. All our intellectual scribes and rulers agree in this, that nature is a *being*, and
not merely a *seeming* or appearance. So far indeed are they
from suspecting that she is but the shadow of the human mind
projected upon the senses whereby the mind comes at last to
adequate self-consciousness, that they look upon nature as the
substance, and man himself as the shadow. Swedenborg alone
disenchants the intellect of this illusion, by denying nature as a
true universal, and allowing her only a relative universality, a
universality in relation to our thought, that is, to the innumerable specific forms our thought embraces. All cognition is of
necessity specific or formal (that is, spiritual) ; and what we
postulate as a generic or universal background to such cognition,
or its subject-matter, is a transparent fetch of our ignorance to
supply the lack of a present or living creator. We are willing
for various decorous reasons to admit that God *may* have created
" once upon a time," at some so-called or imaginary beginning
of things ; but that he and he alone spiritually constitutes the
present life, the actual or identical being, of all that our eyes behold, is what we are by no means prepared to acknowledge, and
in defect of such preparation have recourse to nature as a tem-

porary opiate to troublesome thought. Thus what we call nature and objectify to our sensuous imagination as an absolute universality, is at most only a prejudice or false induction of the mind, whereby in its ignorance of God's creative power, or, what is the same thing, of the laws of spiritual being, it instinctively seeks to supply *a common ratio* — to invent *an identical bond or basis* — for all existence.

Nature accordingly does *not* involve the mind. So far indeed is it from involving the mind, that it is itself rigidly involved by the mind as the necessary subjective base of its own objective evolution; just as the marble is involved in the statue, and the mother in the child, as the necessary condition of these latter's existence. In short nature has no existence save in relation to human thought, or as affording needful relief to the specific contents of our senses; and hence to talk of " the order of nature," or " the laws of nature," as if those cheap phrases expressed something more than a subjective cognition, something objective and absolute, some reality in short out of consciousness and binding upon the divine mind, is to talk childish nonsense. These terms are strictly invalid to philosophic thought, save as indicating the constancy of nature's subjection to the mind, to our mental necessities. They merely indicate the use she subserves in furnishing a hypothetical base to science, or giving it provisional flooring, foothold, fixity, during the protracted period of its spiritual infancy, or while it is still ignorant of creative order, and remains a contented dupe to the illusions of space and time. And to allow them any ontological significance therefore, any really creative virtue, is simply to shut the intellect up to the moonlight and starlight of sense, and exclude it from the fervent splendors of the sun of faith.

Yet it is just this unsuspected superstition and imbecility of our natural science, just this hypothetical or supposititious universality it ascribes to nature, that supplies the main existing obstacle to philosophic thought, or the intellectual progress of society. Our science habitually takes for granted, not merely the relative, but the absolute universality of nature; not merely her universality with respect to all mineral, vegetable, and animal existence, but her universality with respect to herself, her universality so to speak in the divine sight; and hence we habitually rule out the divine or spiritual as a vital element in consciousness, or legitimate factor in existence.* For if there be a generic or universal existence, which is not merely the logical or contingent — but the real or absolute — ground of all specific or individual form, then of course all higher, or spiritual and divine, existence becomes *ipso facto* excluded, and our long and patient hope of immortality turns out unfounded. The essential of nature is passivity or community; i. e. the predominance of substance to form, of subject to object. The essential of spirit again is activity or difference; i. e. the predominance of the formal or objective element in consciousness over its substantial or subjective element. It is obvious accordingly that the spiritual realm must be absolutely barred out of our intellectual cognizance, so long as the mind remains a prey to the illusions of our natural science, or holds nature to be a direct manifestation of divine power. It was the uniform result of Swedenborg's protracted intellectual intercourse with spirits and angels, that he found no form of spiritual existence either intelligible or conceivable, save upon the hypothesis of nature's rigid involution in man, or its essential subserviency to the soul. The fundamental difference he discovers between the good and evil spirit, or angel and devil, is that the latter confirms himself in the persuasion of nature's absoluteness, or her real universality, while the former holds her existence to be purely logical, — i. e. purely superficial and apparitional, like the image of one's person in a glass, — and pronounces every contrary judgment to be a fallacious inference from sense.

XXVI.

But I must bring my labor to a close, or else give my book a bulk which it was not designed to have.

Let me assure the reader, then, that he need not look beyond this doctrine of nature's essential relativity to the human understanding, her strict convertibility in fact with the mind of the race, to find the very clew he craves to Swedenborg's unprecedented and immortal services to philosophy. The sole and complete meaning of nature, philosophically regarded, is, according

* See Appendix, note II.

to Swedenborg, to furnish a logical ultimate or phenomenal background to the human mind in its spiritual infancy, in order that
the mind, being thus objectively mirrored to itself, might present
a subjective floor or fulcrum every way apposite to the opera-
tions of the creative spirit. This, neither more nor less, is
Swedenborg's philosophic secret. If nature, or the realm of the
indefinite, did not at least logically intervene between creator and
creature, or infinite or finite, giving the latter sensible projection
from the former, or provisional reality to its own perception, the
creature might still claim a physical existence conditioned upon
the equilibrium of plenty and want, or pleasure and pain, but he
would be utterly destitute of that moral or rational consciousness
conditioned upon the equilibrium of good and evil, or of the
divine and human *natures*, upon which nevertheless his entire
spiritual being and destiny are grounded. Thus the sole and
perfect key to Swedenborg's ontology, either for the present or
any future world, is his point-blank denial of the ontological
postulate save in the strictest reference to created existence.
His entire ontologic doctrine is summed up in the literal veracity
of CREATION, meaning by that term the truth of God's NATURAL
HUMANITY, or of a most living and actual unition of the divine
and human natures, avouching itself within the compass of man's
historic consciousness, and generating there the stupendous har-
monies of a spontaneous human society, fellowship, or brotherhood.

Let the reader remember then that what forever separates
Swedenborg intellectually from the fanatic, or man of mere
faith, on the one hand, and from the sceptic, or man of mere
science, on the other, is that he never looks upon nature as an
ontological but only as a psychological phenomenon. He does
not regard it as being, but only and at best as seeming to be. It
is an appearance or semblance of being to an intelligence still
uninstructed in the divine perfection. The ontological assumption which is common to our technical faith and our technical
science alike is gross and revolting to Swedenborg, because it
implies that nature not only *actually appears to be*, but in truth
really is, quite independently of such appearance ; that she not
only exists provisionally or in relation to the wants of our intelligence, but exists also absolutely or in herself, and out of rela-

tion to that intelligence. Mr. Mansel and Mr. Mill both alike assume nature's finality, or conceive her to be a veritable divine end, in place of a mere means to an end. They both alike (and quite unconsciously of course) suppose her to be an absolute and not a mere logical existence; suppose her to constitute an obvious objective explanation of our being, and hence are at a hopeless remove from ever so much as suspecting her to be a mere subjective implication of our thought. And being thus identified in their philosophic origin, they can hardly expect to be widely separated in their philosophic destiny. In fact their gathering philosophic doom simulates that of the fabled Kilkenny cats, which having been conjoined by the tail, and then hung upon a clothes-line to struggle together with what hearty mutual aversion they might, could only struggle into, and not out of, each other's fatal embrace. Indeed everybody, religious or scientific, who holds to nature as a true universal and to man consequently as a true individual, is spiritually a Kilkenny cat, with his lower parts affronting the sky, and his higher parts caressing the earth. And precisely what Swedenborg does for the intellect is to release it from this enforced feline posture, and restore it to upright and comfortable human form. That is to say, he teaches us inflexibly to deny and, if need be, to deride nature's pretension to be anything more than a visual surface or shadow of reality stamped upon our mental sensory, just as a photographic negative is only a visual surface or shadow of some person or thing stamped upon a sensitive plate.

Here I suppose I ought to conclude; but I cannot, in fairness to the reader, do so without a word or two in practical application of the doctrine we have been canvassing to the question of idealism.

The foible of our existing metaphysic is, as we have seen, that it accepts without misgiving the scientific postulate of an absolute or ontological basis for existence, and hence utterly voids the spiritual truth of creation. Indeed the only foe philosophy has encountered from the beginning — at least the only one capable of impeding her march to universal empire — is idealism: which is the pretension to confer upon existence a noumenal as well as phenomenal quality, or invest it with its own individuality no less than its own identity. Idealism is philosophy turned upside down. That is to say, it amounts doctrinally to such an affiliation of the objective to the subjective element in consciousness, of the *not-me* to the *me*, of being to existence, form to substance, individuality to identity, as renders creation simply impossible, and puts a point-blank contradiction upon science. It is philosophy mimicking the sport of children, whom we occasionally see bowing their heads till they bring them to a level with their feet, in order that they may catch a glimpse through their legs of an inverted world. And even idealism would have been a harmless foe to philosophy if it had ever been a frank and open one ; if it had not always been domiciled under her roof, and professed a sturdy friendship for her, while secretly working her downfall. For the aim of philosophy is twofold : 1. To discriminate between the spiritual or objective, and the material or subjective contents of existence ; and 2. To hold the latter in rigid and rightful abeyance to the former. And what could be half so sure to defeat these aims as the empiricism of her professed adepts, who in accepting the testimony of sense, or a science conformed to sense, as final, first subvert her lively oracles by sinking the objective being of things in their subjective existence, and then coolly inflate the latter element to divine or absolute dimensions? The idealist maintains that everything visible is exhaustively mortgaged to an invisible essence or subjectivity, which Plato and Hegel call its idea, and Kant its noumenon ; and that this inmost essence or subjectivity of the thing, constituting as it does the very self of its self, is the sole secret of its phenomenal apparition. And what does this amount to, unless it be to supersede the creator by the creature, or, what is the same thing, swamp the wholly unconscious and unselfish being of things in their wholly conscious and selfish existence, and thence reproduce it in glorified egotistic form? In fact creation, according to idealism, and especially according to the Hegelian or consummate form of the doctrine, is the sincere, unaffected, apotheosis of egotism. And when philosophy has grown so anile and so blear-eyed to the proper objects of her contemplation, as to accept this rubbish of idealism, or consent to see in God only the infinite potentiality of our own finite conceit and imbecility, it is no wonder that the common sense of mankind votes philosophy herself a nuisance of the first order, and cries aloud for some fresh resurgent form of heavenly truth.

But idealism is not original even in its aberrations. It is at most an attempted systematization of one of the vulgarest prejudices of the human understanding. What Kant means by his *noumenon* or *thing-in-itself*, what Plato and Hegel mean by their creative *idea* of things, is simply to objectify or render absolute the subjective element in consciousness, by making it supply its own genesis or ground of being; so getting well rid forever of an actual or living creation. And this is exactly what we all mean when, under the coercion of the sensuous understanding, we attribute to ourselves, as we habitually do, an objective individuality answering to our subjective identity; a spiritual reality commensurate with our natural phenomenality. The only difference between these philosophers and the people is this, and it is not to the advantage of the former: they reflectively *confirm* what to the latter remains a mere instinctual fallacy, and so exclude themselves from intellectual daylight. But we all alike instinctively practise the same hallucination. We all tacitly attribute to ourselves a noumenal or real quantity as the background of our actual or phenomenal quality, and on that assumption appropriate to ourselves any amount of absolute good and absolute evil. Our moral instinct, our *feeling* of selfhood or freedom, is so sincere and unhesitating, is so *natural* in a word, that we cannot help claiming an absolute property in every word we say, and every deed we do; so that whenever we happen to say or to do what our conscience approves or disapproves, we never suspect that both word and deed are a strictly normal effect of causes as impersonal or universal as those which regulate the phenomena of physics, but on the contrary flatter ourselves that we are absolutely good or absolutely evil persons, who have the identical power which God has, of originating our own actions, or acting above law.

But however this may be, whether idealism be a mere Adamic taint in the blood, or whether it be the legitimate outcome of exceptional fatuity, it is in all its forms the standing reproach of philosophy, keeping it forever oscillating, as men's temperaments chance to incline them, between a frigid atheism and a torrid pantheism. The one very fruitful idea which it

is pledged to demolish — in the interest of the utterly unfruit-
ful ones it is pledged to maintain — is the idea of creation as a
living or actual operation of divine power; and it does this by
turning the creator logically into undeveloped creature, and the
creature into developed creator. And philosophy has not an
hour's honest vocation upon earth, if it be not to demonstrate
the spiritual or ever-living truth of creation, in showing us that
however much we may subjectively expand and collapse, however much we may rejoice and mourn, however comparatively
enlarged we may become in knowledge and wisdom, or comparatively sunken we may remain in ignorance and superstition,
we are all these things only to the extent of our own finite consciousness, and without the slightest corresponding compromise
of objective or spiritual realities. No doubt the spiritual creation implies the indissoluble marriage of creature and creator in
order to vitalize it, just as the material cosmos implies a union
of substance and form, subject and object, genus and species, in
order to vitalize it. But this union is no passive or barren one
in either case, but a most living or productive union; the parties to it not being united *in se* or subjectively, which would be
to confound or identify them, but only in prolification or objectively, which is to insure their utmost individuality or difference.
It is impossible, in short, that there should be any subjective
identity, but only the utmost conceivable subjective antagonism
between creator and creature; for the one is all fulness, the
other all want; the one all power, the other all dependence.
The only unity they can aspire to consequently is an objective
one, and objective unity is founded upon subjective diversity,
being valid or feeble just as that diversity is profound or superficial. Now manifestly the subjective antagonism of creator and
creature can never become avouched, and consequently their
objective unity never become realized, unless creation be organized first of all on a *natural* basis; that is to say, upon the basis
of the creature's felt or conscious identity in himself, and thence
of his logical diversity from the creator.

In short, the criterion between a true and a false philosophy
is to be found in the estimate they severally put upon the subjective element in experience, or the function of consciousness;
as whether it furnishes a direct or only an inverse analogy of

the creative truth. The absolute truth of course — the truth of which we are wholly *unconscious* — is that God alone gives us being, and that unceasingly; that in him we live and move and have our being at every moment. The apparent or phenomenal truth — the only truth of which we are or can be conscious — is that we have our life or being in ourselves; and hence that the creative relation to us is not inward or spiritual, involving our natural generation, or the gift of selfhood to us, as form involves substance, but exclusively an outward or moral relation, evolving our personal absoluteness towards him, as substance evolves form, and legitimating therefore on our part every extreme of alternate hope and fear. Idealism makes this fallacious testimony of consciousness absolute in objectifying the *me*, or giving it a noumenal as well as phenomenal truth, an unconscious as well as a conscious validity. It first denaturalizes the *me*, or discharges it of finiteness, by making nature properly objective to it under the name of the *not-me;* and then of course it is left free to spiritualize it, or run it into infinitude, by giving it a noumenal or unconscious existence more real and valid than its phenomenal or conscious one. This pretension gives of course an effectual *quietus* to creation, save in the most juggling and mendicant sense of the term; for if I have not only a phenomenal or conscious subjectivity, but also, and much more a noumenal or unconscious one, it is not of the least importance where you see fit to place it, — whether *in* God or out of him, — for it is essentially absolute or underived; and I consequently am an uncreated being, whatever sensible appearances and rational probabilities may be alleged to the contrary.

A true philosophy — a philosophy consonant with the mind's perennial needs — feels none of this morbid itching to inflame the subjective element in consciousness to absolute or objective dimensions, and contentedly leaves it purely phenomenal. Why? Because what alone a true philosophy has at heart is to vindicate the spiritual truth of creation; and it perceives accordingly at a glance that that truth can never be vindicated, but only refuted, if the creature may rightfully claim *in himself* not merely an actual or conscious life, but also a real or unconscious and absolute one. For in that case evidently the created subjectivity overlaps and appropriates to itself the creative one;

and creation philosophically viewed is anything but the subjective
muddling or confounding of creator and creature, which the
Hegelian dialectic makes of it. It is in fact their sharpest possible,
or infinite and eternal, subjective discrimination in order to their
only possible subsequent objective union.   The inexpugnable
necessity of all true creation is, that the creature be subjectively
or *in se* totally alien to, and unidentified with, the creator ; for
unless there be this subjective disunion to begin with, how shall
we claim their subsequent objective or spiritual union ?   Obviously if the statue, the house, the pump, the watch, the table,
the pitcher, the ship, the engine, I make or give ideal form to, becomes actually made only in so far as I concede to the demands
of its subjectivity, in giving it projection from myself by the
mediation of some neutral substance, so *a fortiori* the things
which God creates or gives moral form to can only become
created in so far forth as he endows them first of all with subjective existence or selfhood, which shall eternally alienate
them from — i. e. make them *other than* — himself.   If the lifeless things we make subjectively alienate themselves from us
their maker, and ally themselves exclusively with the base
material out of which they are made, so with far greater reason
must the living creatures of God repugn all subjective identity
with their creator, and tolerate at most only an objective or unconscious relation to him.   I say " with far greater reason " :
for manifestly the disproportion between creator and creature is
infinitely greater than that between maker and made : between
painter and picture, for example : so that whatever can be alleged
in the way of contrast between the constituents of the lesser relation is infinitely more true in application to those of the
grander relation.   If then the unconscious effigy of man I produce from the reluctant marble, vividly disown all substantial
or subjective identity with myself, in restricting my activity to
the interests exclusively of its ideal form, or objective individuality, much more vividly must the breathing, conscious, exultant
man himself refuse to identify his proper subjectivity or selfhood with the power that creates him ; and relegate the total
activity of that power to the depths of his spiritual, objective,
and therefore unconscious being.

Thus a true philosophy will never be found exalting the *me*, or subjective element in experience, out of conscious or phenomenal into absolute or noumenal proportions; for the simple but sufficing reason that any such procedure must be fatal to the integrity of creation, and hence to consciousness. For consciousness is the invariable badge of created existence, being the product in every case of a marriage between creator and creature; and if accordingly you divest my subjectivity of its purely conscious or phenomenal character, as you do when you make it noumenal or absolute, you instantly reduce me to essential unconsciousness, or turn me into uncreated being, which is God. The only guaranty of continued or permanent existence which I as a created being enjoy, is what is furnished by my ineffaceable natural identity. Destroy this, and you destroy my sole and total ground of consciousness, or doom me to absorption in the infinite. The more thoroughly and exquisitely I am myself — the more intense and expansive my self-consciousness — the more thorough and exquisite, of course, on the one hand, will be my subjective or *felt* alienation from God, but also and for this very reason, on the other hand, the more profound and intimate my objective or real sympathy and conjunction with him. No doubt the creative love is infinite, or will always be able to bless its creature beyond his hopes or desires. But a prior condition of such beatitude on the creature's part is, that he exist in himself, enjoy phenomenal selfhood or freedom, undergo subjective or conscious estrangement from his creator. If, for example, the creature should be in himself or naturally godlike, he could not be accessible to the subsequent divine benefaction, because he would already possess in himself or absolutely whatsoever such benefaction implies. But if, on the contrary, he be *self*-alienated, *self*-projected, *self*-distanced from God to the extent of a sheer oppugnancy, he will then be in the best — and indeed only — possible condition of receptivity towards the divine communication, and will react upon it with the total force of his nature. Hence I say that God spiritually creates us or causes us objectively to be, only in so far as he empowers us first of all subjectively to appear, or exist in our own natural lineaments, our own inextinguishable self-consciousness: which is only saying, in a less concise way, that our natural or moral history is a necessary involution, and not evolution, of our spiritual creation.

I hope that none of my readers will dispose himself to reject these observations, simply because they are in advance of received maxims. It is my own firm conviction that the real source of the popular disesteem into which philosophy has fallen, is traceable to nothing in philosophy itself, but exclusively to the indolent and imbecile habit philosophers have of confounding philosophy with science, or identifying the realm of our spiritual being with that of our moral or natural existence.

Our moral existence — our natural manhood — is a mere constitutional implication of our spiritual being ; a mere incident of our God-ward or objective possibilities ; and hence it is void to philosophy of substantive or independent worth. Philosophy — it cannot be too sharply nor too often affirmed — is directly concerned only with truths of *being*, which lie within or above consciousness.   Science, on the contrary, is directly concerned only with facts of *existence*, which lie without or below consciousness. In other words, the realm of philosophy proper is the unconscious realm, the realm of the *not-me ;* while the realm of science is exclusively the conscious realm, the realm of the *me.* Briefer still, philosophy deals only with man's inorganic interests : science with his organic ones.   These two realms — the organic and inorganic one, the *me* and the *not-me*, science and philosophy — are subjectively most opposite, being objectively fused or united only in life, which is the experience of a rational subject.   For example : I am identified to my own consciousness with my organization, that is to say, with the realm of my relations to nature and my fellow-man, and so far of course I am a legitimate object of scientific research, analysis, and augury.   But I am yet all the while being unconsciously *individualized* — i. e. set free from the bondage of my natural identity, lifted above the realm of my relations to nature and society — by a most subtle inward chemistry which converts all that luxuriant show of moral life in me into an evidence or attestation of a profounder spiritual death.   Were I left to the sole tutelage of my rational instincts, or the conclusions of the scientific understanding, I should doubtless never detect this subterranean murmur of death, nor ever dream consequently of that realm of life immortal and ineffable, to which death is the only practicable passage.   On the contrary, I should go on to suppose

that everything really is as it seems; and that our true individuality consequently is not the regenerate spiritual one we derive from God, but the generic moral one which we derive from
our race or past ancestry. But conscience is the divine safeguard interposed to obviate this fatality. It is the cherubic
sword which turns every way to bar all access to the tree of life,
on the part of those who contentedly munch the fruit of the tree
of knowledge of good and evil, and demand no diviner nourishment. Or, to say the same thing in less figurative speech, the
incessant office of conscience, wherever it exists in unadulterate
potency, is to give its subject a pungent conviction of the
spiritual disease, disorder, and death which vitalize his most
flowering and fruitful and faultless moral consciousness; a living
experience of the abject and absolute dearth of good which
underlies and inwardly answers to all that outward vigor and
plenitude of life.

The regenerate individuality which is thus wrought in us by
the divine power, through the humiliation of our moral righteousness, is, I repeat, a totally unconscious one, being made up
of our relations to a good which is infinite, and a truth which is
absolute. It is not therefore, however, any the less, but only
all the more real. The sole realm of unreality is the conscious
realm, the realm of the *me;* because manifestly the *me* is a purely
finite or phenomenal existence, conditioned as to its lower or
sensitive forms upon a rigid equilibrium of pleasure and pain,
and as to its higher or rational and moral forms, upon a rigid
equilibrium of good and evil; and incapable in either case of
surviving a permanent disturbance of such equilibrium. Let
pleasure or pain acquire an absolute ascendency in my organization, and the organization will instantly cease to endure. Let
good or evil obtain an absolute ascendency of my will, and the
will itself instantly disappears. Our voluntary, which is our
moral and rational force, is contingent upon such an exact
though unrecognized balance of good and evil in the social
sphere, or the world of our relations to our fellow-men, as leaves
us *consciously* free, or invests us with the felt ownership of our
own actions: just as our instinctual or sensitive life, which is
what we have in common with mineral, plant, and animal, is
contingent upon such an exact though unrecognized balance of

pleasure and pain in the physical sphere, or the realm of our relations to nature, as makes us *sensibly* free, or invests us also
with the felt ownership of our appetites and passions. We
have no absolute, but only a conscious or phenomenal, control
either of our own actions or our own passions; all the power we
possess in either case being contingent upon our relations to
nature and society. And if this be so, if our conscious life,
the experience we have of ourselves as posited by nature and
society, claim no absolute but only a contingent worth, no objective but only a subjective reality, then clearly we are justified
in saying that the conscious realm, the realm of the *me*, is with
respect to the unconscious realm, the realm of the *not-me*, a
pure illusion or unreality; and hence that whatsoever legitimate
interest it affords to science, all whose research is limited to what
is finite and relative in existence, it yet offers only a reflected
interest to philosophy, since philosophy never sees in the finite
anything but a most specious mask or cloak of the infinite, in
the relative anything but a most subtle revelation of the absolute;
with a view in both cases alike to the gradual and eventually
complete propitiation of our obdurate and brutish intelligence.

Thus philosophy is science no longer controlled by sense, but
enlightened by revelation. Science instructed by sense puts
an eternal divorce between creator and creature, by reciprocally
finiting them, or proving them both alike subject to the laws of
space, time, and person. But science enlightened by revelation
reciprocally infinites creator and creature, i. e. denies every
real and allows only a logical contrariety between them, by
showing the laws of space, time, and person to be sheerly illusory, as possessing a purely subjective and by no means objective virtue. That is to say, it exhibits a doctrine of creation
which perfectly reconciles the creative and the created natures,
by showing the creature (subjectively regarded) to be the
creator himself *naturally finited:* i. e. identified with all animal, all vegetable, and all mineral substance; and the creator
(objectively regarded) to be the creature himself *spiritually
infinited:* i. e. individualized in human form, and eternally redeemed from all mineral, vegetable, and animal limitation. He
is our substance, and we are his form or semblance. He is our
being, and we are his seeming or image. But as the law of the

form or image is, that it be *in itself* an inversion of the substance which projects it, so the whole aim of God's providence in nature and history is to redeem us from the tyranny of this law, by converting us out of inverse natural images of his perfection, into a direct spiritual likeness of it ; which he does by exalting our consciousness out of its physical and moral rudiments, into perfected social and æsthetic form. Practically then, according to Swedenborg, the one thing needful to the permanent reconstruction of philosophy, is its frank, intelligent acknowledgment of the divine NATURAL humanity: crucified, dead, and buried in all the forms of our natural — or physical and moral — consciousness, in which the *vir*, or feminine and individual element, is seen to be pitiably servile to the *homo*, or masculine and universal element ; but glorified, risen again, triumphant over death and hell, in all the forms of our regenerate — or social and æsthetic — consciousness, where the *homo* or created man is seen no longer coercing, but assiduously promoting, the *vir* or creative man. This appears to me the plain philosophic import of Swedenborg's teaching, that our intellectual resurrection out of the mire of sense — which is the final evolution of the human mind in complete harmony with God's perfection — is rigidly contingent upon our renouncing our old and fallacious subjective conception of life, as being primarily universal or natural, and only subordinately thereto individual or spiritual, and cordially acknowledging it henceforth in its new or real and objective aspect, as being essentially spiritual or individual, and only existentially, i. e. by the strictest derivation thence, natural or universal. In other words, the future progress of the mind depends upon our faithfully separating between two things which have been hitherto hopelessly confounded, being and existence, life and death, freedom and bondage : the former interest comprehending the entire realm of man's social and æsthetic objectivity, which lifts him forever out of himself and allies him eternally with God, by making delight not duty, spontaneity not will, freedom not force, the exclusive rule of his action ; the latter comprehending the entire realm of his physical and moral subjectivity, which immerses him eternally in himself, by making him and keeping him the helpless and dishonored tool of nature and convention.

APPENDIX.

APPENDIX.

NOTE A. Page 12.

In recommending Mr. White's biography to my readers as altogether
the best life of Swedenborg extant. I feel bound to say at the same
time that I differ from him utterly in many of his incidental judgments
of Swedenborg. some of which seem to me simply prudish. and almost
wilfully ungracious and ungenerous to his subject, notably those relating
to the inferential injustice done by Swedenborg to woman. I cannot
help thinking that Mr. White's private animosity to the swedenborgian
sect has insensibly tempted him to a somewhat capricious disregard
of his author's fair fame before the world. Every sincere student of
Swedenborg — that is to say, every one who appreciates the enormous
but distinctively impersonal or philosophic benefits his books are destined to confer upon the intellect — must along with Mr. White regret
to see his harmless name perverted to the ends of a petty sectarian
ambition, and even made to sanction what seems to be a particularly
gratuitous exhibition of ecclesiastical zeal. But this sort of thing
should not tempt us into any injustice towards Swedenborg himself,
who has as little responsibility for it as the babe unborn. Indeed I
should be sorry to hold the members of the swedenborgian sect themselves responsible for the glamour they have cast upon Swedenborg's
good name. On the contrary, I feel a sincere respect for these gentlemen, within the very limited range of my knowledge of them, and am
very glad to concede that nothing but the insane spirit of sect could
have tempted men so amiable to engage in their unhandsome enterprise.
None of the older sects parades a pretension at once so senseless and so
blasphemous as they do, when they advertise themselves to the world
as the New Jerusalem, or the end of all divine prophecy and promise
for man upon earth and in heaven. Just conceive of the New
Jerusalem deliberately posing for the world's recognition ! In fact
just think of any one who has ever breathed a breath of God's life in
our nature. turning out such an incontinent peacock as to publish the
fact, or overtly profess to constitute a divine consummation in the
earth ! No doubt these persons would promptly disown, in their civic

capacity, the small and vulgar arrogance they habitually exhibit in their ecclesiastical aspect. But what does this prove? Nothing whatever but that they unwittingly allow their sectarian animus gravely to compromise the unblemished private repute which they would otherwise be entitled to enjoy.

My friend, the Rev. Mr. Barrett, put forth a little book not long since bearing upon the sins of his people, which was entitled *Catholicity of the New-Church, and Uncatholicity of New-Churchmen*, and in which he undertook to show, while viewing the new church as a strict ecclesiasticism, that it had no right whatever to an ecclesiastical temper. I never could comprehend the logic of my friend's demonstration. For surely if the new church be ecclesiastically constituted, its members can hardly do otherwise than cultivate an ecclesiastical spirit. If what my friend calls the new church be catholic in its spirit, then surely new-churchmen cannot be uncatholic in theirs. For, as Mr. Barrett's favorite author would say, churchmen *exist* only from the church, as the church in its turn *subsists* only by them. There is no church without churchmen, and no churchmen without a church; any more than there is a soul without a body, or a body without a soul. Whatsoever any visible church is, its members are, and whatsoever its members are the church is. If Mr. Barrett hold that the new church is a corporate organization with corporate rites and ceremonies, he has no business to go beyond its visible corporeity to get at its soul or spirit. What is visible about it alone declares what is invisible, and he has manifestly no right to allege of the latter what does not strictly belong to the former. If the church be catholic its members must be catholic, for the simple reason that the church has no existence apart from its members. If, again, Mr. Barrett holds that the church is a spiritual institution exclusively, being nothing less than the invisible life of God in the soul of man, then clearly its members are not to be carnally but spiritually discerned and estimated. So far as they belong to the church, they are invisible to the eye of sense, and reveal their existence only to those who are of a similar spirit or character with them. In this state of things Mr. Barrett is entitled to say: "The new church is catholic in spirit, and any specific A, B, or C who foolishly parades its name to the exclusion of the rest of mankind is therefore a spiritual sot." But he is not entitled to say abstractly, that while the new church is catholic, new-churchmen themselves have any power to be otherwise.

The fact is, Mr. Barrett has been keeping bad company, and has thereby got his perceptions somewhat clouded. He is a lover of Swedenborg, a disinterested lover, who values his author for his broad

human worth altogether, and not for any advantage which may possibly
accrue to his own ecclesiastical ambition.   Having this honest admiration of Swedenborg, it naturally afflicts him to see his great services to
mankind attempted to be monopolized by the preposterous little sect
which unblushingly styles itself *The New Jerusalem* (or God's finished
work in human nature), and thus betrays Swedenborg to the just suspicion of all modest persons.   Mr. Barrett's book proves that these
people know nothing worth telling of Swedenborg, and that they are
capable, in their corporate capacity, of a petty ecclesiastical tyranny and
dishonesty which the more experienced sects are getting ashamed of.
But then the wonder is that he should afflict himself with their mis-
deeds.   Why does he not rather abandon the whole concern, and bless
God, as Dogberry says, that he is rid of an encumbrance?   The reason
doubtless is that Mr. Barrett himself is still too much victimized by
that wretched sophistry which forever unspiritualizes the church, in
identifying it with some specific apparatus of priest and sacrifice that
once symbolized it when it was itself nonexistent, or as yet only in
the gristle.

   He is thus all the while unconsciously ministering to the spirit he
condemns.   For it is impossible that any man, or any set of men,
should esteem themselves personally or ritually more acceptable to
God than others, without being to that extent spiritually depraved.
As long, therefore, as Mr. Barrett and other conscientious students of
Swedenborg fidget themselves about *any* ecclesiastical organization
whatever, as falling within the scope of new church principles, this
little sect, that now worries them so much, will never be hurt, but only
helped by their opposition.   For, with the class of people who can be
duped by this shallow conception of the church, a present possession of
the territory in dispute is nine points of the law.   The sect, in short,
needs advertising; and Mr. Barrett, in spite of himself, is made to supply this want, so long as he makes the new church a visible economy
in the earth, and only quarrels with some peculiarities of its transient
administration.

   The swedenborgian sect assumes to be the New Jerusalem, which is
the figurative name used in the Apocalypse to denote God's perfected
spiritual work in human nature; and under this tremendous designation
it is content to employ itself in doing — what? why in pouring new
wine into old bottles with such a preternatural solicitude for the tena-
city of the bottles, as necessitates an altogether comical indifference to
the quality of the wine.   New wine cannot safely go into old bottles
but upon one condition, which is, that the wine had previously become
swipes, or was originally very small beer.   In fact, the swedenborgian

14

sect, viewed as to its essential aims, though of course not as to its professed ones, is only on the part of its movers a strike for higher wages, that is, for higher ecclesiastical consideration than the older sects enjoy at the popular hands. And like all strikes, it will probably succumb at last to the immense stores of fat (or popular respect) traditionally accumulated under the ribs of the old organizations, and enabling them to hybernate through any stress of cold weather, merely by sucking their thumbs, or without assimilating any new material. No doubt the insurgents impoverish the older sects to the extent of their own bulk; but they do not substantially affect them in popular regard, because the people, as a rule, care little for truth, but much for the good that animates it; very little for dogmas, but very much for that undeniably human substance which underlies all dogmas, and makes them savory, whether technically sound or unsound. And here the new sect is at a striking disadvantage with all its more ancient competitors; for these are getting ashamed of their old narrowness, and are gradually expanding into some show of sympathy with human want. The sect of the *soi-disant* New Jerusalem, on the other hand, deliberately empties itself of all interest in the hallowed struggle which society is everywhere making for her very existence against established injustice and sanctified imposture, in order to concentrate its energy and prudence upon the washing and dressing, upon the larding and stuffing, upon the embalming and perfuming, of its own invincibly squalid little *corpus*. This pharisaic spirit, the spirit of separatism or sect, is the identical spirit of hell; and to attempt compassing any consideration for one's self at the divine hands, by making one's self to differ from other people, or claiming a higher divine sanctity than they enjoy, is to encounter the only sure damnation. According to Swedenborg, or rather according to the gospel of the lord Jesus Christ, of which he was in all things the unflinching echo, a literal or differential righteousness among men is incompatible with their spiritual safety; because every man is saved by virtue of his unity with his kind, and not in contravention of it. In short, natural fact or seeming is, according to the evangelic doctrine, the invariable inverse of spiritual truth or being; and the most faultless surface, therefore, of outward or moral decorum, is apt to cover the most odious depths of inward or spiritual obliquity.

Let the reader then, whatever else he may fairly or foolishly conclude against Swedenborg, acquit him point-blank of countenancing this abject ecclesiastical drivel, this sectarian "second childhood and mere oblivion," with which people who ought to know better are availing themselves of the popular ignorance concerning him, to push themselves into ecclesiastical consideration. No one who comes to Sweden-

borg's books without some latent intention to eke out his own dilap-
idated ecclesiastical drapery by skilful picking and stealing among the
angels, can help seeing that no more unsavory name than his could
possibly be employed wherewith to bait sectarian mouse-traps. He is
no blear-eyed Rip Van Winkle dug up out of the drowsy past to affront
the lively present, but a man of the freshest sympathies, and principles
that contemplate only the broadest or most impersonal human issues.
In a word, he is an unaffectedly genial, wise, and good man, all the
higher parts of whose mind are bathed in the peace and light of heaven,
and who aspires to no manner of leadership among men, because the
access of an interior life has weaned him from that restless bondage.
And yet, to say nothing of the endless charm of truth in reference to
the highest themes in which Swedenborg's writings abound, it seems to
me that the unconscious incomparable realism of their style prophesies
a new literature. How a man can leave his own personality so wholly
behind him as to disown every faintest grimace of conventional literary
art, and become absolutely lost to your regard in the sheer splendor of
the truth he recounts, is a daily wonder to me.

The gigantic reach of the man's mind, too, in bringing back every
subtlest ineffable splendor of heaven, and every subtlest ineffable horror of hell, to the purest phenomenality, to the mere shadowy attestation, positive and negative, of a *Divine Natural Manhood*, which
they are both alike impotent to create, or even by themselves to constitute; his vast erudition, untouched by pedantry, and never for an instant lending itself to display; his guileless modesty under the most
unexampled experiences; his tender humility and ready fellowship
with every lowest form of good; the free, unconscious movement of
his thought, reflected from the great calm realities with which he was
in habitual intellectual contact: his unstudied speech, bubbling up at
times into a childish *naïveté* and simplicity, — all these things, while they
take his books out of the category of mere literary performances, and
convert them into an epoch, as it were, of our associated mental history,
— into a great upheaval or insurrection of the human mind itself, — yet
assuredly reduce the feats of our sincerest theologians and philosophers
to the dimensions of ignorant prattle, and turn the performances of our
ordinary literary posturemongers into stale and mercenary circus tricks.

It is sheer fatuity to conceive a man like this aspiring "to clean out
meeting-houses," or projecting any such frivolity and futility as ecclesiastical reform. He was not a bit of a sexton, and the mind of an
undertaker dwelt not in him. His intercourse was wholly among the
living; death, in the undertaker's sense of that phenomenon, having
lost all sanctity to his imagination, by revealing its long imposture, and

confessing itself no more the finished flower of life, but its succulent root and beginning; no more its lurid, menacing west, but its dewy, tender, and most motherly east. In fact, Swedenborg saw that the most sacredly established life of christendom, which was its ecclesiastical life, constituted its profoundest death; and he accordingly never counselled nor contemplated any resuscitation for that life, but only from it. To this figurative extent it is true that no undertaker ever betrayed a jollier scent of mortality than he. But then, unlike the undertaker, he left the dead to do their own burying, and went on himself to describe the New Jerusalem, not by any means as a more trinketted set of literal Jews, complacently arrogating to themselves that sacred repute, in disparagement of an old tarnished set, but exclusively as A NEW LIFE IN MAN, coextensive with the lord's unseen presence and operation in the natural sphere of the mind; or, what is the same thing, with the redeemed and regenerate *nature* of man. He never lets fall a syllable from which you might infer that he conceived the momentous changes taking place in the spiritual world or the realm of mind to involve the slightest interference with the existing ecclesiasticisms. Describing "the last judgment" which took place, he affirms, in the world of spirits about a hundred years ago, and which he professes to have seen in great part, he says that "the state of the church will be henceforth *similar outwardly, but dissimilar inwardly;* because the man of the church will enjoy more freedom of thought on matters of faith, or on spiritual things which relate to heaven, spiritual liberty having been restored to him. For all things in the heavens and the hells are now reduced into order"; and so forth. Again he says: "I have had various conversations with the angels concerning the state of the church hereafter. They said that things to come they know not, such knowledge belonging to the lord alone; but that they do know that the slavery and captivity in which the man of the church has heretofore been is removed, and that now from restored liberty he can better perceive spiritual truths." I quote from his tract entitled *The Last Judgment,* 73, 74.

The moral of my story is that no one has the least right to make Swedenborg the stalking-horse of his own spiritual imbecility; and that if any of my readers would inquire wisely concerning that author, he should by all means consult his writings at first-hand, and leave the swedenborgians diligently alone; just as in inquiring about Moses, he would consult the pentateuch and ignore chatham street; or about Christ, he would consult the gospels only, and give a very wide berth indeed to the pope of Rome and the archbishop of Canterbury.

I may as well in this connection notice a recent work by Mr. Tafel, of Chicago, called *Emanuel Swedenborg as Philosopher and Man of Science*. It is an affectionate and even enthusiastic tribute to Swedenborg's unrecognized merits as a philosopher and man of science, made up of the various eulogistic notices his life and writings have attracted from men of letters. No doubt the world owes it to the memory of its distinguished men to preserve an honest record of its obligations to them ; but Swedenborg would willingly have forgiven it the debt in his own case. I suspect that he would blush crimson if he could once get a sight of Mr. Tafel's book, and discover himself to have become the object of so much cheap personal laudation on the part of people who apparently are quite indifferent to the only claim he himself preferred to men's attention, that, namely, of a spiritual seer. Whatever his scientific and philosophic worth may have been to his own eyes, and we may be very sure that it was never very large, nothing can be more certain than that it became utterly obliterated there by the chance which subsequently befell him of an open intercourse with the world of spirits. He at once deserted his scientific pursuits after this event, and never recurred to their published memorials as offering the least interest to rational curiosity ; while he affirmed, on the contrary, that the facts of personal experience which he was then undergoing possessed the very highest philosophic and scientific interest, as shedding a brilliant light upon every conceivable problem of man's origin and destiny. In looking somewhat attentively through Mr. Tafel's pages, I see no evidence that any of the writers he cites had the least regard for Swedenborg from Swedenborg's own point of view ; while I see abounding evidence of their being disposed to yield him an extravagant personal homage, than which, I am persuaded, nothing could be more offensive to his own wishes. This petty partisan zeal is carried so far as to beget a very revolting note in one place (page 60), in which two men who honestly thought Swedenborg insane are reported to have subsequently gone mad themselves, with such hilarious satisfaction, as leaves no doubt on the reader's mind that the reporter really supposed the divine honor vindicated by that shabby catastrophe. If a suspicion of Swedenborg's sanity were an offence to the gods actually punishable by loss of reason, I know of no hospital large enough to house the victims which would ensue from that judgment within the limits even of my own scant acquaintance. Nothing, indeed, in my opinion, can be more logical and salutary for certain minds than a suspicion of Swedenborg's sanity. And certainly nothing could be more ludicrously inapposite to the needs of those who appreciate his *real*, though incidental, services to science and philosophy, than a certificate to his merit in those respects would be from the hand of all the technical experts on the planet.

Note B. Page 76.

I hope no one will attribute to me the spirit of a textuary in culling the following samples from Swedenborg, or deem me so frivolous as to feel the least solicitude in regard to Swedenborg's private opinions about the church, or about anything else in fact. Any one who in reading Swedenborg conceives that his teaching is intended to be authoritative is very inexcusable for having anything more to do with him on Swedenborg's own principles. For he has done his best throughout his remarkable writings to rob even God almighty himself of all authoritative prestige, of all despotic sway, by proving him instinct with such a tenderness for human freedom, such a reverence for the human selfhood, such a faultless consideration for man's spiritual prospects and possibilities, as to permit every most revolting issue of our moral consciousness, or *quasi* freedom, rather than jeopard it for a moment. Our spiritual dignity and destiny, according to Swedenborg, lie so near the heart of God, as to make hell no less than heaven the argument of his amazing love ; as to make the bosom delight of the tawniest devil, in fact, just as sacred to his tolerance, just as exempt from outside or arbitrary interference, as that of the fairest angel. Only conceive, then, what a perverse — nay, what an idiotic — homage you render Swedenborg, if you attempt coercing him into a relation of petty control over men's faith and practice, which only a very evil person is capable of bearing. Besides, Swedenborg's natural cast of mind is utterly unauthoritative, utterly averse, not merely to command, but even to persuade ; so that if any one will insist upon having an infallible guide as to the truths his own great mind *ought* to acknowledge, and the goods his own large heart *ought* to cherish, Swedenborg is not the least in the world the man he is in search of. Any vulgar catholic or mormon missionary will infinitely better promote his fine spiritual advantage. There is actually no writer worth naming, after Matthew, Mark, Luke, and John, certainly no living writer, whose personality, both moral and intellectual, is so little grandiose as Swedenborg's, i. e. so little melodramatic or impressive ; none who exerts so little voluntary influence upon his reader. In fact the total fashion of the man's mind is in this respect so evangelic or celestial — it contrasts, for example, so vividly with my own depraved intellectual habit — that if it were not for the things he incessantly says, which are manifestly underived from himself, and the clear prophetic glimpses he perpetually gives us into the very heart of creative truth — truth that none of our poets, or visionaries, or sages, or philanthropists begins even as yet to babble — the perusal of his books would be extremely difficult to me, would be in fact little short of a downright penance. As it is, they make all other books seem cheap and trivial, turning them at most into a sort of intellectual " hock-and-soda-water," good to fillip a jaded mental palate into a momentary flush of exhilaration, but not the least fit to organize a new one.

No, all I propose to do in this place is to throw together a few sentences from Swedenborg's multitudinous books, bearing upon the church in man, which may show to those who are curious about his writings what a noble and novel doctrine they yield upon that subject, even in our liberal day and generation. He, good man, would be unfeignedly astonished and disgusted to learn that any persons had been silly enough, or insolent enough, to mechanize a new sect into inglorious existence out of a pretended regard for his writings. But the best counsel I can offer my reader is to give no heed to my opinions about Swedenborg's books, nor any one else's opinions, but to consult them for himself. I am sure he will say in the end that no better counsel was ever given him.

"The church of the Lord is both internal and external; its internal consisting of charity, and whatsoever beliefs are congruous with charity, and its external in goodness of life, or the works of charity and faith." Apocalypse Explained, 403. This of course is the living or invisible church. Thus he says again: "The church's internal consists in heartily *willing* what is good, and its external consists in *doing* what is good." This is the church, the living or invisible church, known only to God, and all unknown to itself. But now he immediately goes on to characterize the sham or visible church: " But the *external* church " — not as before, " the church, internal and external " — " consists in the devout performance of ceremonial worship. But this ceremony, which simulates worship, is like a shell without any kernel, since it is the external surviving the internal; and when the church has come to this pass, it is at an end." Arcana Celestia, 6587.

" Doctrinal differences do not distinguish churches before the lord, this distinction being effected by a life in consonance with the things of doctrine, all of which, when true, regard charity as their base, for what is the end and design of doctrine if not to teach how man should live? The several churches in christendom are doctrinally distinguished into roman catholics, lutherans, and calvinists. This diversity of designations arises solely from the things of doctrine, and would never have taken place if the members of the church had made love to the lord, and charity towards the neighbor, the leading point of faith. Things of doctrine would, in that case, turn out to be mere divergencies

of opinion in regard to the mysteries of faith, which they who are true
christians would leave every one to believe as his particular conscience
directed him, whilst it would be the language of their hearts that *he is
a true christian who lives as one*, that is, as the lord teaches. Thus
one church would be formed out of all these divided churches, and all
disagreements incident to doctrinal differences would vanish; yea, all
their reciprocal animosities would be dissipated, *and the kingdom of the
lord would be established on the earth.*" A. C., 1790.

"All the members of the early church lived together as brethren, in
mutual love. But in process of time love abated, and finally vanished away; and as love vanished evils grew, and with evils falsities,
out of which came schisms and heresies. These would never have
existed, if charity had continued to exist and rule; for in that event
men would not have called schism and heresy by those names, but
would have regarded them as doctrines conformed to each person's
particular way of thinking." A. C., 1834.

"It is false to suppose that the man of the church is constituted, not
by goodness or charity, but by truth or faith." A. C., 2351. "Faith,
in the word, means nothing but love and charity; hence doctrines and
tenets of faith are not faith, but only appurtenances of it." 2116.

"Love to the lord cannot possibly exist apart from neighborly love.
For the lord's love is love to the whole human race, which he desires
to save eternally, and to adjoin entirely to himself, so as for none of
them to perish: wherefore whosoever has love to the lord, *has the
lord's love, and cannot help loving his neighbor.*" A. C., 2023.

"When it is said there is no salvation in any name but that of the
lord, it means no salvation in any other doctrine, that is, *in no other
thing than mutual love*, which is the true doctrine of faith." A. C., 2009.
"The lord is never present in external worship, unless internal worship be contained in it." A. C., 1150. "Many say, there is no internal worship without external. They should say, no external without internal." A. C., 1175. "The new church will be established
only in those who are in a life of good." A. C., 3898. "The church
is necessarily various in doctrine, for one man or one society professes
one opinion, another another. But as long as each lives in charity, he
is in the church as to life, whatever he be as to doctrine." A. C., 3451.

"The belief is very common, that to be received into heaven depends solely upon mercy; and that reception into heaven is the same
thing as being admitted here to a house where a festivity is going on,
and partaking of it. But let persons thus instructed know that affections are *common* in the spiritual world," — just as appetite and passion
are common to men in this world, — "man being there a spirit, and his

life being affection, out of which, and according to which, his thought comes forth ; and that homogeneous affection conjoins spirits, and heterogeneous affection disjoins them, so that heterogeneity makes a devil wretched in heaven, and an angel miserable in hell." A. R., 611.

" The power to think rationally is not man's, but God's in him (dei apud illum)." D. L. & W., 23. " The spiritual world is where man is, and not at all removed from him." Ditto, 92.

" To walk in the light of the New Jerusalem, Rev. 21, 24, means to perceive divine truths from *interior light*, and to live a life in accordance with those truths." A. R., 920. And " to see truths from their own light is to see them " — not from any doctrinal teaching, but — " from one's interior mind, which is called the spiritual mind, and which is vivified by charity. When the mind is thus vivified or spiritualized, light, and the love of understanding truth, inflow out of heaven from the lord, and this influx constitutes spiritual illumination. He who is thus illumined, or has this interior love of truth, acknowledges truths as soon as he hears or reads them," i. e. without needing any argument or persuasion to convince him. A. R., 85.

" It is not the eye which sees, but the spirit by the eye. This may be concluded also from dreams in which we sometimes see as in open day. But this is not all. The same thing is true of this interior sight, or that of the spirit. The spirit sees not from itself, but from a sight still more interior, which is that of the rational man ; nay, even this does not see of itself, but there is a sight still more interior, that of the internal man. Nor can we stop here. For neither does the internal man see of itself, but it is the lord, who, by means of the internal man, alone sees, because he alone lives, and he gives to man the faculty of seeing, and with it the appearance as if he saw himself." A. C., 1954. " There is no such thing in creation as an independent, unconnected existence, nor could anything survive in that condition." A. C., 2556. " No person whatever, be he man, spirit, or angel, can will and think from himself, but from others, nor can those others will and think from themselves, but these again from others, and so forth : thus each from the first source of life, who is the lord. What is unconnected has no existence." A. C., 2886. " It is false that life is implanted or inherent in man ; it is always an influx." A. E., 82.

" There is nothing general or universal, in itself, and apart from the particular or individual things which compose it, and give it name or quality. Hence it is plain that there is no universal providence of the lord possible, save as made up of individual providences, and it is stupid to insist upon such a thing." A. C., 4329. " Inasmuch as life, which is called intelligence and wisdom, is from the lord, it follows also that life *in common* is from him, for the particular things of life which constitute its perfection, and are insinuated into the subject according to his faculty of reception, *are all things pertaining to the common life, which life is perfected in proportion as the evils into which man is born are removed from it."* A. E., 349.

"The eminent life, or excellency of life, of every member, every organ, and of all the viscera of our bodies, consists in this, that *nothing is proper to any of them, unless it be common ;* thus that in each thing there is the idea of a whole man. In man there is no member, nor any part in a member, which does not derive its necessaries, its nourishment, its delights, from what is common or general ; for in the body, what is common or general provides for particular things in proportion to their use. Whatsoever one member or organ requires for its work, it borrows from its neighbors, and this again from its neighbors, thus from the whole ; and it in like manner communicates or makes common to the rest its own, according to their want. The case is similar in the spiritual man, or heaven. Every one is there rewarded according to the excellence of his use, and at the same according to his love of use. No idle person is there tolerated, no slothful vagabond, no indolent boaster of the studies and labors of others, but every one is active, skilful, attentive, and diligent in his own office and business, and places honor and reward, not in the first, but in the second or third place. According to these dispositions, there is an influx among them of necessary, of useful, and of delightful things." (I quote from a charming little tract incorporated in the *Apocalypse Explained,* and entitled *The Divine Love.*)

"As man becomes internal, and instructed in internal things, then externals *are as nothing to him ;* for he then *knows* what is sacred, namely, charity, and belief built upon charity. Wherefore, since the lord's advent, man is no longer estimated in reference to externals, but to internals." A. C., 1003. "External worship is in itself mere idolatry." A. C., 1094.

"Whoso acts from charity is regenerate, and makes no account of the things of faith or truth, because he lives by virtue of the good of faith, and no longer by its truth ; for truth has so conjoined itself to good that it no longer appears as its form." A. C., 3122. "He who has arrived at spiritual good has no more need of doctrinals, which are from others, for he is in the end whither he was tending, and no longer in the means. And doctrinals are only means of arriving at good as the end." A. C., 5997.

"The lord's spiritual church is dispersed over the whole globe, and is everywhere various according to creeds. So in the other world, no one

society, nor any one in a society, exactly agrees with another in ideas."
A. C., 3267. "The spiritual church extends over the whole globe, as
much among those who are without as among those who are with truths
of faith." A. C., 3263. "As internal truths become seen, the external
truths which shrouded them become dissipated, and serve only as means
of thinking about internal ones." A. C., 3857.

"Truth of itself cannot see whether it be truth, but must be enlightened by good." A. C., 4256.

"A holy internal life and a holy external one," such as ritualists
cherish, "are altogether incompatible." A. C., 4293.

"*To know* is not *to believe*. To believe is an internal thing, possible
only to those who are in the love of the good and the true, that is, in
charity towards others." A. C., 4319.

"The man who is regenerating or becoming spiritual is first led *by
truth to good*, because he does not know what spiritual good is but by
truth, or doctrine drawn from scripture; thus he is *initiated* into good.
But when he is initiated, he is no longer led by truth to good, but *by
good to truth*, for he then, from the good that is in his heart, not only
sees the truths he had before known, but *also from this good produces
new truths*, which he had not before known, nor could know. For good
has along with it the property of desiring truths, being as it were
nourished by them, inasmuch as it is perfected by them. These new
truths greatly differ from those he had before known, these latter
having had little of life, while the former are enlivened by good."
A. C., 5804.

"Before regeneration man acts from obedience, after from affection;
these two states are inversely related to each other, for in the former
state truth rules, in the latter good. When man is in the latter state, or
acts from affection, it is no longer allowed him to do good from obedience
merely, or from truth." A. C., 8505. "When man is led of the
lord by good, and not from truth, he is then in charity, i.e. in the love
of doing that good; all in heaven are thus led, since this is to be in
divine order, and thus all things which they think and do are thought
and done spontaneously or from freedom. If they should think and act
otherwise, that is, from truth, they would think whether a thing ought
to be so done or not, and would thus hesitate in everything, and thereby
so obscure the light pertaining to them, as to relapse into an unregenerate condition." A. C., 8516.

"When man is regenerate he no longer asks from truth" (or his
understanding) "what he is to believe and do, but from good" (or his
heart), "because he is imbued with truths and has them in himself, nor
has he any concern about truths from any other source than his own
good." A. C., 8772.

"The divine flowing in former times through heaven, was divine truth, represented by the law of Moses; what is now transfluent there is *good*." A. C., 6720.

"The good appertaining to man makes his heaven, so that every man's heaven is exactly what his good is." A. C., 9741.

"Intelligence is to perceive inwardly in one's own mind whether a thing be true or not. To perceive from teaching is not to be intelligent, but only to know." A. E., 198.

"The ancients did not say *faith* but truth, whereas the moderns say faith instead of truth. The reason is that the former believed only what they saw to be true, or apprehended understandingly, and the moderns profess to believe, though they do not see nor understand. The angels in the superior heavens are not willing even to mention *faith*, for they see truth from the light of good, and call it madness to confide in any one saying that this or that ought to be believed without being apprehended in the understanding. The reason why truth ought to be named in the place of faith is, because by truths come all intelligence and wisdom, but by faith, especially by faith separated from these things, comes all our spiritual ignorance. This is why the higher angels turn themselves away when faith is named, having no sympathy with the thought of those who name it, which is that the understanding is to be held captive to the obedience of faith." A. E., 895.

Note C. Page 92.

The modern sentimental religionist will be shocked at my thus reviving the faded lineaments of his mistress as she appeared in the dew of her youth and unconsciousness, when her service brought sorrow and desolation of spirit to every hearth that harbored her. But I have no disposition to apologize. I am not so presumptuous, indeed, as to quarrel with the peculiar evolution of the religious sentiment which is so rife at this day; for no doubt it is strictly appropriate to the existing needs of the human heart. I only quarrel with the pretension its votaries attribute to it, of being a comparatively pure exhibition of the sentiment, and protest against its being regarded as an absolute advance upon the earlier forms of religion. It is no doubt a providential modification of the old religious conscience, to suit the demands of our comparatively superficial and frivolous spiritual life. But it is absurd, as it seems to me, to talk of it as an absolute improvement. Indeed, to every one studiously familiar with the early religious life of man, the change in question is not from good to better, but only from bad to worse. Religion has undergone so sheer a demoralization since her pure and holy prime — has sunk into such a brazen handmaid to worldliness, such a painted and bedizened courtesan and street-walker, proffering her unstinted favors to every sentimental fop, or clerical *beau diseur,* who has the smallest change of self-conceit in his pocket wherewith to pay for them — that one finds himself secretly invoking the advent of some grand social renovation in order to blot it *as a profession* out of remembrance, and leave it extant only as a spiritual life. Religion was once a spiritual life in the earth, though a very rude and terrible one ; and her conquests were diligently authenticated by the divine spirit. Then she meant terror and amazement to all devout self-complacency in man ; then she meant rebuke and denial to every form of distinctively *personal* hope and pretension towards God ; then she meant discredit and death to every breath of a pharisaic or quaker temper in humanity, by which a man could be led to boast of a "private spirit " in his bosom. giving him a differential character and aspect in God's sight to that of other men, especially the great and holy and unconscious mass of his kind. Swedenborg found hell made up of this oppressive sort of persons, men who claim to be righteous in themselves, and despise the divine or universal righteousness, which belongs to them only as they are in solidarity with their kind, only in other words as the sentiment of *kind*-ness, or charity, in their bosoms, sops up that of self. This is why the New Testament addresses no inviting or soothing word of any sort to the saint, but only to the sinner. In one of those very rare gospel incidents which give us a glimpse into Christ's *personal* temperament, a saintly youth presents himself so aglow with all moral excellence, that Christ cannot help testifying a natural impulse of affection towards him ; but he nevertheless straightway charges him to set no value upon his virtue as a *celestial* qualification. " If thou wilt be *perfect, go and sell all that thou hast, and give to the poor ; and come and follow me.*" No wonder we are told that when " the young man heard that saying, he went away sorrowful ; for he had great possessions." For nothing could well be more preposterous than the recommendation of Christ, if we are to take his words strictly according to the letter, or regard them as devoid of an internal or spiritual and universal sense. Clearly no man was ever divinely authorized to make his private will the rule of my action, unless he were at the same time divinely qualified to prove his will identical with that of all mankind, or exalt it into a standard of universal justice. No, the letter of truth kills, the spirit alone gives life. Thus the " rich man " of the gospel, who finds it so hard to enter the kingdom of heaven, is only figuratively the moneyed man, while in truth it is the "virtuous" man, or the man who in all moral regards is so favorably distinguished from other men as *to feel himself meritoriously related by that fact to God also.* The "possessions" of such a man are a hindrance rather than a help to his spiritual progress, because they induce a belief that the divine righteousness is of a base moral or personal type, and not of an exclusively spiritual or impersonal quality.

One word more. *Consider the lilies,* said he who spake as no man before or since has ever spoken, *consider the lilies, how they grow; they toil not, neither do they spin, and yet I say unto you, that Solomon in all his glory was not arrayed like one of these.* Manifestly, if the subjective or sensitive life of the lily — the life which allies it to the earth as the sole heaven of its nurture and growth — were the same thing with its objective or unconscious perfection, that is, with the beauty and fragrance which alone individualize it to our intelligence, the lesson here conveyed could have no applicability to us, would in fact forfeit its total significance to our understanding. For the whole point of the lesson is, to dissuade us, by the example of the lily, from those subjective cares and anxieties to which we are naturally prone, in the confidence that all our real or objective needs will be infallibly supplied by the supreme care-taker. And if, therefore, the lily could be supposed to be subjectively conscious of its objective charms, or properly solicitous about the impression it produces upon higher natures, the lesson would read exactly backwards, and leave us less void of unwise anxiety than it found us. Clearly the lily offers no fit counsel to us, save in so far as negatively or by contrast it mirrors our inward worthlessness. It is our spiritual habit to be forever seeking the argument of God's good-will to us, not in the infinitude of his love which rejects all worth in its objects, but in our own subjective states by which we are reasonably qualified for his favor. And this vicious habit the lily, by its subjective modesty or serene acquiescence in its native nothingness, eloquently rebukes. It is the exact christian ideal of life, on the other hand, that we should, even while undergoing an experience of our subjective infirmity or unworthiness, amounting to despair in ourselves, yet feel so assured a peace in God, and the constancy of his redeeming love and providence, as virtually transforms that despair into hope. And the lily by its formal or objective beauty, its exquisite unasking and unconscious grace and innocence, exactly reflects or foreshadows these priceless spiritual possibilities in us, and so preaches us, if only our ear is inwardly exercised to hear, a sermon far more evangelic than ever fell from the lips of learned Paul or politic Peter.

Christ's originality — when he interpreted the divine law as meaning in spirit love to God and love to man, or as being fulfilled in our doing to our neighbor as we would be done by — has been of late zealously controverted; some persons maintaining that his doctrine on this subject had been substantially, if not formally, anticipated by pagan sages, while others contend that he was without any rival. How the controversy actually stands I do not know. As a good deal of will energizes it on both sides, it is probable neither party to it is much affected by the arguments of the other. It seems to me, however, that if I were disposed to maintain Christ's absolute originality as a teacher, I should be able to find a much more inexpugnable ground for the claim, in the doctrine he laid down as to the temper of mind which qualified men for the kingdom of heaven, when he likened it to that of unconscious infancy. "Suffer little children," he said to his disciples, "suffer little children to come unto me and forbid them not: *for of such is the kingdom of heaven.*" That clearly was the first time in human annals that the soul of man found itself so level with the divine mind — attained to so clear an insight into the divine perfection — as livingly to perceive that poverty not wealth, innocence not virtue, ignorance not wisdom, was what alone truly qualified men for the divine sympathy. At that period the stoics were the leaders of speculative thought. To fall back on all occasions upon one's moral force, and find a refuge against calamity in one's native strength of will, was the best recognized wisdom of man. Strength not weakness, knowledge not ignorance, virtue not innocence, was the shining panoply wherewith the stoic faith armed its votary against the slings and arrows of outrageous fortune. Christ probably had never heard of the stoics, but if he had he could only have been revolted by their doctrine, since his own was the exact and total inversion of theirs. The ideal of the stoic was rich and cultivated manhood. The ideal of Christ was innocent unconscious childhood. According to Christ, what men need in order to the full enjoyment of the divine favor is, to be emptied of all personal pretension, to become indifferent to all self-seeking or self-providence, and to present to the divine hand the same unaffected submission which the child exhibits to the parent. Thus weakness not strength, ignorance not knowledge, impotence not faculty, affection not intellect, innocence not virtue, heart not head, want not wealth, was what, in his estimation, qualifies men for the skies. And his conviction on the subject, for which also he laid down his life, was so strictly original, that is, it was so little shared by other men, as to have awakened almost no echo up to this day in the bosom of the race, and to have found itself ratified, at most, only by some rare individual experiences here and there throughout history.

Note D. Page 99.

Surely I adore and bless God with all my heart that he has succeeded in putting the scampish or diabolic element in our nature upon the side of public order; that he has so secularized religion, and so popularized government, that whatsoever is basest in our common life tends irresistibly to the highest places, rises spontaneously to the surface like scum or froth, and passes off harmlessly, nay benignantly, in offices of public dignity and use. At least it will be made so to pass off as soon as our owlish vision becomes enlarged to the celestial daylight which is visiting us from on high, and our clownish hearts grow devout enough to acknowledge that evil is a far more vivacious servitor of God, because an interested one, than good has ever been. The good man indeed, if his spiritual intelligence has also been quickened, altogether disowns the divine *service*, in any strict sense of that word. His hearty reverence for God disposes him to a wholly filial recognition of him, and makes him loathe nothing so much as the magisterial conception of the divine name. I suppose the profoundest anguish a really believing mind suffers grows out of the inveterate servility it feels to be imposed upon it by the prevalent thought of God in the church and the world. I cannot imagine, indeed, that the peace of any such mind will ever be perfect, until the divine existence itself ceases to be a tradition of the dead memory, by becoming reproduced in the actual life of its senses.

But all this does not hinder me seeing, on the contrary it insures my seeing, how illusory all our *private* pretension to virtue is, and how preposterous our hope of arriving at true manhood individually, except upon a basis of the amplest preliminary justice to *all* men. Give all mankind relief from abject physical and moral want, by insuring them subsistence and education, and you give them *ipso facto* social recognition; and when society is at last established among men, then for the first time a true, because a really free or spiritual, individuality will be possible. When divine justice or righteousness is universally done upon the earth, or what is the same thing, when every man's natural fellowship or equality with all other men becomes practically organized, then those of us who choose may reasonably aspire to unincumbered spiritual possessions; but as long as every man's soul is mortgaged as now to his suffering brethren, it is hopeless and indeed iniquitous to expect any true spiritual freedom.

Note E.   Page 120.

I SEE no reason why the man of science should not run us physically — run all he can find of physical substance in us — into the
most abject mineral maternity.   And it seems a pity that less logical
men of science should waste their energy in vain efforts to stop him off,
under the impression that he is doing harm to men's spiritual interests.
For after all this is got through with, after we have been scientifically
disposed of and done for to all the extent of our animal, vegetable, and
mineral properties, absolutely nothing at all has been done to account
for our distinctive natural existence or phenomenality.   And this because human nature, unlike mineral, vegetable, and animal nature, is
not physical, but moral or metaphysical.   That is to say, its specific or
free element is one with its generic element, and not servile to it, as is
the case with those lower natures.   No doubt I have all manner of
physical properties, but none of these things is what makes me man, or
constitutes me a subject of human nature.   If I were to embody in my
own person every perfection of the lower natural forms, I should not be
so much more, but only so much less, a man.   You would be obliged
to eliminate all these adventitious quantities, before you would get at
me, at my true human quality, which does not fall within the realm
of science or reflex observation, but exclusively within that of conscience
or living experience.

Understand me.   My morality, or personal quality, the sentiment I
have of a selfhood or freedom over and above my appetites and passions, is what I possess most strictly *in common* with all men, and is
what alone makes me man, makes me a partaker of human nature.   At
first, no doubt, and for a good while, I am apt practically to identify
myself with my appetites and passions, and if it were not for the control
exerted at this period over my action by the public conscience, my
manhood would be swallowed up of sheer animality.   But my parents
and guardians, or the other organized educative force of the community,
stand between me and this disastrous issue, by substituting their manhood for mine, until such time as I myself may attain to moral consciousness.   They lend me their cultivated moral force (while mine is
still dormant) as so much capital whereupon to work out my future
independence, by making their will instead of my own appear to my
imagination the proper law of my action.   They educate my manhood,
or moral consciousness, by leading me to stigmatize myself as an evil
person, and submit to disgrace, whenever I abandon myself to my
animal propensions unreservedly; and to recognize myself as a good

15

person, entitled to honor, whenever I restrain them within certain conventional bounds. But they only *educate* my manhood; they by no means confer or create it. Manhood or moral force is latent in my animal nature, just as the statue is latent in the marble; and what conscience (which in its cruder forms is religion, or the law) does for me is to make it patent, or bring it to consciousness in me, by eliminating to my experience all that is purely animal from it; just as the sculptor brings forth the statue by carefully eliminating from it whatsoever in the marble is pure material, and will not lend itself to ideal form. The sculptor does not create the statue; he only educates it, or leads it forth, out of the obdurate marble into visible form; and he does this by resolutely rejecting or wasting whatsoever in the substance refuses to become form. · So the divine artist, in bringing us to moral consciousness, bestows no objective or real being upon us, but only subjective form, or the appearance of being; and he does this only by resolutely using up and casting out whatsoever in our animal substance insists upon remaining animal, or refuses to take on moral form. If there were not a moral force or force of manhood within all mineral, vegetable, and animal existence, ready to be divinely educated or brought forth in conscious form, all the administrative wisdom of church and state would be thrown away upon me, as upon the tiger or the sheep. Who thinks of educating the tiger or the sheep? And why not? Simply because they are naturally not men; i. e. because their nature is simple not composite, physical not moral, and hence deprives them of conscience, or the knowledge of good and evil. The tiger or the sheep is not, like man, "created male and female"; that is to say, they have science but not conscience, being "created each after its kind," and having no power like man to rise above or fall below that kind. But man *is* created male and female; that is, both physical and moral, common and proper, public and private, bond and free. Thus he alone has conscience, or the knowledge of himself as by nature both chaotic and cosmical, both civic and domestic, both universal and particular, both generic and specific, both good and evil, both sheep and tiger, or the harmony of all nature's contrasts, and hence the analogon of all God's perfection.

And if all this is true — if it be true that my morality is exclusively a *natural* mark in me, and does not give me my spiritual individuality or difference from my brother man, but only a more perfect identity with him, in giving me at the same time an inextinguishable diversity from all that is not him — then doubtless it interests, but it does not alarm me, to hear that Messrs. Vogt and Moleschott and Büchner and Huxley, and all the other *enfans terribles* of science who furnish our newspaper palate with so much pungent provocation nowadays, have serious thoughts of revolutionizing our faith, and making us believe downwards henceforth instead of upwards. Is any one really in dread of science? Science has but one legitimate function, which is obediently to reflect what exists, by no means to conduct or govern it. Can any one imagine a world more utterly farcical than one administered on scientific principles; i. e. on principles *approved* by Messrs. Huxley, Vogt, and the rest? And can anybody suppose that God almighty has at last grown ashamed of having so long misconducted his own business, and is going to transfer it to the *savans?* To the guidance of human science? What sort of a figure would my reader come shortly to cut, if, instead of actively attending to his affairs, he should content himself with standing all day before his mirror, and sinking his real personality in his reflected one? Well, the world would instantly grow just as idiotic, if it could once disown its living inspiration and put up with a scientific one. For science knows and can know nothing of what life is in itself, but only in its effects. It knows and can know absolutely nothing of what life is inwardly or consciously, but only of the outward masks or appearances under which it is unconsciously revealed: just as your mirror knows nothing and can tell nothing of your *morale*, or living personality, but only of your *physique*, or dead one. Life is shut up to the realm of consciousness, the moral or metaphysical realm, in which infinite and finite, God and man, are still inorganically blent or chaotically confounded. But science has to do at most only with the physical realm, the realm of body or substance, where finite is seen divorcing itself from infinite, and life is held hopelessly captive to mere existence, which is death.

Accordingly when the man of science puts his stout tongue in his cheek to deride my old-time beliefs about man's strictly supernatural — i. e. divine or spiritual — origin and destiny, he only succeeds, not in dashing my lawful jocundity even for a moment, but in stimulating me to make a more modest use of my own tongue, by wagging it freely to the following effect : —

"Undoubtedly, excellent observer, the realm of physics in its entirety belongs to us, how little soever we belong to it. It is indissolubly bound up in our *morale*, just as the marble is bound up in the statue, or the organ in its function; and there is consequently no stone so indolent or callous, no fungus so malignant, no ape so unclean, as not to furnish an apt type of our *degenerate* natural possibilities. But only a *type*. For the physical realm no way *involves* the moral, but only *evolves* it, or excludes it from itself; just as the marble evolves the statue or excludes it from itself, the organ the function, the mother the child. And the very oldest of those old faiths which you now innocently because ignorantly despise, was yet beforehand with you in signalizing this natural sovereignty or comprehensiveness of man with respect to all lower natures, inasmuch as it was accustomed to assign to moral existence or human nature infernal no less than celestial capacities ; that is, a power of exceeding the brute himself in brutality, simply by sinking man in animal, or wedding sagacious personality to blind instinct.

"But observe that all this is *degeneracy* in man, or man *falling short* of his nature ; and you, as a man of scientific probity, are bound, if you signalize the fact at all, to signalize it in that striking light. *Naturally* man is not a polliwog nor a baboon ; because the moment he touches these latitudes, we perceive that he does so only by deserting or falling below his own natural level. What I insist, therefore, upon your doing is either to account, *upon scientific principles,* for this natural level in man being pitched so much higher than that of all other existence, as to make it obvious *degeneracy* in him to remind you of polliwog or baboon, or else, incontinently to take your lubberly tongue out of your cheek, and so restore your countenance to its wonted amiable proportions."

The short of the matter is, why does man require to *degenerate* into catamount or peacock, unless his nature be not theirs ? And if his nature be literally not theirs, what philosophic use does it serve to show, by a laborious parade of their organized structural and physiological affinities, that theirs nevertheless is his ? This, no doubt, is praiseworthy science. But science is not philosophy any more than it is religion. If science could only prove to us either that ape can become man by simple education, i. e. without natural *regeneration,* or rising above his own nature, or that man can become ape without natural *degeneration,* i. e. without falling below his own nature and becoming diabolic, then science would put forth a just philosophic pretension, and might shed some light upon the obscurities of our origin and destiny. But so long as it is obliged plumply to deny both of these possibilities, of what conceivable philosophic significance are all the pedantic ostentatious disputes with which it contrives to give temporary eclat to certain rival ambitions ?

NOTE F. Page 149.

THIS Adam and Eve legend is only a gracious allegory, invented to set forth, in exquisite symbols, the invincible blindness in spiritual things which besets our natural intelligence. As a rule mankind never suspects that " great men." as they are called, are the outcome of its own womb exclusively, abject harbingers of its own infinite though still unrecognized wealth of being, but always ascribes to them an independent or outside and exceptional divine significance. It devoutly styles them " providential " men. i. e. men divinely contrived to meet a certain exigency in human affairs, and hence is sure to deem them much above, certainly never below, the average of human nature. Sense never so much as dreams that selfhood, personality, character, is but the badge of our common humanity; and indeed it would be utterly disconcerted if taught to regard its more vivid manifestations as only so many foretokenings of the race's future possibilities. On the contrary, it always concedes a certain absoluteness or infinitude to great character, a certain prestige of preter- if not super-naturalness, which more than anything else retards its own elevation and condemns it to grovel. In short, the moral pretension in humanity — that natural sense of egotism, or *un-kind*-ness, which makes every man deem himself to be something in himself, and apart from his *kind* or nature — habitually arrogates to itself a direct or special divine sanction, habitually prefers specific or class interests to generic or universal ones, habitually disciplines its subject to urge his private claim to the divine consideration, in utter indifference, if needs be, to the ineffable woes and wants of the race.

Carlyle is the boisterous elegist or apologist of this — once crazy and conceited, but now simply effete — faith ; its self-elected Old Mortality, who ever and anon sets himself to furbishing up its martyrology with such a cheerful and profligate contempt for the facts of history, that the world would simply stand aghast, and refuse to applaud the preposterous performance, did it not always discern the inveterate and unconscious comedian in the frowning mask of the moralist. Better than any of our amateur Jeremiahs, Carlyle succeeds in reproducing the flashy but cheap and fallacious conception of man which underlies our old civilization, and is fast hastening its extinction. He has become at last almost the only mouthpiece of that stubborn and vulgar paganism of the heart, which identifies God with the *vir* primarily and the *homo* secondarily ; with our conscious rather than our unconscious personality ; with the lively and muddled but picturesque shows of things, rather than their deep, serene, unostentatious reality. In a word, civilization, not society, is Carlyle's ideal of our eternal destiny; the enforced relation of governed to governor, of an imbecile quantified mass to a qualified minority, and not the frank and free commerce of *universal* fellow and equal with *individual* fellow and equal. His scheme of individual destiny is proportionate. The individual is to remain a distinctly moral or voluntary force, and will never attain to æsthetic or spontaneous dimensions. This fact — let Carlyle continue to ululate as pharisaically as he will — stamps him antediluvian; a very wilful and wicked antediluvian I admit, because he is a sheerly dramatic one: his books being little more than a jocund unconscious harlequinade, in the costume and coloring of our own time, of the old scotch calvinistic cant, now grown rococo and fantastic, and therefore artistically available. But he is at least so very close an imitation of the original article as to be out of all relation to the living intellect and living interests of men.

It is profaning Emerson's chaste and reverent muse to associate it, even in thought, with the *ignis fatuus*, or imp of the bogs, that inspires Carlyle's grim and labored *facetiæ*. But even Emerson, who is so sympathetic with all that is pure and honest and unostentatious in human life, even he is much too apt to confound the children of the bondmaid, born after the flesh, with those of the freewoman, born altogether of divine promise. *Nevertheless, what saith the scripture? Cast out the bondwoman and her son, for the son of the bondwoman shall not be heir with the son of the freewoman.* The gravamen of Mr. Emerson's criticism of Swedenborg, as it strikes me, is, after all, that he is not a spiritual Montaigne; or that in the gossip he gives us about Cicero and Aristotle he drops out the native flavor of those worthies, and substitutes a regenerate one. But this is being too fastidious. For plainly, if these men are, as Swedenborg holds, the respectable men they are in point of spiritual stature, because they are more and not less inspired by the common life of man than it falls to every one's lot to be, were it not better for us to hear of their having made that grand discovery, and demeaning themselves accordingly, than to find them turning out mere immortal mummies, so bent upon keeping up their stale and vapid natural identity as to forego all hope of attaining to a true spiritual individuality? To be sure, if the principle of force or identity in Cicero and Aristotle were more potent than that of individuality or freedom, so that these men were really something in themselves, and not as they stood objectively affected to the common mind, then, of course, Swedenborg was an ass for showing them stripped of their personal prestige, and consenting to sink their fate in that of the ordinary riffraff of mankind. But I have no belief in that hypothesis, and I would not exchange the perspicacious Swedenborg, accordingly, against a shipload of gossiping Montaignes. Nothing has grown so inwardly false to me as this superstition of a distinctive private or personal worth in men. I am sure that if I shall ever have the chance offered me to see any most distinguished man I please in the annals of the race, I shall gladly pretermit every one who has ever been noted for genius, or virtue, or wit, or mere *gift* of any kind, and fasten inexorably upon the interesting person of whom nothing whatever is known, not even his name, but that "he was tired of hearing Aristides called the just." That man, I am not ashamed to own, challenges a perennial freshness to my imagination, which lifts him "above all Greek, above all Roman fame." "What constitutes," says Swedenborg, "the eminency or excellence of life in every member, organ, and viscus of the body, is that nothing is *proper* to any of them *unless it be common:* thus that in every particular thing is contained the idea of the whole."* But this is infinitely more true, so to speak, of life in its spiritual aspect, or in the social body. For in the social evolution of humanity, — which is the lord's second or spiritual advent, — no individuality will ever get itself honored, or even recognized, which does not more or less universalize the subject, by enfeebling his moral or subjective consciousness and inflaming his æsthetic or objective one.

And here let me say one word more to the address of any one whom it may concern.

I have shown in the preceding essay that, whereas morality is commonly reputed to be an attribute of our specific manhood, identifying every man with himself alone, and individualizing him both from God and his kind, it is in truth an attribute of human *nature* exclusively, identifying every man therefore with every other man, while it individualizes or separates him from God on the one hand, and the brute on the other. We suppose it to characterize man spiritually, or in so far forth as he is inwardly at one with God and himself; whereas it

---

* See the beautiful little treatise on the Divine Love at the end of the Apocalypse Explained. "They who belonged," says Swedenborg, Arcana, 1115, "to the most ancient church, called Man or Adam, are above the head in the Maximus Homo, and dwell together in the utmost happiness. They told me that others came to them very seldom, except at times some who do not come from this earth, but, as they expressed it, *from the universe.*" Delicious people! And what a ravishing glimpse is here caught of the soul's future possibilities, if one will only stand faithfully by the soul, and not give up the tradition of such a thing out of deference to the grovelling senses! Should any traveller tell us of a tribe so profoundly human, or largely impersonal as this, dwelling in the heart of Asia or Africa, what could hinder us making off to them at once? But Swedenborg's books teem with similar incitements to cultivated hope and expectation.

characterizes him only naturally, or in so far as he is inwardly at war with all higher and all lower things. In short I have shown that while morality endows man with a subjective or phenomenal consciousness, with a *quasi* or provisional selfhood, adapted to the needs of an immature society among men, there is not the least spiritual or living truth, the least objective reality, in this selfhood: the whole spiritual import of it being to foreshadow the divine natural humanity, or furnish a literal form, a symbolic or figurative expression, to the utterly unsuspected truth of God's essential and exclusive manhood,* and I have also shown that christianity expresses the cordial and intimate, but unsuspected, union which binds together these divided spheres; the sphere of our real or objective being, and that of our phenomenal or subjective existence. It reports, in fact, such a strict relation of cause and effect, of substance and shadow, subsisting between the spiritual and natural worlds, as that the highest, most interior, and incommunicable secrets of creative order stand faithfully, though of course inversely, imaged in every familiar feature of created experience.

Now if all these things be true — i. e. the finiting force I have assigned to morality on the one hand, and the infiniting force I have assigned to christianity on the other — then it seems to me evident that we have an *a priori* right to expect, nay, to demand, some critical moment in the race's progress, in which these contrasted movements shall actually concur, and vibrate thenceforward in unison; some meridian hour which shall lick up the shadow in the substance, or marry thenceforth whatsoever is most phenomenal in human experience with whatsoever is most real; some pivotal life or personality, in short, which shall bring the ritual or representative church to an end, by revealing the infinite divine substance which has hitherto been hid in finite human form, and stamping God and man thenceforth indissolubly one. I say, that these our intellectual data being true, we have an incontestable logical right to demand this historic achievement, and to demand it moreover in duplex historic form: i. e. first, in literal, negative, or obscure form, answering to our natural or superstitious conception of God as a finite, or moral and personal being, having interests essentially at variance with those of the vast mass of mankind; second, in spiritual, positive, or glorified form, answering to our regenerate or cultivated conception of God as an infinite or essentially social and impersonal being, all whose interests are identical with those of the vilest worm that crawls, and whose providence extends to every insensate

---

* Human nature, in its enforced subjection to animal, vegetable, and mineral, is a literal type or shadow of the subjection which the divine nature is obliged to undergo to the human, in the process of man's spiritual creation and redemption.

stone that rests in its place or rolls. The plenary revelation of the creative name, which was intended by the church, is manifestly contingent upon this duplex historic issue. For the church in literal form (the jewish type) supplies at best but a negative witness of God in the earth, inasmuch as it shows the woman in our nature under law to the man. the *vir* subject to the *homo*, freedom prostrate to force. the individual life utterly servile to the common life; whereas in true or spiritual order (the christian type) the individual element, or what the subject is in relation to the infinite, is primary and commanding, while the universal element, or what the subject is in relation to the finite, is altogether secondary and subservient.

Well, what Swedenborg's books practically teach us is, that this last decisive hour of destiny has actually sounded, and that it is big with incalculable issues both to the race and the individual. His doctrine of God's *natural* manhood shows us this grand pivotal life or personality in man, becoming at last enthroned to our rational recognition, in the truth of the broadest human society. fellowship. or equality of man with man upon the earth. Can I not then persuade some fresher sinews than mine to enlist in the study of Swedenborg where I leave off, and patiently run the principles he announces of God's spiritual administration into every detailed natural application demanded by men's enlarging faith and hope? It is of course easy. with our sensuous and childish preconceptions of the divine majesty, to slight the prodigious succor and expansion which Swedenborg's books bring to our husk-fed and famished intellect. But no one, it seems to me, ought ever to open Swedenborg's writings, whose heart and whose head have not been sufficiently revolted both by the awful horrors of our existing civilization, and the merciless complacent moralism of our religious and literary teachers, to endow him with some original and independent insight. I have no fear that any person whose *heart*, especially, has ever been frankly exercised upon any problem of human origin or destiny, will long be disappointed in Swedenborg's lore. I would counsel every such person, to begin with, to dismiss all he has ever heard of the author himself, either from reputed friend or foe. and insist simply upon ascertaining for himself what is meant by his doctrine of the lord, or the divine NATURAL humanity; for there is absolutely nothing worth discovering in Swedenborg, which does not plainly owe all its attraction to that commanding truth. And in order perfectly to grasp this truth, let him start in all his investigations from the axiom which, however poorly, I have endeavored in the text to illustrate to his imagination, namely, that creation is made up to the creature's experience of three successive stages, one primary or essential, another mediatory or existential, and a third the conjoint issue of these two, which is final or characteristic: the first stage constituting a *centrifugal* movement, determined by the need the creature is under to be subjectively pronounced or made self-conscious; the second a *centripetal* movement, determined by his objective or spiritual reaction upon himself, or the need he feels himself under to be reunited to his creative source; and the third a strictly *orbital* movement, presenting the cordial synthesis or living fusion of these two, and full consequently, itself, of immortal peace and power. In other words, let him diligently remember that creation wears first of all a mask of necessity — i. e. of fatality, savagery, or poverty — constituted by the enforced humiliation of creative substance to created form ; by the compression of the *homo* to the compass of the *vir ;* by the subjugation of the wide weltering chaos of mineral, vegetable, and animal existence to the dimensions of the cosmos which is man's compact city or home ; by the reduction in short of man's physical or unconscious being to the measure and pattern of his moral or personal consciousness : and subsequently to that, a free, contingent, cultivated, and affluent appearance, constituted by the creature's reaction towards the creator, or the "desire" of the woman to the man, of the *vir* to the *homo :* and then finally a harmonic, peaceful, sabbatical aspect, constituted by the marriage of these opposing movements, or, what is the same thing, by the conversion of man's natural or subjective force into a spiritual or objective one, which means his redemption out of a loose or profligate natural selfhood into a chaste regenerate one, out of fierce physical want and squalor into social plenty and refinement, and therefore out of a petty moral and finite form of consciousness, into a grandly æsthetic and infinite one.

Note G. Page 183.

I AM prone, on occasion, to bear falsewitness, to steal, to commit adultery and murder; and the world thereupon argues that I am inwardly or spiritually as depraved as these actions report me to be, and so forthwith consigns me to the devil, that is, to the jailer or hangman. In other words, it looks upon my doing as determined by my previous being, and hence feels itself authorized to stamp this injurious being out. But this judgment is childish, and the action based upon it both frivolous and cruel. Doubtless my inherited physical and moral temperament inclines me to do these odious things, whenever I can do them unobserved ; but my inherited temperament is what I am only in the intensest solidarity with my kind, or through that, with all animal, all vegetable, and all mineral existence, and before I have attained to distinctively divine, which is individual, or spiritual, form. What I am in common with all moral and all physical existence leaves me void of spiritual quality, leaves me a form of sheer passivity to the instreaming creative force of things, and hence of mere boundless or unconscious cupidity. And what conscience, or the voice of God in my bosom, does for me in forbidding me to bear falsewitness, or to do any other evil thing, is simply to divinize or spiritualize my consciousness, by arresting this overwhelming passivity to my experience, or identifying it no longer with myself, but exclusively with my inherited nature. When conscience forbids me to do evil, it virtually says to me: "Human nature is inwardly or spiritually enfranchised, i. e. is separated from all lower natures, in being a divine habitation. But man (the *vir*) is altogether unconscious of this fact, being under dominion exclusively to his animal, vegetable, and mineral consciousness (the *homo*) ; so that unless he were made vividly to feel the death he bears in himself, in his own body, he would never be able to renounce his natural genesis, and aspire to a divine or spiritual renewing. And this wilting or withering effect upon consciousness it is my exclusive office to mediate. Thus in forbidding you and all men as I do to steal, to bear falsewitness, to commit adultery and murder, and to covet each other's possessions, I make you each conscious of a power of being or suffering infinitely transcending your power of doing or enjoying ; and *this power it is which alone allies you with God.* I make you aware, in other words, of a freedom or selfhood so completely inward, so wholly your own, as palpably to disclaim any finite origin, or avouch itself a strictly spiritual presence in your nature, connecting it with the skies."

Evidently, then, whenever I do evil, whenever I bear falsewitness, and so forth, I do so, not by virtue of any characteristic quality in me, any quality pertaining to me as a spiritual or cultivated existence, but only by virtue of an unexhausted remainder of that primal and strictly communistic force which belongs to me as a physical and moral existence, and which contrives still to overlap and disfigure my spiritual manhood. My inheritance and my cultivation, my temperament and my character, are two very distinct interests, which moreover never bear a direct but always an inverse relation to each other. If I inherit bad dispositions, as every one must do to some extent who is born of the flesh, and is not destined to remain a spiritual bat to all eternity, these dispositions must come to the surface of action, that I may see them in their true light, and by inwardly loathing them, and outwardly averting myself from them, may attain at last to the free or spiritual individuality for which I am created in the lord. The civil power is of course utterly indifferent to this necessity, and may therefore degrade, or imprison, or kill me at its pleasure, for it is the steward of God in the earth, and all power is committed to it. But it is an essentially corrupt or unjust steward, and it will never conciliate the divine approbation consequently, until it consents to assume its own proper share of the responsibility due to society for our existing crime and vice, by calling every one of its lord's debtors to it and saying to the first, How much owest thou unto my lord? An hundred measures of oil? Take thy bill, and sit down quickly, and write fifty; and so on to the end of the list. No disinterested student of Swedenborg can help perceiving that our moral force is just as truly organic as our physical one, being utterly contingent upon the relations we are under to the world of spirits, by virtue of our existing civic and ecclesiastical organization. And if this is the case, how exquisitely absurd it is to go on confounding a man's spiritual and moral character, or attributing the good and evil, which belong exclusively to his nature or inheritance, to himself, that is, to his character or culture! We have, according to Swedenborg, absolutely no freedom or selfhood, either physical or moral, "as selfhood is commonly conceived," but only the appearance of such a thing, inasmuch as all our power, sensational and emotional, all our appetite and passion, all our affection and thought, all our will and understanding, are an influx to us every moment from spiritual association, giving us each a *quasi* individuality indeed, or a reality to his own consciousness, but restricting the entire truth of the phenomenon to his unconscious solidarity with all other men. How imperative then the obligation upon our existing divine stewardship, whether it call itself church or state, or both, instantly to legitimate all mankind, good and evil, white and black, rich and poor alike, or give every man of woman born equal social recognition, by frankly assuming to itself all the merit and demerit of their physical and moral diversities. No doubt if the steward could only be got to feel his iniquity in the premises, and do at last what divine justice stringently demands of him, he would find men glad enough to receive him into their houses, when he is definitively put out of his stewardship. That is to say, when once human society is fairly inaugurated, by every man becoming endowed with an equal interest in it, then every man will be a law unto himself, and will spiritually execute justice and judgment upon himself, whenever he thinks a thought, or feels a desire, of inequality with respect to the meanest man that lives.

The same error vitiates all our æsthetic judgments. We invariably confound the man and the artist, the substance and the form, the subject and the object, and hold with Horace that the poet is what he is absolutely, i. e. by possession or inheritance, and not contigently, i. e. by doing and suffering. I have a friend, an estimable man enough in all personal respects, who has a great deal of artistic ambition without a gleam of artistic ability. He covers any amount of canvas during the year, as if only to demonstrate that the ambition to excel in any pursuit is always in the inverse ratio of the corresponding power. "I have it in me, however," he cries aloud every year with new emphasis, "and by heaven it shall come out." His friends, alarmed at this unprincipled perseverance, remonstrate with him to this effect : People who have it in them, as you say, are never tempted to swear by heaven, or by anything else, that it shall come out ; for it comes out as infallibly as the small-pox, and always leaves them a mortifying spectacle to themselves ever after, so fatal is the eruption apt to prove to their previous self-conceit, or conception of their own power. The man who starts from a lively conviction of his own genius will probably never succeed in impressing anybody else with a similar conviction. Our current magazine literature, which in great part is a mere flatulent appreciation of distinguished names, has misled you. It has at all events helped if not prompted you to construe your love of fame into genius. You have been wilfully bent all these long years upon proving yourself a painter. But no painter worth naming thinks of vindicating himself in his picture, but only what is infinitely distinct and aloof from himself. No painter, whose soul is docile to the inspiration of art, ever dreams that it is the painter who begets the picture, but is sure rather that the picture begets the painter. The poet does not pretend to make his poem, unless he is a fop to begin with : the poem it is that with infinite maternal ado makes him, educates him out of his puerile vanity, and nurses him up at last into poetic faculty. Painter and picture, poet and poem, are rigidly correlated, or exist only by each other's permission, like subject and object. But it ought to be rooted in your conviction that the objective element in existence or action is alone real, while the subjective element is altogether phenomenal. Shakespeare's dramas were infinitely beyond Shakespeare *himself*, infinitely beyond his own power to produce. How otherwise should Shakespeare himself have so completely faded in all subjective or personal regards out of men's memory ? He is even getting to be looked upon as a mythologic personage. No one from knowing the man Shakespeare all his days could form the least prognostic of his poetic genius, least of all Shakespeare himself. No man is a hero to his friends, unless his friends start with a low conception of the heroic quality. The moral of it all is, dear friend, that art is a literally divine life in man, and that the artist himself contributes absolutely nothing to it, but is in all cases its unlimited servant, a beggarly dependant upon its sovereign mercy; a veritable Lazarus in fact sitting at its gate covered with the sores of his own peccant vanity, and asking to be fed of the crumbs that fall from its table.

NOTE H.   Page 191.

No doubt the literal supernatural deserves the intellectual discredit which is fast overtaking it; that technical supernatural which postulates nature's original objectivity to God, only for the purpose of alleging a posthumous subjective conflict between them. Our knowledge, properly so called, is limited to natural existence, or the field of the senses; and however devoutly, therefore, we may believe in supernatural existence, it is evident that it can never fall within the compass of our proper knowledge, save in the light of a revelation; since its pretension to do so would amount to the destruction of our natural faculty of knowing. If the supernatural can become known to us in an outward or sensible way, as we know natural things, then of course all our knowledge — which proceeds only upon the distinction of things — grows instantly unfixed or uncertain, and the natural world no longer serving as a firm and discrete base to the spiritual, turns out a bottomless morass, which forever swamps its heavenly promise and possibilities out of sight. The most flat-footed and flat-headed materialism of the day, such as that of Carl Vogt and Moleschott and Büchner, is preferable in this state of things, as it appears to me, to our old and fossil supernaturalism, just as the melting of the snows in spring, and the breaking up of the ice in our lakes and rivers, though oftentimes full of damage to private interests, constitute a better harbinger of a renewed life in nature than its continued immobility would be.

POSTSCRIPT.

As my book is passing through the press, a friend calls my attention to some paragraphs in a recent english work, calculated, as he thinks, to prejudice Swedenborg's good name. The work is entitled *Spiritual Wives*, and has for its author Mr. Hepworth Dixon. It is a book conceived and written under such a palpably obscene inspiration that one must be thankful, I suppose, for the comparative pusillanimity which has presided over its execution. A thin gauze of decency is doubtless furnished by the language of the book, but its whole atmosphere is odiously foul, not because the facts with which it abounds necessarily suggest uncleanness, but because the author's scent is apparently so sensitive in that line that he sniffs corruption, where a blunter faculty would shrink from suspecting it. The *auri sacra fames* is tolerable only within certain well-defined limits, and it is a discredit to english literature, generally so manly, that a person of Mr. Dixon's fashion should have been allowed to thrust himself into provinces of thought and experience so essentially morbid as those here canvassed, and, therefore, so justly remote from a profane scrutiny and appreciation, without receiving an instant rebuke from the more respectable members of the literary guild.

The facts which Mr. Dixon relates — if his information can be relied on, which seems a very doubtful point — are full of interest to philosophic thought, and do not of their own accord either invite or tolerate the coarse commentary and exposure they get at his hands. Mr. Dixon himself does not conceal that the victims to these delusions were eminently religious persons, filled with a fanatical or frenzied thirst of the divine approbation. Why then does he not show the same respect to the fantasies of their sincere faith, that he shows to the more commonplace phenomena of the religious life? Why, for example, does he cruelly revive the names and private histories of these suffering zealots, most of whom have passed to their final audit, and insidiously appeal to every denizen of the gutters to come and hold obscene carnival over their graves? I myself knew in my youth two young ladies, sisters, whose name Mr. Dixon wantonly parades to a mocking and lascivious gaze; and they were persons of such an exquisite feminine worth and loveliness in the estimation of all their friends, and in spite of their religious aberrations, that no violets of the wood, nor any lilies of the valley, ever owned a deeper heart of modesty, or exhaled a breath of chaster fragrance. What a horror then to encounter their stainless name in this depraved book!

If religion mean — as it is commonly held to mean — a strictly personal tie between God and man, then of course the tie is one exclusively of *privilege;* and I do not see accordingly how any consistent religionist is ever to stop short of fanaticism in his approaches to God. Of course the vast mass of religious professors are insincere — i. e. as Christ said, are unconsciously acting a part imposed upon them by circumstances — and obey only the logic of expediency; but I am not talking of these. I am talking only of the sincere religionist, of the man who feels himself so committed to the religious instinct in his soul, both for time and eternity, as to take no counsel of the flesh, that is, of his ecclesiastical connections, as to how far he shall obey it. If I am a person of this loyal make, and am actually able to feel a good conscience towards God, giving me an unquestionable advantage in his sight over a sinful world and a careless ungodly church, I do not see how I can help expecting, and hoping, and even craving that the divine love avouch its approbation of me in some signal or supernatural manner, — *in giving me exemption, for example, from the ordinary limitations that impend over human freedom.* I am, no doubt, an abject fanatic and fool to a spiritual or cultivated regard in cherishing such aspirations. But no one making a religious profession has the least right to call or to deem me one. For I am a fool, not because my conduct is logically inconsistent with the intellectual principles we both avow, but because those principles themselves are flagrantly insane; and here he and I are under the same condemnation. Such is the palpable and pitiless logic of the situation. What, then, is the remedy? Surely not to trample me under the hoofs of your clownish envy and hypocritical commiseration, but patiently to show me that I fatally misconceive the aim of all true religious discipline, which is not to give me a sense of safe and pleasurable personal relations with God, but on the contrary so to inflame a sense of personal hostility to him in my bosom, that my otherwise implacable self-love may feel itself remorselessly slain in its inmost fastnesses, and I may thenceforth freely identify my private hopes towards him, with the promise of eventual and indiscriminate mercy he has made to my race or nature, and to that exclusively.

But I only intended, when I began, briefly to stigmatize Mr. Dixon's absurd misrepresentations of Swedenborg's writings, which he strives by indirection to make more or less responsible for the disorders he paints. Of course it is worth while to say to a man who is ignorant of Swedenborg, that there is not one particle of truth, nor, perhaps, in any nice sense of the word, of veracity, in any of the insinuations Mr. Dixon lavishes on this subject. But it is not worth while to say so to any one else. Every one familiar with Swedenborg knows that he who finds impurity, as to matter or form, either in Swedenborg's ideas of marriage, or of any interests relating to marriage, will, if he look a little deeper, probably come to the conclusion that his judgment was premature, that it reflects in fact far more truly upon himself or his own subjective states, than it does upon Swedenborg, and his objective teaching. It would be amusing to hear the derisive shouts with which the wandering Brook Farm ghosts must receive Mr. Dixon's discovery, that that movement was greatly due to Swedenborg's influence upon New England thought! One is at a total loss, indeed — so habitual, so reckless, and so gross are Mr. Dixon's misstatements — to name the people upon whom he depended while here for information. But it is easy to divine that they must have been a sort of people unused to intellectual daylight, a sort of people towards whom the inquirer was bound to gravitate, and not "levitate," as the "spiritualist" lingo has it. For example, Mr. Dixon condescends, *inter alia*, upon my unworthy name in connection with the Brook-Farmers, a community with which, while it existed, I was in no relation whatever, either of knowledge or of sympathy. He manages, indeed, in the brief paragraph he devotes to me, to tell as many untruths, very nearly, as there are words in the paragraph. He first gives me the title of "reverend," and calls me a "Brook Farm enthusiast"; the facts being that I never belonged to any ministry ordained or unordained, and that I almost never heard of the Brook Farm association till it failed to exist. He next says that I "scandalized society by making a public confession of my call to the New Jerusalem"; the fact being that I never heard such a call, nor even suspected the possibility of it, and never, therefore, scandalized society by confessing it in public or in private; my idea of the New Jerusalem having always been that it is quite too divine a life in the earth to make its voice heard in the streets "calling" anybody, or even returning anybody's own "call." Mr. Dixon next proceeds to say, that I filled many pages of the Harbinger with proofs of Swedenborg's and Fourier's doctrinal identity in respect to sexual morality; the fact being that I never had a suspicion of any such identity, nor ever, therefore, alleged it. And then finally he says: "In fact, this reverend author, a man of very high gifts in scholarship and eloquence, declared himself, on spiritual grounds, in favor of a system of divorce which is hardly to be distinguished from divorce at will." The one grain of wheat in all this chaff is, that I have always declared, and do now declare, myself in favor of a systematized divorce; but it is a monstrous stupidity to say that this divorce is nearly equivalent "to divorce at will." No doubt my idea might bear that interpretation to some persons, but only because these persons are profoundly sceptical as to marriage having any diviner sanction than social convention, and hence suppose that to release married partners from the *enforced* homage they owe to each other — this *enforced* homage being the only thing that distinguishes our present marriage sacrament from concubinage — would be to destroy the marriage sentiment in their breasts and turn them into incontinent vagabonds. My hope in enlarging the grounds of divorce, on the contrary, is based exclusively upon my conception of marriage as furnishing the *essential* bond of the sexual relations, and as only awaiting, therefore, the disuse of force, and the inauguration of perfect freedom in those relations, to prove itself also an *indestructible* bond. That a "learned pig" may turn up his nose at this logic, and refuse to commit his delicate interests to it, is quite conceivable, and is doubtless a salutary thing on the whole for the sty. But I have no idea of the sty as furnishing an architectural equivalent to our divinely human house, or home, which is still to come; and I have no aspiration accordingly for its amendment. In fact the more uncomfortable and uninhabitable the sty becomes to human beings, the brighter the prospects of that "holy and beautiful house." * That is to say, the more we are forced to suffer as mere porkers, revelling in the trough, the more we are likely to enjoy as men when once we shall have come to spiritual manhood.

But enough of Mr. Dixon, who is certainly not worth referring to in his own right, but only as a sign of our growing moral decrepitude, which tolerates a literary man in betraying so cynical an irreverence for his own nature, as to make its most dolorous plague-spots an occasion of pecuniary gain, by using them as a vehicle, at best, of heartless rhetorical grimace, and a provocative of lascivious curiosity. The facts with which Mr. Dixon deals are facts of religious disease or disorder exclusively, demanding, therefore, above all things else, a sympathetic or reverential treatment. The sauce of indecency consequently with which he serves them up no way belongs to the facts themselves,

---

* This is the lovely spiritual house typified in Deut. xxvii. 5, 6, and 1 Kings, vi. 7, "And the house, when it was in building, *was built of stone made ready before it was brought thither:* so that there was neither hammer, nor axe, nor any tool of iron, heard in the house while it was in building."

but is either a helpless secretion or a calculated oblation of his own prurient fancy, the lord alone knows which; and no one else, I suppose, feels concerned even to inquire. What is palpable on the face of the book is that it is a mere pecuniary speculation; but what can one say of a man who, in the sight of such woes, has no other thought in his heart than how he can most make money out of them!

THE END.

Cambridge: Stereotyped and Printed by Welch, Bigelow, & Co.